A MOTHER'S SPIRIT

Anne Bennett was born in a back-to-back house in the Horsefair district of Birmingham. The daughter of Roman Catholic, Irish immigrants, she grew up in a tight-knit community where she was taught to be proud of her heritage. She considers herself to be an Irish Brummie and feels therefore that she has a foot in both cultures. She has four children and four grandchildren. For many years she taught in schools to the north of Birmingham. An accident put paid to her teaching career and, after moving to North Wales, Anne turned to the other great love of her life and began to write seriously. In 2006, after sixteen years in a wheelchair, she miraculously regained her ability to walk.

For more information, visit Anne's website,
www.annebennett.co.uk.

D0785884

By the same author

ANNE BENNETT

A Mother's Spirit

HARPER

Harper
An imprint of HarperCollins*Publishers*
77–85 Fulham Palace Road,
Hammersmith, London W6 8JB

www.harpercollins.co.uk

This paperback edition 2009
1

First published in Great Britain by
HarperCollins*Publishers* 2008

Copyright © Anne Bennett 2008

Anne Bennett asserts the moral right to
be identified as the author of this work

A catalogue record for this book is
available from the British Library

ISBN: 978-0-00-789669-1

Set in Sabon by Palimpsest Book Production Limited,
Grangemouth, Stirlingshire

Printed and bound in Great Britain by
Clays Ltd, St Ives plc

Mixed Sources
Product group from well-managed
forests and other controlled sources
www.fsc.org Cert no. SW-COC-001806
© 1996 Forest Stewardship Council

FSC is a non-profit international organisation established to promote the
responsible management of the world's forests. Products carrying the FSC
label are independently certified to assure consumers that they come
from forests that are managed to meet the social, economic and
ecological needs of present and future generations.

Find out more about HarperCollins and the environment at
www.harpercollins.co.uk/green

*To my grandson Theo, the youngest Bennett boy,
with all my love*

ONE

'Please let me come with you, Daddy?' Gloria Brannigan pleaded with her father that afternoon, as he prepared to leave the house.

Brian looked into the appealing eyes of his daughter, the child he loved more than life itself, and shook his head. 'I cannot take you to the docks, my dear,' he said. 'Your mother would—'

'Mother has retired to bed with a sick headache,' Gloria said, almost triumphantly.

'And what about the cold that has laid you low now for almost a week so that you have been unable to go to school?' Brian asked with a wry glance at her.

'That is quite gone, Daddy, and I could have gone to school today but you know how Mother fusses so!' Gloria told him. 'The fresh air might even be good for me,' adding, as her father seemed unconvinced, 'You could even claim the trip to be educational.'

'And just how do you work that one out?'

'Well, the things unloaded in New York are from all different countries, aren't they? I could make a list of them and later I could look them up on my globe.'

'I think not, darling,' Brian said regretfully.

'Oh, go on, Daddy,' Gloria urged. 'I am so bored, and the docks are exciting. I like to hear the sailors calling to each other in their own languages.'

'It's the languages you can understand that worry me,' Brian said grimly. 'Sailors' talk is not for the ears of young ladies.'

'Oh, Daddy, don't be so stuffy,' Gloria said. 'Anyway, I shall be too interested in everything else to listen to anything unsuitable.'

Brian gave a throaty chuckle. 'All right, you cheeky monkey,' he said. 'You win. I was taking the smaller carriage anyway, because Bramble can pull that and a bit of exercise will do him good. The pony's been a bit skittish of late, with you not being able to exercise him. I suppose you know that I will catch it in the neck good and proper for encouraging you to play truant?'

'You didn't encourage me, Daddy,' Gloria protested. 'It was me persuading you.'

'Your mother will not see it that way,' Brian said, with a rueful grin. 'It's a good job that I have such a broad back.'

'Well, I think you are a lovely, kind daddy,' Gloria said, winding her arms around his neck. 'In fact, the best daddy in the whole world.'

Brian felt tears prickle the back of his eyes. This child was the only one he would ever have, because of what Norah had suffered at their daughter's birth. Gloria, however, made up for any son Brian may have hankered after. Her hair was the colour of spun gold and hung in natural ringlets, which she tied back with a ribbon that always matched her dress. Then there were those unusual and very beautiful violet eyes, encircled with long, black lashes and the wide and generous mouth, the only feature she had inherited from him.

'We must hurry,' he said. 'There is not much daylight in these winter days. I will send Tilly in to you to help you get dressed in your outdoor things. The day is bone-chillingly cold and you will need to be well wrapped up.'

Gloria watched her father leave the room with a smile playing around her mouth. At fourteen years old, she was well aware that she could twist him around her little finger.

Joe Sullivan had been appalled by the conditions on board the liner bound for New York. It had been anchored in the deeper waters of Lough Foyle, and he had boarded it from a tender sent out from the pier at Moville in southern Donegal in Ireland two weeks before. He had been excited and in good spirits at being en route to America – the one place to which he had so longed to go.

However, all the steerage passengers had been housed in the bowels of the ship, and many, including Joe, had been sick for the first few days as the ship was tossed about in the turbulent ocean. The weather had been too bad for the hatch to be opened often, to enable the passengers to climb on deck, and so the air in their quarters quickly grew fetid and stale, and soon smelled of vomit.

Joe took every opportunity to be outside, despite the fact that the wind cut through him. Throughout the voyage, the wind whipped the waves into gigantic breakers fringed with white, which constantly crashed against the ship.

November was not a good time to travel the ocean, Joe decided and he would remember that in future, and he had been extremely glad to reach Ellis Island. As he queued to disembark, he looked to the New York skyline with its skyscrapers, which some of the fellows on the ship had told him about. What a sight it was, and as unlike the skyline of his home town of Buncrana, County Donegal as it was possible to be.

The huge Statue of Liberty dominated the waterfront. Liberty was what every Irishman dreamed of. His young brother, Finn, had given his life in the Great War because Britain had promised the Irish their freedom if they helped them fight the Hun. Here in New York, America, Joe was sure he would experience real freedom, and he was filled with exhilaration at the prospect.

First, though, he had to go through the procedure on Ellis Island, where he would be prodded, poked, examined, tested and questioned, to ascertain that he was fit to enter America. He wasn't worried about the physical examination, for he knew he was as fit as anyone else – fitter than most, in fact. Work all his life on the farm had seen to that.

The three Rs Joe had learned at the school in Buncrana run by the Christian Brothers where, if you weren't inclined to learn in the normal way, the lesson would be beaten into you. Joe had always had a healthy respect for the cane. His mother had had a similar one and he had felt its sting often. So he had learned as much as he felt he needed, and more than enough to please the Brothers, and now could give a good enough account of himself.

Everyone entering America had to have a sponsor waiting for him or her. Joe might have easily been on the next boat back if it hadn't been for a neighbour, Patrick Lacey, who had travelled the same route as Joe five years earlier. He would never have touched American soil himself if it hadn't been for an uncle willing to sponsor him until he got settled, and he offered to do the same for Joe Sullivan.

Joe stood at one side of the table and three stern-faced men sat the other side of it, checking all the tests he had passed and scrutinising the letter closely. Then one said, with a slight smile as he returned the letter to him, 'That seems to all be in order, Mr Sullivan, and as you passed everything else satisfactorily, there will be no need to detain you on Ellis Island any further. Pack up your things. You will be leaving on the tide today.'

'Yes, sir,' said Joe. 'And thank you, sir.' A *frisson* of excitement began in his toes and spread throughout his whole body. Friday, 18 November 1921, and he was on his way.

Gloria was blissfully happy having her daddy to herself. The steamship he was waiting for hadn't begun unloading yet, so Gloria was able to drink in the sights, sounds and smells of the docks as they walked together.

There were sailors everywhere, shouting and calling out to each other, and the steamship funnels belching out grey smoke into the much greyer sky. Goods being unloaded clattered down the gangplanks, and barrels being rolled rumbled along the dockside.

And everyone was so pleasant. Some of the sailors, mostly the foreign ones, Gloria noticed, gave her a wink or called out to her, for she was a pretty child with a ready smile.

Bert Clifford, who managed the factory that her father owned, was especially nice to her and always called her Miss Gloria, as if she was a real lady. He knew which side his bread was buttered, for his boss doted on the child. It was easy to be nice to her too, she was such a comely little thing.

Whispery trails of vapour escaped from people's mouths when they spoke, and yet Gloria hardly felt the cold, wrapped as she was in a beautiful blue woollen coat with a cape of the same material over her shoulders. A matching bonnet was tied under her chin over the golden ringlets, framing her face and making her eyes look bigger than ever, thick black stockings encased her legs, soft black leather boots went halfway up her calves, and her hands were buried in a black fur muff.

'Funny how you like the docks so much,' Brian mused. 'I must admit I was much the same when I was young. Course, there were some sailing ships about then, but not many. Some ships used steam, but had sails as well. What a sight it was to see those – majestic almost – and yet totally inefficient. A ship could be becalmed for days, weeks even sometimes, whereas now, why, the passage from England takes two weeks or less, they tell me. Like that one there, with the passengers waiting to disembark.'

The passenger ships' pier was a little further along the harbour than those of the trading boats.

'So, that one's from England?'

'Aye, and Ireland,' Brian said. 'It picks up first at a little place called Moville and then Belfast and on to Liverpool before coming here.'

'I'd love to go to Ireland,' Gloria said. 'See the place where you were born and raised, Daddy.'

'And so you shall, my dear, one day,' Brian said. 'But Ireland at the moment is not a place for anyone to visit. It is a bed of unrest, I believe. And for the life of me I cannot see what is so wrong in wanting to govern your own country. Anyway, it means the poor unfortunate people are all coming here, hoping for a better life, though it often turns sour for them.'

There was a sudden cry from Bert Clifford and Brian turned. 'They're beginning to unload,' he said to Gloria. 'You sit in the carriage for a while now and wait for me.'

'Oh, Daddy . . .'

'No,' Brian said. 'You must obey me in this. You will only be in the way and anyway, I'll not be able to watch you.'

'I don't need watching, Daddy.'

'You think not?' Brian said, with a lift to his eyebrows. 'I didn't at all like the way some of the sailors were smiling and winking at you.'

'I didn't think you noticed.'

'I notice everything about you, my dear,' Brian said with a smile. 'Now then, you be a good girl and I will take you for tea at Macy's afterwards. What do you say?'

Gloria's answer was in the smile she gave her father, as she kissed him on the cheek before climbing into the carriage without another word of complaint. Macy's afternoon teas were not to be sniffed at.

She watched her father hurry away towards Bert. She knew there was no reason for him to do this himself, as her mother had said the previous evening. Bert Clifford was an honest and trustworthy man and she couldn't understand why Brian didn't just leave him to it.

'Because it is my business, not his,' Brian had said. 'And I want to count those supplies coming off the boat myself, and that is the end of the matter.'

Her mother hated the thought of her husband consorting with common sailors, considering it so unnecessary and degrading. Gloria understood, however, how much her father liked the vibrant clamour and bustle of the docks. He was now lost to her sight in the crowd, and she turned her attention to the immigrant ship just in time to see the gangplanks lowered.

Joe couldn't wait to explore the place. Those on Ellis Island had changed his money to the American currency before he left, and he jingled the coins in his pocket and thought of the wallet packed with dollar bills, pleased that he had so much of it left. He had been careful and taken part in none of the card schools so many of the other men seemed hooked on. His father had never approved of cards and none had been played in their cottage to while away the winter evenings.

'A fool and his money are soon parted,' Thomas John had said when Joe had queried this. 'Gambling can get a grip on a body. I have seen more than one bet his whole wages on the throw of the dice or a card game, and lose the lot. However did they explain that to their wives and hungry weans when they got home? I often wondered about that and decided a long time ago that gambling wasn't for me.'

It wasn't for Joe either because his brother, Tom, still back on the farm in Buncrana, had sold a field and the sheep in it so that Joe could have this chance in America. It had been incredibly generous, and he had been extremely grateful, but he knew there would be no other money if he was to squander this. Although officially Tom was owner of the farm, now that their father had died, their crabbed, spiteful mother held the purse strings. Joe knew he would

7

never get a penny piece from her, and he didn't know how long the money he had would have to last him until he landed himself a job.

He hoped, though, that Patrick Lacey would help there. Joe's sponsor had said he would offer him lodging, at least until he got himself straight, and Joe intended looking him up as soon as possible.

The gangplank was down, a cheer went up, and the passengers moved slowly forward, hampered by their cases. Joe's attention was taken by an altercation on the dockside between a well-dressed man and a sailor over a cask that the man seemed to be demanding the sailor open.

Once it was open, the man withdrew a piece of linen or cotton that had obviously been used as packing. He waved the material aloft, and as he examined the contents of the barrel he started berating the sailor, who appeared to be foreign and was opening his arms helplessly.

It was causing great amusement amongst the disembarking passengers, until suddenly a gust of wind whipped the material out of the man's hand. It swirled and danced in the air for a while, before settling across the nose and eyes of the pony coupled to a small carriage.

With a shriek, the pony reared on its back legs. The coachman made an abortive dive for the pony, but was struck on the temple by one of its flailing front legs and fell to the ground. Then the pony made a headlong dash for the exit and the main road beyond, people scuttling out of its path.

Inside the carriage, Gloria tried to see what was happening before she was cast to the floor of the carriage where, tossed from one side to the other, she began screaming her head off.

Joe, nearly at the end of the gangplank, spied a face briefly at the carriage window, and realised that it wasn't empty, as he had supposed, but that there was a child inside. He dropped his bag and case, leaped to the rail, vaulted over the two people in front of him, hit the ground running and took off after the pony. His father always said he could run like the wind and it was true that he could always beat Tom in a race and he ran that afternoon like the very devil.

As he was drawing level with the pony, he wondered how to get it to stop. He wouldn't be able to hold it by the reins; the panicked pony would just pull him over and drag him along the ground. There was only one thing for it. Joe knew he had just the one chance and he thanked God that the pony was not large. As he drew almost level he made a superhuman leap and landed on the pony's back, remembering how, as a game, he and Tom had tried leaping onto their old horse at home.

This, however, was no game. If he was thrown from the pony he would be crushed by the carriage. His heart thumped in his chest as, for quite a few moments, he thought that might happen, as he was at the back end of the frightened and panicky animal, which was desperately trying to dislodge him. His relief when he managed to catch hold of one of the reins was palpable, and he began to pull himself towards the pony's head.

The animal was scared witless, but Joe began to stroke its mane gently and rhythmically, talking to it softly as he had done to their own horse at home when it had been spooked by something.

At first, he wasn't sure he was doing any good, and he was only too aware how near they were to the main road. He could hear the traffic and knew if he didn't stop the pony before the road, it was highly unlikely any of them would survive.

However, though his mouth was dry with fear, he kept the panic out of his voice and hands as he continued to stroke and talk as gently as he could. Gradually, he felt the pony begin to respond and to slow slightly. Then people came forward to hold him. He was eventually brought to a halt only a couple of yards from the road.

9

He stood with his head down, his sides heaving and gleaming with sweat. Joe slid from his back, ran to the carriage door and opened it.

Gloria was lying curled in a ball on the floor of the carriage, certain she was going to die. She had begun to uncurl herself stiffly as the carriage stopped, though she still shook.

Joe climbed inside the carriage and lifted the child gently to her feet. Her bonnet had become dislodged and her hair was tousled around her head, and although her face was brick red, it didn't detract from her beauty at all.

'Are you all right, miss?' Joe asked solicitously.

Gloria opened her mouth to speak, and began to weep in fear and relief. She put her arms around Joe's neck, and he didn't protest, knowing that she probably needed the comfort of another human being. She cried into his shoulder as he lifted her in his arms and carried her from the carriage.

They were still clasped together like this when Brian reached them, red-faced and panting. From every side people told him of the bravery of the young man, newly arrived in the country, who, without a shadow of a doubt, had saved the life of young Gloria Brannigan.

Brian knew that without being told. He had died a thousand times as he pounded after the careering carriage, and even as he watched the young man from the immigrant ship leap on to the back of the terrified pony, he feared he would not be able to stop the pony in time.

He peeled his still distraught daughter from Joe's arms as he said to him, 'I owe you a debt that it will take a lifetime to repay. Brian Brannigan is my name, and this is my daughter, Gloria.'

'Joe Sullivan, sir,' Joe said. 'And as for what I did, I am just glad that your daughter is unharmed.'

'Thanks to you,' Brian said, looking Joe up and down. He liked what he saw. Joe was a handsome man, with expressive dark eyes. He stood straight and tall, and looked fully in command of himself, and only his tousled brown hair and his rumpled suit were evidence of his act of bravery. 'None but my coachman, Tim Walsh, tried to stop the pony,' Brian went on, 'and now the poor man is lying comatose on the ground awaiting an ambulance. Everyone else kept out of the way.'

'You can't blame them, sir,' Joe said. 'I would say the pony was too panicked to stop in any way other than the one I tried, and even I wasn't sure that it would work.'

Gloria was looking at Joe with a sort of awed expression. 'What did you do?' she asked.

'Leaped on the pony's back, that's what,' Brian told his daughter. 'And in doing so saved your life and risked his own.'

'I . . . I don't know what to say,' Gloria said. 'Thank you, I suppose, but that doesn't seem very much really.'

'It isn't,' Brian agreed, 'but here is a better offer.' He turned to Joe. 'You have just come off the immigrant ship?'

'Aye, sir.'

'Have you a job?'

'No, but I have a neighbour looking out for me.'

'Well, I own a factory and I sure could use a brave young fellow like yourself. How d'you feel about that?'

Joe couldn't believe his luck. In payment for saving this man's daughter, he was being offered employment. And though the man was still red-faced and breathless from his unaccustomed exertion, he looked to be honest and straightforward.

'I feel grand about it, sir,' Joe said.

'Are you looking for that sort of work?'

'I am looking for any kind of work that pays a wage, sir,' Joe said. 'But I have to tell you that I have never done work in any sort of factory before.'

'Are you willing to learn?'

'Certainly, sir.'

'That's all I wanted to hear,' Brian said. 'Now I have to

find out what is going to happen to my coachman and sort out stabling for the pony, because I will leave him and the carriage here tonight. And I dare say you have to collect your belongings. Let's say we meet back here in about half an hour and we will go home by taxi.'

'Home, sir?' Joe repeated.

'Yes, home, Mr Joe Sullivan,' Brian said, clapping Joe on the back. 'Where my wife, Norah, will, at the very least, want to shake you by the hand.'

TWO

'We must go straight home, my dear,' Brian said, as he helped his daughter into the taxi. 'It would never do for your mother to get wind of your mishap before I have a chance to tell her. I am afraid we will have to forgo tea at Macy's.'

'I don't mind that, Daddy,' Gloria said plaintively. 'I ache everywhere, to tell you the truth, there is a pounding pain in my head and everything is wavy before my eyes.'

Brian felt guilty. He saw that Gloria's face was as white as lint and that her eyes seemed to stand out in her head and were glazed slightly with pain. By giving in to Gloria's demands that afternoon, he knew he had put her life in danger. 'That's not to be wondered at, my dear, after the way you were thrown about in that carriage,' he said gently. 'You are probably suffering from shock too. As soon as we get home, you are going to be tucked up in bed and I am sending for the doctor.'

The fact that Gloria made no comment about this was not lost on her father. 'Lean against me, my dear,' he suggested, 'and close your eyes. That was a dreadful and frightening thing to happen to you, but we will have you home and comfy in no time at all.'

Joe was waiting for them, excited at the thought of riding in a taxi, for he had never done that in the whole of his life before, but as he climbed in he noticed the pallid face of the child, Gloria, as she cuddled up to her father and he said, 'I hope you are not too uncomfortable, miss?'

Gloria sighed as if the effort of speech was too much for her and it was her father who answered. 'Battered and bruised and in shock, I think,' he said. 'We'll have the doctor look at her when we are home.'

'Have you heard how the coachman is, sir?'

'No,' Brian said, 'only that the poor fellow was unconscious and taken to the hospital, but my factory manager, Bert Clifford, is going to see how he is as soon as he can, and he will send me word. I hope that he will be all right. Tim is a fine man and a good worker, and has been with me for years.'

Joe, though, doubted that the man could have escaped without serious injury because he had caught the full power of the frantic rearing pony's hoofs.

But it wouldn't help to say that. Anyway, he was soon distracted by his first journey in a taxi through the traffic-filled streets of New York, and he turned his head this way and that, taking in all the sights of the city. He was awed by the sheer size of some of the buildings, so high they did indeed appear to scrape the sky.

Brian watched his amazement for some time before he asked with a smile, 'Glad you are here, Joe Sullivan?'

'Oh, yes, sir,' Joe said. 'It has long been a dream of mine to come.'

'It wasn't my choice originally,' Brian said. 'It was my father's. I was twelve years old when we first arrived in America. We came here after the death of my mother.'

'And how did you like America, sir?'

'I liked it well enough when I came to terms with the fact that I would never see my mother again,' Brian told him. 'Though America then, or New York at least, was a different place altogether. There were not that many fine buildings, but a great many ruffians, and the city was ruled by the gangs roaming the streets. My father, though he had a factory in the city, would not live there and so he bought a plot of land in an area to the north called Queens and had a house built that he called Stoneleigh. Then it was all countryside, but the city is creeping towards it now. You'll see it for yourself in a minute.'

'Yes, sir,' Joe answered. 'But I am a bit concerned about my sponsor, Patrick Lacey. He will be wondering if I do not call, for he knows I was arriving today.'

'Don't worry about that,' Brian said. 'When we get home, if you give me his address, I will dispatch my man to tell him you are dining with us tonight.'

'Dining, sir?'

'Yes,' Brian said. 'It's the least I can do, and just a small measure of my gratitude to you.'

'But won't your wife mind my just turning up like this?'

'My boy,' Brian said confidently, 'after she hears how you saved Gloria in the way that you did, there is nothing you can do that will annoy my wife, though she might not be as pleased to see me.'

Before Joe was able to form any sort of reply, the taxi suddenly turned through ornate gates and down a gravel path. Even in the descending dusk, the magnificence of the Brannigan residence could be plainly seen. The only large house that Joe had any experience of at all was the one that his sister Nuala worked in. Even so, he knew that the Brannigan house was in a league of its own. It was built of honey-coloured brick and had more windows and chimneys than Joe had ever seen in his life. He trembled in apprehension at even entering such a place.

The taxi drew to a stop before the house, the wheels crunching on the gravel, and Joe was alarmed to think that he was going to go up those marble steps and in at the front door as if he was someone of importance.

Suddenly, the door opened and a man in some sort of livery ran towards them.

'My butler, Planchard,' Brian said in explanation to Joe as the man reached them.

Gloria had fallen into a doze in the taxi and only murmured drowsily as Brian gathered her into his arms.

15

The butler's eyes were full of anxiety as he cried, 'What's happened, sir? Can I help you at all?'

'There was a bit of an accident in the town, concerning the carriage,' Brian said, 'and I left it there. Pay the driver, will you, like a good chap? My hands are rather occupied at the moment.'

'Do you want help with Miss Gloria, sir?' Planchard said as he paid the driver, picked up his master's bag and cast a curious look at Joe, who had climbed out of the taxi and was looking around, not quite sure what to do next.

'I'm all right,' Brian said as they walked towards the house. 'There is no weight to Gloria. But you might look after this brave man here beside me. Name of Joe Sullivan, hailed recently from one of the immigrant ships from Ireland. He will be staying to dinner tonight.'

'Yes, sir,' the butler said, dutifully enough, and yet in the light spilling out from the hall Joe caught the man's surprised eyes alight on him speculatively as he bent towards Joe to take his case.

Joe hid his smile, for he guessed that New York was full of people from immigrant ships from all over the world, but none of them had been brought to the Brannigan house for dinner before. He also knew that he would probably be the talk of the place by morning.

'Now, Joe,' Brian said as they reached the house, 'Planchard will take charge of you, while I get Gloria sorted out.'

Planchard nodded in Joe's direction and, leaving his case in the hall, he said, 'If you leave your bag next to the case, sir, I will show you into the drawing room.'

'And when you have done that,' Brian said, 'perhaps you will tell your mistress what has happened and inform her that I am taking Gloria straight to her room. Summon Tilly too, for Miss Gloria may have need of her, and someone had better go for the doctor urgently.'

'I'll attend to it all directly, sir,' Planchard said.

16

Brian began to mount the ornate staircase, still with Gloria in his arms, while the butler said to Joe, 'If you would follow me, sir . . .'

Joe smiled ruefully because it was a novelty being called 'sir' and it had happened twice. Wondering what sort of room a drawing room was, he left down his bag and followed the butler, who crossed the black-and-white-tiled hall and opened cream double doors to a low and elegant room with a carpet so thick Joe's feet sank into it. 'If you will just wait here, sir,' the butler said, 'I am sure that Mr Brannigan will be with you shortly.'

Left alone, Joe glanced around the room with interest and a little fear, for he felt totally out of his depth. The room was lit with electric lights set around the walls and in a huge glass chandelier, which hung from the patterned ceiling. A gold suite was drawn up in front of the white marble fireplace where a welcoming fire blazed in the grate. Joe delicately ran his hands over the brocade pattern of the upholstery and wondered if he would ever dare to sit on one of those chairs.

He glanced at the small ornate clock on the mantelpiece. It was made of gold, which sparkled in the firelight, and had a glass front so the swinging pendulum was visible. 'Almost six o'clock,' Joe said to himself and, looking out where the silken curtains to either side of the large window had not been drawn, he saw the evening was as black as pitch.

He crossed the room and stood for a long time peering out at the grounds surrounding the house, marvelling at it all. He thought back to his many, uneventful years in Ireland. He knew that when he thought about his new life in America he could never have imagined the chain of events that had landed him in a house such as this, as the invited guest of such an obviously prominent and wealthy man. He tingled with excitement for he just knew that his life would take off from this point.

17

He wished no harm at all on the beautiful young lady he had rescued from danger and yet he couldn't but thank his lucky stars that her father was a factory owner. He just knew that Brian Brannigan could shape his future in America.

'Ah, there you are, my boy.'

Joe swung around from the window. Brian was standing in the doorway arm in arm with a lady whom he introduced as his wife, Norah. The resemblance to Gloria was marked. Joe guessed that once the older woman's hair had been just as strikingly blonde as her daughter's, but now it was much duller and tied from her face in a sort of fancy bun at the nape of her neck. She had the same high cheekbones, and the same-shaped eyes, though Norah's were plain blue. Behind them Joe saw the resentment and he knew that Mrs Brannigan didn't want the likes of him sitting down at her table.

When Brian had told Norah of the accident and of Joe's part in it and went on to say that he had invited the man to dinner, she had looked at him as if she couldn't believe her ears. She had been up to see Gloria, and she was distressed and worried, and now this other bombshell.

'You have invited that man to dinner, here?' she'd repeated.

'Aye,' said Brian. 'I did.'

'And why, pray, did you do that?'

'Do what, my dear?' Brian had asked mildly.

'Oh, don't be so obtuse, Brian,' Norah asked. 'Why ask a common workman to dinner?'

'Didn't I explain what he did, and that if he hadn't been there—'

'Of course you have explained,' Norah snapped. 'Though if you had acted as a proper father and refused to take Gloria to such an unsuitable place then she would have been in no danger whatsoever. But whatever he did I'm sure the man would hardly have expected to be asked to dine with us. Why didn't you thank him sincerely, as I am prepared

18

to do, offer him a sum of money and send him on his way? Find him a job if you must, but to ask him to dinner is madness. Surely you can see that he is bound to feel out of place and uncomfortable.'

'It was done in the heat of the moment,' Brian admitted. 'However, he is here now and you must accept it, my dear.'

'You do not have to explain manners to me,' Norah hissed. 'I know how to behave and conduct myself, and much better than you.'

Despite her views, though, Norah was quite impressed when she saw Joe. He was a handsome and well set up young man, and had a way of carrying himself. Added to that, his brown eyes looked honest and steady and he was at least respectable.

Norah Brannigan extended her hand to Joe and said, through pert, thin lips, 'I believe my husband and I have much to thank you for, Mr Sullivan? He tells me you saved our daughter's life today.'

'I happened to be in the right place at the right time, ma'am, that was all,' Joe said. 'I was just glad to be of service.'

'Gloria is much more comfortable now,' Brian said. 'We are awaiting the doctor and her maid, Tilly, is sitting with her.'

'I trust she will make a full and speedy recovery,' Joe said.

'So do I,' Norah agreed. And then she cast a venomous look in her husband's direction. 'Of course, the whole thing should never have happened in the first place.'

'Now, Norah,' Brian said in a placating tone, 'we have been all through that.' He turned to Joe. 'Now if you give me the name and address of your sponsor, I will send him word where you are.' Joe gave it to him and he wrote it on the pad he lifted from the desk, then pulled the bell rope by the side of the fireplace. 'We will have dinner shortly after the doctor has been, but in the meantime would you like a drink?' he asked Joe.

Joe thought about what the men on the ship coming over had said about the Prohibition Law in America forbidding the sale or production of alcohol, but from the vast array of bottles in the cabinet, he could see no sign of it in the Brannigan household. This didn't surprise him for, in his experience, most rich people seemed to be able to sidestep the law.

'I don't know what to ask for, sir,' he said. 'I understood that Prohibition would—'

'I saw the way the wind was blowing before it became law,' Brian said, 'and was able to stockpile a fair bit in the cellars. Ridiculous notion to try and turn a whole nation like this one teetotal.'

'I couldn't see it working in Ireland, sir,' said Joe with a smile.

'I couldn't see it even being proposed in Ireland,' Brian said. 'Doesn't work, of course. It will be two years by the end of January next year and already the gangs that used virtually to run the underclass of the city that I spoke about in the taxi have sprung up again. They are now in control of nearly all the illegal liquor smuggled in. Mark my words, that law will cause more problems in society, not less. Still, that doesn't answer my question. As this isn't a dry house yet, what would you like to drink?'

A pint of cold Guinness would have gone down a treat, but Joe couldn't see anything remotely like that and Brian, seeing his dilemma and guessing how he was feeling, said, 'Will you join me in a whiskey?'

Joe sighed inwardly. Whiskey at least he knew, though he hadn't drunk it often, so he said, 'A whiskey, sir, would be very good.'

A young maid dressed in a white apron over her black frock appeared then. 'Ah Mary,' Brian said, passing the paper into her hand, 'give this to McManus. Tell him to go to this address and inform a Mr Patrick Lacey that his friend, Mr Joe Sullivan, is dining with us this evening.'

Mary gave a little bob as she took the letter from Brian, and Joe realised how easy life was for a person rich enough to employ a bevy of servants.

'Now,' said Brian, passing a generous glass of whiskey to Joe, 'Sit down, make yourself comfortable and tell me a bit about yourself.'

Joe sat very gingerly on the gold suite, and told Brian of the small town of Buncrana in northern Donegal and the farm near to it where he had been born and reared. He went on to tell him of his young brother, Finn, who had enlisted in the Great War and was killed in 1916, and his elder brother, Tom, who now owned the farm after the death of his father, and his sister Nuala living in Birmingham, England. He didn't speak of Nuala wanting to marry a Protestant man, or that when she wrote the news of this to her parents her father had had a heart attack and died with the letter still in his hand.

Nor did he say that his mother, who had become almost unbearable to live with, had disowned Nuala because she blamed her for her father's death, and he never mentioned Aggie, his eldest sister, either – another one his mother disowned – who had run away from home when he was just a boy, because these were personal family matters and not for sharing.

'The place was not the same at all after Daddy died,' Joe told Brian and Norah. 'It was as if the heart had gone out of the place. And then I felt that life was passing me by and, well, I was breaking my back for a farm that would never be mine and so I decided to give America a try.'

'And how did your brother take that news?' Brian asked.

'Oh, Tom understood,' Joe said. 'In fact he—' But Joe got no further for at that moment the doorbell rang.

Knowing that it was probably the doctor, Norah was crossing the room before the maid appeared at the door. 'Have to leave you to your own devices, Mr Sullivan,' Brian said.

'Don't worry, sir, really,' Joe said. 'I am anxious as you are to hear what the doctor has to say about your daughter.'

'Help yourself to another drink and make yourself comfortable,' Brian said as he left. 'We will both be back directly.'

Joe didn't help himself to a drink, but sipped the one he had slowly as he again looked about the room in wonder. He thought of his brother on the farm and what he would say if he saw him now, sitting in such a room in such a house, as if he had a perfect right to be there, and supping whiskey, no less.

He knew that Tom, in similar circumstances, would probably be paralysed with shock and fear, and unable to take joy in any of it. He, on the other hand, intended to make the most of every minute because he knew it would be nothing more than a glimpse into how the toffs lived, and that when this bizarre day was at an end, his life would return to normal.

The doctor stayed about half an hour and by that time Joe's stomach had begun to grumble.

'The news is good,' Brian said as he re-entered the room. 'The doctor said there were no bones broken. Of course the poor girl is bruised all over and badly shaken up, and might be slightly concussed, but he said there's nothing a few days in bed won't cure.'

'I'm pleased, sir,' Joe said with a smile. 'You must both be very relieved.'

'We are,' Brian answered. 'I told the doctor what you did and he said you undoubtedly saved Gloria from a much greater injury. Now, I suggest that I let Cook know that we will be ready for dinner in half an hour or so.'

The dining room was even more opulent than the drawing room. It was dominated by a large table laid with a white lace cloth, and more cutlery and glasses than Joe had ever seen in his life. He knew that he would have to watch and copy Brian's use of them very carefully or risk making an utter fool of himself.

Before they had the chance to start their meal, though, there was a knock at the door and the butler came in and said that Bert Clifford was outside and would like a word. Brian was on his feet immediately. 'Excuse me,' he said throwing his napkin down onto the table. 'He probably has news of Tim.'

Brian's face when he returned was very grave. 'The news is that Tim has a fractured skull,' he said, 'and it's touch and go whether he will pull through at all, or if he will be any use if he does survive. It is a terrible tragedy altogether.'

'Has he a family?' Joe asked.

'No,' Brian said. 'He has always lived alone in a little place above the stables. I will go up to the hospital myself tomorrow, have a word with the doctors and see what's the prognosis, but for the moment I am without someone to see to the horses.'

And then he took Joe totally by surprise by asking, 'What about you, Mr Sullivan? Could you take over for a few days until we find out what's what with Tim?'

'Me, sir?'

'You seem to know about horses.'

'Not horses like these, though, sir,' Joe said. 'I only had dealings with farm horses, not thoroughbreds, and then only one at a time.'

'I thought many of our countrymen did a study of thoroughbred horses, especially those thundering around a race track.'

'You are right, sir,' Joe said, 'but not me. I have never backed a horse in my life. There was little money, for one thing, and I have never liked the idea of throwing hard-earned money away. So you see, sir, I wouldn't be the man for you at all.'

'You are exactly the man,' Brian said. 'These are not racehorses, and I need no gambler in my employ.'

23

Joe didn't know how to get out of this because he was sure that Brian thought he had more expertise than he had, but how could he refuse? Wouldn't he scupper his chances of employment of any kind if he did? And then there was Patrick Lacey. 'I'd like to help you out, sir, really I would, but you see, my sponsor may have already arranged a place to stay and—'

'Naturally he would be informed of the change of plan if you agree to do it.'

Despite the benign look on Brian's face, Joe saw the determination to have his own way in his steely brown eyes and heard it in his voice. Patrick would be informed, not asked if that was all right or convenient. That was the rich for you.

He suppressed the sigh as he asked, 'How many horses are we talking about, sir?'

'Not that many,' Brian said reassuringly. 'There's Gloria's pony, Bramble – the one you stopped so admirably today – my hunter, the matching pair for the large carriage and the mare Norah likes, which often pulls the small dogcart. Think about it, for you would be getting me out of a fix, and you seem to have a fine empathy with horses.'

Joe's heart sank. Five horses and all thoroughbreds, he could bet, and he hadn't a clue how to deal with them.

'Mr Brannigan,' he admitted, 'I have never even saddled a horse in my life. If we rode one at all, it was bareback.'

'Well, you can learn, man,' Brian said. 'It's not hard, and you will have the stable lad, Bobby, to help you. What that boy doesn't know about horses isn't worth knowing. What do you say?'

There was nothing Joe could say but yes. He had known from the start that he would have to agree to anything Brian planned. Joe could not afford to upset him, for he held his future in the palm of his hand.

'Right, that's settled then,' Brian said, beaming approval. 'After the meal I will send my man McManus to your

24

sponsor's house again to tell him of the change of plan and have a room made ready for you in the basement with the other servants. Then early tomorrow I want you to fetch the carriage back from the docks.'

'Yes, sir,' said Joe, and though nervous of doing a job he knew so little about, he was relieved to have employment and a place that night to lay his head.

'Mind you,' Brian went on, 'I think the day of the horse, except for recreational use, is at an end. It is getting too dangerous to take them on to the streets these days, and I have ordered myself a motor car, so that will mean the carriage and the matching pair will probably be leaving us.' He leaned towards his wife and, seeing her disgruntled look, said, 'Do take that frown from your face, my dear. I have made my views abundantly clear. In fact, Bramble too is on borrowed time,' he added, turning back to Joe.

'Not because of the incident earlier, sir?' Joe asked.

'No,' Brian said. 'That really wasn't the pony's fault, but Gloria has nearly outgrown him now anyway, and then after Christmas she is off to a convent school in Madison. If she wants to ride when she comes home in the holidays then I will hire from the local riding school. So whoever is taken on in the stables will have to see to the car too, of course.'

'Tim won't do that,' Norah said. 'You know he won't.'

'Well, you can't teach old dogs new tricks, I suppose,' Brian said. 'In fact, I have been thinking that it was about time Tim was pensioned off. If he pulls through from this then I will talk it over with him. I've no idea how old he is, but he is no spring chicken and I'll see to it that he is all right.'

Norah laughed. 'I wish you well of it,' she said, 'because he won't take kindly to that.'

'Then that will be an obstacle to overcome in the future,' Brian said. 'What I want to know, Joe, is what do you think of me getting a car?'

Joe didn't know how to answer this because he was far

more nervous of dealing with a car than horses of any description. At least they were familiar. In the end he said, 'I . . . I don't really know what to think, sir.'

'Think you could drive a car, Joe?'

'Oh, I really don't know about that, sir,' Joe said agitatedly. 'I have never had anything to do with cars.'

'Not many have,' Brian said. 'Let's just say that you are not opposed to the motor car, which will soon be the only way to travel around this city and any other too?'

'No, sir,' Joe said. 'It's progress, I suppose, like the steam ships taking over from the old sailing ships.'

'That's true enough,' Brian said. 'What I am asking you, Joe Sullivan, is when the car I have ordered is delivered, are you prepared to learn to drive it so that you can take me to the factory each day and bring me home each evening?'

Joe thought about it, but not for very long, because in his heart of hearts he thought he would probably settle to it better than factory work. He knew too that Brian wanted him to do this for him and he was a man used to getting his own way. If he refused he'd get someone else who was willing to do it and that would be an opportunity lost to Joe, and he sensed that Brian would be disappointed in him. So he said, 'This seems to be a country where life refuses to stand still so I am willing to learn to drive a car if you want me to.'

'Can't say fairer than that,' Brian said in approval, and he clapped Joe on the shoulder.

THREE

After dinner that first evening, Planchard introduced Joe to the rest of the staff. They had heard how he had rescued Miss Gloria, and at great risk to his own life, and so he was welcomed as something of a hero. Joe hadn't grown up in a home where praise was customary and so he was embarrassed at the fuss made. He was also very tired, and was pleasantly surprised to be shown to the room in the basement that, Planchard told him, Mr Brannigan senior had specially built to house the servants.

He didn't notice that it was basic and spartan, for he'd never had a bed, never mind a whole room, to himself before. And it had everything he needed. It housed an iron bedstead, a chest of drawers and a hanging rail, and to him it was like a little palace. He lay in that comfortable bed that first night amongst crisp clean sheets, under plenty of warm blankets covered with a bedspread, and was so happy that he had taken the plunge and come to America. He had the feeling that this was the sort of country where anything could happen, a true land of opportunity.

The following morning, Brian ordered a taxi for himself and Joe, using a telephone that he had had fitted in the house. Joe was astounded when he told him this.

'You mean, sir, that you can just pick up a machine and talk to people miles away?'

Brian smiled at Joe's astonished face. 'That is the general idea,' he said. 'How else would the taxi firm know that I wanted them this morning?'

'It's almost unbelievable to me, sir,' Joe said. 'I know that you said I was to go into New York this morning to fetch the carriage back and I wasn't sure how I was going to go in except maybe to use one of those frightening tram cars.'

'No, Joe, not this morning,' Brian said. 'Though you will have to get to grips with those sooner or later. Today I am going with you because I want to see how Tim is faring. And don't be in too much of a hurry to fetch the carriage back. Familiarise yourself with the place before you collect it because as it is Saturday today I will not be going to work and will have no urgent need of it.'

'Thank you, sir,' Joe said, grateful for his employer's consideration, because he had had only a glimpse of the city as the taxi had sped through the deepening dusk the evening before and he was dying to see more of it.

Just a short while later, after his second ride in a taxi, he stepped from it onto one of the crowded streets and looked about him. He could hardly believe that he was here at last, standing in New York City.

Used to winding country lanes, he was fascinated by the wide and perfectly straight streets and the way many of them had numbers instead of names. The city's skyscrapers towered above him, and the size and variety of the shops and the goods they had on sale in their huge glass windows fairly dazzled him.

To all sides, people, seemingly of every colour and creed, thronged the pavements which Joe had heard tell were called sidewalks. He noted that though many folk spoke with the American drawl, there were plenty more with foreign accents or inflexions in their speech, and he knew it wasn't just the Irish who were flooding American shores. New York truly was a cosmopolitan city and he felt privileged to be part of

28

this New World. He vowed to store it all up to tell Tom in his letters home.

When he arrived back, later that morning, it was to learn that Tim the coachman had died in the night.

'Poor fellow,' McManus said. 'Been here years, and then to end his days like that . . .'

All the staff were upset over Tim's death, as was Brian Brannigan, although he was heartily glad that Joe had agreed to step into Tim's shoes. Joe had surprised himself that morning by quite enjoying bringing the pony and carriage home. Bramble was a lovely little pony when he was not spooked by anything, and rattled along at a fair old rate.

Joe couldn't help comparing Bramble to the farm horses back home. Their top speed was little faster than a man could walk briskly. He did agree with Brian, though, that the city streets were not so safe for horses any more. Soon Bramble would be sold on and it would be a car that Joe would be driving. That thought was a scary one. However, for now he had to care for the horses and it was Joe who drove the sombre Brannigan family to St Bridget's church a few days later for Tim's funeral.

The next day was Thanksgiving and a half-day off for Joe. And so, after tasting such delights as apple and butternut squash soup, pumpkin pie and Mayflower pudding, he decided to look up Patrick Lacey. He braced himself and went into the city on his first tramcar. Patrick lived in a downtown tenement, and McManus had given Joe instructions on how to find him in that maze of streets on the East Side. He found 57 Orchard Street fairly easily, but stood outside it for a moment or two, surprised by its seediness. It had not been what he had expected at all in this brave new world.

The tenement was just one of many, and built of dull grey brick, with an iron fire escape fitted to the side of it, running down to the ground, and which, to Joe's surprise, was festooned with washing. There were few people about, but then the day wasn't a pleasant one and the other servants had told him that on Thanksgiving Day most people got together with their families if they had any close by.

As he entered the tenement door, his nostrils were immediately assailed by a pungent smell that came, he supposed, from so many people crowded in together and he was glad that the smell got fainter when he reached the third floor where Patrick's rooms were.

Patrick was delighted to see him and Joe noted his friend seemed taller somehow, and certainly broader than the man he remembered leaving Ireland's shores.

'Well, the American life seems to suit you well enough,' he said as Patrick drew him inside. 'You're looking grand.'

'Never mind me, you old codger,' Patrick said. 'Sit you down there and I will rustle us up some tea and then maybe you will tell me what has happened to you because all I have had so far is cryptic messages.'

Joe sat down on the battered sofa and in no time was nursing a cup of hot strong tea and regaling Patrick with his adventures since the incident at the docks.

Patrick listened flabbergasted. 'You are one lucky sod,' he remarked good-naturedly when Joe had finished. 'Tom always used to say if you fell in a dung heap, you would come up smelling of roses and he is damned right.'

'I can't help being in the right place at the right time.'

'Where was the imperilled heiress when I was ready to disembark?' Patrick asked. 'That's what I want to know.'

'If there wasn't one, then there wasn't one,' Joe replied with a grin. 'I'd say that heiresses, imperilled or otherwise, are in pretty short supply, and you can't lay the blame for that at my door either.'

Patrick shrugged. 'I suppose not,' he conceded. 'And I haven't done that badly myself either.' He caught sight of Joe's disbelieving eyes and said, 'I know what you are thinking and you are right – it isn't that damned pretty a place and not one half as good as where you are living. But it is a good deal better than some, and better than when I first came when I was lodging with another family. Talk about cramped.'

'How many rooms have you?'

'Three,' Patrick said. 'If you have finished your tea I'll show you.'

'Well, this is the living room, I suppose?' Joe said.

'Yeah, and the only room with windows,' Patrick said. 'Though the view is not one to write home about, so I am not really bothered about that anyway. Next door to it is the kitchen.' And as Patrick led the way to it Joe caught sight of a few cupboards and a sort of stove with a couple of gas rings. 'Fairly new innovation, the gas,' Patrick said. 'These tenements were thrown up with no form of lighting, heating, no running water, nothing, but now we have gas lights, gas rings to cook on, and a toilet just down the corridor. 'And this,' he said, opening the door off the kitchen, 'is where I sleep. You see there would have been plenty of room for you too.'

There would have been, Joe saw, for Patrick had a size-able double bed, but Joe thought of his own little room and bed for him and him alone – his little oasis of calm where he could hide away in his off-duty moments – and he knew he would never change places with Patrick. He didn't say this, however, because he had no wish to alienate his friend.

'At least you are almost right in the city,' he said, 'and I bet there is fine entertainment to be had in New York on Thanksgiving Day?'

'Entertainment?' Patrick cried. 'Man, there is everything here. Catch up your coat and we'll hit the town and you'll see for yourself.'

Joe never forgot his first foray into New York at night and he wrote in all down in a letter to Tom the following day.

Dear Tom,

Last night I was out with Patrick Lacey, who wanted to show me what New York is like at night and we went in on an underground train that they call a subway. We went into what looked like a large metal box on the street to find hundreds of steps leading down. And you went down so far I began to think that we were descending to the bowels of the earth.

Suddenly, we came out at a platform, not unlike those at Derry with the ticket office at the end and it was hard to believe that above us were roads and houses and shops and people carrying on as normal. However, everyone else seemed to be taking it in their stride and the platform was fair teeming with people. I didn't want to make a holy show of Patrick and so I said nothing and got in the train behind him as if I had been doing it every day of my life and it seemed no time at all till we were at Times Square.

Full darkness had fallen then and oh Tom there are not enough words to tell you about the lights. Patrick said he was fair mesmerised at first and so was I. The colours were so bright, so vibrant. It was amazing. There weren't just one or two, you understand. Whole sides of buildings were lit up in every colour you could think of and some were fixed to flash on and off.

Eventually Patrick dragged me away to a place called a speakeasy, because though there is supposed to be no alcohol allowed in America at the moment, at the speakeasies they serve it in teapots and give you a cup to drink from, with a saucer as well, so any taking a casual look in would think we were all taking tea.

They play something called jazz. It's really catchy, foot-tapping music, and played with such energy on big brass instruments. The dance floor was full.

32

The way some of the women dance the Charleston and the Shimmy and the like, though, would be frowned upon in the whole of Ireland. And many of the young women have their hair cut short, and their dresses go straight down and have a little bit of skirt at the bottom with hems just below the knee. And some smoke and nearly all wear cosmetics. Imagine a few of those walking the streets of Buncrana?

It was a truly amazing night and at the end of it, I took a streetcar that brought me most of the way home. This truly is a wonderful country, Tom, and I cannot thank you enough for giving me the opportunity to come here.

But when Joe had sealed that letter and sent it, he wondered if Tom would feel any resentment when he read it, knowing that he would never experience any of these things himself. All Tom's life he had sublimated any desires of his own and bent to the will of a crabbed old woman who never had a civil word for him. Joe knew at the end of it, with their mother gone, eventually Tom would inherit the farm, but he thought it a high price to pay.

As the months slipped one into another, Joe considered himself a very fortunate man. He had a job he enjoyed, especially when the car arrived. It was a magnificent, dark green Cadillac, and Joe thought that the idea that he would sit behind the wheel and drive it was both terrifying and thrilling. But he had readily taken to driving, and so the carriage and matching pair that pulled it had been sold, and so had Bramble, and Joe was by then so mesmerised by the car that he hardly missed them.

He was truly content. He had a generous employer that he respected, good wholesome food, a warm bed and a room of his own. Added to all this, he enjoyed the camaraderie of the staff and had a good friend in Patrick Lacey. What more could a man want?

And all this had come about because he'd rescued the daughter of the house from danger. He would have hated anything to have happened to Gloria because she was a lovely young thing. Not that he saw much of her because after his first Christmas in the house she had started at her convent boarding school in Madison.

She had told him that as well as academic subjects, she would learn the sort of attributes she needed to take her place in society. 'Isn't it odd, Joe?' she went on. 'Mother says I have to learn how to be a lady. I thought you just grew into one, but apparently not.'

Joe had laughed at her gently and said, 'And I'm sure that you will make a fine lady at the end of it.'

While Gloria had settled down happily at the school almost immediately, she was missed by everyone at home. Her parents were like two lost souls. Brian eventually started going to his old club two or three evenings a week, and Mary reported that even on the nights he was home, he and the mistress hardly said one word to each other while she was in the room serving dinner.

They both lived for the holidays when the house would come alive and ring with the sound of chattering, giggling girls running up and down the stairs. They danced to the pulsating jazz that Gloria played on her phonograph, or played tennis on the court Brian had had made in the paddock at the back of the house.

Kate, the cook, would moan that she didn't know whether she was coming or going, but Joe knew by her twinkling eyes that really she loved to see the house full. She made sure the cookie jar was never empty, and there was always homemade lemonade on offer.

Joe was also pressed into service to fetch and carry girls around the city. He knew he was a favourite with them all because he never told tales on them. Gloria's friends also thought it the most romantic thing in the world for a man to rescue a girl in the way he had Gloria, and Gloria claimed he was her own knight in shining armour.

One day in the autumn of 1923 Brian asked Joe if he had ever thought of taking any of the courses being advertised in the city institutes. Shock ran through Joe at Brian's words, because he knew his employer well by now, and when he spoke like that, it wasn't really a question at all. It was more like the iron fist inside the velvet glove.

Yet Joe answered, 'No, sir. Things like that are not for the likes of me. I am not brainy enough.'

'Who says?' Brian said. 'You have to have a brain in your head to understand the mechanics of a car, and they are always praising your knowledge at the garage.'

'That's different, sir, and—'

'They do courses in typewriting and accounts, and I need a man in the office,' Brian said.

'Oh, sir, it is kind of you and all, but I am not fitted out for office work.'

'Kind be damned!' Brian cried. 'You would suit me very well. I am impressed by your common sense and your intelligence. Will you do this for me, Joe?'

Joe shook his head helplessly. 'I honestly don't know if I will be able to make head nor tail out of any of it,' he said. 'And I would probably need a typewriter.'

'Leave that to me,' Brian said. 'Your job is to take the course and get Bobby ready to take over from you in a year or so.'

Joe sighed and yet he knew the hand of opportunity was being extended to him again, and he would be a fool if he didn't grasp it tight.

A month or so into the course Joe thought he had made a vast mistake. He found it the hardest thing he had ever done in his life. He had always been good at figures and thought he would find accounts not that difficult. He was wrong, but he found typewriting much worse. Memorising the keyboard was hard enough and his fingers seemed too big and cumbersome for the keys.

He laboured on and didn't bother complaining because he knew that Brian would obviously want some return on the money he had spent educating him, and he hoped that his employer's belief in him was not misplaced.

None of the Brannigans' staff could understand why he was doing all the book work, and neither could Patrick. Joe told none of them, not even Tom, what Brian had said about being taken on in the office if he should pass the exams, because he could not visualise himself in such a role. He didn't know if he wanted it, certain he would feel out of his depth. Anyway, there would be no possibility of it if he were to fail his exams, as he was certain sure he was going to.

In one way, though, Joe was pleased that he had so much going on in his life because that summer he had found himself attracted to Gloria physically for the first time in his life. He had been appalled and disgusted that he should have such feelings for a young girl, and the boss's daughter, no less, and seventeen years younger than he was. He knew he wasn't just lusting after her beauty and her developing figure, for his love for Gloria seemed to fill every part of him. Just to be near her caused the heat to fill his body as the blood coursed more quickly through his veins and he knew that he would willingly lay down his life for Gloria and feel it an honour to do so.

He recalled the day she had left to start boarding school she had sought him out in the garage first and put her arms around him and kissed him on the cheek. She had been a child then, though, and he had thought of her as a child. But two years down the line she was a child no longer. He wasn't sure that he could trust himself not to betray his feelings if she were to do anything like that again, and he knew there was no way that he would ever risk that.

This meant that his manner towards her changed. They had always had a special relationship. Gloria never forgot that Joe had possibly saved her life, and so they had always been free and easy with one another, and she never thought of calling him 'Sullivan', as her mother did. But suddenly Joe became very stiff and proper, as that was the only way he could deal with emotions that he had never imagined he would have.

Gloria had been confused and hurt at first. She assumed that she must have said something to offend, though Joe denied she had, nor would he admit that there was anything wrong. Then she became irritated by his remoteness and the peculiar way he was behaving, and one day she had stamped her dainty little foot on the floor and almost hissed, 'Joe, if you say just one more time that it is not your place to comment on something I say then I will get very cross with you.'

Joe had no reply to that, and in the end Gloria had barked out, 'Are you going to say nothing at all?'

Joe shrugged. 'What is there to say, Miss Gloria? You and your parents are the bosses around here.'

'Joe Sullivan, you must be the most aggravating man in the whole world,' Gloria cried.

'So you say, miss,' Joe had replied, and she had flounced back to the house.

He was sad that he had made her so angry, and from that point her attitude to him had been cooler, and although that made life easier for him, he missed the camaraderie that they'd once enjoyed.

But he didn't allow himself to dwell on any sort of relationship with Gloria. He knew the only way to get rid of any madness of the mind – and this was a form of madness – was to work harder until he got over it, as he knew he would in the end.

However, Joe's hard work paid off because in the summer of 1924, he took exams in accountancy and typewriting and in the autumn of that year found out that he had passed both with high grades. He was delighted, but unaware that his results meant that his life was going to change completely. Brian clapped Joe on the shoulder, said that he had always had faith in him and that he would be an invaluable help to him in the office.

That was enough of a sea change for Joe to cope with, but then Brian dropped another bombshell.

'Of course, now that you are going to be working for me in the office a servant's room in the basement will no longer be suitable accommodation for you,' he announced.

Joe was astounded. 'But why, sir? I'm very comfortable there.'

'Joe, this is an opportunity to better yourself,' Brian said. 'You must trust me in this.'

'But where will I stay, sir?' Joe asked.

'Why, in the house, of course,' said Brian, as if the decision had all been signed and sealed. 'You'll be put in one of the guest rooms.'

Joe's whole being recoiled from living in the house. It was the largest and most sumptuous dwelling he had ever seen, but it was someone else's house, and he really didn't want to leave his room in the basement.

But Brian had decided that that was how it was going to be, and Joe was to take his meals with the family in the house too. Joe remembered the only other meal he had had in the house, the evening he had arrived in New York, and the way that Norah had resented his presence then. He had no reason to think that she thought any more of him now, for all Brian's praise. He would much rather have taken his meals in the kitchen and knew he would miss the banter and companionship.

But never in his wildest dreams had Joe thought the other servants would act the way they did when he told them what Brian had in mind for him. Kate actually called him an upstart and made a few pointed references about people not knowing their position in life and aping their betters.

Joe didn't even try to explain or justify himself, for surely they knew he had to do what his employer wanted, just the same as they did, but he was sorry to lose their friendship. Only Planchard, himself in a privileged position, congratulated him and said he deserved every success, and Joe was grateful for his support.

To his utmost surprise, Patrick reacted the same way as most of the Brannigans' staff when Joe told him of Brian's plans for him. 'Well, you've done well for yourself, all right,' he commented sourly. 'I'm surprised you still come to see a common man like me.'

'Come on, Patrick. It's still me – Joe.'

'No it isn't,' Patrick said. 'The Joe I know would never have sucked up to his employers the way you must have done.'

Joe was surprised and a little hurt. He considered Patrick a really good friend; surely, he thought, you want a friend to achieve good things in life. He hoped that he would have reacted differently if the positions had been reversed.

However, Joe knew that something had been severed between him and Patrick that night and he felt heart sore about it. In fact, he felt so deeply hurt that he was determined at the first opportunity to tell Brian he wanted no fancy job in a fancy office and he would like to turn the clock back and just go back to his room in the basement and let everything go on as it had before.

In the cold light of day, though, he knew he couldn't do that. His future was inexorably linked to Brian's, for better or for worse.

For his second dinner in the house, Joe dressed with meticulous care. He knew that Brian's wife would be the kind of person who had never really seen him as a person; to her he would just be one of the servants. But she would probably remember that the last time he had dinner in this house, he had been wearing soiled and travel-weary clothes, the hand that he had extended to her had been rough and calloused, with blackened nails, and his brogue had been so thick it could have been cut with a knife.

That night he wore a dark blue suit and a snow-white shirt, the striped tie matched the handkerchief in his top pocket, cufflinks sparkled at his wrists, and the black leather shoes were so highly polished he had almost been able to see his face in them. Added to this, his hands were much softer than they had been and his nails spotless. Mustering as much confidence as he could, he extended his hand to the woman whose eyes had opened wider in approval and said, 'Good evening, Mrs Brannigan.'

She smiled at the charming lilt to his voice and her smile was a genuine one as she shook his hand and said she was pleased to see him. However, her eyes were shrewd and Joe wondered if she couldn't understand why her husband had paid for the man to have lessons in accounts and typewriting when there must be many already trained for such work. Sullivan, after all, was just a chauffeur.

She betrayed none of this in her manner to him, though, and when Joe showed how embarrassed he was to be served by people he had once counted as his friends he saw Norah's sympathetic eyes on him. She understood perfectly how he was feeling, and she was also aware of how servants often reacted with someone they thought was stepping out of their class. Brian, on the other hand, was unaware of Joe's discomfort and saw no problem at all, and Joe knew that that was just one more thing that he would have to overcome.

'And how did you like the work in the office today, Mr Sullivan?' Norah asked him as the meal was served and the servants left the room.

'Oh, I liked it fine, ma'am,' Joe replied. 'Of course, there is still a lot for me to learn.'

'Plenty of time, Joe,' Brian said. 'And at least you have made a good start. Those letters you did for me today were first class.'

'Thank you, sir,' Joe said. 'Tell you the truth, I never expected to have a job like this. To go to work every day in a suit was never in my line of thought at all.'

'America truly is the land of opportunity,' Brian said.

'It is, sir, right enough,' Joe agreed. 'But it was you, not America, that gave me this chance and I will never forget it.'

'Thank you for that, Joe,' Brian said. 'But in the Ireland I remember, and the Ireland some of the migrants tell me about, such things as I did for you couldn't be done. If your father is a drunk or a layabout then it is almost assumed his offspring will be the same. Your future and expectations would be fixed in the minds of those around you. It was America, Joe, that gave me the opportunity to help you get on.'

'You are right there, sir,' said Joe. 'And tonight I intend to write a letter to my brother and tell him all about the good fortune that has lighted on me, and all about my first day at work.'

'Have you given him no hint of it before this?'

'I have told him very little, sir. I was going to tell him what I was doing, but I found it all so hard at the beginning I didn't think I would ever make a hand of it, and was positive I would fail my exams. There seemed no point in saying anything until the results were in, but now he needs to know. He will be delighted for me. You'd not find a better man than Tom, for it was his generosity of spirit that allowed me to come to America in the first place.'

'How's that?' Norah asked.

'He sold a field of sheep,' Joe said. 'He wouldn't have been able to manage the sheep on his own once I had left, but he sold the whole lot to a neighbour who had been after them for some time. And he gave the money to me to pay for my passage over and to keep me for a few weeks in case I couldn't get employment straight away.'

41

'What a wonderful gesture,' Norah said. 'He surely is a brother to be proud of. And now if everyone has finished maybe, Brian, you will ring for the next course?'

Joe's presence at meal times was a very beneficial one for Norah, because he soon became aware of her unhappiness. He sensed that she was lonely and missing Miss Gloria, and he found himself feeling sorry for her and so often tried to keep the conversation going.

A few weeks after Joe had moved into the house, Brian said one morning at the office, 'It's obvious that you are enjoying yourself at work because the way you talk about it over dinner you have even got Norah interested.'

'You don't think that I am talking too much, sir?'

'I do not, Joe. I tell you, I have never seen Norah so animated.' He thought for a minute and added, 'Well, if I'm honest she was like that when Gloria was smaller. Sometimes we even had guests for dinner. Seems a long while ago now. You seem to have rejuvenated something in her.'

Brian was right. Norah was greatly attracted by Joe. She didn't think of him in a sexual way – she wasn't going to be that stupid, – but she thought that if she'd ever had a son, she would have liked one like Joe and she couldn't for the life of her think why he was still unmarried.

'I haven't found the right woman yet,' he told her when she asked him.

'What!' she exclaimed. 'I can't believe that in the whole of New York you haven't found a girl to suit you. Are you difficult to please, Mr Sullivan?'

'I wouldn't say so,' Joe said. 'I mean, not more than most men, but I may be more on the cautious side.'

'I wouldn't have said that that was part of your personality at all.'

'Ah, maybe not generally,' Joe said, 'but I think it pays to be a little hesitant when someone is making a lifelong commitment.'

'And there you have it, my dear,' Brian said. 'The man rests his case. Anyway, a wife might bring further problems. It suits me to have Joe as free as a bird just now. Anyway,' he went on, 'Gloria will be home in a week and your time will probably not be your own then, for, going by past performances, you will be called on to be a taxi service to Gloria and her entourage of friends.'

'I shan't mind that, sir.'

'That's what I like, an adaptable man,' Brian said. 'And you know I can barely wait to see my little girl again.'

Nor can I, thought Joe, but kept that thought to himself. He had no intention of rocking the boat. Many men had to cope with the fact that they loved a woman who was unattainable and he was just one more. He was sure he would get over the fixation he had for Gloria Brannigan in time. He had to, and that was all there was to it.

FOUR

When Gloria arrived home in the summer of 1925, she had finished school for good. To celebrate, Brian bought her a car.

'A Model T Ford,' he told Joe. 'And a snip at three hundred and fifty dollars. I don't know why you don't buy a car of your own. You said to me one time that you had a heap of money stashed away and you have had a rake of rises since then. Why don't you spend some of it?'

'I suppose if I am honest, sir, it is because I have been encouraged to be frugal all my life,' Joe said.

'What are you saving for?' Brian asked, adding sarcastically, 'Your marriage?'

'Hardly, sir, with no one on the horizon.'

'Well, your funeral then?' Brian said. 'And after your death you can have a great mausoleum built and people will come and look at it. "Joe Sullivan," one will say to another, "Who was he now?"

'"Well, now, I am not too sure," will be the reply, "but he must be someone important to have this huge monument built."'

Joe was laughing as he said, 'Not that either, sir.'

'Then what, for God's sake?' Brian said. 'What is the point of saving for saving's sake? As you are not prepared to enter the marriage stakes, there won't even be a son or daughter to leave it all to after your day.'

Joe said nothing, but he knew there would never be a child for him, because he had given his heart to Gloria Brannigan. That was a great cross for him to bear, especially as he knew that all he could ever be to her was a friend.

Everyone, even the servants, had looked forward to Gloria coming home for good. Joe felt the same, but with some trepidation because he knew what a strain it had been living in the same house as her in the holidays, and yet he couldn't wait to see her. She had always been like a ray of sunshine in the house and brought the whole place alive, and Joe knew that Brian and Norah looked forward to having their little girl back home again, where they thought she belonged.

But it was soon apparent to Joe that Gloria had changed. She had finally grown up, he supposed, but there was no trace of the fairly compliant child about the girl that faced them across the table on her first night home.

They had almost finished the meal when she said, 'I am tired of learning now. I want to live a little and have some fun with my friends.' She turned to her parents. 'You have to realise that I am an adult now and entitled to more freedom.'

Joe could see her point, though he didn't say so. He found while he could chat easily to Brian and Norah when Gloria wasn't around, he was much more reticent with her there because her nearness affected him alarmingly.

He doubted that Brian or Norah noticed this for they were used to their daughter holding the floor. He too loved to hear her talk, the words tripping over her pretty little lips; he liked to watch her face light up and her eyes sparkle as she told them all some amusing tale, and to hear her tinkling laugh. To him she was a perfect being, truly beautiful, and although he knew it was futile to love her as he did, he couldn't seem to help himself.

'Really, women today want to have the same freedom as men,' Gloria was saying.

Joe heard Norah's sharp intake of breath, but Gloria either didn't notice or didn't care because she continued, 'Many of my friends have older brothers and they have all sorts going on at the colleges they attend – ball games, crew races and college hops. Oh, the list is endless. They want us to go along and enjoy it and, really, why shouldn't we?'

'Are you out of your mind?' Brian exploded. 'A little freedom is one thing, but this is nonsense, Gloria. You must see that.'

'No, I don't see that at all,' Gloria stated flatly. 'What's wrong with what I said?'

'This silly nonsense about being equal with men, for one thing. It isn't how respectable women talk at all.'

'And you can't go to events at men's colleges unchaperoned,' Norah put in.

'Will the pair of you stop being so old-fashioned and stuffy?' Gloria cried in exasperation. 'And if Joe will show me how to drive the car, how will you stop me going out when I want to?'

'I could forbid it,' Brian said.

'Yes, Daddy,' Gloria said. 'And I could just as easily take no notice.'

Brian's face went puce with temper, but Gloria ignored him. She leaped to her feet, saying as she did so, 'Anyway, no time like the present. I'll wait for you outside, Joe,' and she disappeared out of the door.

She had put Joe into an intolerable position. He looked across the table to Brian and said, 'What d'you want me to do, sir?'

Brian shook his head. He looked like a defeated man and Norah seemed horror-struck at the turn of events. Joe felt sorry for them both, though. In a way, he thought, they had brought it upon themselves because the two of them had indulged Gloria for far too long to start denying her things now and expect her to just accept it.

This was proved when Brian said, 'I don't know, Joe.

I am not sure that I know anything any more. But you best start teaching Gloria to drive the car if she is so set on it. Better that than she takes it onto the roads without the least idea of how to drive it and ends up having an accident.'

Joe went, but he was cross with Gloria and within a few minutes of him getting in the car, she was aware of it.

'You're annoyed with me, aren't you?' she said.

Joe was too angry to be his usual cautious self when dealing with Gloria and he burst out, 'Yes I am, Miss Gloria. You were totally inconsiderate of your parents' feelings tonight and put me in a devil of a fix, and really the only crime they have ever committed is that of loving you too much.'

'I know, Joe,' Gloria said. 'And I am sorry for them really. I am not completely heartless, but I know them, and if I'd shown any sign of weakness, they would have ground me down like they have in the past. Do you know, Joe, I had more freedom at the convent than I have ever been allowed here. What madness is that?'

Joe sighed. 'And I have seen how frustrated you have got at times, but really it's because your parents love you and don't want anything to happen to you.'

'I know, but, Joe, they are smothering me,' Gloria cried.

'Miss Gloria, they have missed you sorely when you have been away at school,' Joe told her softly. 'It isn't unreasonable for them to want to spend some time with you now that you are finished with education. I bet that's what they were looking forward to. Couldn't this great declaration of your need for freedom have waited at least until you'd been home with your family a while, and then introduced it more slowly?'

'I had to do it while I had the courage,' Gloria said. Then, catching sight of the reproach on Joe's face, she cried, 'Don't look at me that way. I talked it over with the girls and we all agreed that it was best to be straight with them from the start.'

47

'Better for you,' Joe said. 'Sometimes you have to consider other people's feelings too, and if necessary put them first for a change. Still,' he said heavily, 'I suppose the damage is done now.'

'I suppose so,' Gloria said, 'though I promise that I will try and make amends, and one thing I can be grateful for anyway is that you have lost that artificial and stiff way you used to talk to me, even if you are taking me to task.'

'Miss Gloria –'

'Why did you change so completely, Joe?' Gloria said. 'I often wanted to ask you.'

Joe's heart was hammering in his chest so loudly that he was surprised that Gloria couldn't hear it, and the roof of his mouth felt unaccountably dry. He forced himself to speak slowly and calmly. 'I changed because you changed,' he said. 'As you grew from a child to an adult, I could no longer treat you in the free and easy way that I once did.'

'Oh, stuff and nonsense, Joe!' Gloria exclaimed.

'It wouldn't have been appropriate.'

'Joe . . .'

Joe knew that he had to put an end to the questions before he betrayed himself altogether and so he faced her and said, 'Miss Gloria, do you want me to teach you to drive this car or don't you, because we are losing all the light and there are many other things I could be doing?'

'In other words,' said Gloria, 'end of conversation.'

'Unless it concerns the motor car or driving, yes.'

Gloria had no desire to alienate Joe. To obtain true freedom she had to learn to drive the car and to do that she needed him. 'All right then,' she said. 'You win. Show me what I have to do.'

Gloria soon picked up how to drive the Ford, and Joe was glad, for it had been agony for him to sit so close to her, to breathe in her heady perfume, longing sometimes to kiss those luscious lips. He was often truly uncomfortable because she did use the confines of the car to ask him personal questions and tease him in the way she had used to. He was glad when he felt that she had the confidence and skill to drive the New York streets in comparative safety.

After that there was no holding her at all. She'd be off to New York on vast shopping trips, returning with her friends, the car packed to the gunnels with bags full of clothes. They would often be wearing the new creations as they sat down to dinner, dresses made by the most fashionable designers, Chanel, Lanvin and Patou.

The girls were inspired by the styles of stars of the cinema screen, such as Lillian Gish and Mary Pickford, which they'd discuss endlessly and in glowing terms, and would scrutinise the fashion magazines like *Vogue*, or *Queen* or *Harper's Bazaar* to be sure they were up to the minute.

These clothes were nothing like the conservative outfits Norah wore in mainly pastel shades. The majority of the new fashions were in vivid vibrant colours of green, blue or red, or in loud floral designs. The young were done with restricting corsets too, and instead wore silk camisoles, which flattened their chests in line with the fashion for the slightly boyish figure, suited to shift dresses with no waist and knife-edge pleats in the skirts.

'Jean Patou has a darling little suit in wool and jersey,' Gloria said one day, drawing the pillar-box-red illustration from her bag. 'Just right for the cooler days of summer, don't you think?'

'I'd think more of it if there were more to it,' Brian growled. 'That skirt is far too short.'

'Oh, Daddy, you're funny,' Gloria said. 'Most skirts are short now.'

Gloria was right: nearly every outfit she owned was like that, the skirts with gathers, pleats or splits in them. She seemed oblivious to the disapproval of her parents, and the day she came home with her hair bobbed in the Eton crop Joe thought

Brian was going to have an apoplectic fit, but Gloria was unabashed at the furore.

'Stop roaring at me, Daddy,' she commanded. 'And stop glowering at me in that way. I don't know why you are so cross or, indeed, what it has to do with you either. Since it is my hair on my head, surely I should be the one to decide how to wear it, and anyway, with long hair how could I put on my new cloche hat?'

'That's hardly a good enough reason for having all your hair cut off like that,' Norah said.

'On the contrary, Mother, it is a perfectly good reason,' Gloria retorted. 'Louise Brooks looks divine in hers and everyone wants to copy her. And she has her hair cropped too. Many girls do these days, Daddy. I am afraid you and Mother are very behind the times.'

That wasn't how Brian saw it at all, but the deed was done now and he could do nothing about it, especially as all Gloria's friends had had their hair bobbed too and were similarly unashamed about it. They seemed remarkable close, the friends Gloria had made at the convent, and when they weren't meeting up, Gloria would be having long and involved conversations with them on the telephone.

Gloria's friends' parents seemed incredibly lax and lenient with their daughters, which Brian found hard to accept. Not that the girls cared a jot for how he felt. They visited often, and the rooms rang with their laughter, jazz would reverberate all over the house, and the girls would be dancing together or else trying out Gloria's cosmetics. A couple of them actually took up smoking.

'It's so different from when I was growing up,' Norah said one day as she sat down to dinner with Brian and Joe. 'You had to wait first to be introduced to a young man, and then if he asked permission from your parents to walk out with you, then that was the young man that you would become engaged to and eventually marry. This way . . . well, there are so many men, but when I cautioned Gloria that she would make a name for herself, she laughed.'

It was the men that bothered Joe too. Brian always worked shorter hours when Gloria was at home – that is, if he went in to work at all – and so Joe often saw the young men, sometimes known to the Brannigans in only the vaguest way, who would come scorching up the drive in their sports cars. They would stop suddenly with a squeal of brakes and a spray of gravel, and Gloria would come running from the house and be spirited away to some venue or other, from which she might not return for a day or two.

But what really disturbed Joe were the languid young men who turned up to play tennis. He considered the girls' attire almost indecently short, and these people were so easy with one another that a young man seemed to think nothing of throwing a casual arm around Gloria's shoulders, or even embracing her if he felt they had played well together.

And yet as the summer passed, Joe sensed that Gloria was not truly happy, that her gaiety was forced. Eventually the frivolity and freedom would end, and when that happened, he imagined Gloria would probably have chosen one boy over all the others. That was the one she would marry, and the day she did that would be the day that he would leave the Brannigans' household. He couldn't have stayed and watched her married to another.

Summer gave way to autumn and then winter, and the dresses were swapped for thick skirts in bright colours, lurid jumpers and multicoloured scarves, which the girls wore with their 'up-to-the-minute' checked and baggy coats.

Joe watched Gloria anxiously. She seemed more dejected than ever. The frenetic pace of her social life had slowed somewhat as the colder weather settled over the city, but when she didn't pick up in the early spring either, and was still listless and eating less than a bird, Brian and Norah

51

were all for calling out the doctor to her, though Gloria wouldn't hear of it.

And then just a week away from her nineteenth birthday she went to her room even earlier than usual. Joe had watched her moving her dinner around her plate and fully understood her parents' concern. He decided that he would seek her out at the first opportunity and try to get to the bottom of what was wrong with her. So engrossed was he that he didn't notice that Gloria's door was unlatched as he passed her room on the way to his own further down the corridor.

He'd hung his jacket over a chair and had removed his tie and loosened his top button when the knock came to the door and he was stunned on opening it to see Gloria there.

'Are you all right, Miss Gloria?'

Gloria didn't answer. Instead she said, 'Can I come in?'

It was the last thing that Joe expected her to say, and he looked down the corridor to see if there was anyone about who might have overheard her, before replying, 'I don't think that's a very good idea.'

'I need to talk with you privately and I can't think of any other place where we can do it,' Gloria said. 'Please let me in?'

Joe was in a quandary, but he couldn't leave Gloria standing there and so he opened the door and she walked past him and sat on the bed. He sat on the dressing-table chair opposite her, and for a second or two they stared at one another.

Gloria looked terrible, Joe thought, and with his heart in his boots he asked tentatively, 'Are you in trouble of some sort?'

Gloria shook her head. 'No, it's nothing like that,' she said, and Joe let his breath out in a sigh of relief.

He was totally shocked when Gloria went on, 'It's just . . . Joe, what do you really think of me?'

'What tomfool question is that?' Joe got to his feet. 'I really think it would be better to return to your own room now, Miss Gloria.'

'Hear me out,' Gloria pleaded. 'Please sit back down, Joe, and let me finish.'

Joe sat down heavily, aware that the hairs on the back of his neck were prickling with apprehension and his palms felt clammy. He said almost gruffly, 'Miss Gloria, why are you asking me this question?'

'Because I need to know,' Gloria said. 'I don't want you to think of whether it is right or wrong and whether it's your place to say anything about it. I just want to hear what you really think of me from your own lips.'

Joe couldn't trust himself to speak and eventually, when the silence had stretched out between them, Gloria went on, 'All right then. I guess it is up to me to bare my soul.'

'Please, Miss Gloria,' Joe pleaded, 'don't say anything that you are going to regret.'

'Will you shut up, Joe?' Gloria retorted. 'I must tell you. I think that I have fallen in love with you.'

Joe just stared at her. He felt as if he had been kicked in the stomach by a mule. He couldn't believe what he had just heard. The words he never imagined would be said to him had been said, and by the young woman he loved with all his heart and soul. Yet he had to reply. 'Miss Gloria, don't be cross at what I am about to tell you. You are young still, and the young often get crushes on people. You will probably fall in love many times before you are ready to settle down.'

Gloria leaped off the bed and stamped her foot. 'Don't you dare patronise me, Joe Sullivan!' she cried. 'I have loved you all my life, since that day on the docks when you opened the carriage door and asked me if I was all right.'

'Miss Gloria, you were a child then.'

'I know that,' Gloria snapped. 'And then I loved you as a child, but that love has changed as I have grown. Now I love you like a woman, and for God's sake will you stop calling me Miss Gloria?'

Joe just stared at her without a word and when the silence

got uncomfortable Gloria sighed and said sadly, 'All right then. You can't blame yourself for not being able to love me in return. At least now I know where I stand.'

Joe felt as if he was breaking up inside at seeing Gloria so upset. As she reached the door, he cried, 'Wait, please . . .'

Gloria turned. 'What for? More humiliation?'

'No,' Joe cried. 'Oh God, I have no wish to humiliate you or hurt you in any way, for you are dearer to me than anyone, and that is why I cannot take what you offer. A fortnight ago I was thirty-six and you aren't quite nineteen yet.'

'I don't care how old you are.'

'You must care. I care. And I am also employed by your father. I am a working man, Mi— Gloria.'

'And none the worse for that,' Gloria said. 'But none of this – your age or what you do for employment – has any effect on one's love for another.'

'Gloria, I cannot return your feelings because I will not allow myself to,' Joe said. 'You know many young men, who move in the same circles as yourself, who speak the same language. Any of those—'

'All of those young men were measured against you and found wanting,' Gloria said. 'I was hoping that being in their company would help me to get over the feelings I had for you, but in fact seeing them made me value you more.'

Joe felt as though all his limbs had turned to jelly, but there was a pain around his heart.

Gloria, watching his face, suddenly said in a voice that shook slightly, 'You said that I am dearer to you than anyone. D'you think you could ever come to love me?'

Joe looked at the face of his beloved, at the tears now seeping from her eyes and trickling down her cheeks, and knew she deserved the truth, even if he was to go no further than this. 'I love you with all my being,' he said gently, 'and have done for a long time. I love you so much it hurts.'

'Then, Joe, if we love each other, together we can conquer the world.'

Joe smiled. 'It would be nice to think so. But there are numerous obstacles in our path. Your parents will never agree to any sort of match between us. They will have a much better marriage planned for their only child. In fact, they might send me packing for even considering it.'

'No,' Gloria declared. 'I won't let them. No one will part us. I will speak to my parents – not now, for they have probably retired for the night, but certainly in the morning.'

Joe nodded, but he was certain that they wouldn't stand for any sort of union between their daughter and Brian's secretary, but he didn't say this, for he couldn't bear to dim the light that was setting Gloria's face alight. When she asked, 'Will you kiss me, Joe?' he could no more have stopped his arms going around her than he could have stopped the sun from shining, but he knew that for him it was the end of the road for his career with Brian, which had once seemed so promising.

The next day Gloria faced her parents over the breakfast table and told them point-bank that she and Joe had discovered that they loved each other.

Brian was both astounded and furious. Banging his fist on the table, he said, 'Well, my dear, you will have to unlove Joe, for I am afraid I will not have it. By God, the barefaced nerve of it amazes me. I have taken that man in, given him a leg up, thought of him as my right-hand man, and this is how he repays me – taking advantage of my own daughter. Talk about biting the hand that feeds you.'

'It wasn't like that, Daddy. It wasn't at all,' cried Gloria. 'You have no right to say any of this. I had to almost drag the words from Joe, yet I know that I have always loved him. And don't say that I loved him as a child alone. He said that too and I gave him the same answer as I give you: that as I have grown and matured, so has the love I have for him. Does my happiness mean nothing to you? Why d'you think I have been so miserable for months?'

'Gloria, you really have no right to speak so to your father,' Norah said. 'As for not caring about your happiness, you know your father and I have tried to make you happy since the day you were born.'

'Then let me marry Joe!' Gloria demanded.

Brian rubbed his chin while he looked at his defiant daughter. 'It's such a surprise,' he said, 'the last thing I had expected, to tell you the truth, and judging by your behaviour of the past months.'

Gloria sighed. 'I went about with those boys to try and erase thoughts of Joe from my mind.' She shook her head. 'It didn't work, though, and in fact it only made me love him more.'

'And you say you truly love this man?'

'Oh, yes, Daddy, with all my heart and soul. I ache with love for him. He feels the same, though he would say nothing at first because he is so much older than me and employed by you.'

'What do you make of it, my dear?' Brian asked Norah, who was looking at Gloria with a slight frown puckering her brow.

She often thought afterwards that had Gloria not been so wild for almost a year, not in the least circumspect or prudent as became a young lady, her reaction might have been different, for all she liked and admired Joe greatly. She feared that Gloria's antics with hosts of young men had laid her wide open to ridicule and scorn, and possibly damaged her reputation. If that had happened she knew the doors to any form of respectable society would be closed to her and an advantageous marriage out of the question. Far better surely to have her safely and respectably married before more damage was done. However, marriage was a big commitment and not one to be entered into lightly.

'You are still very young, my dear,' she said to her daughter. 'Are you sure this is what you want?'

'Absolutely sure,' G[...]
don't have Joe then I will [...]

'Do you not mind, thoug[...]
than you?' Brian asked.

'No,' Gloria replied. 'Whatever [...]
the man I love and the man I want [...]

Norah thought of the often brash [...]
men that had been Gloria's companions of [...]
to have no aim in life other than the pursu[...]
She doubted that any one of them had ever d[...]
work in his empty life. She would have hated her [...]
to have married one of those people.

Joe was different. He was the sort of man that could [...]
relied upon, one who knew what hard work was and thrived
on it. It didn't matter a jot to her about the age difference.
In fact, she saw it as an advantage. Joe had his feet firmly
on the ground and she felt Gloria would be much safer with
someone like that.

'Well, at least we can't say we don't know the man,'
Brian said. 'We have had years of getting to know him.' He
gazed at the daughter he loved so very much and felt a lump
form in his throat as he realised that another man was now
more important in her life than he was, and so his voice
was husky with emotion when he said, 'If this is really what
you want, my love, then you have my blessing.' He gazed
at his wife, saw her smiling and relieved face, and added,
'And I can see your mother approves too. Now where is
the man in question hiding away?'

'In his room,' Gloria said, leaping up from her chair. 'I'll
tell him now.'

In the cold light of morning, Joe had gone over the scene
of the previous evening in his bedroom and regretted it
bitterly for he had no doubt that Brian would send him
packing now and he had only himself to blame. If he didn't
love Gloria so very much, he could have parried her questions. Too late now. With a heavy heart he dragged his case

othes in it while

rst through the
n she told him
l for the match.
ated joy, for it
ntented himself
er close.
ce had been lit
re was one that
e, but this kiss
when they even-
desire.
altogether, and
ee your parents

loria said determinedly. 'In fact, if I
not have anyone.'
, that Joe is many years older
age he is, Joe Sullivan is
o marry.'
and rootless young
te. They seemed
r of pleasure.
ne a day's
laughter
be

immediately. Hand in hand, they left the room and ran down the stairs.

'Well, well, well,' Brian said when he saw Joe at the door. 'Fine turn-up for the book this is. The minute my back is turned you are making love to my daughter.'

Joe smiled. 'Not quite, sir. But I do love her very much and would like your permission to marry her.'

'And you have it, Joe,' Brian said, going forward to shake him by the hand. 'And I hope you know what you are taking on. She can be the very devil when she doesn't get her own way.'

'You really can't tell me anything about Gloria that I don't know, sir,' Joe said. 'And there is nothing about her that I do not love.'

Gloria gazed at Joe and thought her heart would burst with happiness.

Everyone in the house seemed stunned by the news, and not everyone was that pleased either.

Kate said, 'There is bettering oneself and taking advantage, and that's what the young pup has done, setting himself up to marry that pretty young thing and him near old enough to be her father. Mark my words, it never works trying to mix chalk and cheese.'

Joe knew what they thought but there was nothing he could do about it, and anyway he was taken aback by the speed at which everything was decided. Gloria was now sporting a platinum engagement ring with a huge diamond in the centre of it, and Brian declared there was no need to delay the wedding.

'The autumn I always think is a nice time of year,' he said.

'It is, sir,' Joe agreed, 'and though I am immensely grateful that you are taking over the entire cost of the wedding, I need a little time to save up enough for a deposit on some suitable place for the two of us to live in.'

'What are you talking about, man?' Brian said with a laugh. 'You will live here, naturally.'

That hadn't been what Joe had anticipated at all. He imagined he and Gloria in their own little house or apartment somewhere, but when he said this, everyone seemed to think it was all rather amusing.

'Darling, I wouldn't have the least idea how to keep house,' Gloria said. 'I have never had to do it, and as for cooking anything, well, I have never done that either. I honestly don't know how to boil an egg.'

'But did you not have any sort of cookery lessons at school?' Joe asked.

'Well, no,' Gloria said. 'Why would we? And I have never washed dishes, or really cleaned anything, and wouldn't know how to start dealing with the laundry. We have servants to do those types of things.'

Joe realised then that after his marriage everything would go on as it always had done, and the only thing that would alter after he put the ring on Gloria's finger was that she would share his bed.

Three rooms were being amalgamated to make a suite

for Joe and Gloria, and when Joe was shown the plans for his approval he was staggered at the size of it. He knew he wouldn't be sorry to leave the room that Brian had assigned to him when he had moved into the house. It had a carpeted floor, a blue fluffy rug by the large and comfortable bed that matched the drapes at the windows, a wardrobe, chest and dressing table in light wood, and a bathroom for his use off to the side. It bore no resemblance at all to his spartan cellar where he had felt so contented, and yet he had never felt at home in the luxurious and comfortable room.

The bridal suite was at least being planned specifically for Gloria and himself, and he was sure he would be happier there with Gloria by his side. In fact, if he wasn't then he was a hard man to please

'What is this room to the side?' he asked Brian.

'That is your dressing room,' Brian said. 'Will I have a bed installed in there too?'

'What on earth for, sir?' Joe asked. 'The bed you tell me you have ordered for Gloria and me would accommodate half a dozen with ease. What use would we make of another bed?'

'There are times when a woman might like to sleep alone,' Brian told him. 'Or when you are home late perhaps, or have to get up early and don't wish to disturb. Believe me, a separate bed is essential.'

All of it was out of Joe's understanding. In the world he came from, when a man and woman married, they bought a double bed and slept in it together thereafter night after night. They made love on it, babies were born on it, small children sometimes shared it and the marriage bed was often the most important purchase ever made.

He thought of the huge and beautiful bed Brian had ordered. Was it possible that Gloria would lie encased in that magnificent bed all alone, while he lay in another bed, the other side of the wall?

Brian saw the confusion on Joe's face. 'A dressing room and a separate bed were among the first things I insisted on when I married Norah,' he said. 'And she has been as grateful as I have been at times. I know that this is all new to you, but trust me in this.'

'Yes, sir,' Joe said, knowing he had no alternative.

FIVE

The news that he was engaged to Gloria Brannigan, Joe found opened doors to him, even if many people did view him with suspicion, doubting his intentions were really honourable. One of those doors was to the club that Brian attended.

Brian had taken Joe to the club quite a few times but he had always had to sign him in as a guest, but after the engagement he had been made a full member and he enjoyed the privileges this offered, though he always kept well away from the gaming rooms. He had gone in with Brian once and had been appalled at the money gambled away. Brian loved the thrill of it and was a regular, but it left Joe feeling cold and rather odd when he saw Brian raise the stake in a poker game for the amount that the average working man would barely earn in a month of back-breaking work.

He was amazed too by all the fuss a marriage of this magnitude caused. Norah and Gloria were either poring over fabric patterns for the drapes and discussing colour schemes, or shopping together for Gloria's trousseau. The wedding dress she was having made seemed to need endless fittings, as did the bridesmaid dresses for three of her school friends. Then there the flowers to choose, cars to order and invitations to send.

'Let them be,' Brian advised when Joe complained of this. 'Women and weddings go together like peaches and cream.

Mind you, we'd better be thinking about ordering our suits soon.'

'I have half a dozen decent suits,' Joe said. 'I wasn't going to go to the expense of buying another. I was just going to buy a new shirt.'

Brian smiled. 'You really have got to stop thinking of the expense of things all the time,' he said. 'Those days are over for you and, anyway, you haven't a morning suit or top hat, and that is what will be required on the day.'

'Oh, surely not, sir,' Joe said.

'I am afraid so. All the men will be dressed the same,' Brian said. 'And you will have to think of your best man. Will you be asking the man that sponsored you? Patrick something, wasn't it?'

Joe shook his head. 'The friendship was spoiled between us when I passed my exams and you took me into the house to live. I haven't seen him since then.'

'Hmm, a pity.'

'A great pity, sir,' Joe said. 'But there it is. In fact, the only one in the house that was pleased about my success that time was Planchard, and I think that he will do well enough.'

Brian nodded. 'He is a good man. So he will have to get kitted out as well.'

'Couldn't I just hire a suit, sir?'

'Stop calling me sir,' Brian said. 'You will be my son-in-law soon and my name is Brian. No, it would not be good form for you to have a suit on hire. The bridegroom needs his own.'

'But when would I ever need it again, sir?'

Brian shrugged. 'Who knows? Another wedding maybe, or other society dos where a morning suit is the appropriate and expected dress. Look,' he went on as Joe still looked doubtful, 'on your marriage you will become my business partner. Whatever people say, first impressions count, and so it is important to me that you have the correct clothes to fit these occasions.'

It was the first time a partnership had been mentioned and though Joe was undoubtedly pleased he was also a little unnerved. But if Brian had decided then that was how it would be, he knew, and it would be another change in his life that he would eventually get used to.

The morning of the wedding, 16 October 1926, Joe was spirited out of the house and into the white limousine to take him to the church early, lest he should cast his eyes on Gloria's dress before the service and so bring bad luck upon the marriage. His morning suit felt stiff and uncomfortable, and he marvelled that Planchard looked so good in his. Brian was right, though, Joe noticed, as the car pulled up in front of the church and he saw some of the guests arriving: the women were dressed in a variety of outfits, but the men, without exception, were wearing morning suits. He would have looked decidedly out of place in anything else.

The church was filling up nicely as he and Planchard walked side by side down the aisle to sit in the pews to the right and await the bride. Joe felt as if all his nerve endings were exposed and he found it very hard to sit still.

'You're like a cat on hot bricks, sir,' Planchard said.

'I know,' Joe said. 'It's the waiting. I never could abide waiting. You sure you've got the ring safe?'

'We checked before we left the house, remember?' Planchard said with a smile.

'Just wanted to be certain.'

'Relax.'

'God, I only wish I could,' Joe said. 'We seem to have been sitting here for ages.' But then the strains of the Wedding March could be heard, and he followed Planchard out of the pew to stand before the altar. Behind him, he could hear the shuffling of feet as people stood, and he was aware of sniffing and snuffling as some women began to cry.

He turned and watched Gloria, on the arm of her father, walking slowly towards him. She looked so lovely, so utterly radiant, that he felt as if his heart had stopped beating for a moment or two and he knew he loved her with all his heart and would do so till the breath left his body. He stepped forward to stand beside her. Her father released her into Joe's care and Gloria passed her bouquet to one of her bridesmaids. Then, taking each other's hand, they kneeled together at the rails as the Nuptial Mass began.

Joe was pleased, walking out of the church with his new bride on his arm, to see so many had come to wish them well. As it was Saturday the factory was closed. Bert Clifford and his wife had reserved seats towards the front, but Joe was touched to see how many other employees had turned out too.

There were others from the church, and some of the men he knew from the club, with their wives and families. He saw many of the men's eyes were on Gloria and he knew that more than a few would be envious of him.

Kate had surpassed herself with the sumptuous meal she had prepared. She might not approve of the wedding at all but she was too proud of her culinary skills to produce anything substandard. The centrepiece was a four-tier wedding cake. Brian cracked open wines he had laid down in the cellar before prohibition began, and a fine time was had by all.

Joe and Gloria were spending that night in their suite of rooms in the Brannigan house before setting off the following day for a fortnight's honeymoon at Lake George in the Adirondack Mountains. Brian had highly recommended the location, where he had been himself as a young man.

All in all, the day had been almost perfect and Joe settled in his bed that night with a sigh of contentment. Gloria went into his arms willingly and when he kissed her lips, teasing them open with his tongue for the first time, she murmured and held him tighter. When he went on to kiss her neck and then her throat she moaned with pleasure. That moan inflamed the impassioned Joe further, his pulse raced and he felt himself harden. He forced himself to go slowly knowing that, despite all her wildness, Gloria would be a virgin.

'Don't worry, darling,' he said huskily, 'I will try not to hurt you at all,' and he began gently to remove her nightdress.

Immediately Gloria slapped his hands away. 'What are you doing?'

'Didn't your mother speak to you about what might happen tonight?'

'A bit . . .'

'What did she say?'

'She said that you might ask me to do things I might find strange, but I must submit to them because I am married to you now.'

'Is that all she said?'

Gloria shrugged. 'Mostly. At least she said that men always seem to set great store by it, and that it's really not so bad when you get the hang of it; that I might even get to enjoy it myself sometimes.'

Despite Joe's frustration he laughed. 'Did you understand one word of what she was talking about? And did she explain what "it" was?'

'No,' Gloria admitted. 'She might as well have been talking double Dutch, but I felt I couldn't ask anything because she seemed so embarrassed, but I do know she never said anything about taking my nightdress off. I have never gone naked to bed.'

'Darling, how can I make love to you if you are keeping your clothes on?' Joe asked.

He suddenly felt sorry for Gloria. He had held back during the courtship and wanted to hold back no longer, for, though he hadn't expected Gloria to be experienced, he did think she would at least have been informed. But now he dampened down his ardour, cuddled her in his arms and told her what married men and women did in bed together.

She was shocked initially, there was no denying that, but

she wanted to please Joe and so she allowed him to remove her nightdress and submitted to his kisses. At least she began by submitting to them, but then it was as if Joe's kisses unlocked the passion Gloria had suppressed. Joe's hands stroking her body, fondling her breasts, and his lips nuzzling at her nipples caused sharp shafts of desire to shoot through her and she moaned and groaned with ecstasy. When Joe's fingers slid between her legs, she arched her back. Joe knew she was ready and he was smiling as he entered her.

The sudden sharp pain caused Gloria to cry out and then it was forgotten as waves of exquisite joy swept over her again and again.

'All right, my darling?' Joe asked as they lay still, entwined together. 'Did I hurt you?'

'A little.'

'I'm sorry.'

'Never be sorry for what we did tonight,' Gloria said. 'You have made me happier than I can ever remember being.'

And she was, for she felt as if she had been engulfed with total bliss and her love for Joe was greater than ever.

Gloria and Joe returned from their wonderful honeymoon to find that Brian had bought them a Cadillac as a wedding present. With Joe at work all week, Gloria had charge of the car to go into New York on shopping trips, or to meet her friends for lunch, and in the evenings and at weekends she and Joe would often take off in it somewhere together. They had thought to begin a family straight away but each month they were disappointed.

They assured each other that these things take time, and meanwhile there were any number of distractions to be had in New York, and they had good friends to visit at weekends. They told themselves that they were young and free, and maybe it was as well to stay that way for a while.

However, they were fooling themselves. Each month Gloria's longing for a child grew greater and she dreaded feeling the drawing pains in her stomach that meant they were once more unsuccessful.

Then just after Easter, Brian had a funny turn at work and Joe drove him home and sent for the doctor. He advised Brian that he had to take life at a slower pace if he didn't want his heart to give out altogether. Joe had seen his father have the same warning and not heed it, but he had been a younger man then with no authority to tell his father what to do.

With Brian the relationship was totally different. 'You have to do as the doctor says,' Joe said. 'What's the point of having him come to see you otherwise? After all, I am here now. Over the years you have taught me well and you will be near at hand if I need advice.'

Brian knew that Joe spoke the truth, but he growled, 'And what will I do all day? Now if you were to do the business and give me a grandchild, which I thought you would have done by now, I would be as happy as Larry to stay at home more.'

'You can play about with your stocks and shares,' Joe told him. 'It's what you love to do anyway. And didn't the doctor tell you to take more exercise? A brisk walk every day would use up some of your excess time.'

'You are ducking the issue, man.'

'What issue?' Joe asked, though he knew full well.

'I want a grandchild to gladden my heart and give me a reason for living long enough to see him or her grow up.'

'Aye,' Joe commented wryly. 'Well, we can't always have what we want.'

'Why's that?' Brian demanded. 'Is there a problem? Shall I ask the doctor to take a look at you both?'

'There is no problem,' Joe said. 'Leave well alone. These things take time.' And surely, he thought, there couldn't be anything serious wrong. He was as fit as a fiddle and so was Gloria, and he saw no reason why they wouldn't soon have a child of their own.

*　　*　　*

However, the years passed and each month Gloria was sunk in despondency, especially as she knew her parents were waiting anxiously. She had a wonderful, happy life, money was no object, and she could have anything for the asking. Added to that she had loving parents and an adoring husband, and yet the thing she wanted above all this, a child, eluded her.

In the summer of 1929, when Gloria and Joe had been married almost three years, she said to him, 'Don't you think it's strange that there has been no sign of a child, Joe? Maybe I should do what Mother wants and see the doctor?'

'What can a doctor do about something like that?' Joe asked.

'I don't know,' Gloria said. 'But it wouldn't hurt to have a word.'

Joe said nothing else, but Gloria knew he didn't want her to go to the doctor and discuss their most intimate affairs with him, and so she said, 'I won't bother the doctor yet. Maybe I'll go next spring, if it doesn't all begin naturally.'

She felt, rather than heard, Joe's sigh of relief as he said, 'Your father at least has something else to occupy his mind for now. He is buying shares left, right and centre, by all accounts. He doesn't have to come into the office each day, but he insists, but I don't let him do much. Actually he seems to spend most of the day on the telephone to the Exchange, buying and selling shares.'

'He's always been the same with stocks and shares,' Gloria said. 'I don't really understand it.'

Joe shook his head. 'I don't want to understand it,' he said. 'Seems like a mug's game to me. Even Bert's at it. I thought you had to be really wealthy, but apparently not. You buy on something called a margin, Bert said. First a person borrows the money and then uses that to buy stock, so he can put the stock up as collateral. The whole thing is decided by the value of the shares, which apparently go up and down continuously. When they rise, you collect the dividend. Then if they drop, as they did earlier this month, he said you raise some more cash and wait for them to go up again. He wanted me to go in with him.'

'I'm surprised that he wasted his breath on you,' Gloria said. 'You don't even trust banks. You have a stash of money in a biscuit tin.'

'What's wrong with that?' Joe said. 'I have got along without stocks and shares this long while, and I will continue to give them a wide berth.'

About the middle of October, Joe became aware that Brian was worried about something and he asked him about it.

'It's nothing that you need concern yourself about,' Brian snapped.

'Stop that sort of talk, Brian,' Joe snapped back. 'I am your son-in-law and so everything that bothers you this much is my concern too. If it is connected to the business in some way, then I need to be told what it is.'

'It only loosely concerns the business,' Brian said. 'And it's all to do with the shares. They dropped in early October, but they did that last month too and recovered.'

'And this time they haven't?'

'Not yet,' Brian said. 'They will eventually, but they are still dropping at the moment.'

'Why don't you sell up while you have the chance?'

'I can't do that, Joe,' Brian said. 'You don't know how much is at stake. I would lose a packet if I sold at current rates.'

'I hope for your sake that prices soon rise then.'

'You worry too much, Joe,' Brian said. 'I have been doing this for years. And the uneasiness sort of adds to the excitement.'

It was excitement that Joe could well do without, and he saw Brian develop deep furrows across his brow and down each side of his nose, and sometimes he looked quite grey. Joe knew he was more worried than he was letting on and he was very concerned about him, but Brian refused to talk about it.

The following week, Bert sought Joe out. 'I am selling my shares back to the bank tomorrow,' he said. 'The boss should do the same. I tried telling him and got my head bitten off for my trouble. He said he'll lose money. Hell, I will lose money, but at least this way I'll get something back. People say the stock market is going to crash. Try talking to him, Joe. He listens to you.'

'Not at the moment he doesn't,' Joe said grimly. 'But I will do my best.'

Brian, however, was intractable. 'People are getting fearful, that's all,' he told Joe. 'They just have to hold their nerve and sit tight.'

The following day, Bert told Joe of the agitated crowds of people who had flooded the Exchange, frantically trying to redeem their shares. 'Good job I went early,' he said. 'For all that there was a mile-long queue already there, at least I got in. Some poor devils didn't. When the hall reached what they considered capacity, they just shut the doors. People were hollering, crying, screaming in the streets, banging on the doors. I tell you, Joe, it was mayhem, and some of those who got in got no money, for the Exchange just closed down, couldn't cope at all. God Almighty, Joe, where will America be after this?'

Over the weekend, the market seemed to recover a little and there was a glimmer of hope that it would bounce back as it had so many times before. Brian had a smug, 'told you so' look on his face as he read the financial papers. But, by Monday the shares began spiralling down again and the evening papers were full of doom and gloom, and bad forecasts of worse to come. Brian decided he had to go down to the Exchange and see how things were for himself, and so on Tuesday morning, without a word to anyone, he got up early and left the house.

The streets around the Exchange were busy for that hour in the morning, and in the milling crowds around the closed doors the desperation and panic could almost be felt. Brian felt the knot of worry he had carried for a few weeks harden and he was suddenly filled with dread. No one spoke to everyone else, and even avoided eye contact. Brian admitted for the first time that he might have made a ghastly mistake. It seemed hours later that the staff began arriving and then the crowds surging against the doors burst them apart.

The sheer number of people streaming in that day made it impossible for the staff even to attempt to try to close the doors again. Brian stood cheek by jowl with his neighbours and saw the shares drop that first hour more than they had ever dropped before.

The ashen-faced people began to shriek and scream, and then the massed crying of wretched people settled to a loud hum of profound distress that filled the room and rebounded off the walls. There was pandemonium on the Exchange floor, and Brian saw some men grab frantically at their collars before collapsing beneath people's feet. Brian didn't blame them; it was only the people pressed all around him that were keeping him upright, for he knew he too was ruined. His major investments were in radio and steel, and when the value of them dropped so low they were worthless he knew his life was effectively over.

Stumbling through the door and into the street, he began to lurch from one side of the sidewalk to the other as if he was in the throes of drink when really he was trying to come to terms with the anguish and wretchedness that he was going to inflict on those he loved best in all the world. He walked for miles and for hours, trying to ignore the sharp pains shooting across his chest, but when eventually the cold and darkness caused him to head for home he knew what he was going to do.

There had been a little concern when there had been no sign of Brian when the house was astir that morning. When he hadn't made an appearance or contacted anyone, either at the factory or the house, Joe had come home early, intending to take the car out and look for him.

He was in the bedroom, changing from his suit when he heard the loud hammering on the front door.

'Thank goodness, that must be Daddy now,' said Gloria, who had followed Joe upstairs. And then, just a few minutes later, they heard Norah's cry of distress.

The knocking on the door had been so loud and insistent it had brought Norah from the drawing room, and so she was in the hall as Planchard crossed it and opened the door to see his master holding the evening paper in his hand, leaning heavily against the doorjamb. He looked as if he had had a skinful, although there was no smell of drink upon him at all.

'Are you all right, sir?' Planchard said, going forward to support him.

Norah gave a little gasp of shock, seeing Brian brought into the light, leaning heavily against the butler. His face was grey, even his lips had no colour, and his rheumy eyes were red and bloodshot with huge fleshy bags beneath them.

'Oh, Brian, my darling,' she cried. 'What in God's name has happened to you?'

She went forward, her arms outstretched, but before she reached him he said sharply, 'Leave me be.' Norah stopped, unsure what to do as Brian said to Planchard, 'You leave me be, too.' He pulled himself away from his butler's arm, stood for a moment as if to regain his balance, and staggered off towards the study. Planchard and Norah looked at each other, worry etched on both their faces as Joe and Gloria came running down the stairs.

'What is it, Mother?' Gloria cried. 'What's happened?'

'It's your father, dear,' Norah said. 'There is something the matter with him. He is ill. I have never seen him like that.'

73

Joe looked across at Planchard, who said, 'The mistress is right, sir. There is certainly something very amiss.'

'Where is he now?'

'He went towards the study,' Norah said.

Joe was his making his way there when he heard the shot and it galvanised him into action. Norah gave a shriek and Planchard, who had been returning to the kitchen, was side by side with Joe as they reached the study door with Norah and Gloria behind them.

It was locked and bolted, as Joe had expected, and he rattled it and shouted, but there was silence.

'We will have to break it down, sir,' Planchard said, and Joe nodded.

The panel split the second time they hit it, and then Joe was able to get his hand in and open the door from the inside. They were too late, Joe saw that at a glance, and he felt his heart contract as he saw Brian at the desk, his head fallen forward in a pool of blood. There was a neat bullet hole in his skull and the gun that fired it had fallen from his hand on to the blood-splattered paper that read

I'm sorry.
Love you all.
Brian

It was so absolutely horrendous it was almost unbelievable. Joe steeled himself to put his fingers to the pulse on Brian's neck, knowing it was useless, and then Gloria burst away from Planchard, who was trying to prevent her and her mother going too close. But they had seen enough. Gloria let out an almost primeval howl and sank to her knees, and Norah fell unconscious to the floor.

Joe felt numb with shock, but his first duty was to his wife and then his mother-in-law. He lifted Gloria into his arms and held her shivering form as he said to Planchard, 'Can you manage to get your mistress upstairs?'

'I'll see to her, sir,' Planchard said. 'And shall I phone the police after I have phoned the doctor?'

'Police?' Joe repeated. 'I hadn't thought of the police but I suppose they need to be informed, so if you would . . . And anyone else you think we might need to call. I can't seem to be able to think straight at the moment.'

Planchard looked at Joe's drawn, ashen face. 'Don't worry, sir. Leave that side of things to me.'

The servants, many in tears, were clustered in horrified confusion in the hall, unsure what to do. When Mary stepped forward to help Joe with Gloria he waved her away. 'I will manage her,' he said. 'But your mistress might need your attention.'

Gloria leaned against Joe as he carried her up the stairs. Laying her gently on the bed, he said, 'Planchard is calling the doctor, darling. I'm sure he will be able to give you something to ease you.'

'What good will the doctor do me, Joe?' Gloria asked sadly. 'He cannot bring Daddy back.'

Joe sat down on the bed and tenderly stroked Gloria's hair away from her forehead. 'I really do understand how distraught and devastated you are feeling at the moment.'

'I will never see him again,' Gloria said, covering her face with her hands. 'I'm not sure I can bear it.'

Joe put his arms tight around her and murmured into her hair, 'You will, my dearest, darling girl. It will take time, but I will be by your side always, helping you in any way I can.'

'Oh, Joe!' Gloria cried, and the tears came then, not the quiet, controlled weeping she had already done, but like an outpouring of her very soul. The sound of Gloria's sobs rasping in her throat cut Joe to the quick, and he held her shuddering body in his arms.

He remembered the doctor expressing surprise and concern that his mother hadn't cried when his father had dropped dead of a heart attack. Whether tears would have helped a woman like his mother he wasn't sure, but in Gloria he saw them as a good sign, and so he didn't urge her to stop crying, but just held her trembling body close, rocking her slightly and feeling her tears dampen his jacket.

Eventually, when she was calmer, he laid her head down on the pillow. Her face, he noticed, was as white as lint and her eyes looked larger than ever and puffed up from the tears.

'Why did he do it, Joe?' she asked. When Joe shook his head helplessly she added, 'It's something to do with those blessed shares, isn't it?'

'Quite possibly,' Joe said. 'But we might know more later. Planchard is informing the police, but you needn't concern yourself with any of that. To sleep would be the best thing for you.'

Gloria said nothing. She knew that the only way sleep would help her was if she were to wake up afterwards and find the whole thing had been some horrible nightmare.

'I must find out what is happening,' Joe said. 'I will send Tilly to sit with you.'

Downstairs he found Planchard waiting for him with the evening paper in his hand. 'The master was holding this when he came in,' he said, handing it to Joe. 'Look at the Stop Press, sir.'

There in the hall, Joe learned what had caused his father-in-law to take his own life. He read of the Wall Street Crash, which had begun on a day the paper called Black Tuesday. Many people faced ruination because of it, and some men, seeing this, found their hearts couldn't take it and they had died there on the Exchange floor.

'If it is as bad as that, maybe in the end Brian's heart might have given out too,' Joe said. 'That would have been tragedy enough, but doing it this way – that's so . . . well almost unbelievable. He is the very last man that I could imagine doing such a thing.'

* * *

The doctor, who had known the Brannigan family for years, was terribly shocked and upset by the news that Brian had felt driven to kill himself after the news he had heard about his shares. He went into the study first, looked down on the body of the fine man he had known Brian to be, and felt the pity of it all wash over him.

Brian had no need of his services now and he followed Joe up the stairs to see how the man's wife and daughter were coping.

'I am worried about the mental state of both your wife and your mother-in-law,' he told Joe, after examining them both. 'I have given them each a strong sedative for now. At least they will sleep tonight and I will be back in the morning.'

'The police are on their way,' Joe said.

'Well, I would say neither woman could help them in what is so obviously a terrible and tragic accident,' the doctor said. 'It could be very detrimental for them to be disturbed tonight.'

'I'll see they are not,' Joe said firmly. 'And I will make that clear to the police.'

In the end, he didn't have to because the police saw straight away that Brian's death was a suicide and they praised Joe for having the foresight to leave everything as it was until they arrived. Once the police left, Planchard phoned the undertakers to take the body away.

'Would you like me to phone Bert too, sir?' he asked. 'I don't think news like this can wait until the morning.'

'No, you're right,' Joe said, 'and he was worried enough when I told him that Brian had gone out this morning without a word to anyone. He was all for me leaving a little earlier so that I could look for him before true darkness really descended.'

Over the next few days, there was so much to do that Joe didn't know whether he was coming or going. Everyone now knew what had happened, and not just in the Brannigan household either, for it was widely reported in the newspapers. An estimated thirty billion dollars had been lost in the Crash, and Joe felt as helpless as though he were on the edge of a precipice and about to fall into the dark void beyond.

Everything Joe had to do seemed to take so long and there were only so many hours in the day. He had thought arranging the funeral would at least be straightforward. However, when he went up to the presbytery to make arrangements with the priest, he told Joe that Brian should not be buried in consecrated ground because he had taken his own life.

Joe glared at him for a moment before saying, 'And exactly who would that punish?'

'It's the law of the Christian Church, Joe.'

'You can't put the word Christian to a law like that, which serves only to shame and stigmatise the people left behind,' Joe snapped. 'They are already coping with the fact that their loved one is dead, and by his own hand. Have you the least idea what that feels like?'

'But, Joe—'

'There isn't a but here, Father,' Joe said. 'Brian has donated enough money to this church over the years and, added to that, his plot where his father is buried, and where Norah will lie eventually, is bought and paid for.'

'Money and even ownership of a plot doesn't come into this, Joe. It's a question of doing what is right.'

'You will be doing something badly wrong if you refuse to bury Brian's body in the churchyard,' Joe said. 'The doctor said the balance of Norah's mind is precarious.'

The priest shook his head. 'Obviously I feel immensely sorry for Norah, for all of you.'

'Oh, good,' Joe said sarcastically. 'That will make all the difference. Look, Father, when Brian came home from the Exchange he was in a bad way. Planchard said that he thought Brian wasn't totally sane at that point, which was just a couple of minutes before he turned the gun on himself. If he wasn't in his right mind surely he can't be blamed for his actions?'

'Not if he wasn't sane.'

'Well, you know the manner of man he was,' Joe said. 'Could you see him ever even thinking about killing himself?'

'No, Joe, I couldn't.'

'Well then, Father?'

'All right, Joe, you argue well,' the priest said at last. 'Brian can have his Christian burial.'

Joe had been expecting the call from the solicitor, though he thought they might get the funeral over first, but it was the day before it that he was called to the office urgently. He was deeply shocked by what the solicitor had to tell him for he hadn't dreamed that things could be so bad. He knew he had to deliver two new hammer blows to his beloved wife and his mother-in-law, and he didn't know how in God's name they were going to cope with them.

He decided to say nothing until the funeral was over, but that meant carrying the news alone, and he found it to be a heavy burden. He felt totally isolated, and bad that he hadn't even had proper time to mourn the man that he owed so much to and thought so much of, for both Gloria and her mother looked to him for support. He couldn't ever remember feeling so sad or so lost, not even when his own father died.

SIX

The church was packed out for the funeral, for Brian had been a popular man, but Joe was worried about his mother-in-law, who looked gaunt and frail. He knew, though, however gruelling she found the occasion, she would carry it through to the bitter end for she was that type of person. And so would Gloria, for she had her mother's backbone. He had such admiration for both of them as he helped them into the funeral car that led the cavalcade of motor vehicles back to the house for refreshments.

He knew the two women might collapse when the mourners left. When the last one went home and Norah announced she was going to bed, Joe wasn't surprised.

'Aren't you ready for bed yourself, my dear?' he asked Gloria.

'Not yet,' Gloria said. 'I will go up in a little while,' but she barely waited until her mother had left the room before she asked, 'What is it, Joe?'

'What do you mean?'

'You are holding something to yourself that I fear probably affects us all. Your eyes are quite haunted by something and you have been like this since you came back from the solicitor's yesterday.'

Joe shook his head. 'You don't want to hear this today.'

'D'you know, Joe, I have the feeling that I won't want to hear it any day,' Gloria said, 'but the burden isn't one that you should carry on your own.'

'Are you sure?' Joe said. 'It's bad.'

'Then tell me and let me share it,' Gloria urged.

Then Joe told her, and watched her eyes widen, her mouth tighten and heard her gasp with shock. Her voice was little above a whisper as she gasped, 'You mean we have lost everything? The factory? Even the house? Everything?'

'It certainly looks that way,' Joe said. 'I don't know yet how much your father actually owed.'

'He knew this,' Gloria said. 'When Daddy took his own life, he knew this.'

'Your father wasn't himself then.'

'He couldn't face it,' Gloria said. 'That was all. He took the easy way out and, whatever you say, Joe, he knew what he was doing all right when he put the house and the business at risk. He has left us destitute.' She looked at him in desperation. 'Joe, what are we going to do?'

Joe put his arms around her and said, 'Survive, my beautiful, darling girl. We won't be the only people that this has happened to. I will find us a place to live and take a job. While I have a pair of hands on me, I will not let us starve, never fear.'

Joe was to find that, as Brian's partner, he was responsible for all his debts, which were considerable. In that first week after his funeral, he seemed to discover one shocking fact after the other.

As the shares had begun to fall Brian had borrowed more and more money, probably hoping to make a killing when they rose again, and he'd used both the factory and then the house as collateral. Quite apart from this, he owed money to many traders in the town. Then the club contacted Joe about the quite excessive gambling debts from Brian's card games. When he thought he had learned everything, he discovered to his horror that the last two batches of stock had not even been paid for. He had been unaware of this because although he did the accounts, it was left to Brian to pay the bills, and he had neglected to do this. All these creditors would have a claim on the estate.

There was money in the bank to pay the workers for just one more week. Joe went to talk over the future with Bert.

'There is no point going on making the components anyway,' Bert said. 'The industries that we were supplying have gone to the wall themselves. The factory and all in it are worthless. Pay the men off, sir, tell them to go home, and hope to God most of them find jobs elsewhere before too long.'

'What about you?'

'Well, I was coming up for retirement anyway,' Bert said. 'I have had good wages for years and invested much of it. In the old days I did make money from shares and although I lost money recently, I had cashed in most of my shares in September when they eventually rose again after the dip at the beginning of the month, so I am all right. Don't you worry about me.'

Most of the workforce knew what was coming too, Joe realised when he spoke to them, and though they were worried, they didn't blame him. They knew whose fault it was.

That didn't help Joe much. He locked and barred the factory doors for the last time, shook Bert warmly by the hand and returned home an unhappy man.

'Don't feel too sorry for them,' Gloria said when he told her how bad he felt about making his workforce redundant. 'We'll be in the same boat soon, and you might be competing with them for the few jobs there are about, for places are closing down every day.'

'It's a dreadful time for the whole of New York,' Joe said. 'I don't know whether it will ever recover from this. It might be better for us to try our luck somewhere else, and yet we might be no better off. I think what has happened in New York is going to have repercussions throughout the whole of America.'

'To move might totally unsettle Mother too,' Gloria said. 'I mean, she has lived here all her life, she knows nothing else, and Daddy and her parents are buried here.'

'Yes,' Joe said. 'We must stay here and weather the storm the best way we can.' He gave a sudden sigh. 'Now I must speak to the indoor staff and I am dreading it.'

'Have you money for their wages?'

'Not in the bank,' Joe said. 'There is very little there, but I have got a stash in that biscuit tin you used to tease me about.'

'Good job you took no notice of me then,' Gloria said. 'It's money that the bank need know nothing about.'

That was true, and Joe was glad that he was able to pay the wages of the staff for the last time, but he found telling them how bad things were very hard, although they knew that with Brian's suicide the news would hardly be good.

'I wish you all the very best,' Joe told them. 'I will of course give you all excellent references. I wish I could ask you to stay on longer, but we have to be out ourselves next week.'

'Have you some place to live?' Planchard asked.

Joe nodded miserably. 'A two-bedroomed apartment downtown.'

Planchard shook his head. His mistress and Gloria living in an apartment seemed all wrong to him.

It seemed all wrong to Norah too – in fact, so wrong that she refused to accept that it was going to happen. 'Don't be so ridiculous,' she said to Joe when he tried to explain. 'You cannot expect me to leave here and go into some slummy apartment block.'

'Norah, it's all that we can afford,' Joe said. He felt sorry for her because she had been in a privileged position all her life and any other way to live was alien to her.

'There must be money in the bank.'

'There isn't, Norah,' Joe said decidedly. 'And that is why we will have to sell the factory, and this house, and so we

83

can't live here any more. In fact we no longer own it, because Brian borrowed against it. The bank now owns this house.'

'I have never heard anything so absurd in the whole of my life, and I will not move from here and no one will make me.'

Joe could see that Norah was getting agitated and upset, and he left her and appealed to Gloria. 'Talk to your mother,' he pleaded. 'I know she is fighting the inevitable because she's scared. See if you can get her to understand.'

'I'll do my best,' Gloria said, though she too was frightened of the future and hated the thought of leaving her home. She knew there was no alternative, however, because Joe had written all the figures down for her. That was what she must make her mother see.

Gloria tried hard. For a long time she explained how bad the situation was for them all, but Norah wouldn't listen.

'Ignore her,' Joe said eventually. 'You have done your best. Pack up her stuff along with your own. Take none of your fancy dresses or ball gowns, though you can take any personal items and gifts you have been given, so you can take your jewellery and your mother's. We may well have need of it yet.'

'Can we take nothing else?' Gloria said.

'I'm afraid not,' Joe said. 'It has to be sold to pay off the creditors. The bank has agreed, however, that I can take the everyday crockery and cutlery from the kitchen, and a selection of cooking utensils.'

'Cooking utensils will be wasted on me,' Gloria said. 'I told you before we married that I couldn't cook and didn't know the least thing about keeping house.'

'It can't be that hard,' Joe said, 'for there are plenty of people at it. Anyway, I should think not being able to cook a four-course meal will be the least of our troubles.'

Adamant to the last, even when the bailiffs entered the house, Norah sat on an easy chair in the drawing room and refused to move.

Outside, a man with a clipboard gave a perfunctory look over the truck that Joe had hired to ascertain they hadn't squirrelled away the family silver. They were ready to go, but Norah wouldn't budge.

'Lady, if you don't move then we will lift you up and dump you on the drive outside,' one of the men told her eventually. Norah's lips were clamped shut and she glowered at him. He went out to where Joe stood leaning against the truck and said, 'By, but she's one cussed old bird.'

'She's scared and saddened,' Joe said. 'Let me talk to her again.'

The man shrugged. 'All right, pal,' he said. 'She's all yours, but remember we haven't got all day.'

Joe went into the drawing room and faced Norah. 'Come on,' he said. 'What's this about now? Both Gloria and I explained it to you.'

Norah didn't answer that. Instead, she said in an outraged tone, 'He said – that man said – that he would pick me up and put me on the sidewalk.' She gave an emphatic nod of her head and added, 'He wouldn't dare.'

'He might well,' Joe said. 'He has a job to do.'

'Then let him try,' Norah said fiercely. 'The audacity of it! Carrying me out of my own house.'

Joe kneeled down and, taking Norah by the shoulders, he looked her straight in the eyes. 'Norah,' he said. 'Listen to what I am going to say. This is not your house, not any longer, and you have no right here. The bank owns it now, and you must leave it to them and come with me and Gloria. She is waiting for you in the truck.'

'Joe, it will break my heart to leave this place,' Norah said, and Joe's own heart turned over in sympathy for her, but this wasn't the time to soften.

'No it won't. You are stronger than that, Norah, and anyway, there is no alternative.' He stood up and put out his hand. 'Come on,' he coaxed.

He saw the tears trickle down Norah's lined cheeks, but she took Joe's hand and he led her outside.

Joe was very proud of the furnished apartment that he now rented in Manhattan West Side. It was expensive, though, and he knew that he would have to find a job as quickly as possible to pay for it. It was on the fifth floor and had two sizeable bedrooms, a living room, a separate dining room, a roomy kitchen and bathroom, and a balcony.

Gloria could see that Joe was pleased with it and so she didn't say that she thought it awful, cramped and squalid. She knew her mother felt the same, because she saw it in the disdainful curl of Norah's lips and the set of her jaw. She said nothing, but then since the day she had been taken from her home she had said very little at all.

From the very first day in the apartment Gloria's life changed beyond all recognition. She had to learn to wash dishes, launder clothes and clean the apartment, and though she found things extremely difficult, she complained little, knowing that it wouldn't help. She also looked after her mother, who was so sunk in melancholy that she seemed unable to rouse herself at all and spent most of her time in bed.

In the early days, Joe showed Gloria how to cook porridge, bacon and fish, eggs, both boiled and fried, and how to make tea and boil potatoes. Apart from that they lived on sandwiches and pies they bought from the shop.

Gloria had no idea of budgeting either, in the beginning, for in her old world, if she had money she spent it on anything she wanted. Much of what she bought was put on her father's account before her marriage, and Joe's after it. Now Joe had to explain about putting aside the money for bills and rent, and saving any spare in case he had difficulty in finding work, and she found this very hard to take.

He thought he would find work with little trouble, but he soon realised there were few jobs to go around and many people after them. Men would cluster around the gates of one of the factories still operating, and that way might be picked for a day or two's work. That work might consist of anything and whatever wage you were offered, however paltry it was, you took it, for if you didn't someone else would.

Their poverty frustrated and angered him because it was the result of nothing he had done wrong. And the worry that he wouldn't earn enough to keep them alive never really left him. He certainly wasn't earning enough to pay the rent. Every week he had to dip into the biscuit tin and he knew things couldn't go on like that indefinitely.

By 1930 more factories had gone to the wall and it was harder than ever to get work. The cold was intense throughout January and February, and there were many snowstorms. Joe was often soaked to the skin after standing for hours in the hope of employment, only to be passed over for younger, fitter-looking men. That was a real problem, for in March that year Joe was forty and since finding Brian in his study that time, and the dreadful days following it, he really did look his age.

Gloria, however, was still optimistic that their fortunes would improve and this seemed to be the case when Joe was taken on as a labourer in the building of the Empire State Building in March. She began to believe their troubles were over, but Joe told her to go easy, for the work would not last for ever. He was proved right too. The job was good for the months that he had it, but although the building was set to be the tallest skyscraper in the whole of America, it was going up far too fast for Joe's liking and was finished by May of the following year.

Gloria felt engulfed in panic and misery when Joe told her that his job was at an end, because she knew he had nothing else lined up. He would be back to hanging around the factories, hoping to be picked for a job of work, and whether they ate or not depended on him.

So the following morning, when Joe got up a little later than usual, Gloria assumed that he was going to be doing a tour of the factories, as he had done before.

'No, not yet,' Joe said, when she asked him. 'I am off to see the Empire State Building opened officially by President Hoover first. D'you want to come along with me and see it for yourself?'

Gloria stared at him as if she couldn't believe her ears. What good was watching the opening of the Empire State Building – or any other building, come to that? It wouldn't affect their lives in any way. They needed money and Joe hadn't time to go gallivanting.

'See it for myself?' Gloria repeated scornfully. 'I have no desire to see it and I am surprised that you want to. As you have no work, shouldn't you be out looking for something?'

'I will look for something,' Joe said. 'The opening shouldn't take all day.'

Gloria, however, was dreading going back to the way they had lived before, and worry caused her to lash out at him. 'Joe, I don't believe that I am hearing this,' she cried. 'You know yourself that there is not a chance of a job unless you are out early. You have said so yourself. When you are watching the President cutting the tape, as if you are a man of leisure, just remember that.'

'And when have I ever wasted time?' Joe ground out.

'Well, you are proposing to now,' Gloria retorted.

'Dear God, woman . . .' Gloria saw the rage building up in Joe. His face was crimson and his eyes flashed fire. She waited for the onslaught, but it didn't come. Joe didn't trust himself to speak. He couldn't trust himself to stay in the same room as Gloria either, and he wrenched the door open, then slammed it so hard behind him that it shuddered on its hinges.

Gloria sank onto a kitchen chair, and burst into tears. She knew how unjust she had been. Joe was out every day, in all weathers, and was willing to work his fingers to the bone for them. Why hadn't she gone with him to see the opening of that magnificent building? He would have been so pleased if she had, but instead she had driven him out with her angry words.

Norah lay in bed and listened to her daughter weeping. She knew Gloria was very near breaking point, for she had heard it in her voice, and now she faced the fact that she was partly to blame. Instead of being a help to her – to them both – she had been more of a hindrance. True, the way they lived now was as far from her former life as it was possible to be, but it was the same for Gloria and she hadn't crumbled, but had soldiered on, making the best of it, though she was now at the end of her tether.

It was time that she herself took an active role in the family again, Norah decided, and she threw back the covers.

Gloria heard her mother's approach with surprise. She lifted her tear-stained face and said, 'Are you all right, Mother?' for Norah spent much of her time isolated in her room. 'Is there something I can get for you?'

'There is nothing you can get me, girl, and yet I am definitely not all right,' Norah said. 'I am selfish and self-centred.'

'Oh, Mother . . .'

'Hear me out, Gloria. I have watched you and Joe struggle for months and as yet have not lifted a finger to help you.'

'Mother, we understand. What has happened was a terrific shock for you.'

'It was a terrible shock for all of us and my withdrawing from life helped no one. Your father took the coward's way out, Gloria, and yet I envied him. At one point it crossed my mind to make an end to it all when I realised that I had lost the house. I felt that I was in despair. But I have finally got over that nonsense now, and for all he seldom complains I imagine Joe gets as fed up as the rest of us.'

'Yes,' Gloria said. 'And I have driven him away.'

'You are under strain as well,' Norah said. 'And that is

why you said what you did – because you know your man works himself to death for the pair of us.'

'I know,' Gloria said, 'and I will apologise to him as soon as he comes in.'

Many hours later, when the early summer's evening had a dusky tinge to it, Joe arrived home, worn out and footsore. His face was grey and lined with fatigue. Norah, looking from him to her daughter, felt that her presence wasn't necessary and took herself off to her room.

Gloria said gently, 'I was worried about you.'

'Were you?' Joe asked wearily. He looked at her steadily. 'I don't think you were. You probably just wanted to establish that I was out looking for work and not wasting time.'

'No, Joe,' Gloria maintained, 'I was truly worried. I thought something might have happened to you and I couldn't have borne that. I am so sorry about what I said to you this morning. I was wrong and I regretted the words as soon as they left my mouth.'

Joe's face lightened a little, but still he asked, 'Do you really mean that?'

'Yes, Joe,' Gloria replied earnestly. 'I mean it from the bottom of my heart.'

'That, my dear girl, is all I wanted to hear,' Joe said, and as he held her closer she heard the rumble of his stomach.

She pulled away from him slightly. 'Joe, you're hungry.'

'Well, I haven't eaten all day,' Joe said. 'You can't buy anything when you haven't even a dime in your pocket.'

'Oh, Joe,' Gloria said, 'I only have bread in, but I have milk and tea.'

'Tea and bread is a banquet to a starving man,' Joe said, giving Gloria a peck on the cheek. 'Lead me to it. You must feed me up anyway, for I have at least a day's work at the docks tomorrow.'

Gloria used to love the docks, she remembered, and would nag her father to take her as often as she could. It had all stopped when she was fourteen and Joe had put his life on the line to save her from greater injury or death. That, however, had been in her other life when she had been living, rather than merely existing. Now she said, 'Oh, Joe, that's wonderful.'

'Aye, isn't it,' Joe said. 'I would have hated to come home with nothing, and I only got this because I can drive.'

'Oh? What are you driving?'

'Trucks. One of the hauliers is a driver down, and I wish the man no harm, but I hope he takes a while to recover from whatever it is he is suffering from.'

'Ooh, yes,' Gloria said. 'A whole week would be lovely.'

'A week,' said Joe. 'That is nothing at all. I was thinking more of six months or so.'

'And I would say you were tilting at windmills.'

'You shouldn't be saying anything at all,' Joe said. 'You should be putting food on the table before I start gnawing on the table leg.'

Two months later Gloria looked down from her fourth-floor window to the dusty yard below and thought she had died and gone to hell. She could see the doors to the communal lavatories sagging open on broken hinges, and the dustbins spilling onto the yard, and she wanted to die. She never in all her life thought that people lived like this, let alone that she would be counted as one of them.

She faced the fact that she was no longer a person in straitened circumstances, but part of New York's poor, and that realisation was hard to take. They no longer had an apartment, for despite Joe's semi-permanent jobs at the docks, they couldn't pay the rent. Instead they had rooms in a tenement building. Her mother had the one bedroom, and in the other room the family had to live, Joe and Gloria sleeping on the settee, which opened up as a bed at night. Any basic cooking would have to be done in what was laughingly called 'the kitchen', which housed a battered table and four rickety chairs, a sink under the one cold tap, a couple of shelves and two gas rings. The lighting too was from gas. They had no bathroom, and the toilet was a shared one, with access to it across the dusty yard. Gloria bitterly resented Joe bringing them there.

She hadn't really believed Joe when he told her in July that they were going to have to move to a cheaper place because the money in the biscuit tin was almost all gone and they could no longer afford the rent of the apartment. When Joe had taken Gloria to see this place she had been appalled. She couldn't believe that he could possibly think she could live here. Now the apartment she had once thought of as small and squalid seemed like a palace in comparison.

Joe knew how she felt and he felt a failure because he could provide nothing better. In fact they were lucky to have anything at all, for many in the same circumstance as Joe lived on the streets. A man he worked with at the docks, named Red McCullough because of his shock of red hair, had told him of the vacancy, in one of the tenements in Ludlow Street, nearby where he lodged in Orchard Street.

As Orchard Street was where Patrick Lacey lived, before Joe went to look at the place Red had mentioned, he looked him up. He was, however, long gone, the neighbours said, and none seemed to know or care where.

Later, when he saw the rooms at the tenement in Ludlow Street, he realised that, with no indoor toilets, they were far worse than those in Orchard Street. The whole area was more run down and shabby, yet Joe knew he had to take tenancy on those rooms, though he guessed what Gloria's reaction would be.

She didn't disappoint him. Like her mother before her, she tried to pretend the move wasn't going to happen. It was Joe who packed their few meagre possessions and he bore Gloria's glares of resentment and barbed remarks, for he knew she was dying inside at the thought of moving to the place she had seen for the first time the previous day. He knew even the day they were leaving, as he was stowing their things away in the truck that he had hired with the last of their savings, she was hoping that Joe would relent, or something else would happen to prevent them leaving the apartment.

Nothing had happened, however, and as she surveyed the room that first day she looked at Joe, her eyes full of reproach and said, 'What are you thinking of, bringing me to a place like this? Mother and I cannot stay here, Joe. You must find somewhere else. In the whole of the city there must be somewhere better to stay that we can afford. It's just a question of looking, I'm sure.'

Joe had had enough. 'Look, Gloria,' he said, 'there is nowhere. I know that this is not what you or your mother are used to, but I am doing my level best to stop us all dying of starvation or exposure. Just at the moment this is the best that I can do, for it is either this or the streets. Sorry if it isn't good enough.'

Gloria heard the hurt in Joe's voice and so did Norah. She was hiding her utter shock well, for even as Joe told her about the place she hadn't been really prepared, but she heard his words and knew he spoke the truth. She knew that Gloria had taken almost as much as she could, and it was up to her to try to rally her daughter, and so she said, 'Come, come, Gloria. The place won't look so bad when it has had a thorough clean. And any day now Joe may get a regular job and we won't be here that long.'

Gloria knew what her mother was about and she felt mean. Joe was trying so hard for them all. She felt a momentary flash of anger for the father she had once adored who had got them into this mess and then couldn't stay around even to attempt to put some of it right.

'It's me that should be saying sorry, Joe,' she said. 'I know you are trying always to do the best for us. It's just this place . . . It's such a shock. Maybe, though, Mother is right and we won't have to stay here for too long altogether.'

'Perhaps,' Joe answered. He didn't believe that for a

minute, though. He knew just how bad the unemployment was and he couldn't see any let-up in the grip it had on the city.

Month after month passed and the recession worsened. In the winter of 1931 severe blizzards began to paralyse the whole city and early in 1932, a gold pendant of Gloria's and a set of pearl earrings had to be sacrificed to prevent the family from starving or freezing to death.

By 1933 food became less freely available and more expensive, because a severe drought had followed the blizzards of the previous year, turning the farming areas into huge dust bowls. Farmers began leaving the land in desperation and seeking other forms of employment in the towns and cities, adding to the problems already there and causing a food shortage.

The country had elected Theodore Roosevelt President in 1932. He was a popular man and people said he would be good for the country, but even a president has no control over the weather, and Joe began to wonder seriously how much longer they could survive.

Eventually, the churches began to work with the poor and starving people. St John the Baptist, the church that Joe, Norah and Gloria attended every Sunday, was no exception and they operated soup kitchens. Each person was entitled to one bowl of thick, nourishing soup and one thick slice of coarse bread every day, which was dispensed from the streets to the homeless and destitute, and from the church hall to those in the tenements. For many that meal was a life saver.

Gloria also thought it was good for her and her mother to get out of their small rooms, where they lived on top of one another. As the summer passed and autumn brought the cold and the damp, it was good to gather in the warm church hall, thereby saving money on coal. They met some of the people who shared their tenement and the neighbouring ones.

Norah and Gloria had never associated with such people, and though many cursed and swore worse than any rough man, Gloria enjoyed listening to the ribaldry and banter between them.

It gave them something to talk to Joe about in the evenings too, for though he had met many of the men as they roiled around the streets together looking for work he had had little to do with the women. 'They are destitute, Joe, some even poorer than we are but many refuse to let life wear them down. You can't help respecting an attitude like that.'

'I agree,' Joe said. 'Sometimes life seems one wearying and never-ending struggle.'

'And yet you wouldn't think some of these people had a care in the world,' Norah said. 'Today for example a few of the Irish women lifted up their skirts and danced a jig for us.'

Gloria smiled at the memory and added. 'Yes, and a boy, little more than a child, was there playing the tune for them on a battered old violin.'

Unbidden there flashed into Joe's head the picture of himself and Tom playing the music for Aggie to dance to. He remembered her plaits bouncing on her back and her eyes alight with delight, for she adored Irish dancing and yet, in the end, dancing had been her downfall.

Gloria saw the shadow flit over Joe's face and she stopped talking and said, 'What is it, Joe?'

Joe shrugged. 'Just memories. Nothing important.'

'Important enough to put a frown on your face.'

Joe sighed. 'Well, I suppose I might as well tell you,' he said. 'I was remembering a time when my brother and I would play the Irish music at home. He played fiddle or violin as you call it, and I would play the tin whistle and our sister Aggie would dance.'

'I never heard you mention anyone called Aggie,' Gloria said. 'I thought you only had the one sister Nuala who worked for the Protestant people near your home in

Buncrana. And then in the Troubles she went with them to their second home in England and never came back. You never said why not.'

'I'll tell you about Nuala another day,' Joe said. 'It was my elder sister, Aggie, that used to do the dancing and,' he added grimly, 'she disappeared off the face of the earth at fifteen years old.'

Gloria's eyes grew wide with surprise. 'Why did she do that?'

'Because she was raped by the dancing teacher,' Joe said simply. 'When Aggie discovered she was expecting the man's baby she knew she would have to leave her home, because for an unmarried girl to have a baby is just about the worst thing in the world to those over in Ireland.'

Gloria was incensed. 'That is monstrous. What of your parents?'

'They knew nothing,' Joe said. 'And they were never told. Tom is the only one who knew all about it and he told me just before I came here. The man McAllister said he would deal with things and Tom said he was sure that he was sending Aggie to his sister in a place called Birmingham in England. Aggie agreed to go to save the family's shame. From the night Tom saw her being driven off in the man's cart in the early hours of the morning, he hasn't a clue what happened to her.'

'What a perfectly dreadful story,' Gloria said. 'That poor, poor girl, driven to such lengths. I know such things go on and the man is seldom held responsible for anything, but I have never met anyone affected in such a way.'

'And it gets worse,' Joe said. 'The dancing teacher died shortly afterwards and when the man's wife contacted his sister to come to the funeral, the letter was returned saying she didn't live there any more, so Aggie truly did disappear into thin air. That thought haunted Tom for years. He wonders if he could have handled things differently, but he was only thirteen himself.'

Norah noted Joe's doleful face and she said gently,

'However dreadful it is, Joe, you must put it out of your mind because all the fretting and worrying in the world cannot change what is past and gone.'

'You're right, of course,' Joe said. 'And I really have got quite enough to worry about now without looking for other things I can have no control over.'

Gloria knew that was only too true for despite the daily soup ration, life was still a struggle, but she was glad that Joe had told her about his sister Aggie. It was good to share burdens. And so she would get him to tell her about his other sister, Nuala, too. There was another mystery there, she was sure.

October was drawing to a close when Gloria suddenly leaped out of bed one morning and just made the chamber pot in time, for the nausea had risen inside her as soon as she'd opened her eyes.

Joe looked across at her with his eyebrows raised. 'What was that all about?' he said. 'It couldn't have been something you ate. You eat so little.'

Gloria shrugged. 'Could have been anything,' she said. 'I am fine now, anyway.'

In fact she felt far from fine, but Joe couldn't afford to lose time from the job at the docks that he had had for three days now, and she waited till the door had closed behind him before she allowed herself the luxury of a groan.

Gloria was sick the next day and the day after that, and Joe was beside himself with worry. He was still at the docks and well liked because he worked hard and never refused to do anything. He would work till the job was done whatever time it was, so sometimes the hours were long. He knew that if he didn't go in one day someone else would take his place, and yet he was so worried about Gloria he wanted to stay at home and have the doctor brought out.

Norah wouldn't hear of it. 'D'you think I can't look after my own daughter?'

'You'll call the doctor out to have a look at her?' Joe asked, as he hovered at the door, worry lines creasing his forehead.

'I will if I think it necessary,' Norah said. 'Now, for God's sake, will you go to work before someone else is given your job?'

The door had barely closed behind Joe when Norah looked at her daughter and said, 'You couldn't be pregnant, could you? I know you haven't had your monthlies for ages.'

'They have stopped before when I haven't had much to eat for a while.'

'But you have a big bowl of soup every day at least,' Norah said. 'And there is a sort of bloom to your face that wasn't there before.'

'Oh, Mother, do you really think I could be having a baby?' Gloria cried, hardly able to believe it.

Norah laughed. 'I don't need to ask how you would feel about it.'

'I'd be ecstatic if it were true,' Gloria said, 'and that's even taking into account the situation we are in. It is what I have longed for most, the one thing I thought I would never achieve.'

'Well,' Norah said, 'let's just wait and see, shall we? Wait until Joe hears.'

That night when he came home Gloria was up and dressed, and he asked immediately how she was. She smiled at him. 'Me? Joe, I am as fit as a fiddle.'

Joe was puzzled by her answer, by her very manner, and said, 'Is that what the doctor said?'

'I went to no doctor,' Gloria said, 'because I am not ill, you see. I am just expecting our child.'

Joe's first reaction was a feeling of unparalleled elation, and then realisation kicked in and the burden of keeping a child hale and hearty and well fed and warm in this beleaguered city seemed almost insurmountable. And so his first words were, 'Oh my God, Gloria! How the hell are we going to cope?'

Gloria leaped to her feet and stamped her foot angrily. 'Shame on you, Joe Sullivan, to greet the news that you are to be a father that way.'

Immediately, Joe felt ashamed. Whatever his worries, it was no way to respond, and it was news he had never expected to hear. He put his arms around Gloria and said, 'I am heart sore for what I said earlier. You have made me one of the happiest and proudest men in the whole wide world.'

Joe never expressed any negative feelings again in front of Gloria or her mother, who both seemed on top of the world at the news. Only in his letters to Tom did he confess his true feelings. Tom had been devastated at what had happened to his brother and he understood his concern about caring for a child in the penurious way they were living. But despite that, Tom envied him that he would soon hold his own child in his arms.

SEVEN

Gloria had a trouble-free pregnancy. As her stomach swelled, her skin took on a glow that seemed to radiate the happiness inside her and she could hardly wait for the baby to be born so that she could hold him in her arms.

For much of the pregnancy, Joe had had fairly regular though not permanent employment, and so was able to give Gloria extra money to buy some flannelette material that she and Norah made into soft nightgowns, and towelling that they hemmed to make diapers, and he made a rocking crib from orange boxes and scrap wood that he found at the docks.

The whole tenement had taken an interest in Gloria Sullivan's first baby, including Red McCullough, who had become such friends with Joe. It was an odd friendship for Joe was twenty years older than young Red. He had arrived in America the spring of 1929 and so he had just had a short taste of what New York had to offer before the Crash.

'I suppose because of that, I have no great affinity for the place,' he said to them all one night.

'I can understand that,' Gloria said. 'But my home is New York and I would hate to leave it. Wouldn't you, Mother?'

'I wouldn't leave it,' Norah said emphatically. 'I have put up with a lot of changes in my life in recent years, but that would be one change too many for me. My husband did a bad thing in killing himself, but before that he was a good husband and provider, and a wonderful father. He is buried here and so here I will stay too.'

'Well, London is my home,' Red said, 'and I would return to it tomorrow if I could, but they are in a recession as bad as this in America, which is why I left in the first place. My parents are managing because the family all lives around the docks, on one another's doorsteps really, and it's share and share about, but I would be just one more mouth to feed.'

'Well, then, I see no advantage in moving anywhere,' Norah said, 'especially when you say that England is the same. I think most of Europe is affected in some way.'

'You're right, Norah,' Joe said. 'And, apart from the unemployment situation, Europe is a hotbed of unrest just now. So we will just sit tight and wait for that baby to be born and hope America pulls herself out of this in time.'

'And I wish this baby would hurry up.'

'Well, you know, I would say it takes time to grow a baby to be fine and healthy,' Joe said, 'and that's what we want, isn't it?'

'Oh, yes, Joe,' Gloria said fervently. 'More than anything in the whole world.'

At last, on Friday 6 April 1934, Gloria had her first pains. Initially, they weren't that strong and so she said nothing before Joe left for work, knowing he would worry about her if she did. Her mother, though, had been aware of her slight grimaces of pain and so when Joe had gone she asked if she should go for Bella Turner, a retired nurse who helped out at most deliveries in the tenements. Gloria shook her head.

'Not yet,' she said. 'Bella says first babies usually take some time.'

'Well, she's right there,' Norah said. 'I mean, I know I only had the one, but you were in no hurry, as I remember.'

'We'll leave it a little while then,' Gloria said.

By the afternoon, though, the pains were stronger, and by the time Joe came home, Gloria was installed in Norah's bed in considerable discomfort. Norah was mopping her glistening brow and Bella was also in the room. She had tied a towel to the bedhead for Gloria to pull on when the pains got bad, and it worried Joe greatly to see Gloria suffering the way she was. Bella shooed him from the room as she assured him everything was completely normal and nothing to worry about at all.

Expelled from the bedroom, he was too anxious about his wife to be able to rest. He paraded up and down the room, like some sort of untamed beast, suffering with her at each anguished shout as the clock ticked and the hours passed.

Joe had been home three hours when he heard the first new-born wail, and he burst into the bedroom before either of the women was able to stop him.

'Mr Sullivan,' Bella said crisply, 'your wife is hardly decent enough to be seen.'

Joe barely heard her. He was gazing with awe at the tiny bundle Norah had, which she wrapped in a shawl and gave into Gloria's waiting arms. Joe saw that Gloria looked tired and her face was damp with sweat, her tousled hair plastered to it, and yet to him she had never seemed lovelier. When she smiled at him, he was across the room in seconds.

'You have your son, Joe,' Gloria said.

'A son,' Joe repeated, as if he wasn't quite able to believe it.

He was so small and fragile-looking, with hair so fine it was like down covering his head. His milky blue eyes tried to focus. 'Isn't he just magnificent?' Gloria said. 'This is our little Benjamin Thomas.'

Joe just nodded. He was unable to speak, for a huge lump was lodged in his throat. He traced a finger gently down the baby's cheek and sudden overwhelming love for him washed over Joe. He knew that he would willingly lay down his life for the two people who mattered more to him than any others on earth.

His biggest worry was earning enough money to put food on the table. This was especially so for the baby, who needed good, nourishing food to grow up healthily and able to fight the many infections that spread rapidly in those teeming tenement buildings. The burden of worry that he would be unable to do this lodged between his shoulder blades. As the weeks and months passed this concern often drove much-needed sleep from him as he lay in bed at night, and many more trinkets of Gloria's had to be sold to provide nourishment for the child.

And then a letter came from Tom that put his own problems into perspective.

Ben had passed his first birthday and now that he could walk, he would toddle over to his father as soon as he saw him come in and Joe would lift him high in the air. And so, he had his son in his arms when Gloria handed him the letter and, still holding Ben, he sat in the chair to read it.

Gloria was in the kitchen doorway, waiting to hear what Tom had to say, when she saw the blood suddenly drain from Joe's face. 'What is it?' she said, taking the child from him as she spoke.

Joe didn't speak but the eyes he turned to her were full of pain and anguish, and bright with unshed tears.

'Joe, for God's sake,' Gloria cried in alarm. She passed Ben over to her mother, disregarding his protests, and then she put an arm around Joe. 'What is it? What's happened?'

Joe's voice was husky as he said, 'Do you mind the time I told you about my wee sister, Nuala, that my parents thought the sun shone out of?'

Gloria nodded. 'I remember it well,' she said. 'I thought at the time that it was like a fairy story. She married a Protestant and when she wrote to your parents and told them that, your father had a heart attack and died.'

'Yes,' Joe said. 'We were not allowed to speak her name after that. I was all for writing to her and telling her what happened, but Tom was afraid of Mammy.'

'Afraid?' Gloria said incredulously.

'Mammy's rages have to be seen to be believed,' Joe said. 'But it wasn't just himself he was worried about. He was afraid of Mammy attacking Nuala if she did come home, so she didn't even know her father had died. How I wish now we had taken the chance while we had it.'

'Is it too late?'

Joe nodded. 'Far too late,' he said. 'Nuala and her husband, Ted, were killed ina car accident over a week ago, leaving behind two children: Molly, a girl of thirteen, who Mammy claims looks the spit of Nuala, and a wee boy of five.'

'Poor children . . .'

'Ah, yes indeed,' Joe cried. 'Especially as Mammy is intending taking them home to live with her.'

'Well, isn't that the best solution all round?' Gloria asked. 'I mean, I can't think of anything worse to happen than for the children to lose both their parents in such a tragic way, so isn't it better that they are with their grandmother? If, Heaven forbid, anything should happen to us, I would like Mother to take care of Ben.'

'As I would without hesitation,' Norah said.

She put down the struggling child as she spoke and he toddled round to his father. Joe took him on to his knee before he said, 'I can understand you thinking that – anyone would – and there is no one but Norah that I would like to have the care of Ben in such a circumstance. But you are talking about a rational person and one who would love and care for our son as we would.'

'But your mother will know what a tragic loss the children have suffered,' Gloria said. 'I know you have often said your upbringing was a harsh one, but these are her grandchildren and—'

'Gloria,' Joe answered, 'when I left Ireland my mother was still full of resentment and spite against Nuala, and according to Tom she has got no better as time has gone on. If this girl looks anything like Nuala then I worry that Mammy will make her pay for what her mother did.'

'You can't be sure of that!'

Joe shook his head. 'You don't know her like I do. I should have defied my mother and made contact with the sister I loved so much. Now I will never see her again and will never have the opportunity to get to know the children. They must think themselves so alone in the world.'

'Ah, yes,' Gloria said, and her heart turned over in pity for them. And yet, she thought, Joe might be building up a worse scenario than it was. Maybe his mother had been hard on him as a boy, but usually grandparents were far more lax than the parents.

In the following weeks, Tom's letters told Joe only the bare minimum about the situation, though Tom did write that Molly so resembled her mother it was like having the young Nuala returned to them. He also told him that the boy had become so ill they had decided to leave him in the care of his paternal grandfather.

However, Joe was no fool, and he knew Tom well enough to realise it was more what he didn't say than what he did that was worrying. Reading between the lines he could only feel for the young orphaned girl, at the mercy of his mother.

He knew Gloria, who didn't know Tom as he did, would just take his letters at face value. Joe didn't say anything to Gloria, either; he couldn't expect her or Norah to understand his worries over his mother's behaviour when they had never met her. And he had always kept a lot of his mother's letters to himself and so Gloria was unaware of her true nature.

Joe did worry about the girl, though, but, helpless to change the situation in any way, he told himself in time she would grow up and leave the farm. She could go back to the grandfather and brother she had been wrenched from and Tom, who had evidently become so fond of her, would get over it in time.

Larger-scale news made an impact on their lives, and Joe often spoke about it when he came home from work. 'The immigrant boats have begun arriving again,' he said to the two women in the autumn of 1935, 'only now they are full of Jews.'

'Jews?' Norah and Gloria said together, in astonishment.

'Aye, and mainly from Germany.'

'Why come here?' Norah asked. 'Isn't America in the greatest recession it has ever experienced?'

'Well, that chap Hitler appears not to like them at all,' Joe said.

'Isn't he the one who became the Chancellor of Germany a few years ago?' Gloria asked.

'That's the chap.'

'So what has he got against Jews?'

Joe shrugged. 'Search me. But for whatever reason, he has got it in for them. Jewish children aren't allowed to go to school now, so one man was saying, and they can't hold citizenship. As some of them say, they considered themselves German and fought in the last war for a country that has now rejected them. Between you and me I think we might have trouble with that Hitler.'

'Europe might,' Norah said dismissively. 'But their problems needn't involve us.'

It was an attitude that Joe had come across before. Norah, Gloria and all native-born Americans seemed immune to what was happening elsewhere in the world. It wasn't that they didn't care; it was more that they honestly thought European concerns couldn't and shouldn't affect America in any way.

What did shake their composure and stir their national pride, though, were the Olympic Games held in Berlin in

August 1936, when the African-American athlete Jesse Owens won four gold medals. In fact, in that Games he broke eleven Olympic records and beat the favoured German athlete Luz Long in a very close long jump final. While the German athlete was the first to congratulate Owens, Hitler, regarding him as racially inferior, would neither shake his hand nor place the winner's medals around his neck. The American people were incensed by that.

Some now started to look with new eyes towards the racially prejudiced Hitler, Chancellor of Germany and leader of the Nazi Party. Many initially might have thought the immigrant Jews' tales of persecution far fetched, but now they were beginning to wonder if they were true after all.

But none of this essentially touched the lives of Joe and his family, while poverty did. Joe continued to trawl around the docks picking up what work he could and with the help of the sale of Gloria's jewellery they were able to scrape by.

Ben was the light of all their lives. By the time he was three he strongly resembled his mother, with his mop of blond curls, violet-blue eyes and the long black lashes. He would have looked angelic, if it hadn't been for the wicked glint in his eyes. When he was playing in the yard of the tenement with the other children, if there was mischief to be had, he would be in the thick of it, and that just made Gloria and Joe love him all the more.

It was that autumn that Gloria realised her mother wasn't well. Her face, she noticed, was grey and drawn, the lines of strain more prominent than she had ever seen them. She also walked stooped over and seemed easily out of breath. She told Gloria when she asked that she felt quite all right and she should stop fussing, and she refused point-blank to see a doctor.

'It's money for the doctor's bills that she is worried about,' Gloria said one night as she lay in bed beside Joe. 'I think

I'll ask Bella to look in. Mother likes Bella and she just might take notice of her.'

When Joe came home the following evening, he guessed something was bothering Gloria by the shadows behind her eyes, but he knew she would say nothing until Ben was put to bed in the shakedown he had in his grandmother's room.

When he had gone, Joe looked from one woman to the other and said, 'What is it?'

Norah looked at Gloria before saying to Joe, 'Bella thinks I have a growth, a tumour. She can feel the lump just below my left breast.'

'I said she needs to see a doctor,' Gloria said. 'He can send her to the hospital. They can operate and take the tumour out and she will be as good as new again.'

'But I don't want that,' Norah said softly. 'Hospitals cost money, and anyway, it's too late. I have had this lump for some time. Forgive me, but I didn't want to be a burden to you, or have you spending money on me when you have so little of it.'

Gloria was stunned by her mother's words, Joe could see, but he knew that he was looking at a dying woman and he had respect for her courage. But when he tried to say this, Norah cut him off. 'Without you, Joe, both Gloria and I would have been lost after Brian killed himself. It is due to your valiant efforts that we have survived at all. Now my time is running out, but yours is just beginning and after I am gone—'

'Mummy, don't let's talk about this now.'

'Darling, I don't know how long I have got,' Norah said. 'There are things that have to be faced and if I can bear it, then so must you.'

The whole ethos of the family changed from that day. For a few weeks it seemed the same, though Norah's illness was always in the forefront of Gloria's mind and she would have felt terribly alone if it hadn't been for Joe's understanding.

He thanked God that they had Ben for Gloria to focus her mind on.

Even when Norah took to her bed most of the time in mid-December, Ben accepted what his mother told him, that his grandmother was very tired. He even accepted the priest coming to the house regularly, for he was familiar and someone that he saw at Mass every Sunday. It was only when Norah eventually decided to see the doctor, a fortnight before Christmas, that he asked if his grandmama was sick.

'It was pointless to lie, Gloria thought, and so she said, 'She is, darling. Grandmama is very sick. In fact, Ben, she is going to die . . .'

'What's die?' Ben asked.

'It means that Grandmama will go away to live with Jesus.'

Ben was totally surprised. 'Oh,' he said. 'Does she want to?'

'I think she does, Ben,' Gloria said. 'She's very tired.'

'Will she come back when she is feeling better?'

Gloria had to swallow the lump that threatened to choke her as she answered, 'No, Ben, she will go to sleep and not wake up again, and there is nothing that we can do about it.'

It was Thursday 6 January 1938, and, knowing the end was near, Gloria had sat beside the bed all night and held her mother's hand. Norah was not conscious, and yet her contorted face showed the level of her suffering and Gloria prayed for God to give her peace.

Suddenly, there was a rattle in Norah's throat and then there was a deathly silence, the only sound the muted tick of the clock from the other room. And yet, Gloria felt that her mother's spirit was like an actual presence in the room.

It was only seconds later, but it felt longer, that the room grew suddenly very cold, still and empty, and Gloria knew that Norah's suffering was finally over. She got to her feet with a sigh, and laid her mother's hands across her chest. Then she bent over and kissed her cheek. 'Bye, Mummy,' she whispered. 'I love you and I will miss you to the end of my days.'

She thought she had accepted her mother's imminent death, but she suddenly felt so bereft and forsaken.

In the other room Joe was already getting dressed and he looked at Gloria standing in the doorway, her eyes glistening with tears. He didn't need to speak, but opened his arms and Gloria went into them with a grateful sigh. The tears that she had been holding back all night began to seep from her eyes and slide down her cheeks, and Joe held her tight until she was calmer once more.

Ben had been sleeping in the room with his parents when his grandmother took to her bed and when he opened his eyes a little later, Gloria told him his grandmother had died. Joe though wondered how much he really understood, for all he was a bright and very articulate child. He lifted Ben into his arms as he said gently, 'Would you like to see her?'

Ben remembered what his mother had said about his grandmother going to live with Jesus when she died and so he said, 'Is she still here, then?'

'Of course,' Gloria said. 'Where else would she be?'

'I want to see,' Ben said.

Joe set him on his feet, took his hand and they went into the room together.

'She's asleep,' Ben whispered to his father.

'It's the sleep that I told you about,' Gloria said.

Ben's eyes were confused. 'So when is she going to live with Jesus?'

'The important part of her has already gone,' Joe said. 'But you will hardly understand this yet for you are too young. But the priest will understand it, and you and I will take a walk up to tell him as soon as you are dressed.'

'Aren't you going to the docks today then?' Gloria asked,

because it was a quarter to seven and Joe would usually have left by now.

'Not today,' Joe said. 'There are things to do. And I'm sure if you ask her Bella will give you a hand, while I take charge of Ben.'

Despite the loss of money, Gloria was glad that Joe was going to be there that day for she was bone-weary. She was also very glad Bella was near at hand, and so obliging, for she had never laid out a dead body before. She had to do it, though, because it was the last service she would do for her dear mother.

There was a good turnout for Norah's funeral although the only Mass card on the top of the coffin was from Tom. They were all quick, though, to shake Gloria's hand and commiserate with her in her loss. Norah had been well liked and it helped Gloria to know that.

She was also well aware of the fact that ideally her mother would have liked to be buried beside her husband in the churchyard not far from their old home. But Norah had a good idea of what it would cost to transport a body halfway across the city and then reopen a grave, and so she said that Gloria wasn't even to consider it. 'It's money that you can ill afford to waste and it is a waste because I won't know a thing about it,' she had said. 'Let's face facts. It is only my body that you are disposing of. The important bit of me will have gone heavenward, I hope.'

'Oh, Mummy, don't.'

Norah grasped her daughter's arm and said gently, 'My dear, I must. I couldn't bear it if you were to beggar your-self to bury my body somewhere you thought I might prefer, so I am telling you straight now that the county cemetery will do me fine.'

'Mummy, you must have thought, expected, that your body would lie beside Daddy's when you died?' Gloria said.

'You know what I expected?' Norah said. 'That I would

111

end my days in the house your father brought me to when he married me, that I would see you and Joe rear my grandson there in comfort and ease. If I ever looked ahead to the future, that is what I saw and that has crumbled away like so much dust beneath my feet, so that at times it has been difficult to cope with. How does all that compare to where my body lies when I am dead and gone? The county cemetery is where I wish to be laid.'

Joe tried to hide his relief when Gloria told him what Norah had said. He wouldn't allow his mother-in-law to lie in a pauper's grave, but even the most basic of funerals cost money they didn't have and Gloria had to sell the last of her trinkets and her wedding ring to pay for it.

One late February day Red McCullough said to Joe, 'Aren't you fed up with this life, Joe? Living hand to mouth, never sure whether you are going to earn enough to keep body and soul together for another day?'

'Course I am fed up,' Joe said. 'Who wouldn't be? But there is nothing to be done about it.'

'Well, I intend to do something about it,' Red said. 'And that is make for England as soon as possible.'

'You'd be no better off,' Joe said. 'Didn't you tell us England has been hit by a slump as well?'

'It was,' Red agreed. 'But England is over it now.'

'How can you be so sure?'

'My cousin, Pete, works down the docks and he says there are jobs for all that want them,' Red said. 'And if you don't fancy dock work there are factories galore, he says. He claims he could get me set on easy. You too, I would imagine.'

'Oh, what I would give for a steady and regular job that pays a living wage,' Joe said. 'But what has brought about the change? America seems as depressed as ever.'

'Yeah. Between you and me, Pete thinks England is preparing itself for trouble with Germany.'

'Doesn't that worry you?'

'A bit,' Red said. 'But I'll take my chance. This is like a living death anyway, and in the end the whole thing with Germany might blow over.'

'I thought Hitler might prove a problem,' Joe said. 'I really hope it doesn't develop into anything more serious. My young brother lost his life in the Great War – and that was supposed to be the war to end all wars. Surely no one in their right mind would want to repeat that.'

Red shrugged. 'Probably not. For now, though, it is good news for us and I am willing to give it a go. My parents are only waiting for me to send word and they will buy my ticket because I couldn't afford it.'

'Neither could we, normally,' Joe said. 'But my mother-in-law had kept back some nice pieces of jewellery that we could sell.'

'Are you for it then?' Red asked.

'Well, I am willing to give it a go, if just for my son's sake,' Joe said. 'But Gloria . . . well, she won't want to leave here. She said as much to you.'

'I know she did,' Red said. 'But remember there was no alternative then. Couldn't you talk her round?'

Joe shook his head. 'I don't know. She is as stubborn as a mule about some things. And then her mother is not long dead. They were very close and she still gets upset at times. But she just might see the sense of us moving if it is to give Ben a better chance. I will sound her out and see.'

A week went by and Joe couldn't seem to find the right words to say to Gloria. By then, Red had written to his parents and they were in the process of wiring him the money to buy his ticket, and Joe knew he would have to say something to Gloria.

That night, Joe only waited till the meal had been eaten and Ben had gone to bed before drawing his wife down on the settee before the fire.

'What is it, Joe?' Gloria asked. 'There has been something on your mind all evening.'

Joe told her all that Red had said to him, leaving out any talk of conflict between England and Germany, but when he suggested leaving America, she pulled away and looked at him with horrified eyes.

'Leave here?' she said. 'Surely that's madness?'

'Not as I see it,' Joe said. 'It's madness altogether if we stay.'

'America is my home.'

'I know that, and in the normal way of things I never would have thought of leaving,' Joe went on gently. 'Even after the crash, I honestly thought that we could ride out the storm. But it has gone on and on, and shows no sign of easing. England then had a recession to match America's, but apparently it has pulled itself out of it. It's Ben that I am really concerned about if we stay here much longer.'

'D'you think I'm not concerned?' Gloria asked. 'I worry about him all the time.'

'I know that you do,' Joe said, pulling her close to him again. 'We both of us love our child dearly and want the best for him, so don't just reject this out of hand. Because I wasn't set on for two days this week we have finished all the food in the house, and then all we had was bread, and not much of that. What nourishment is that to a growing boy? He will live on fresh air tomorrow, the same as the rest of us, and God knows what we will do when the coal runs out.'

Gloria knew Joe was right. Her stomach still yawned emptily because she had eaten sparingly so that Ben and Joe might eat their fill. In fact, she had done that so often, her clothes hung off her gaunt frame and she took care to ensure that Joe never saw her naked. But she didn't want to leave her place of birth and so she said, 'I'll get some money together. My mother had some lovely pieces of jewellery and I—'

'And what will you do when they are gone?'

'Joe, there is unrest in Europe,' Gloria said. 'You have said so yourself.'

'There is unrest in America too,' Joe maintained. 'Because people are hungry and destitute and have lost all hope, and we will be counted among them unless we have the courage to get out while we can.'

'Can't we just wait for a while and see if things change?' Gloria pleaded.

Joe shook his head. 'Gloria, we must go while we have enough of Norah's jewellery left to pay our passage. Remember you are doing this for Ben, giving him the chance of a future.'

How could Gloria deny that to the child she loved more than life itself? She sagged against Joe and so he knew he had won even before she said glumly, 'All right then. We will play this your way.'

EIGHT

Ben had never been so excited as the day when his father told him he was going on a ship to a place called England, so far away that it would take days and days to get there. Gloria wasn't one bit excited. The loss of her mother was still like a gaping hole in her heart, and had it not been for Ben she would have stayed in America and waited for things to get better.

They would eventually, she was sure, just as Red told her they had in England, because after Joe had talked to her she had questioned Red closely the next time he had come to the house. Joe had anticipated this – he knew his Gloria – and he warned Red to say nothing of the possibility that there might be a war.

'You didn't have to warn me of that, Joe,' Red said later. 'I'm not some sort of halfwit, and I didn't want to upset Gloria further. She is breaking her heart already at the thought of leaving this place. It's written all over her face and, to be honest, I feel sorry for her. I will do all in my power to make it easy for all of you when you land in England.'

'Thanks for that, Red,' Joe said sincerely. 'I owe you one.'

'Make it a pint when you finally get to good old Blighty,' Red said with a grin.

'You're on,' Joe laughed. 'Oh, won't it be a wonderful

feeling to have money in my pocket for the odd pint or two?'

'It will be,' Red said. 'But that isn't a good enough reason to leave. I know why you are going, and that is to give your lad a chance. I would do the same if I had a son, and that is also why Gloria has made the heartbreaking decision she has.'

Joe knew that only too well and he was very gentle with Gloria as they packed up all their possessions and made plans to leave. Red left three weeks before the Sullivans sailed. He said he would secure them a place to stay and look into the job situation before they arrived. Joe was grateful, for with a family to think of he didn't want to move from the frying pan into the fire. And so he waited to book their passage until he had heard from Red that he had found them temporary lodgings in a place called Stepney and had secured Joe an interview at the docks office.

While Ben and Gloria said their goodbyes to the people in the tenements, Ben's mind was more focused on the trip to England than leaving the friends he had played with and would probably never see again. Gloria was bitterly upset at bidding farewell to the women who had become friends, especially Bella Turner. Most of the neighbours had been kindness itself when she had been pregnant, and had rallied around and supported her when her mother died. Gloria knew that she would miss them all dearly, but she had to do as Joe advised and look forward.

Ben had never been so thrilled in his whole life as the day he walked up the gangplank of the ship. He saw the churning water in the distance, which his dad said was called the Atlantic Ocean. 'We have to sail over that to get to England,' he told Ben. 'It will take some time, like I told you before.'

Ben didn't care how long it took, for the ship was such an exciting place to explore. Gloria felt desperately home-sick almost as soon as the ship pulled away from the harbour.

It didn't help that she felt decidedly queasy and very glad that Joe took almost full charge of Ben.

Ben would go off exploring with his father and could barely wait to relate all the exciting things he had seen to his mother, and his high, piercing voice would often make Gloria's head ache. She was very glad to be feeling halfway human by the morning of the fourth day and after that, the next four days, until the ship docked at Southampton, were far more pleasant. She even ventured on deck a time or two, though the sharp late March wind sending the clouds scudding across the sky, or the sleety rain, didn't encourage a person to linger.

Joe was pleased to see eventually the shores of England in the distance and felt a tingle of anticipation. England promised to give him employment. He didn't care where, just as long as it paid enough to enable him to bring up his family decently, and he felt as if another, different phase of his life was beginning.

As arranged, Red McCullough met them at Euston Station. Gloria was as glad as Joe to see his familiar face grinning at them, though she wasn't a bit impressed by the view of London from the windows of the taxi that they took from the station. Red was pointing things out with a hint of pride, but Gloria considered London grey and terribly drab, and many of the people appeared the same. She tried to hide her distaste, but Joe knew her too well.

Red's parents, Dolly and Jim, at whose home they stopped first, were warm and welcoming, but they spoke so fast and with such strong accents that Gloria couldn't understand everything they said. She couldn't fault their hospitality, however, and the meal they sat down to was delicious.

Then Red took the Sullivans round to the lodging house that he had found for them to stay in until something better should come up. Mrs Bullock, who spoke in a sort of strident boom, showed them their room, which was at the top of the house, and though it was sparse it was clean, and there was a shakedown bed for Ben.

'You will see,' said Mrs Bullock, pointing to a list of rules on the wall, 'breakfast is served from seven o'clock until eight thirty daily, and the evening meal is at six thirty sharp. There is a strict timetable for using the bathroom – please stick to it – and there is a charge for the using the geyser. And remember, all rooms have to be empty by ten thirty each day so they can be cleaned.'

'She's not very welcoming,' Gloria said when she had gone.

'What do we care?' Joe said. 'For the past years we have put up with far more than a disgruntled landlady. Let's all go to bed now, for I am fair tired out. Things always look better in the morning.'

The next morning, though, Gloria woke up feeling quite miserable and dispirited, and homesickness stabbed at her like a nagging tooth. But she knew that there was no point in saying any of this, what couldn't be cured had to be endured and she knew that if they were to make a go of living in London she had to be more positive. She was glad, however, that Joe had nothing to do for a day or two, and before they left the lodgings that morning he tried to explain to her the money, which she found really perplexing.

'I had to learn all about American money when I went over,' Joe said.

'But American money is logical,' Gloria said. 'There is no uniformity to English money at all.'

'Look, I will explain it all to you,' Joe said, as he laid the coins down on the small table beside the bed. 'But the best way of understanding it properly is to use it. Honestly, you will pick it up in no time.'

'Hmm, no doubt,' Gloria said. 'But just go through it with me now and I'll try to remember.'

'All right. There are twelve pennies to a shilling and twenty shillings to a pound.'

'And what are these little things that look like American dimes?' Gloria asked.

'The larger one is half of a penny, and the smaller one is a farthing, which is a quarter of a penny,' Joe told her. 'And this here is a thrupenny bit, which is three pennies, and this silver one is worth six pennies. But sometimes the money is called by different names.'

'Like what?'

'Like a sixpence is sometimes called "a tanner" and a shilling is "a bob", and ten bob could be a note like the pound note,' Joe said. 'Then there are florins, which are two shillings, and half a crown, which is two shillings and sixpence. As for a guinea—'

'Stop!' Gloria said. 'My head is reeling already.'

Joe laughed. 'Don't worry about it.' He pulled her to her feet. 'It will get easier, I promise. Now get your coat on and let's go and explore the place we are living in.'

Some of the London streets, Gloria found, were knobbly, which Joe told her were called cobbled, and some were lined with barrows piled high with all manner of produce, which were sold on the streets. When they came upon a whole area like this Joe said it was a market. He told her of the Market Hall in Buncrana, the nearest town to the farm, where they would sell any surplus goods, but they didn't shout their wares like the costers in the market in London. Gloria found that quite entertaining. She couldn't understand all they said but that didn't matter; it was just fascinating to listen.

For the next two days she toured the streets with Joe and Ben, and on the third day Joe had his interview and was taken on at the docks as a stevedore like his friend Red. Joe was delighted because in New York he had just been a longshoreman, employed on a temporary basis, often daily, and it was up to the stevedores, who were in regular and better-paid employment, which of the longshoremen they took on. To ensure a temporary job a person had to pay eight cents to the stevedores, but the work was so badly paid and spasmodic that Joe couldn't always raise the money until he had sold a trinket or two.

Now, however, he was one step up, with a regular wage. Gloria thought that wonderful too. Regular and full-time employment were words that she never thought she would hear, and she felt the knot of worry slide from between her shoulder blades. This was the first step in the new life they had begun to carve for themselves, and she hoped that soon perhaps they could get out of the lodging house and into some place of their own.

Until that time came, though, Gloria had to vacate her room each morning. From the first, Red's mother, Dolly, had said she should come in to them each day, and for the first three days Gloria had done just that. She was always made welcome and, not having any grandchildren to spoil, Dolly had a soft spot for Ben and always had some little treat in for him. However, Gloria knew she couldn't keep imposing on the McCulloughs.

The first time she and Ben went out alone she did feel very lonely and lost. She knew that it would help no one to say this, and certainly not her son, who was manfully coping with a massive change in his own young life. For his sake as much as anything else, she decided they would use the time they had to be out of the lodging house to find her way around the city that they were hoping to make their home.

She didn't stray far in the first few days because she was afraid of getting lost. She was amazed by some of the historic buildings and churches that New York lacked. Sometimes they came upon another street market, or small ornate parks with well-tended flowerbeds almost hidden away behind wrought-iron railings.

She also saw more horses than were ever seen in New York. These were no sleek, fine-boned animals, but large and beefy, with shaggy feet. They pulled carts piled high with barrels, or sacks of coal, or even bottles of milk, and Ben was enchanted by them.

'We had a horse the same on the farm in Buncrana,' Joe told his young son. 'They are the sort of horses built for strength, not speed, and one day we will go to Ireland on a visit and then you will see for yourself.'

When Gloria and Ben got hungry and footsore they would find a small café somewhere, or eat from one of the stalls in the markets selling food, and Gloria would battle with the money, glad that so many were willing to help her. Despite this, though, as the weeks passed, she found Londoners not exactly unfriendly, but busy, as if everyone passing had more and better things to do than stop to chat. That happened even at Mass on Sunday. She was finding it really hard to make friends, and was glad of Ben's company, though she knew he too was lonely and missed the children of the tenements that used to play all together, and she envied Joe his job.

One day, Gloria decided to take Ben further afield. With great daring they took the underground to the city centre. It was the first of many trips, because Ben particularly liked walking along the banks of the grey, torpid Thames. It was such a busy river, housing even some big boats and Gloria had wondered if the boats ever got out into the open sea and, if so, how they did it. Both of them then were surprised and delighted one day to see Tower Bridge raised right up and the traffic stopped either side of it while the large ship, pulled by small tugs in front of it, sailed through. What a sight that was!

They always found things of interest, like the day they stumbled upon Regent's Park, and amongst the ornamental flowerbeds and fountains they discovered a zoo. Ben had no idea what a zoo was, but Gloria had visited one in New

York when she was small and described it to him. 'Can we go in?' he asked, his face alive with excitement. It was expensive, but Ben had been given so little all his young life, and so Gloria nodded and caught up his hand. That night he told his father all about the marvellous day he had had, tripping over his words in his haste to tell all.

A couple of days after this, they saw the Houses of Parliament, where Gloria told Ben all the laws of the land were made, and then found Downing Street where the Prime Minister, Neville Chamberlain, lived. On another, they walked down The Mall to Buckingham Palace, and Ben was thrilled when smart soldiers astride beautiful bedecked horses passed them by.

At the gates surrounding Buckingham Palace, Ben watched the guards changing places and listened earnestly as Gloria told him that that was where the King lived. He wasn't sure what a King was, but it sounded important, especially with all those soldiers that his mother said were there to guard him. He was enthralled, though, by the soldiers that stood in the sentry boxes as still as if they were statues.

'They got bright red things on top,' he told his father that evening. 'And they got big furry hats on their heads, and they've all got guns as well.'

'Red told me all about them,' Joe told his young son. 'They have to stay as still as still and the funny hats they wear are called busbys. And they are the King's own guard.'

'We saw the big house that he lives in,' Ben said. 'Mummy said he was a very important man.'

'Oh, easily the most important man in the land, I would say.'

'Golly,' said Ben, and then for the first time he said, 'I like it here in London, Daddy.'

'I'm glad, Ben,' Joe said. 'Really glad, because so do I.'

The only thing that worried Joe, apart from finding somewhere to live, was the unsettled rumbling around Europe.

Power-hungry Germany had already taken over Austria in March, but the Austrians had seemed not to mind, possibly because Hitler was an Austrian by birth.

Joe thought it was as well to keep abreast of things and he suggested getting a wireless.

Gloria clapped her hands in delight. 'Ooh, Joe, it would be marvellous, as long as we can afford it. It is a great entertainment to have, with the music and the plays and all, and there is bound to be something on for children that Ben would like.'

There was also the news, which was what Joe really wanted it for, but when he said this Gloria told him that he was an old worry guts. Then when Joe got home the last Friday in September Gloria thrust the evening paper in front of him.

'All your fretting was for nothing,' she said. 'They were shouting it out all over the newsstands and so I bought a paper to see for myself.'

She handed it to Joe and there on the front page was a picture of Neville Chamberlain waving a piece of paper and declaring, 'I believe it is peace for our time.'

Joe had heard about the meeting Chamberlain and the French Prime Minister were having with Hitler in Munich, and as he read the report detailing the land Czechoslovakia had agreed to hand over to Germany in exchange for peace, he felt suddenly cold inside.

'What are you looking so gloomy for?' Gloria demanded. 'It's there in black and white. What more do you want?'

'Oh, I don't know,' Joe said. 'I suppose I want the assurance that Hitler would honour any agreement made. As for Czechoslovakia giving away part of their country, well, I hope they don't live to regret it. In my experience partitioning countries only causes more problems, not less.'

'Let's wait and see, shall we?' Gloria said.

'All we can do, I suppose,' Joe said.

However, he didn't seem able to lift the mood he was in,

and in the end he wrote an impassioned letter to Tom and urged him to get a wireless, to keep abreast of important developments.

Gloria was not looking forward to the deepening autumn and the colder weather for there was no let-up in the rules that the rooms had to be vacated by ten thirty every day. Joe too was quite desperate to find somewhere more suitable and everyone they knew was looking out for them.

Three weeks after the triumphant Chamberlain declared that he had averted conflict with Germany, a docker called Dermot Shields approached Joe one dinner-time. 'Red says that you're looking for a flat. Is that right?'

Joe nodded. 'We're in lodgings at the moment, and my wife and son have to leave there every day at ten thirty and trail around the streets. 'Do you know of some place?'

'Aye,' the man said. 'My brother Michael has a place in Tottenham, but he is going back home to take over the farm from my father. You have a good chance of getting the place if you are quick because he hasn't told the landlord he is leaving yet.'

'Is it around here?'

'No,' Dermot said, 'I told you, it's in Tottenham.'

'Where's that then?'

'Miles away.'

'Yeah, but what about my job?' Joe said. 'I don't suppose that I could live there and carry on working here.'

Dermot shook his head. 'Hardly likely. You would spend more time travelling than you would working.'

'Then . . .'

'My brother had a job in an armaments factory,' Dermot told Joe. 'And he could put in a word, if you fancied working there.'

'I will work anywhere that pays a decent wage,' Joe declared. 'But I have never had anything to do with making guns.'

Dermot shrugged. 'It's a job and it pays well. I'm sure you would get on as well as the next man. The point is, do you want to keep the job you have and stay in the lodging house, or take the flat and find some other employment?'

Joe didn't need to think about that for very long. He liked the work on the docks, that was true, but he loved his wife and son and couldn't condemn them to the conditions they were living under one moment longer than necessary. It was now October, and since they had come to Britain in late March this was the first sniff they had had of any accommodation. Who knew how long he would have to wait for another, and that might not be near the docks either?

'Could we go and look at it?'

'Of course,' Dermot said. 'But like I say, the sooner the better.'

'Tomorrow,' Joe said decidedly. 'I'll take the time from work.'

'Right,' said Dermot. 'It's wise to move fast. I'll go over tonight and tell Michael to expect you, and I will write down the directions and address.'

'It's very good of you,' Joe said. 'My wife will be ecstatic.'

And Gloria *was* ecstatic when Joe went home with the news that night. 'I long to move out of here and have our own home,' she said. 'Is it near here?'

'No, it's in Tottenham,' Joe said. 'Miles away.'

'What about your job at the docks?'

'Well, I couldn't work there and live in Tottenham.'

'Oh, but, Joe . . .'

Joe saw the worry lines furrowing Gloria's brow and he took her in his arms. 'I know what you are worried about,' he said, 'but we will never go back to that uncertain and terrible way of living that we had in New York, believe me. There is work about for anyone and everyone here now, and I will soon get another job. In fact, Dermot said his brother works nearby in a factory and he might be able to put in a word for me.'

Joe didn't tell Gloria what the factory made and was glad she hadn't asked. He didn't want her to know that he might be making guns or ammunition. She might then begin to wonder why a country so seemingly bent on 'peace for our time' had need of so many weapons. He had wondered himself, but not for long, because he didn't like the answers his mind was coming up with.

'And shall we will go up tomorrow and look at the place?' Joe asked, with a twinkle in his eye.

'Oh, yes, Joe,' cried Gloria. 'What do you think?'

Dermot had given good directions to his brother's place, with the number of the tram and where they caught it from. 'The tram will take you up Broad Lane, and you tell the conductor you want the Stamford Road stop. Newton Road leads off it. The flats are right at the end of the road, and the one you want is the one to the right, Horton Tower.'

Gloria was in a fever of excitement and yet she enjoyed that tram journey, and she was particularly interested as the tram passed a goodly selection of shops just as the conductor came to them to tell them that the next stop was theirs.

When they alighted from the tram Ben was excited by the sight of children playing in the streets. There were mothers at some of the doors keeping a perfunctory eye on the children and they nodded and smiled at Joe and Gloria as they passed but Gloria had eyes only for the red brick building in front of her. She remembered the apartment that Joe had taken her to initially after the Crash and how rundown she had thought it at the time. How snobbish she had been then. But all that was behind her now, and she would welcome living in this place. Number 8 Horton Tower might soon be their new home, and she felt a tingle of excitement begin in her toes and fill her whole body, for she longed to be able to call somewhere home.

Michael and his wife, Lynne, were welcoming, and showed them over the flat eagerly. It was well furnished and they said that they were leaving most things for a fee to be agreed between them. 'We can't take it all with us, even if we wanted to,' Lynne said to Gloria, hitching her plump and gorgeous baby further up on her hip. 'In fact the only furniture we are taking is the baby's cot.'

Gloria laughed. 'Well, we will have no need of that at least,' she said. 'It would be a bit cramped for Ben. But,' she turned to her young son, 'what do you think about having your own room at last?'

Ben didn't speak, and didn't have to because, as Lynne said, 'I think that beaming smile is answer enough. Come and I will show you the kitchen.'

Gloria loved the modern kitchen as she loved the bathroom with fitted hot water, and the large living room with its picture window overlooking the whole of London.

She turned to Joe with shining eyes and he was smiling as he said, 'You like it then?'

'No, Joe,' Gloria said, spinning around in delight. 'I love it, just absolutely love it. If we take this place then I would think I had died and gone to heaven.'

Red and his parents were thrilled about Joe and Gloria securing the flat, and came over to see it after Michael and his family had moved out.

'With the flat so well furnished, there is little to buy,' Gloria told Dolly.

'No,' the older woman agreed, 'though I'd buy a new mattress for the bed.'

'Yes, I will,' Gloria said. 'And I need a proper bed for Ben. The poor child has never had one. And he needs a cupboard or something for his clothes.'

Dolly went with Gloria to buy these items, showing her where the bargains could be had, so that Gloria had enough over to buy pretty bedding, and towels, a few rugs to cover the lino on the floor and cushions to brighten up the sofa.

When it was all installed, Gloria looked at her home with

a sense of pride. She was surprised to find how much pleasure she took in housework. In her old life, which seemed aeons ago, anything that fell on the floor lay there until a servant picked it up. Her clothes were always at hand and ready to wear, and her meals were put before her and cleared away afterwards.

She had never had to lift a finger and, in the first apartment they'd had, she had not been good at it even though she had tried. Then in the slummy rooms of the tenement, it didn't matter what a person did, the place never looked any better. With first Ben and then her mother to see to as well, it was often Joe's efforts in his scant time off that had prevented them drowning in squalor.

But in this wonderful apartment she really wanted to make a cosy and comfortable home for Joe to return to each evening. He had started a job at the factory where Dermot's brother, Michael, had worked. It was in Fore Street, so close he could walk, but if he was running late there was a tram all the way as well.

Added to this, St Ignatius' Roman Catholic Church was only a short walk away, and there was a school attached, which Ben would be starting after Easter of the following year.

'Oh, Joe,' Gloria said one evening as they snuggled together on the sofa, 'I know we can be really happy here.'

Joe kissed Gloria tenderly and said gently, 'I know, my dear, and isn't it about time we had some good fortune?'

NINE

The dangerously unsettled times continued, and the wireless brought it all into the Sullivans' living room. In November, with heavy sheets of rain falling through the black night, they heard of news that had been leaked out of Germany of what was being called 'Kristallnacht'. The newscaster said that it meant Night of Broken Glass and described a rampage against Jews in Berlin that had lasted three days. Nazi storm troopers threw Jews, men, woman and children, out of their homes and onto the streets, and any who protested were beaten up. Then the Nazis smashed and ransacked their homes before setting them alight. They set light to the synagogues too until, the report said, the sky was blood red from so many fires.

When the news had finished, Joe was not that surprised to see Gloria was in tears. As for the people subjected to these attacks, he could only imagine their abject fear and helplessness. He remembered seeing the frightened and often confused and disoriented Jews that had arrived in New York, and realised that they were the lucky ones.

'How utterly, utterly cruel,' Gloria said. 'What if it was us – you, me, Ben, and all our neighbours on the streets on this filthy night – and the churches we might have sought shelter in set on fire? What would we do, Joe? What are any of those people going to do?'

'I don't know,' Joe said miserably. 'I can only imagine

130

many of them will perish. Maybe you see now why I was so sceptical about the agreement Chamberlain drew up with a man who can order savagery like that?'

'Yes, Joe,' Gloria said. 'And I am frightened of what lies ahead of us.'

In March, Hitler's armies invaded Czechoslovakia and just after Easter, Joe began to worry about what would happen to his family if war came. He didn't think that it was going to blow over, and he had to admit that for some time he had seen the war clouds gathering. What if he had brought his family to something worse than they had left behind? That thought haunted him.

Gloria had known for a while that there was something bothering Joe. She waited for him to discuss it, but when a few more days went by and he still hadn't spoken, she waited until Ben was in bed and then said, 'What is it, Joe?'

Joe sighed. 'Oh, I don't know really . . .'

'Come on,' Gloria said almost impatiently. 'Something has been eating away at you for ages. Can't you share it with me?'

'All right then,' Joe said. 'You have a perfect right to know anyway. The fact is, I think the whole world is balanced on a knife edge. If it comes to all-out war, then civilians will be as much at risk as serving men. I have been thinking about it seriously: if you want, I will take you back to America.'

Gloria stared at Joe, hardly able to believe her ears. She thought of the life they had had before they left. She remembered the deprivation, the poverty, the constant hunger and she shook her head.

'To what?' she said. 'I couldn't go back now to the life we had in New York, and there is no guarantee that we would be returning to anything better.'

'No,' Joe had to admit. 'But—'

'Look at the life we have here now, Joe,' Gloria went on. 'I am happy here. I feel I have settled at last.'

Joe knew that Gloria was happier than she had ever been, certainly the happiest he had seen her since they had arrived in England. Even though he had sometimes seen the homesickness in her eyes, he knew that she hankered for the New York that she remembered from her youth and the early years of their marriage, a New York that he feared was lost and gone for ever.

'You have a good job here and Ben has just started school,' Gloria reasoned. Ben really enjoyed school and he was proving very popular amongst the other children. Most of them had never heard an American accent, unless it was on the cinema screen, and so Ben was looked upon almost as a celebrity. His hair was like a golden halo around his head and with the large violet eyes he was also a very handsome child. He was a favourite with many of the teachers too. Gloria knew that even if she had wanted to go back to America, she would have hated to wrench the child away from where he was happy and had made friends, and she couldn't return him to the hardship they had come to England to escape.

'There is nothing for us in New York, Joe,' she said firmly.

'And if war comes?'

Gloria gave a sudden shiver. 'Well,' she said slowly, 'that thought does scare me, but if it does happen, the whole of London isn't going to empty, is it? We have weathered so much already, and come through it. I want to stay put here now and I imagine that most people will feel the same.'

'I agree with you really,' Joe said, 'but I think that war is inevitable now. I heard a couple of weeks ago that the TA is being recalled and there is conscription beginning for men aged twenty and twenty-one.'

'It's just a matter of time then?'

'I'm afraid so.'

Just a few weeks later, Gloria waited until Joe had finished his evening meal before saying. 'I want to get a job.'

Joe was taken totally by surprise. 'I don't want a wife of mine to work,' he answered rather stiffly. 'There is no reason for it.'

'Don't be so stuffy,' Gloria complained. 'Everyone has to do their bit and the government are recruiting people. They've put leaflets through the letter boxes.'

'And what about Ben if you take a job?'

'He is at school all day.'

'It isn't a full day,' Joe pointed out. 'And what about in the holidays?'

'I enquired about that,' Gloria said. 'There are clubs being set up before and after school and to run through the holidays for children with mothers doing war-related work. Lots of the mothers I meet at the school gates are taking up some type of work.'

'And will you like that, Ben?' Joe asked.

Ben shrugged. 'Dunno,' he said. 'But if it's like school it would probably be all right, 'cos I like school.'

'I'm lonely here all day,' Gloria said. 'I can't even see Dolly easily now that we are so far away. You have your job all day, and you see Red once a week but I often have nothing to do and no one to talk to.'

Joe sighed. 'All right. I see you have a point. So what sort of work are we talking about here?'

He thought of the factory that he worked in where he spent the day at a machine that bored holes in the barrels of rifles. It was dirty, greasy and noisy, and ribaldry and coarse jokes and language were just part of the working environment, but he didn't want his Gloria to be exposed to that sort of thing.

So, he was quite relieved when she said, 'Well, there are all kinds of jobs they want women for, but I have been talking to Elsie Bannister about it. She only lives up the road and has a little girl, Sally, in Ben's class that he is quite sweet on. They often come out of school holding hands. Anyway, she fancies having a go at sewing parachutes.

I wouldn't mind that either and we could go together. It isn't as if it's really hard work.'

Joe wasn't very surprised. It was so typical of her to want to do her bit rather than sit back and do nothing. She looked so delicate, but he knew she had such admirable reserves of strength and fortitude.

Gloria, however, watching Joe's face intently, had no idea of the thoughts tumbling about his head and took his silence for disapproval. 'Come on, Joe. Let me try at least?' she pleaded. 'If you're right and we do go to war, won't our airmen need parachutes? And if the men are sent out to fight, won't it be the women that will have to do that kind of thing?'

Joe grinned at her. 'All right,' he said. 'You've convinced me. You can go and do your job, as long as Ben doesn't suffer.'

Gloria and Elsie got their jobs at a place that had been a corset factory in Phillip Lane. It was on a direct tram route ten minutes beyond the school and so they would take the children as far as the school gate first.

Gloria loved the camaraderie of the team she worked in and the women would all eat dinner together in the canteen, though what they had to eat was sometimes questionable. The canteen's shepherd's pie seemed to consist of much potato and hardly any meat at all.

'Probably be worse when this blessed war actually begins,' one of Gloria's team, Maureen, said one lunchtime when the food was particularly grim. The other women agreed, for there was no question that war was inevitable and people spoke of 'when' not 'if'.

'I've heard there's going to be rationing, and each person will have just so much.'

White-haired Winnie, older and chubbier than the rest, said, 'Fairer if they do. I lived through the last lot and the nobs would buy up all the food in the shops. They didn't go in themselves but would send their servants. Disgusting, it was. Course, some grocers caught on what was happening and would only sell them so much, but others were out for all they could get and would sell them as much as they wanted.'

'Not fair, is it?' Violet said. 'Nobs seem to get away with murder.'

'Yeah,' Elsie said. 'And I bet they will find their way around this rationing as well.'

Gloria could have said that that was true. In the years of Prohibition in America her father never went without anything. Restrictions were for other people and didn't bother him in the slightest, but she never discussed her privileged upbringing with anyone.

'Well, that will be up to the shopkeepers, I expect,' Winnie went on. 'Though if it is a government thing they might keep more of an eye on it than they did last time. Anyroad, we paid out the shopkeepers who hadn't played fair because we boycotted the shops afterwards.'

'I'd say that served them right,' Elsie said.

'Well, it's the kids you worry about most,' Winnie said. 'I mean, kids've got to have summat decent to eat, don't they? I had twin boys three years old when the war began, and a little girl born when the war was a few months old. The hardest sound in the world to bear is your children crying with hunger and you unable to do anything about it.'

'I agree,' Gloria said. 'We left America to prevent that happening to Ben – all of us really, but him in particular – because children don't flourish just on fresh air.'

Violet laughed. 'I'll say not. My two lads are always stuffing their faces. Mind you,' she went on, 'the two boys are a dream compared to their sister. Coming up to her teens now and a proper little madam. She would argue all day if I let her. What's your Sandra like, Maureen?'

'Not so bad now that she's been working for a year. It soon sorts them out when they have to get up and out for work each day, and the bosses don't stand no nonsense. In our house it's Charlie that is the little bugger. Sandra says that it's our own fault because we've spoiled him, but she's as bad as me and the old man.'

'Whatever they're like, enjoy them while you can,' Winnie said. 'Before you know it they'll be grown and gone, like my three, and my two lads I reckon will be in the thick of it before long.'

'What you talking about, Win?' Violet replied. 'From what I hear this ain't going to be a war like no other and we're all going to be in the thick of it, every man jack of us.'

No one argued, only too aware that Violet was right. A shiver of fear trailed down Gloria's spine and she was glad of the hooter calling them back to work.

Ben didn't mind at all that he had to go to clubs before and after school.

'They're fun,' he told Joe. 'Even more fun than school. We play games and that, and the ladies are real nice and new kids come all the time.'

'See,' Gloria said. 'I am not the only wife and mother doing this. More and more women are getting involved. When war comes, we will all have to pull together.'

Joe nodded. 'You're right. And I was wrong to even hesitate. And I suppose it is no good asking you if you want to go and hide away in Ireland like Tom is always urging us to do?'

'It's not in my nature to scuttle away at the first sign of trouble,' Gloria answered.

'Nor mine.' Joe surveyed his wife and there was pride in his voice as he said, 'You are a truly amazing woman. Not many would have coped as well as you have with all that life has thrown at you so far.'

'I coped because I had you by my side,' Gloria said simply. 'I would have folded in two if I hadn't had you.'

'You will always have me, my darling girl,' Joe said

huskily. 'For I will love you, body and soul, until the breath leaves my body.'

'Ah, Joe,' Gloria said, leaning against him with a sigh, 'I count myself a lucky woman to have fallen in love with such a fine man, and this war is just one more trial that we will face together.'

Being together meant Ben as well. He had already been with them through thick and thin and they couldn't bear for him to be sent away. So when they were contacted about sending him to a place of safety, Joe and Gloria rejected the idea, and that was what she told the official who came round to see her.

On the last day of August, as they sat eating their dinner in the canteen, Violet asked Gloria if she had finished her blackout curtains.

'Yes, but only just in time because it comes in force tomorrow and I don't fancy a two-hundred-pound fine because I have a chink of light showing.'

'It was a right hard slog doing all those curtains by hand,' Maureen put in. 'I was at it night after night, and I did the ones for my mother as well. She said she wished she had kept hold of the sewing machine she dumped only a few years ago when her arthritis made it difficult to use. If I'd had that I bet I could have made them all in a couple of hours.'

'Joe made me shutters for the kitchen and bedroom windows that I just had to stretch the material over,' Gloria said. 'That helped a bit. But I made curtains for the windows in the sitting room and they look awful.' She wrinkled her nose and said, 'I have never had black curtains on my windows before.'

'Ah, but then you have never lived through a war before like I have,' Winnie said. 'Not that anyone bothered about blackout curtains then, of course. There weren't the planes about, though Zeppelins dropped some bombs on London. I think this war is going to be very different.'

'Why bomb innocent people anyway?' Gloria asked. 'Isn't it soldiers that are supposed to fight wars?'

'That's how it used to be, girl,' Winnie said. 'It ain't like that any more. We'll have to wait and see what he's got in store for us.'

'Ooh, don't, Win,' Violet said with a shiver. 'You're giving us all the willies.'

'Talking of war, I'm going up for my gas mask after work,' Elsie said. 'You coming, Glor?'

Gloria made a face. 'Do you think we need those horrid things? I can't see myself ever putting it on.'

'You might be glad of it, girl, if them Jerrys launch gas attacks like they did in the last war,' said Winnie. 'Even if you have the slightest whiff of it, it buggers up your lungs good and proper.'

'Anyroad, you ain't got no choice,' Maureen said. 'You have to carry it round your neck in a box. Our Charlie's is red and blue, not the usual black, and it looks a bit like Mickey Mouse.'

'Bet it don't make it smell any better,' Winnie said.

'No, it don't,' Maureen grumbled. 'It stinks to high heaven, to tell you the truth. He said it makes him feel sick and I am not surprised. But he will have to wear it the same as the rest, and I bet he won't play the teachers up like he does me when he goes off with the school tomorrow.'

'Oh, ain't you going to miss him, Maureen?'

'Course I will, and my old man says we'll bring him home again if there ain't a lot doing. They don't expect you to send much with them, though. We had a list and all he had to take was one vest, one pair of pants, one pair of trousers, two pair of socks, handkerchiefs and a pullover.'

'Is that all? No coat?'

'Yeah, there is a coat and toiletries as well, but that is all he has for goodness knows how long.' Maureen gave a decisive sniff and went on, 'Point is, when we decided to let him be evacuated, I got him kitted out and I've packed a case of stuff. I'm having no one think that mine's a pauper's child.'

'Ah, bleeding shame, ain't it?' Violet said. 'Hope you packed plenty of grub. My lads are always claiming they're hungry.'

'He has enough to feed an army, don't worry,' Maureen said. 'And a couple of comics – and the government recommended barley sugar, in case any feel sick, I suppose.'

Gloria thought it monstrous to send young children all over the country to unknown destinations. Maureen's son, Charlie, was only seven years old.

She was still thinking about it that evening as they collected their gas masks. Just as Maureen had said, all the children's masks were red and blue, and, stretching the imagination, did look a bit like Mickey Mouse. That didn't impress Ben in the slightest. He said it was still horrible and he wasn't going to put it on. Gloria said nothing. Time enough to fight with him when she had to.

The next morning Maureen came in late, her eyes were puffy and there were tear trails on her cheeks.

'I don't know how she is able to bear it,' Gloria said that night to Joe. 'Mind you, she isn't bearing it so well because every time I spotted her she was awash with tears. She doesn't know if she has made the right decision or not, that's the trouble. You are persuaded to do this and then you begin to have second thoughts and it's too late. I don't think I could ever send Ben away.'

'No,' said Joe. 'Nor me, but war has moved one step closer today.'

'Why? What's happened?'

'It was on the news on the wireless just before you came home,' Joe said. 'Germany has invaded Poland, and the Poles are fighting for their lives.'

The Prime Minister, Neville Chamberlain, was giving an address on Sunday 3 September, at about eleven fifteen in the morning. Everyone knew what he was going to say, but when he actually said those words, that Britain was now at war with Germany, Gloria felt the hairs on the back of her neck stand up.

The wail of the air-raid siren suddenly rent the air and Gloria felt as if the blood in her body had turned to ice. She looked at Joe in sudden terror. Neither of them knew what to do. Then she ran, frantically collecting coats and gas masks as the all clear was sounded.

'Must have been a false alarm,' Joe said.

'Thank God,' Gloria said fervently. 'But we are at war now and the attacks *are* going to come. That showed me that I am totally ill prepared and for a few minutes I had no idea what to do.'

'Neither did I,' Joe admitted.

'It said in the paper to pack a shelter bag but I didn't,' Gloria said.

'A shelter bag?'

'Yeah,' Gloria said. 'It said to put in rent books, insurance policies and identity cards, and things you value that you couldn't replace, like treasured photographs. And then you could have maybe a packet of biscuits and drinks and things for the kids – books they especially like and a pack of cards or a set of dominoes. The point is you haven't time to hunt around the house for these things when you should be busting a gut getting to a place of safety as soon as possible.'

'So it's good advice then?'

'Yeah, it probably is,' Gloria conceded. 'There are lots of government guidelines and articles about coping in wartime like crisscrossing tape over the windows. I mean, flying glass can cause a lot of damage, but I didn't do it because I hadn't wanted to think about war and yet I've known for ages that this day would come. How stupid is that?'

'What is war?' Ben said.

'A terrible tragedy that should never ever happen,' Joe said. 'But Hitler's armies keeps marching into other countries and taking them over and they have to be stopped.'

'How?'

'Well, lots of our soldiers are probably going to have to go over there and fight the German soldiers.'

'One of the kids at school said Hitler will send planes over here full of bombs and that they will blow us all up,' Ben said.

Joe couldn't refute what the child said and claim he was spouting rubbish, for he knew that he couldn't protect Ben from war and the effect it would have on his life. It was far better, though, for Ben to get the facts from him or Gloria rather than listening to the lurid and gruesome talk in the playground.

'The planes will carry bombs, and they will try and blow us up,' Joe said, 'but the government know all about this and they have built shelters for us to stay in while the bombs are coming down.'

'So we will be all right then?'

'I sincerely hope so.'

Later that night, when Ben was in bed, Gloria said, 'One of the women told me the other day that there aren't half enough shelters for the people of London.'

'I read it too,' Joe said, 'but it wasn't something that I thought I should share with a five-year-old child.'

'It is right, then?'

Joe shrugged. 'I would say that it is true enough. But if they had a shelter on each street corner, it would hardly suffice.'

Gloria shivered. 'Some of the women I work with say they're going down the Tube if the raids come. They say they would just feel safer so far underground.'

'Yes, and the sounds of it would be sort of muffled,' Joe said. 'But I doubt the authorities would let anyone do that. There's bound to be some regulation about it.'

'Yeah, there probably is,' Gloria agreed. 'There is about most things these days.'

Cinemas, theatres, dance halls and other places where a lot of people might congregate together were closed, and Ben's school didn't reopen after the holidays because most of the teachers had gone with the evacuated children. Ben was very lonely and missed his friends a great deal, and Gloria had to take leave from work to look after him.

Then she missed the company of the other women and the money. However, the biggest bugbear to them all was coping with the blackout. It made life very difficult for those who wished to go about their daily business and it was hard to see the point of it when there had been no raids at all.

Eventually, towards the first Christmas of the war, so many people had been injured or even killed in accidents because of the blackout that the rules were relaxed. Shielded torches could be used and shielded headlights were allowed on vehicles.

Immediately torches disappeared from the shops' shelves at a rate of knots and batteries were at a premium and often unavailable. But Joe was successful and he showed his to Gloria with great pride.

'Make it easier to get about,' he said.

Gloria turned on the torch's feeble light. 'Huh, not very.'

'Better than the nothing we had before.'

'I suppose so,' Gloria said. 'I hear they're thinking of reopening the cinemas and theatres. I wish they'd reopen the schools too.'

'They'll have to,' Joe said. 'Half the kids that were evacuated are trickling back home, according to the papers. Mothers don't see the point of them living with strangers when not a single bomb has fallen anywhere. School will probably be open again in January.'

'January,' Gloria repeated, and gave a sudden shiver. 'The government said rationing will come into force then. It's supposed to be a fairer system, but there is little in the shops now. Every time I hear of another merchant ship being sunk I feel sick. It's Christmas in less than a fortnight and half the things I wanted I can't get, and there are hardly any toys either to make the day a bit special for Ben.'

'And if you complain about anything they remind you there's a war on,' Joe said.

'Yes,' Gloria agreed. 'Just as if that fact might have slipped your mind.'

Ben's school did reopen in January with some teachers that had been brought out of retirement, and Gloria was delighted to be back at work. She had also registered with a grocer and was allowed four ounces of bacon, four ounces of butter and twelve ounces of sugar per person per week to start with.

By March, meat had been added to the rationed goods, and most of the evacuated children had come home again, including Maureen's son. The war was being dubbed the Bore War, and Joe had been thinking about his role in it for a week or two. Then when he went for his weekly pint with Red, he told Joe that he and his cousin, Pete, had both received their call-up papers, and this galvanised Joe into making a decision.

Why should he languish at home in a war that threatened to imperil them all? A war in which everyone had to do their bit if Britain wasn't to be overwhelmed by Germany, as so many nations already had been. He didn't tell Gloria until the next evening, after Ben had been put to bed.

As the play drew to a close. Joe stood up, switched the wireless off and then, with his arms around Gloria, told her he would like to train as a volunteer fireman. Gloria jumped out of his arms as if she had been shot and stared at him as if she was unable to understand what she had heard.

'But you know nothing about putting out fires, and anyway, you already have a job,' she said eventually.

'This is as well as the job, not instead of it,' Joe said. 'And I would be trained to do it properly. That's why I want to join up now. I mean, it's no good waiting until the bombs are dropping and fires blazing all over London, is it?'

'I see that,' Gloria said. 'But why you?'

'Why not me?'

'Isn't it dangerous?'

Joe didn't answer that. Instead he said quietly, 'Gloria, Red and his cousin got their call-up papers last week. He told me when we were down the pub together. How dangerous do you think that is?'

'It's just—'

'Look, pet,' Joe said. 'I will not be asked to fight, because I am too old, and anyway, I am an Irishman and so couldn't be conscripted. That suits me, because if I was, I would feel then I was working for the British Government. I can understand Ireland's neutral stance in this war. But I am staying put, not because of any government, but because of the people. I want to feel I am doing my bit just the same as you.'

Gloria knew by the determined look on Joe's face that she would be wasting her time saying anything more about it. His mind was made up. But later, in bed, she lay thinking about that. Once Joe had decided something he wouldn't allow himself to be deflected from it for any reason. That could be deemed a good attribute, but he seemed to make his mind up without taking the thoughts and feelings of those closest to him into consideration.

She didn't want him to be a fireman, but he would go ahead anyway. She wondered about the future, whether there might come a time when he went totally against her wishes, and how she would feel about that.

Joe and Gloria took more interest in the war now that Red would soon be involved in it. He had almost finished his training when Hitler turned his attention to Belgium and the Netherlands. Gloria always bought a paper on her way to work and read with horror of the raid on Rotterdam the previous evening that it was estimated had killed nine hundred people. The scale of it was shocking and everyone at the factory was talking about it.

'All those poor people,' Gloria said. 'You can only imagine what they went through.'

'Aye, and what was done in Rotterdam could be done just as easy in London,' Elsie remarked dourly. 'The thought of it gives me the creeps.'

'Listen to this then,' Winnie said, still scrutinising the paper. 'The Germans have taken a fort in Belgium thought to have been impregnable and broken through the French defences.'

'You mean the Maginot Line that the French were always crowing on about?' Maureen asked. 'They always claimed it was unbreachable.'

Winnie shrugged. 'Maybe it was, but from the map in the paper it looks like, by gaining control of the fort, they were able to avoid the Maginot Line altogether and get to France through Belgium.'

'God Almighty!'

'It gets worse,' Winnie went on. 'It says here that lots of our soldiers are there too and in retreat.'

'Where are they retreating to?' Maureen asked. 'Hitler seems to rule more than half of Europe.'

'Well, if you study this,' Winnie said, 'there is nowhere but the sea, so I suppose they will eventually be making their way to the beaches.'

'Come, come, girls,' the supervisor said, coming in at that moment. 'The news is bad, I know, and I also know many of you have loved ones in the forces. But if we talk about it from now till doomsday it will not make a ha'p'orth of difference, so let's get back to work, eh?'

Grumbling slightly, the women bent to the task in hand, for they knew the supervisor was right. She wasn't that hard a taskmaster as a rule, and she knew what many of the women were going through because her only son was in the army now, and in the same danger as everyone else.

TEN

As the war news worsened, the call went out for men to form the Local Defence Volunteers. People joined in droves and despite the seriousness of the situation it was quite comical to see them drilling. The units were composed of the very old, very young and the infirm, and most had no idea about any sort of marching, let alone marching in unison.

Initially they had no uniforms either, other than a black band around their arms. In place of rifles, which were in short supply, they practised with broom handles.

'If these are the only defence Britain has against Hitler and his disciplined armies then God help us,' Joe remarked one day over breakfast. 'And how the hell do they hope to defend us with broom handles?'

'Be fair,' Gloria said, though she too was laughing. 'They'll get organised in the end. They're having uniforms made, I know, because a few of those who work with me have got fathers or sometimes brothers in the Volunteers. And they are getting rifles.'

'God, are you hoping to make me feel better?' Joe said in mock horror. 'If they let that lot loose with rifles they will likely shoot each other.'

'Give them a chance,' Gloria laughed.

'Have we the time to give them a chance, is all I'm saying,' Joe said. 'I sometimes wonder if anyone has a chance against Hitler anyway. He seems unstoppable.'

'I often think that too,' Gloria confided, serious now too. 'Doesn't do to say it because it's bad for morale and that, but most must think that if they read the papers or listen to the news.'

The veil of secrecy was lifted and people read of the Allied troops massed on the beaches. Naval troopships were waiting in deeper waters to bring them home but they couldn't get close enough to the beaches to reach the men. Those living on the South Coast with boats of all sizes capable of crossing the Channel went out to help ferry the men to the ships.

Pictures of the soldiers waiting to be evacuated, standing in line on the pierheads they had made from discarded vehicles and anything else that they could find, were splashed across the pages of the newspapers. Even in the grainy newsprint, the fatigue and the desperation on the soldiers' faces were evident, and Gloria's heart went out to them.

But of course the Germans did not wave them off joyfully. The reports told of Stukas raking the soldiers unmercifully as they hurried across the sand, or stood in line waiting to be rescued, though some of the soldiers had hastily erected field guns to try to shoot the planes down. They had to cope with bombs too. The bombers also targeted the naval ships full of soldiers and a fair few were sunk.

By 4 June it was all over and Britain seemed to be looking at defeat. More soldiers had been rescued than had been thought possible, but still there were too many left behind, either dead or captured, and added to that was the colossal loss of equipment that all had to be replaced if Britain was to have any sort of chance against Germany at all.

France surrendered on 21 June. Most people were only too well aware that only a small stretch of water separated Britain from the French coast where German armies were massing prior to invasion, while Hitler's bombers pounded the coastal towns.

Invasion was on everybody's lips, and the government

directives sent to every household urged people to hide maps, and disable cars and bicycles not in use. At the same time, signposts were removed from roads and the names on the train stations were painted over. Railings surrounding parks and gardens were sawn off, and households were urged to take all unwanted metal objects to their nearest metal collection point. Every bit was needed to make planes, and in particular Spitfires.

Sometimes the skies were filled with these doughty little planes and whenever Gloria heard the drone of them in the distance she would feel her stomach contract with fear for the young pilots. Everyone knew Britain's only hope of survival rested on the slim shoulders of these young men, and many lost their lives in their bid to hold supremacy in the skies, aware that unless Hitler crushed the air force, he wouldn't risk an invasion.

While the battles were raging overhead, Tom wrote that the war was getting nearer to the farm, for a party of soldiers had arrived in Buncrana to protect Ireland's neutrality.

'Listen to this,' Joe said to Gloria. 'Tom says that Lough Foyle has been commandeered and is full of military craft now – warships, destroyers, frigates, all sorts. He has heard talk that they are making extra runways for military planes in the Six Counties all to protect the Merchant Naval ships. I wonder what happened to the fishing.'

'What d'you mean?'

'Well, Lough Foyle used to be full of fishermen,' Joe explained. 'There's fishing to be had in the Swilly, but it is a much smaller lough altogether and couldn't possibly accommodate all the men who used to fish the Foyle. It used to be grand on Saturdays in Buncrana. The fishing fleets would be in and selling their fish at the harbour, and boy, was it fresh. When we got in, we would have it for dinner, fried up in butter. My mouth would be watering just at the thought of it.'

'Well, you won't be treated that way here these days,'

Gloria said. 'The grocer was telling me this week that he has heard the butter ration is being cut to two ounces very soon.'

'Aye, I know,' Joe grumbled. 'And soon I won't be able to have a cup of tea when I want one because they say that is being rationed from July.'

'Honest to God, Joe Sullivan, aren't you a first-class moaner?' Gloria cried. 'You have to make some sacrifices for the war effort, you know. And if all you have to worry about throughout this war is getting hold of a cup of tea, then you can count yourself as one lucky man.'

'All right,' Joe said, and added with a twinkle in his eye, 'I consider myself suitably chastened. I shall never moan about rationing again all the days of my life.'

'Hah,' said Gloria. 'And pigs might fly!'

On Saturday 7 September, the sirens went off the first time since the day of the false alarm when war was declared. It was only four o'clock in the afternoon, but Gloria was taking no chances. Ben, like most children whose mothers could afford it, had a siren suit, which could be zipped over any clothes he had on, and Gloria helped him into it and hung the gas mask in its box around his neck before attending to herself. In seconds the two of them were out on the street where they could plainly hear the drone of approaching planes.

This, then, was the real thing. Gloria was scared and wished that Joe was with them, but he took any overtime that was offered, and he was on duty as a volunteer fireman later as well, though up until now the nights had been quiet. The streets were no place to linger and, anyway, an ARP warden was at her elbow. 'Hurry along do, ducks,' she said, and Gloria threw the shelter bag and gas mask over her shoulder so that she could hold Ben's hand.

She had already worked out the quickest way to the nearest shelter, which was in St Ann's Road, and they hurried down Harold Road, crossing over Wakefield Road. By the time they were scurrying down the High Road, following the streams of people, the first of the falling bombs could be heard. Everyone put on a spurt, and then St Ann's Road was before them, and the reassuring sight of the reinforced sandbagged shelter.

The place was packed when Gloria and Ben arrived, but more and more piled in, so there was barely room to move. And there they stayed for two hours, while the explosions and thuds and thumps and crashes went on all around them. Gloria battled with a primeval fear, such as she had never felt before. This fear wasn't for herself as much as for her young son, whom she had to protect at all costs. Other people were just as frightened as she was, and she heard their cries and screeches all around her. Mixed with the sound of the falling bombs, the noise was almost unbearable.

Her arms encircled Ben as he jumped when a bomb fell very close. Babies were wailing, and the strident sound seemed to resound off the walls.

Eventually the reassuring sound of the all clear cut through everything, and Gloria gave a sigh of blessed relief. When she took hold of Ben's hand, she realised that he was shivering and she willed her voice to have no hint of a tremble in it as she said to him, 'That was a bit scary, I must say. But thank goodness it was over fairly quickly, and Daddy might be home when we get in.'

Joe wasn't in the apartment, but he must have been home, for his fireman's uniform was gone. Gloria guessed he had gone straight on duty to fight the raging fires.

Two hours later, the bombers were back. Gloria could hardly believe it. Ben was in his pyjamas ready for bed, and she pulled a jumper over them for extra warmth before zipping him into his siren suit, then put his socks and boots back on with hands that shook.

As they scurried through the streets once more, Gloria

looked back and saw the menacing planes in the sky, their intermittent drone filling the air. The ferocious fires were still burning brightly, lighting up the sky for the bombers, and she felt more terrified than ever.

Later, cowering in the shelter, everyone was aware that the pounding intensity of the raid was coming closer. Some people began to pray, and others to wail and cry. The bombing went on all around them for hour after hour, until Gloria felt she had always been there sitting on that hard bench, gasping in the rank, fetid air, holding her terrified son in her arms while the booms and thumps and crashes shook the walls.

When the all clear roused her, she was leaning against a perfect stranger with Ben cuddled between them, fast asleep despite the noise, and she lifted him in her arms for she knew he was in no fit state to walk.

When they reached home, the clock read a quarter to five, and Gloria carried Ben through to his room and laid him in the bed just as he was, pausing only to remove his boots. Then she went back through to the kitchen and put the kettle on. She ached with fatigue and her eyes felt sore and gritty, but she knew she was too churned up and worried about Joe to sleep.

In the end she made a cup of tea, hoping that it would warm her, for she felt as if she had ice running in her veins, but she drank the scalding liquid without really tasting it. It was as she drained the cup that she heard the dragging sound outside the door and she went to open it.

Joe almost fell through it. Red bloodshot eyes stood out in his blackened face, and a foul, caustic smell emanated from him. He was also barely able to stand with weariness.

'Almighty God, Joe!' Gloria cried. 'What on earth has happened to you?'

Joe didn't answer and, seeing his jacket was mud-smeared and dripping, Gloria unbuttoned it, eased it from his shoulders and let it fall to the floor before taking some of his weight as she led him to the sofa and lowered him down gently.

She poured him a cup of tea and pushed it into his cracked and begrimed hands. 'Drink that,' she said. 'It's well sweetened.'

Joe took it from her gratefully, hoping it would help to stop him shivering. His trembling wasn't from cold, but came from deep inside him, reaction to the God-awful things he had seen and done that night.

Gloria was sobbing, seeing Joe in such a state, and as she kneeled to unlace and remove his wet and muddy boots Joe ran a hand over her hair. 'Don't cry,' he said. 'I'm all right.'

Even as he spoke he wondered if he would ever be all right again. The tea did revive him a little and as he handed the drained cup back to her his tortured eyes met hers as she sat back on her heels staring at him, tears trickling down her face.

'I was helping with the fires,' he said.

She nodded.

'There were so many dead, so many suffering,' he went on. 'Fires were like raging infernos, breaking out everywhere. They needed everyone to help. I just couldn't leave. I knew you would be worried. I'm sorry.'

Gloria put her arms around him. 'Hush,' she said. 'None of this matters. Have you eaten?'

Joe gave a brief nod. 'At a WVS van. I really need to sleep.'

'Come on then,' Gloria said. 'Let's get you into bed.'

'No, not bed,' Joe said. 'I'm far too dirty and too weary to wash.'

'Don't be silly.'

'Please. I just want to stay here,' he said, sagging back on the sofa.

He closed his eyes as if the effort of speaking had totally tired him out, and Gloria had no desire to fight with him.

He had gone through quite enough already that night, she guessed. She lifted his legs up gently, and he lay back and sighed. By the time she returned with a blanket to cover him, he was fast asleep.

She envied Joe that sleep. She lay awake for hours, for her mind refused to close, and she went over and over the events of that evening and night. She had the feeling, now the raids had begun, they would continue as they had in other towns and cities. She might spend many nights in the shelter, while Joe would be in the thick of it just as much as any fighting man. And she would have to draw on every vestige of courage to learn to cope with it as the wives of the servicemen did.

The next morning, Ben and Gloria were sluggish, and Joe still lay like one dead on the sofa. This surprised Ben greatly for he had never seen his father spend the night that way before and he had never seen him so black either.

Gloria saw his confused eyes and, knowing the rousing power of his high-pitched voice, drew him into the kitchen, saying, 'Leave your questions till we are on our way to Mass, and eat your breakfast. I don't want you to disturb your father.'

Once out in the streets, Gloria was appalled by the bomb damage they saw, only some of which had been apparent in the dark. There were many craters and gaping holes, and some of the stacks of debris were still smouldering. Burst sandbags had bled onto the street and a discarded hosepipe dribbled into the gutter. The putrid, pungent stink in the air lodged in their nostrils.

'Why did the Germans drop bombs on us?' Ben asked suddenly.

'I think it's just something that happens when one country is at war with another,' Gloria said.

'Will they do it again?' Ben asked, and though Gloria was pretty certain they would, she said, 'I don't know, Ben, but we have to stand firm and not run away in fright. Think how brave the soldiers are, fighting for us all, and your daddy helping to fight the fires last night.'

'He got very dirty,' Ben said. 'You would shout at me if I got that dirty.'

Despite herself and the desolation all around them, Gloria smiled as she said, 'I might not if you had been fighting fires last night too. The point is, you can get dirty without even trying. Come on now, we'll be late for Mass if we're not careful.'

Outside the church was a cluster of people all talking about the raids. 'There will be more than a few that hasn't a place to live this morning,' one woman said.

'I know,' said Gloria. 'I was amazed at the devastation as we were making our way here today. Each mound of bricks and debris we passed represented someone's life. Where do the people go? What do they do?'

'I don't know,' the first woman said. 'But I'd take a bet the government haven't put anything in place.'

'And they will have to do summat, and quick, if that raid is one of many,' another said.

'As it's likely to be,' the first woman said. 'That was just a taste of what is to come.'

Gloria caught the look of sheer terror on Ben's face and wished she could reassure him that the woman was spouting nonsense, but she couldn't. She felt worn down by foreboding and hoped the Mass would help lift her mood.

It didn't do much for her, though the priest did speak of the raids and the need to have courage. Gloria didn't know what to pray for. Peace? How could there be peace when an evil man had to be stopped before peace could be secured?

She was glad when the Mass was over, and didn't linger because she was anxious to get back to Joe. He was stirring when she and Ben went in. He peeled his eyelids back slowly and immediately wished he hadn't bothered for a pain beat in his temples. However, far, far worse were the images of events of the previous night that flooded across his brain. He accepted the fact that he had seen and heard things that no man should ever see or hear, and that none of his training had prepared him for.

The charred bodies haunted him, and those burned black, some of them children younger than Ben. The first time he had carried a child so badly burned he was unrecognisable, Joe was sick into the gutter. He was never sick again. It was a luxury he couldn't allow himself when so many people needed help, so when the nausea rose in his throat, he swallowed it and carried on.

He had gone into buildings searching for people, feeling that any minute his lungs would burst with the heat. The blackness and swirling smoke often meant he could see nothing, and his hand would come into contact with a body burned almost to cinders, which crumbled at his touch. Far worse than this, though, were the screams of the dying in blazing houses that the firemen were unable to reach because of the intensity of the fires, which the hoses seemed to have little effect on.

Through it all the bombs would continue to hurtle from the sky. The smell that lodged in Joe's nose and throat, over the smell of burning buildings and smoke and cordite, was the stinking and nauseous reek of burning human flesh. He didn't think that he would ever be free of that smell – that it would live with him for ever.

He was certain of one thing: he would never bring the things he had had to do, and he knew he would do again, into the life he shared with Gloria and Ben.

Gloria, seeing him awake, said, 'How are you feeling now?'

'Never better,' Joe said, and he smiled at her.

But Gloria was no fool. She had seen the haunted look on his face and the desolate look in his eyes, even through the dirt. She wondered what harrowing scenes he had witnessed the evening before. She wouldn't ask him, and certainly not in front of Ben, but later, if he wanted to talk, she would make it clear that she was ready to listen. So she said, 'You're one hell of a bad liar, Joe Sullivan. What d'you want to do first, eat or wash?'

Ben's eyes opened wide, for his mother would never let him sit down at the table looking half as bad as his dad did. She was forever going on about him washing his hands. Sometimes he thought he would have them washed away before he was grown up.

Joe saw Ben's face and guessed his thoughts. 'I think I'd better have a bath first, and I am sure that Ben would agree with me, wouldn't you?'

Ben nodded. 'Not half, and I'll say what Mommy says to me sometimes. You are so mucky make sure you don't block up the plughole.'

Joe laughed, glad he was still able to do so, glad of his son for lightening the atmosphere and chasing some of the demons away.

The bombers returned that night, and Gloria managed to grab just two and a half hours' sleep after the raid had finished. It was hard enough work even getting out of bed the next morning, never mind the thought of putting in a full day at the factory. However, she forced her reluctant body out from under the covers because she knew Joe had had even less sleep than she had, and he had already left for work.

Ben was dead to the world and when Gloria roused him he was crotchety and bad-tempered. 'I don't want to get up,' he said mulishly. 'I'm still tired.'

'I didn't want to get out of bed this morning either,' Gloria admitted. 'And I am more than just tired – exhausted, in fact – but we still have to get up.'

'Why?'

'Because that is the way life is at the moment.'

'I'm too tired to go to school.'

'You know, Ben,' Gloria said, 'I could take a bet that a lot of children in London feel as you do now, and a lot of parents feel as I do, but say all the woman I work with didn't come in today, then there would be no parachutes made for the airmen who need them. Or just suppose no one turned up to drive the buses, or the lorries? Where would we be then?'

Ben shrugged. 'I don't care, 'cos I'm too tired.'

'Come on, Ben,' Gloria urged. 'You'll be late if you don't hurry up, and so will I.'

Ben still lay in the bed with his eyes shut, and Gloria said through gritted teeth, 'Hop out of bed now, there's a good boy.'

'No,' Ben said. 'I don't want to.'

'Haven't you learned yet that you can't always have what you want?' Gloria said impatiently, stripping the covers from Ben's bed as she did so. Ben gave a yelp of surprise and Gloria said almost fiercely, 'If you don't get out of bed this minute I will come in with a jug of water to tip over you.'

Ben wasn't sure that his mother was joking. She didn't look like she was, and though she had never even hinted at anything so drastic before, everything had changed because of this war. With a sigh he slid out of bed and began to dress.

Even then, he didn't seem to have a hurry bone in his body. Gloria did feel sorry for him, but she wasn't at her best either, and so it took her all her time to keep her temper because she feared that she would be late for work.

In the end she made it by the skin of her teeth. Elsie was just the same, and as they hurried to the tram stop she said to Gloria, 'They say four hundred and thirty were killed that first night, and sixteen thousand injured.'

'God, such numbers,' Gloria breathed. 'It doesn't bear thinking about. Such tragedy and sadness, and more homes destroyed.'

When they reached work, everyone was discussing the air raid.

'So many were killed 'cos there ain't enough shelters,' Maureen said. 'Fancy declaring war when you haven't enough shelters to keep the people safe.'

'I thought you'd be coming down the shelter in St Ann's Road with me,' Gloria said to Elsie.

Elsie shook her head. 'You know we live with our mom?' she said. 'Well, she won't leave the house. We had to sit it out under the stairs.'

'Oh, I wouldn't do that,' Maureen answered. 'Mind you, I couldn't find a shelter for love nor money that first night. They was all full up by the time I got there, but by the second night we found out about a deserted warehouse and we bedded down there. There were a fair few of us using it in the end, and it's half underground, see, and feels safer, like.'

'How come they're deserted, these warehouses?' Gloria asked.

'Oh, well, that's the best yet,' said Maureen. 'There are hundreds of these places scattered around London if you are in the know, but this one we were in last night, this geezer was telling me used to house dray horses and they moved the horses out to a place they consider safer. Priceless, ain't it? They did sod all for the people and now we are bedding down each night in places they didn't consider safe enough for their precious horses.'

'Huh, think Churchill cares about the likes of us?' Winnie said. 'Like hell he does. We got to look after our own.'

'I took my lot down the Tube last night,' Violet put in.

'And didn't the authorities try to stop you first, Vi?'

'They did and all, but they gave up in the end,' Violet said with a grin. 'Had to really 'cos there were just so many of us. I mean, it ain't as if they've done anything for us, and all we're doing is trying to keep our families safe. For Christ's sake, what's wrong with that?'

The Blitz, Hitler's promised Lightning War, continued night after night, and Gloria prepared for it. Joe had got hold of a vacuum flask – Gloria didn't ask from where – and each night she filled it with hot sweet tea as soon as she got home from work, then made up sandwiches to pack in the shelter bag, including biscuits, if she had any.

Each time the siren shrilled, she felt as if a lump of lead had landed in her stomach, but she had to cover her fear for the sake of her terrified son. The sound seemed to lend wings to their feet, and often before the strains of the siren had died out, Gloria, Ben and sometimes Joe would be hurrying through the streets where they usually didn't need the torch, for search lights would be streaking across the sky.

Gloria always felt better, though, when she was in the shelter, in the company of others. The stale air, stuffiness and the often clamorous noise now didn't disturb her as much as it had done. Instead, she began to feel a cama-raderie with the others because they were all in this together.

She wasn't the only one either to feel better when the drone of planes and crash of bombs were answered by the ack-ack guns barking into the night sky. 'Go on. Give it to them, the dirty buggers,' was the general consensus voiced. Gloria could understand that perfectly because it was like they were not just sitting there, putting up with it, but hitting back.

It was usually hours later when the all clear would shrill out its reassuring sound. Gloria would then have to rouse Ben, whose eyes would be glazed with fatigue. He was too heavy for Gloria to carry any more, and so if Joe wasn't there he would stumble in weariness as he filed out of the shelter. Outside, as they hurried home, they would see the blazing fires licking the black night with orange and red flames. They would lend a rosy glow to the sky, and the air would smell of smoke and cordite and brick dust with sometimes the merest whiff of gas.

Gloria felt sorry for Ben, who would be so tired the next morning he was either like a bear with a sore head, or prone to tears, and Gloria found him hard to deal with; she too had never felt as tired in the whole of her life. However, she knew she wasn't the only one to feel such utter exhaustion and it was just one more thing she had to learn to cope with.

As October drew to a close, the papers were estimating that two hundred and fifty thousand Londoners were homeless.

'God!' breathed Gloria. 'It's hard even to visualise that number of people without anywhere to live.'

'It affects us all,' Violet said. 'After a raid we don't know if we will have our house left standing when we come out. 'What would I do with the kids if that happened? It's them I worry about most.'

'I know,' Gloria said. 'My son is scared to death nearly all the time. Joe even brought up the subject of evacuation again, and he was dead against it at first, same as I was. He said he didn't think the raids would be as heavy, nor go on so long.'

'Did any of us?' Violet said. 'But I ain't sending mine away.'

'Nor me,' said Maureen. 'I mean, I tried it the once, didn't I? God, I missed him so much. When we fetched him back we promised him that we wouldn't send him away again.'

'How do they know these areas are so safe anyway?' Gloria said. 'Joe once said that there were few places in the whole of Britain that could be deemed safe.'

'Yeah,' Elsie said. 'Look at all them kids that were sent down to the South Coast that had to be brought back after Dunkirk when everyone thought we might be invaded.'

'Well, Ben is not going anywhere,' Gloria said. 'And I told Joe that. I reckon being separated from us would upset him even more. He is staying here with his family, where he belongs.'

At home that night, Joe had a letter waiting for him from Tom. Since Molly had arrived at the farmhouse in 1935, he always asked after her in his letters, and since the war had begun, and particularly when the bombs started falling in Birmingham, he had also asked after her little brother, Kevin, as well. And so Gloria, seeing the frown on Joe's face as he read the letter said, 'What's the matter?'

'Tom writes that Molly hasn't heard from them in Birmingham for a while. Here, read it for yourself,' and he passed the letter over.

It's been three weeks now since Molly has had any letters from Birmingham, though they usually write every week. She is worried, naturally, with the pounding the city is having. I said that we don't know the state of play there at all and it is best to have patience, but you can't blame her for being anxious.

'What d'you think has happened?' Gloria asked.

Joe shrugged. 'There's a hundred and one reasons why letters won't have arrived from a city getting almost nightly bombardment, but I will write and reassure Tom. Then I will just hope and pray that Molly hears something soon and that nothing awful has befallen her grandfather and her brother.'

Then towards the end of November, Joe had word from Tom that Molly, fearing for the safety of her loved ones in Birmingham, had left the farm and travelled to Birmingham to find them. Joe knew just how naïve and inexperienced she would probably be, and she would have nothing to prepare her for a city in the throes of a desperate and violent war, and he hoped and prayed that she would be all right.

He remembered the ferocious attack on Birmingham on the 19 November, which was the very day that Tom said Molly had left, and he hoped that she had reached Birmingham safely and found shelter. However, when later Tom confessed he had heard nothing from her, Joe imagined that Molly had become just one more casualty of war and wrote and told him this.

On 29 December London suffered another stupendous attack. The first wave of planes dropped incendiaries, thereby lighting the way for the bombers that followed them. The next morning, even seasoned Londoners reeled under the assault, which had destroyed eight churches designed by Christopher Wren, Paternoster Row, the Central Telegraph Office and the Guildhall. The bombs had also seriously damaged five mainline stations, sixteen underground ones and nine hospitals.

St Paul's Cathedral was spared, and the papers printed pictures of it standing straight and tall in a sea of rubble like a beacon of defiance, only its beautiful stained-glass windows lost. When the papers claimed by New Year's Day 1941 that 13,339 Londoners had been killed and 17,937 seriously injured since the blitz had begun in September, Joe and Gloria were stunned by the enormity of such tragedy.

ELEVEN

The war trailed on through 1941. There were a few skirmishes that amounted to very little, and then a massive raid in March and another in mid-April, but from then there was nothing more.

'If Hitler is finished with us at last,' Elsie said one day as the women sat in the canteen, 'then all we've got to worry about is the blackout and rationing.'

'Rationing! God,' said Violet, 'they will ration the air we breathe soon, no doubt, and trying to feed a family on what they allow us is a joke.'

There was a murmur of agreement, because now jam, marmalade, treacle and syrup were on ration, joining tea, margarine, cooking fat, cheese, meat, bacon, ham, sugar and butter, and every housewife, especially those with families, was finding it a struggle.

What they had a lot of was home-grown vegetables. 'What we need is tips on how to make carrots, swede and turnips into some rivetingly exciting dish to feed the family,' Elsie said.

'Well, there is always Woolton Pie,' Winnie said. 'Lord Woolton says it's patriotic to eat that and things like it.'

'Ugh,' Maureen said.

Violet put in, 'Oh, yeah, I wonder how many times a week he has it served up to him. Mind you, this is little better.' She poked her dinner with her fork. 'Poor man's goose, this is supposed to be.'

'And there's no goose been anywhere near it,' Maureen said. 'It's liver.'

'And not much of that,' Winnie added, 'but stacks of potatoes and swede and turnip.'

'My mum heard of a recipe on the wireless the other day called vegetable and oatmeal goulash,' Elsie said. 'The meat ration was gone and so she wrote it out and that's what was waiting for me when I got home.'

'Sounds terribly exciting,' Winnie commented drily.

'Tasted worse,' Elsie said, making a face at the memory. 'I ate it, though. We all did because there wasn't any choice.'

'That's it,' Violet said. 'And that Charles Hill bloke on the wireless, going on about Potato Pete and Dr Carrot doesn't make any of them taste any better.'

'Still, it's better than having nothing at all,' Gloria said. 'Believe me, I had a touch of that in New York and it wasn't pleasant.'

'Yeah,' Elsie said. 'There might be no danger here of actually starving to death, but the peril of being bored to death is very real.'

About this time, Joe received a very confusing correspondence from his brother, which he told Gloria about.

'So this woman said Molly had been around asking questions about her brother and granddad a few weeks before,' Gloria said. 'So she isn't dead after all.'

'Well, she wasn't then, anyway,' Joe said. 'Tom reckons that it was probably about February that all this happened.'

'But why didn't she write to Tom?' Gloria demanded. 'You said yourself that he has been crazy with worry about her.'

'I don't know,' Joe said. 'That letter from the neighbour can hardly be any sort of comfort to him. All he knows is that the grandfather is dead and that Kevin is probably in an orphanage, but he doesn't know where.'

'Oh God! That really is so sad,' Gloria said. 'I wish we could do something for Kevin at least.'

'So do I,' Joe said. 'I would hate a similar thing to happen to our own son, but there is nothing we can do.'

Gloria knew that Joe was right. After that Kevin was often in her thoughts, though she felt anger against Molly for causing her uncle such anxiety.

Warmth began to steal into the dusty London streets as the spring took hold and as day followed day, with no sign of a raid, many hoped and eventually began to believe that their ordeal was over. By the first sunny Saturday that Gloria could remember there had been no raid for almost three weeks. She knew Joe would be working, but she announced at breakfast that she didn't intend to waste the day and that she fancied going to the Recreation Ground at the top of Grovelands Road. This pleased Ben no end because he was never allowed to go on his own.

They had a wonderful day. It was, Gloria thought, just what they needed. The park was packed with people doing the same, and she spoke to many other mothers as they watched their children playing together.

It was such a normal thing to do, when life for everyone hadn't been normal for a long time. Surely now the air raids were over, though, and the tautness and tension in her began to ease, melted away in the heat of the sun that seemed to hint of better days to come.

Gloria had packed a picnic, and when the sandwiches had been eaten Ben got involved in game of football with some other boys. Gloria watched Ben pounding over the grass and thought that that was what he should be doing: playing in the park with others his age, not terrified out of his life, cowering in a shelter.

Going home later, she thought Ben looked happier and grubbier than he had for a long time. And then he glanced up at his mother and said, 'That was terrific today. Are the bombs really and truly gone now, Mom?'

'I can't promise,' Gloria said. 'Not totally, but it would be nice if they were, wouldn't it?'

'Not half,' Ben agreed with a sigh. 'I suppose we have to wait and see. That's what you always say.'

'Well, that's because I don't know,' Gloria said. 'No one does, and I suppose that's all part of the plan to keep us on our toes. Come on, Dad might be in when we get back and you can tell him all about our magical day.'

Joe was home and already changed to go on firefighting duty, though he wasn't due at his post for a couple of hours. Ben was chattering fifteen to the dozen, telling him about the park and the football match, and Gloria was putting a meal together.

'You just have time for a quick bath,' she said to Ben. 'And you can take that look off your face, mister,' she added at the disgruntled expression Ben turned to her. 'You're like a child a tinker would be ashamed to own, and you can tell your dad all the rest while we eat.'

Later, leaving him to dry himself and get his pyjamas on, Gloria returned to the kitchen to put the final preparations to the meal as Joe, sitting at the table, scanned the newspaper.

'That seems to have been a resounding success today,' he remarked.

'Yes,' Gloria said. 'And yet it was only a day in the park. I mean I could have done it before but you have a sort of shelter mentality – you know, rushing back home each night to prepare the shelter bag for another night of terror. Course, what made today more special was the football match. Ben would just love a ball of his own.'

'I know that,' Joe said. 'But I guessed we wouldn't track one down for his birthday. I never had a ball either – none of us did – but we would beg a pig's bladder from someone we heard was slaughtering a pig and use that in the rare free moments we had.'

Gloria wrinkled her nose. 'Wouldn't fancy that, and I don't think asking for a pig's bladder is quite the thing to do in London.'

'No,' Joe agreed. 'And the bloody thing is likely rationed anyway.'

'Sure to be,' Gloria agreed sagely, and they burst out laughing. In the middle of this, the wail of the sirens rent the air. For a split second they both froze and it was the blast of a bomb falling close to them with a resounding crash that galvanised them all into action.

'Almighty Christ!' Joe exclaimed as the drone of the planes was heard above their heads. 'The watchers must have been half asleep. They're on top of us.'

Gloria didn't bother to answer. She was too busy trying to turn off the meal she had been cooking and then filling the shelter bag, calling to Ben as she did so, 'Hurry up, Ben. Pull a jumper over your pyjamas and get your siren suit on.'

There was no time to make sandwiches so she threw the makings into the bag along with a packet of biscuits. There was no time to boil the kettle to fill the Thermos and so she filled two bottles with water.

'I don't need my siren suit,' Ben said. 'It's too hot and anyway, the legs are too short.'

'For God's sake, Ben,' Gloria cried, tucking a blanket into the top of the bag, 'we could be in the shelter hours – you know that – and it could be cold when we come out. And who cares about the legs, being a bit short? No one is going to be looking at you.' She tried to keep the panic out of her voice as she said, 'Get it on, and fetch your gas mask and mine, and be quick, for Christ's sake. Can't you hear the planes all around us?'

Ben could hear them all right and they almost paralysed him with fear. He struggled into his suit with hands that shook so much, Joe had to help him. But at last they were out in the street where the search lights showed up the German planes above them like menacing black beetles. Joe delivered his wife and son to the shelter door, before taking off to join his unit, knowing somehow that this raid, after such a lull, was going to be a big one.

And it was. Soon, all around Gloria, people were crying, screaming, praying and the keening of the babies was a constant thin sound, cutting through everything.

Gloria had the urge to sit on the floor, wrap her arms around herself and howl like a wounded animal might. But she couldn't do that. However scared she was, Ben was worse. His teeth chattered together and his eyes stood out in his white, exhausted face as if they were on stalks.

Gently Gloria drew him onto her lap, knowing that in ordinary circumstances Ben, now that he was a big boy of seven years old, would never submit to being nursed. This time he snuggled right into her and she held him tight and wondered whether she was giving comfort or taking it.

They had sat out many raids in that same shelter, but few had been as fast and as furious as this. The German planes, with their distinctive intermittent sound, roared and thundered overhead and the sickening thuds, booms and crumps of explosions were constant.

Some fell so close that the shelter walls shook, dust trickled out from between the bricks and swirled in the air. Any moment, Gloria thought, the ceiling would descend on them all and this place where she had sought shelter might end up as a tomb for her and her son, and she held Ben even tighter.

She heard muffled screams and cries from outside and then the bells of the emergency services ringing frantically, and she sent a prayer up to keep Joe safe, though she doubted that anyone could possibly be safe.

When the all clear went, Gloria felt almost light-headed with relief and almost surprise. She roused her son, who had eventually fallen into an uneasy slumber against her, and he slid from her knee and stood in front of her, swaying and disorientated.

Outside the sky was blood red. 'That's London burning,' said a man passing her at that moment. Gloria nodded dumbly; she knew it too.

She took Ben's hand and he seemed grateful, for the horror of that night was still with him and evidence of the destruction was all around them, with fires blazing everywhere. Pockets of flames crackled and sparked as they greedily consumed the contents of people's houses now reduced to piles of smouldering rubble.

When they turned from High Road it was to find many of the streets around them had been reduced to rubble too, but Newton Road and the two blocks of flats were unscathed. Gloria was so relieved to be inside her own front door, and she thought of her neighbours that had lost everything that night. She felt so saddened and depressed that, but for her son, she would have put her head in her hands and wept.

The following day the full magnitude of that night's raid unfolded. On the wireless Gloria heard that five hundred and fifty bombers had attacked all parts of London the previous night, killing one thousand five hundred people and injuring one thousand eight hundred. They had also hit the Chamber of the House of Lords, Westminster Abbey, Westminster Hall, St James's Palace and Lambeth Palace, fourteen hospitals, the British Museum, the Old Bailey and almost all major mainline stations.

Knowing where the targeted areas were, Joe went off the following afternoon to see that the McCulloughs were all right, as he had promised Red he would keep his eye on them. Gloria opened the door to him a little later and knew by his face that the news was bad.

'They're gone, Gloria,' he said, and his eyes were like great pools of sorrow. 'The whole area is flattened. They didn't stand a chance.'

Gloria could hardly bear to hear the words. She thought of the motherly Dolly and her gruff though kindly husband, Jim, whom she would never see again. Her eyes filled with tears and she asked brokenly, 'Have any of them survived?'

Joe shook his head. 'Not one. Living on top of one another as they did, they have all gone: Red's grandparents, aunts, uncles and cousins, even his cousin Pete, who was home on leave, all blown to bits.'

Gloria was distraught. 'God, Joe, this is terrible,' she said. 'I can hardly bear the thought that I will never see any of those lovely people again. And what of Red? What has he got to come home to?'

'Bugger all! That's what,' Joe burst out angrily. 'He's away fighting for his country and his good, kind and totally innocent family is wiped from the face of the earth. And I will have to write and tell him. How the hell do you break news like that to anyone, least of all a man you are so fond of?'

'I don't know, Joe,' Gloria said, crying in earnest. 'I really don't know . . .'

Gloria and Joe's distress was so profound that Ben couldn't be protected from it, and when he heard of the death of Dolly and her husband he was upset too. They had shown him nothing but kindness and had been like grandparents to him. Despite the death and destruction all around him, this was the first time that he had encountered death on a personal level, for he couldn't remember the death of his grandmother, and he was as saddened and tearful as his parents.

But still the horrors hadn't finished. Elsie was not waiting for Gloria at either the school or the tram stop the following morning. Gloria carried on into work, not knowing what else to do, and found that Elsie, Maureen and their children were among the dead. She thought of the tragedy of Maureen bringing her small son back, only to have him blown to smithereens along with his teenage sister.

Elsie had been her special friend, and they would meet up and their children would all play together. She remembered Elsie's pretty little daughter, Sally, whom Ben had been sweet on, and her son, David, three years older, whom Ben was always trying to emulate. Gloria felt desolate that she would never see any of them again.

It was too much. There was only so much tragedy and sadness that the human brain could take at one time. She was no good at work, for the tears constantly welling in her eyes were blinding her. Ben too would be coping with this loss. He would have heard about Elsie's children at school, and really she needed to be with him so they could mourn together.

The supervisor was upset herself and knew that Gloria was in no state to be at work.

'Take a couple of days off,' she advised. 'The news has knocked me sideways, to tell you the truth, and I think you need time to come to terms with it.'

Gloria thanked the supervisor and left to collect her son from school. His teachers too were sympathetic and agreed with her that Ben would be better at home. Ben's face was chalk white and lined with tear trails and his eyes reflected his sadness.

Later Gloria learned that Elsie's children hadn't been the only friends he had lost that day: there were many empty desks in the school. Her heart went out to him, and to Joe as well, who settled down straight after the evening meal to write the hardest letter he would ever write to his mate Red McCullough.

Less than a month after those very sad successions of funerals, Joe received a letter from a friend of Red's in the forces, saying that he had been killed in action. Though Joe knew he would miss him, he was glad in a way, because the McCulloughs had been a close-knit family and he knew Red would have been lost without them. But he grieved for him none the less. Red had been a good mate to him and a great friend to them all.

There was a lull in the air raids through the summer, and when they did resume in the autumn of that year they were sporadic and far more localised.

Then on 7 December, the Japanese attacked Pearl Harbor and America was pulled into the war.

Gloria was unaccountably upset about it. 'It might shorten the war, though, Gloria,' Joe said.

'No one knows whether it will or won't in the end,' Gloria said. 'All I see it as now is an escalation of hostilities.'

No one could argue with that, and Christmas was again a very muted affair. Gloria looked forward to the New Year of 1942 with little enthusiasm.

The sirens blared out one mid-February day when Joe had only just left the house to go on duty. Ben had been about to get undressed, but Gloria told him not to bother.

'It's too cold,' she said. 'Just pull your siren suit over your clothes. I got it roomy.'

'You got it so I could grow into it,' Ben said. 'You said so at the time, and the legs are so long that if I don't turn them back on themselves they drag on the floor.'

'Some people are never satisfied,' Gloria replied. 'You said the legs on your old one were too short.'

'They were,' Ben maintained. 'And they cut me up the middle too.'

'Ben,' Gloria said in measured tones, 'will you stop talking, get into your siren suit and fetch your gas mask? In case it has escaped your notice, we are not going to a Sunday school outing.'

Ben did as he was told and a few minutes later said, 'I'm ready. Look, I'm waiting for you now.'

'Watch it,' Gloria said, lifting her coat off the hook. 'Come on.'

The shelters weren't as full as they had been the previous year, as many chose to stay at home and only sought shelter if the raids came closer, but Gloria didn't think her nerves would have stood that.

'Someone's getting a good old pasting tonight,' remarked the shelter warden when the raid had been going on an hour or two.

And they were, and not that far away either. The droning of the planes, the whine of the bombs and the resultant explosions were perfectly audible. The planes came no nearer, however, and eventually, about two hours later, the all clear blared out reassuringly, and Gloria and Ben stumbled out into the night. They could see the raging fires spitting orange and crimson sparks into the sky, and scurried past, breathing in the familiar tang of acrid smoke mixed with the stink of cordite.

Gloria gave a sudden yawn. 'Gosh, I'm tired,' she said to Ben. 'Bombing raids permitting, I will probably go to bed not long after you tonight.'

She was about to start getting undressed for bed when the knock came to the door. Alarmed at someone coming at that time of night, she called out, 'Who is it?'

'The police.'

'Oh God!' Gloria felt as if an icy hand had suddenly taken hold of her heart and she fumbled in her haste to open the door. A grim-faced policeman stood there, and with him the shelter warden she had been with just a few minutes before. 'It's Joe, isn't it?' Gloria cried. 'It has to be Joe.'

'Can I come in, Mrs Sullivan?' the policeman said. Gloria let them though the door, her eyes never leaving the policeman's face.

'Would you like to sit down?'

'No, I don't want to do anything but hear what's happened to my husband,' Gloria said. 'Tell me, please.'

'Your husband has been injured, Mrs Sullivan.'

'Injured, not killed? Oh, praise be to God,' Gloria cried and then she caught sight of the policeman's sombre face and swallowed the lump that had formed in her throat. 'Is he likely to die from his injuries?'

The policeman shook his head. 'These are questions I can't answer. You must ask the doctors at the hospital.'

'Which hospital?'

'Well, they were trying Highgate Hill Infirmary as it was one of the closest,' the policeman said. 'It does depend on beds, though. We have a car at your disposal in case you have to travel some distance.'

'But I can't come with you,' Gloria cried. 'Not now. I have a son.'

'That's why I am here,' the shelter warden said. 'I will look after your son until your return. Go off with the policeman and find out how your husband is.'

Gloria nodded, took her coat from the hook and followed the policeman. She sat on her hands in the car to prevent them shaking, and held herself stiffly erect because she was afraid of losing control. She knew if she lost Joe, she wouldn't want to go on. How would she cope without her beloved Joe, and how would Ben cope?

But he wasn't dead, she reminded herself, and when she saw him she would will him to stay alive. But she didn't see Joe when she arrived, because he had already been taken for emergency surgery. One of the doctors on duty said that he was extensively burned but also had internal injuries. 'Brave man, by all accounts,' he went on. 'The fire officer who came in with him said he held up the entire weight of a house so that a family trapped beneath it could escape. And then with the last one through, it sort of caved in and crushed him.'

Gloria sank onto a seat. She really felt as if she couldn't take any more, and she wanted to tell the doctor that she didn't want a dead hero, she wanted a live husband, but she didn't say this; she didn't try to say anything for she knew if she tried the tears would have overwhelmed her.

She sat for over two hours in silence, praying inside her

head for the survival of her beloved husband before a young doctor, a harassed-looking woman in a white coat, with a stethoscope around her neck, came to see her.

'Mrs Sullivan?'

'Yes,' Gloria said wondering if she had come to tell her that Joe had died on the operating table.

'I examined your husband initially. He is a very sick man and will be in surgery many hours yet. It might be best if you come back in the morning.'

Gloria would have liked to have camped in the hospital overnight, but there was Ben to consider. She would come down first thing in the morning, though, and bugger the job. They could get someone else to sew the parachutes. Her first priority had to be her husband.

'What are his chances?' Gloria asked.

'That is impossible to answer,' the doctor said. 'But he is gravely ill. The next twenty-four hours will be crucial.'

When Gloria was dropped outside her block of flats, she was aching inside with sadness.

'Is there anyone you can ask to stay with you tonight?' the policeman asked.

Gloria shook her head. 'I have no family and no friends left now.'

She said a similar thing a few minutes later to the shelter warden.

'My missus will come and stay with you, if you like,' he said. 'You shouldn't be on your own.'

'No, really, I will be fine,' Gloria said firmly. 'It is very kind of you, but I want to be by myself for a while.'

'You sure?' the shelter warden asked anxiously.

'Quite sure.'

Still, the warden left reluctantly but Gloria shut the door behind him with a sigh of relief. She wanted to be alone, to be able to release the tears that had been threatening since the police had knocked on her door.

And when the tears were spent, she felt light-headed and sluggish, and longed to lie down and sleep. But her mind was too active to allow her to do that and so instead she sat down at the table to write to Tom. He needed to be told, she thought.

Though she had never met Tom, Gloria felt she understood him a little because of his letters, and what Joe had said about him. She had never written to him herself, though, and she found it difficult to write for the first time to someone to tell them bad news, and so the letter was a brief one.

Dear Tom,

I have never written before, but I thought you ought to know that Joe was injured last night helping people escape from a burning building, which later collapsed on him. They told me that he had quite extensive burns and internal injuries as well. He is a very sick man, Tom, and I am sorry to be the bearer of such bad news.

Regards, Gloria

Gloria put the letter in an envelope to post on her way taking Ben to school in the morning and eventually she went to bed, where she tossed and turned through what was left of the night.

The next morning, Ben was surprised that his father had left for work before he had got up, which was what his mother told him. Other things were wrong that morning too, and his mother was tetchy and short with him.

Then, as they were ready to go, Ben said, 'Why are you wearing the coat you wear for Mass to work? You have never done that before.'

'It's warmer than the other,' Gloria answered shortly.

'And you've done your hair different.'

'I fancied a change, that's all.'

'And you've got black rings around your eyes.'

'Ben, for heaven's sake!' Gloria exclaimed. 'Don't you know that it is very rude to make personal comments about people?'

'Well, you have,' Ben stated flatly.

For the first time in her life, Gloria really wanted to shake her son. She felt as if all her nerve-endings were raw and exposed. Every time she remembered the doctor's eyes she felt sick with fear, and she could do without Ben going on and on. But she controlled herself and said, 'I didn't sleep well last night and that's why my eyes are ringed with black, and don't ask why I didn't sleep well,' she went on, with the ghost of a smile for his benefit, 'or I just might clock you one.'

Ben grinned back and retorted, 'Wasn't going to ask anyway.'

Joe was a fighter and the doctor who came to see Gloria said he was delighted with the way he had pulled through the series of operations he had had through the night, though it was still touch and go, and the burns were also giving them cause for concern.

'However,' the doctor went on, 'your husband seems to have the constitution of an ox. To be honest, I didn't expect him to pull through last night or be half as well as he is this morning, so that is good news.'

'Thank you,' Gloria said. 'Can I see him just for a minute?'

The doctor nodded. 'You can peep in. But he won't know you because he is heavily sedated and might be for some time yet, because he will be in tremendous pain from the burns.'

Joe lay like one dead, his shallow breathing the only sound in the room. Most of his body was covered in thin gauze strips that the nurse explained were to protect the burns. Gloria's heart was filled with love and pity for her poor, brave Joe and the trials he had yet to go through.

Her boss at the factory, where Gloria went after she had

visited the hospital, understood about her need to take time off. 'Mrs Sullivan, you have holidays owing to you,' he said. 'So take what you need now and you will still be paid if you take it as holiday pay.'

'Thank you,' Gloria said. 'You are very kind.'

'Not at all,' the boss said. 'It is only what you are entitled to.'

Gloria popped in to see the women too, to tell them why she hadn't turned in that day, and they were all sympathetic and understanding about her need to be with her husband. As Winnie said, 'I mean, this war work and being patriotic is all very well and good, but your own has to come first.'

Ben was pleased that his mother picked him up after school and he hadn't to go to the club but he thought it odd. 'You've never come to pick me up before,' he said.

'Well, normally I can't,' Gloria said. 'But I haven't been to work today.'

'Why not?' Ben asked because it was almost unheard of for his mother to take time from work.

'I'll tell you when we get home,' Gloria said. 'I am perished with cold.'

'All right,' Ben said, 'but let's hurry then.'

They did hurry through the dank, damp streets with the clammy fog swirling around them, and Ben was as pleased as Gloria was to reach the warm flat. She pulled the blackout curtains across the windows so that they could turn the light on before she took off her coat. Ben said, 'Go on then.'

Gloria sat on the settee, drew Ben down to sit beside her and put an arm around him as she said, 'The reason that I didn't go to work today is to do with what happened to your daddy last night.' And she went on to explain things to Ben.

She wasn't aware when he began to cry, but when he looked up at her as she finished talking she saw the tears trickling down his cheeks. He scrubbed at them with the sleeve of his jumper and said brokenly, 'Is Daddy going to die?'

Gloria swallowed the lump in her throat and bit back the hearty reassurances she had been going to give her son. He deserved the truth, she thought, and so she said, 'We hope not, Ben.'

'But you said you'd seen him today. You must know.'

'He is very sick, but he is holding his own, and the doctors are pleased and a little surprised,' Gloria said.

'Daddy is hardly ever ill,' Ben said.

'I know,' Gloria said. 'They said that your daddy has the constitution of an ox, and I will see him every day and stay with him as long as the hospital will let me stay,' Gloria said. 'I have taken time off from work to do just that.'

'And he will get better in the end, won't he?'

Gloria gathered Ben into her arms and the tears seeped from her own eyes as she said firmly, 'I promise you I will do my level best to see that he does just that.'

TWELVE

The day after Gloria told him about his father, Ben declared there was no need to take him to school each day as if he was a baby. Gloria knew that he was saying that it was his dad who needed her attention, not him, so each morning they set off in separate directions.

The hospital was always bustling and busy, whatever time of the day Gloria arrived, and the staff seemed rushed off their feet. She'd wondered at first if they would allow her to visit daily, but they seemed to have no problem with that, so she sat in the room, holding Joe's left hand because it wasn't burned like the right one, and told him how much she loved him, and that he had to recover from this because she needed him and so did Ben.

On the third day, Joe opened his eyes. They were vacant and unfocused, and she doubted he was aware of anything much. He had shut them again by the time the doctor Gloria had summoned had come to examine him. However, the doctor told her it was a very good sign.

She went home not long after this, glad that she had something positive to tell Ben that evening, and then when she reached home she found a letter on the mat from Tom. In it he said that he had been so shocked at the news and that all of them were in his thoughts and prayers constantly. He expressed the deepest regret that he couldn't travel over to give her some practical support, and if there was anything else she wanted, then she only had to ask. The love and concern that dear man had for them all could almost be lifted from the pages of the letter, and Gloria put her head on the table and cried as if her heart was broken because she had felt so alone.

She wrote back to Tom, thanking him and telling of the small sign of recovery Joe had made. When Tom sent his next reply it was in a parcel addressed to Ben, and inside the package were sweets, chocolates and comics for him. Ben had never ever received a parcel in his life before and he was almost speechless with pleasure. He wrote a thank you letter straight away.

Joe continued to recover very slowly, and Gloria kept Tom updated on his progress so he was aware of when he passed the crisis, when he fought against the fever that threatened his life, and when he began the first of the painful skin grafts. Each time in his reply Tom included something for Ben, often with a little note attached.

Gloria began back to work when her holiday pay was used up, but left at dinner-time so that she could spend time with Joe and still be home for Ben when he had finished at his after-school club. At weekends she took Ben to the hospital with her, but had to leave him in the visitors' room, for the hospital was adamant that children under twelve were not allowed on the wards. Ben was more than grateful then for the comics and sweets his uncle kept sending him because they whiled away the hours very pleasantly until his mother came back and told him all the news about his father.

In the middle of April, there was another raid. Ben was in bed and asleep, and Gloria roused him quickly. He struggled into his siren suit while she packed the shelter bag.

'It will likely be a light skirmish like the last few,' the shelter warden said, 'but better safe than sorry, I say.'

He ruffled Ben's hair in a way Gloria knew he hated and said to Gloria, 'How's your husband?

'He's doing all right,' Gloria said. 'He's been having skin grafts for three weeks now.'

The shelter warden whistled. 'Very painful business, I hear that is.'

Gloria pursed her lips and gave an almost imperceptible but definite shake of her head. She never discussed the pain Joe was in with anyone when Ben was in earshot, feeling the separation from the father he loved was enough for him to cope with.

Before Gloria could say anything, however, there was a terrific explosion that seemed to be right above them. Ben gave a yelp of terror and the shelter warden exclaimed, 'Christ Almighty! That was close.'

But the words had barely left his lips when there was another explosion just as close and then another. He looked at Gloria and said, 'I think it might be Tottenham's turn tonight.'

It soon became apparent the shelter warden was right. As the relentless attack continued, people streamed in from the neighbourhood, seeking some sort of refuge from the harbingers of hell spilling down on top of them. The raid went on for hours, and so close around them that Gloria almost waited for the shelter to be hit. The whistle of the descending bombs made her insides crawl with fear.

When the raid was over at last, she stumbled out of the shelter with Ben to scenes of utter devastation, a large sea of rubble stretching out as far as the eye could see.

With fingers of apprehension trailing down her spine, Gloria, with Ben by her side, walked down the short streets to where their small block of flats had once stood. All that was left was a gigantic mound of rubbish, littering the pavements and most of the road.

Gloria stood and stared at it, as if unable to believe the evidence of her own eyes. She tried to tell herself that she should be grateful they were not hurt at all, that all the planes had destroyed was bricks and mortar, but it wasn't just bricks and mortar to her. She had loved her flat, had kept it spotless and was always buying things to make it cosier. It symbolised the new future she was building with Joe and Ben, and now it was gone for ever.

'What we going to do now, Mom?' Ben asked, and Gloria didn't answer him because she hadn't the least idea. All she and her son had in the world were the clothes they stood up in – pyjamas, in Ben's case – the shelter bag and their gas masks.

Just then an ARP warden approached them. 'You used to live here, ducks?' he asked.

Gloria nodded dumbly.

'Have you got any relatives or friends who might take you in, like?'

Gloria shook her head. Tears seeped from beneath her lashes and trickled down her cheeks.

'Here now, ducks, you don't take on so,' the man said. 'I'll take you round to the WVS van and give you a feed first. It puts a new complexion on things on a full stomach, I always think.'

Gloria wasn't the slightest bit hungry. She felt sick with worry and thought that food would probably choke her.

'But where will we sleep?' she cried.

'Don't you worry about that,' the man told her cheerfully. 'Woodberry Down Mission has been taking people in. You won't be the first I have taken there this evening. Now you follow me and I will soon sort you out.'

Two days later Gloria wrote to Tom, but knowing what a worrier he was, she played down the despair that she was feeling.

Dear Tom,

Another bit of bad news, I'm afraid. Our flat was demolished in a raid the night before last. We were taken to a church hall nearby where we have been made very comfortable. You are not to worry about us; there are plenty in the same boat. Please don't tell Joe what has happened either when you are writing to him. He can do nothing about it but worry, and he is doing so well, I would hate him to suffer a setback now.

I have printed the address of where I am staying now at the top of this letter and look forward to hearing from you.

In fact Gloria was trying hard to keep a brave face on everything, for Ben's sake, and particularly for Joe, who knew nothing about the way they were living now. Inside, though, she really grieved for her lovely flat, which she had lavished such love and care on, reduced to a pile of masonry and everything in it crushed to bits. They had been down in the depths of poverty and despair for years, and the flat had been the outward sign that they were on their way up again, that the future was rosy once more.

She had shed tears at night when all were asleep, muffling her sobs in her pillow, but after a few days she knew she really had to get over it. What she told Tom was right: she was by no means the only person in such circumstances, and some were far worse off than she and Ben. Anyway, moaning never did any good and the kind people at the mission were doing their level best to help them.

So when they were sorted out with clothes – a couple of shirts and pairs of trousers, socks and shoes for Ben, and a couple of dresses and cardigans, and shoes that had seen better days for Gloria, and the bare minimum of underclothes for both of them – she accepted them with good grace. Such few clothes, though, did mean that she seemed to be constantly washing them in the big laundry room at the back of the mission hall, but there again she wasn't the only one.

Gloria forced herself to get into the routine of living there, though the lack of privacy did bother her, and there was often too much noise for Ben to sleep very well.

She had given her ration books in to the mission hall staff, and they provided the meals. It was always porridge in the morning and slices of the grey national loaf spread with margarine, and at night a stew of one kind or another with lots of vegetables and little meat, which they were all well used to now, and there was never much left.

But however Gloria looked at it, she thought it a depressing way to live, and the only bit of good news as the spring unfolded into summer was that she could see Joe improving week by week. But when the doctors suggested discharging him at the beginning of July she was thrown into a panic.

'We can do no more for him here,' the doctor told her. 'He will not be able to do much yet, and he needs peace and quiet in order to rest and recover properly.'

Gloria thought of the noisy, clamorous mission hall and knew Joe would never recover there. But she knew where he would recover, and that was back in his old home in Ireland, where she imagined he would get all the peace and quiet he would need.

Her mind recoiled from such a move, yet what was the alternative? In her heart of hearts, she knew there wasn't one, and not one person who would be able to help her except kindly Tom Sullivan.

All night she tossed and turned, but by the morning no solution had presented itself. So before she went to visit Joe that day she wrote a letter to Tom, explaining everything. Tom's answer came by return of post.

Dear Gloria,
    You can come and welcome, and as soon as you like. You do right bringing Joe here. He will I'm sure be fit and well again in no time and I really can't wait to see you all.
    Love, Tom

All Gloria had to do then was tell Joe, and in such a way that he would have no idea of the desperation she felt at the thought of living for months in a remote cottage in the back of beyond. He was delighted that the doctors thought him well enough to be discharged, but not so happy about the things his wife and son had endured.

'Why didn't you tell me that you had been bombed out?' he asked.

'For what purpose?' Gloria replied. 'You would have fretted and worried, and that would have done nothing to change the situation, but could easily have made you ill again.'

'And now you are proposing to go back to Ireland with me,' Joe said. 'In fact, you have it all sorted, but you hate the countryside and this is as rural as it gets.'

Gloria leaned forward and kissed Joe gently on the lips. He felt his heart turn over with love for this wonderful women when she said, 'You need a place where you can get the peace and quiet that the doctor prescribed, and that is all that matters to me. Now all I need are some clothes for you, for yours were crushed in the flat, and I need a case or something to carry our possessions, though there are precious few of them. Everything else is in hand.'

Ben was waiting for his father in the visitors' room of the hospital, and though it was very early, the place was all astir. He watched all the white-coated doctors with their stethoscopes swinging, striding about importantly, the nurses scurrying from place to place, the porters pushing trolleys or wheelchairs around, and the cleaners with their mops and buckets tackling the corridors.

He was impatient to see his father and wished he would hurry up, but when he did appear in the threshold of the room, Ben was shocked to the core. He knew his father had been very sick, but when his mother said he was well enough to leave hospital, as far as Ben was concerned, he would almost be back to normal.

187

However, the man that shambled into the waiting room just a little later bore little resemblance to the father that he hadn't seen for over four months. The clothes his mother had got for him seemed too big, his face was grey and his cheeks sunken.

Ben knew that he couldn't rush at him the way he usually did, the way he wanted to, and so he approached him slowly and Joe saw him biting his lip in agitation.

Joe felt like death warmed up. Even dressing had exhausted him, and the material felt rough against the newly grafted skin, but he forced a smile and said, 'Hello, Ben. Haven't you a hug for your dad?'

'I might hurt you.'

'Away out of that,' Joe said. 'When did a hug ever hurt anyone?' He put his arms around his son and had to bite back the grimace of pain as Ben's arms tightened around him.

Ben gave a sigh of relief, turned to his father and said, 'You'll get properly better soon, won't you, Dad?'

'I will certainly,' Joe said. 'I need good fresh Irish air in my lungs and nourishing food in my body and I will be as right as rain in no time.'

'Mom said there won't be no bombs in Ireland,' Ben said. 'So we won't have to go to the shelter in the middle of the night, and you won't have to go out and fight fires any more, will you?'

'No,' Joe said. 'That's one good thing, anyway.'

'Come on,' said Gloria. 'If we don't get a move on we will miss the train. Come here, Ben, and I'll help you put that haversack on.'

'Let me carry it,' Joe said. 'Or give you a hand with the case at least.'

'Joe, we have such few possessions now that there is no weight in the case,' Gloria said. 'All you need to do is put one foot in front of the other and you can take my free arm to help you, if you need it.'

'It doesn't seem right.'

'None of it is right,' Gloria said. 'War isn't right. What happened to you isn't right. Let me and Ben take care of you now, Joe, and try and make you well again. OK?'

'Have I a choice?

'No,' Gloria said firmly.

Joe shrugged. 'I had better say OK then,' he said with a ghost of a smile.

'Yes,' Gloria said. 'You had best had. Now come on, let's get going.'

Ben knew that he had been on a boat before. His mother had showed him America where he had been born and the big expanse of sea they had crossed called the Atlantic Ocean to reach London, but he had only been four at the time, little more than a baby and only had vague memories of it. This time the sea they had to cross was called the Irish Channel and his dad said as it was only a small stretch of water the boat wouldn't be so big, nor the journey so long.

Ben was pretty impressed just the same. The boat was the *Ulster Prince*, it had three black funnels and it looked massive. Ben felt his stomach turn over at the exhilarating thought that he was actually going to get on board and sail away.

'Isn't it just grand, Dad?' he said, as they stood on the deck together and looked out over the rails to the grey scummy water lapping the sides of the boat and then to the activity on the dockside.

Joe smiled. 'It is, son. Another new chapter of our lives is opening up.'

'I am dying to meet Uncle Tom.'

'You will like Tom,' Joe said confidently. 'You'd be hard to please if you didn't like Tom, mind you, for he is a grand man altogether, and I am looking forward to seeing him again myself.'

And then the engines throbbed into life, black smoke billowed out of the funnels, and there was a sudden screech from the hooter, so loud and strident that Ben had his fingers in his ears. Then the boat moved ever so slightly and they were on their way.

Ben was tired by the time the train was pulling into Derry station. He just wanted the journey to be over. Joe wanted that too, because he was feeling very jaded and sore. He got up and stood in the corridor as the train began to slow down.

As the platform came into view he said with relief, 'There's Tom waiting for us.'

At this Ben got up to join his father, anxious to catch sight of this uncle who had been so kind to him. Gloria too wanted to see the man she had got to know through the many letters exchanged while Joe had been in hospital.

She saw that Tom was still a handsome man with a fine head of hair. Once it had been a vibrant brown, though it was now liberally laced with grey, as was Joe's. Like Joe he was of medium height and had cheery ruddy cheeks, from life in the open air, she guessed. When he spotted them his whole face broke into a beam of happiness and Gloria felt herself relax.

The train drew to a halt and the family began to alight as Tom hurried across the platform to meet them. He thought he had never seen anyone as thin as his brother. Joe had never carried excess weight, but now he was positively gaunt, and holding himself stiffly as if every movement was painful, and his eyes were slightly glazed.

Tom's heart turned over in pity for the discomfort Joe was so obviously in, but he wiped this from his face as he bid him welcome, because Joe had always hated people feeling sorry for him. Then he turned to welcome Gloria, whom he felt he knew from her letters, and realised that she was as beautiful as Joe always claimed she was, with her blonde hair, flawless skin, high cheekbones and those vivid violet eyes.

Tom put his arms around her. 'Welcome to Ireland, my dear,' he said.

'Thank you, Tom,' Gloria said. 'I am so glad to meet you at last and I know this is the right place for Joe just now.'

'It is indeed,' Tom said. 'We'll have him as right as rain in no time at all. What do you say, Ben?' he said, turning to the boy, who was the image of his mother.

Ben looked at this man, his uncle who spoke in such a slow and easy way and had really kind-looking eyes, and despite his weariness he felt safe and secure in a way he hadn't done for ages. 'That's what Dad thinks as well,' he said, remembering his father's words in the hospital.

'Well, then,' said Tom, 'let's get you up in the cart and we'll have you home in no time at all.'

As they walked towards the cart, Joe gave a laugh and said sardonically, 'I hardly think so, with this horse.'

'Not five minutes in the country and you're complaining about the horse already,' Tom grumbled. 'I told you before and I will tell you again, there is nothing wrong with this horse.'

Ben didn't think there was much wrong with it either. 'That horse is like the ones in London that pulled the beer barrels and the coal!' he exclaimed, and said to his father, 'You said you had a horse with the shaggy feet on the farm here.'

'Ah, yes,' Joe said, as he helped his wife and son up into the cart. 'But what else did I say? Do you remember that?'

Ben shook his head, 'I don't think so.'

'I said those type of horses are built for strength not speed. Tom's claim that he would get us home in no time is not a strictly truthful one.'

Gloria shot a glance at them, alarmed that they had begun to argue within minutes of meeting, but she soon saw that it was all play-acting, ongoing banter between the brothers.

'Well, it will be a damned sight quicker and more comfortable than walking,' Tom said. 'So stop your blether and get up beside your wife.'

'I'm riding with you,' Joe said.

'You would be more comfortable in the cart,' Tom told him. 'I have cushion and blankets ready for you.

Joe said nothing but just stared at Tom with an almost challenging look in his eyes. When Tom's eyes met Gloria's, she gave a slight shrug that said quite clearly that he was wasting his time, that once Joe had decided on something that was that.

'Please yourself then,' Tom said, getting up behind the horse and pretending not to notice the grimace of pain that Joe made when he hauled himself up and the cautious way he sank onto the seat beside his brother.

As the horse plodded steadfastly down the road, Joe began pointing things out to Gloria and Ben. Gloria saw how important it was for him to bring his wife and son back to his birthplace, especially as Ben loved everything he saw. Raised in London streets, he was amazed at so much greenness and space. He admired the sheep that dotted the hillside, and the little white cottages they passed. They each had a plume of smoke rising from the chimneys, and Ben asked what it was.

'When you have a fire in the grate, the smoke comes out the chimney,' Joe said.

'Why would anyone have a fire today?' Ben asked. 'It's boiling.'

'I know, but you see most people here cook on the fire.'

'Oh boy, do they really?' To Ben that seemed the most amazing fun.

Tom and Joe laughed, and Tom answered, 'Aye, and to tell you the truth it is not always the most convenient thing. On a day like today, for example, you are sweltered indoors and so the door has to be left open, and if you're not careful the chickens from the yard will find their way in too.'

Gloria thought chickens running around a kitchen disgusting, but Ben thought it sounded magical. 'You have chickens?' he said.

'Yes, Ben,' Tom said. 'We have many chickens. In fact, it will probably be one of your jobs to collect the eggs each morning.'

'Oh boy!' Ben cried. 'Eggs as well?'

'They come from chickens,' Tom said. 'Didn't you know that?'

Ben shook his head. 'I don't know much at all about eggs.'

'Small wonder,' Gloria put in. 'Eggs don't feature much in a wartime British diet. Each person is supposed to have one egg a fortnight, and we are lucky if we see one egg a month.'

'That's dreadful.'

'God, Tom,' Joe said, 'in the end, with the blackout and the bombing and all, the food or lack of it was the least of our problems.'

'The Americans brought dried egg powder with them,' Gloria said. 'It started appearing in the shops just as we left and I suppose that might help the situation a bit.'

'Well, there're plenty of eggs here,' Tom said. 'And we have cows too for the milk. Have you ever seen a cow, Ben?'

'Yeah, from the train,' Ben said. 'I've never seen one close up. I went to a zoo once with Mum, but they didn't have any cows.'

'Well, do you know cows give the milk you drink?'

'Yeah,' Ben said. 'Dad told me. I thought that he was joking at first.'

'Oh, it's no joke, believe me,' Tom said. 'Cows have to be milked twice a day every day, even at Christmas.'

'Golly.'

Tom was tickled with Ben's enthusiasm. 'I'll show you how it's done, if you like; let you have a go.'

'Oh, you bet,' Ben cried.

'You mustn't get under your uncle's feet,' Gloria said. 'I am sure that he is a very busy man.'

'Not too busy to take my nephew around and show him things, though,' Tom said. 'It's bound to be strange to him.' And then, as they passed fields of ripening hay, he went on to Joe, 'We'll have a grand year for the harvest as long as the weather doesn't break.'

'No sign of it so far anyway,' Joe said. 'And I will be fit enough by then to give you a hand.'

'Why make promises you might not be able to keep, Joe?' Gloria chided. 'How d'you know that you will be recovered enough to help at the harvest? For goodness' sake, don't try to run before you can walk.'

'I will help you, Uncle Tom,' Ben said, 'if you show me what you want done. And I will have plenty of time because Mum says I will not be going to school until September and that is ages and ages away.'

'Think you will be able for it?' Joe asked him with a twinkle in his eye, and when Ben answered firmly, 'You bet I will be,' the two men laughed uproariously and laughed even harder when Ben asked, 'What is harvest, anyway?'

Gloria actually was feeling quite panicky and this seemed to increase with every step the horse took. She felt she had left civilisation way behind in Derry, and she had a genuine horror of being buried in the country.

'How far away is Buncrana from the farm?' she asked Tom.

'About two and a half miles by road,' he said. 'Slightly less if you go over the fields.'

God Almighty! Gloria thought. Two and a half miles up hill and down dale to buy a loaf of bread. But then, she told herself they probably didn't buy bread, they made it, and as they were living here she would probably have to learn to make it too. And cook it over the open fire, what was more. God Almighty, what had she come to?

'All right?' Joe said, glancing back and seeing the look on Gloria's face.

Gloria knew she couldn't say what was really on her mind. She had made the only decision she could have done for Joe's sake. What was the point of whining about it now? And so she said, 'I'm fine. It is certainly very beautiful and I am sure that I will soon settle down.'

'That's my girl,' Joe said proudly. But he was well aware that Gloria was just putting on a brave face, and she hadn't met his mother yet.

'How does Mammy feel about us just landing on her like this? he asked Joe quietly.

There flashed into Tom's mind the scene when he told her that Joe and Gloria and Ben were coming to live with them in order that Joe recovered totally from his injuries. She had been furious but he had stood firm and reminded her that it was his decision to make, not hers, that the farm belonged to him and she had better remember that.

'Mammy came round to it in the end,' he said.

'Tom, you are talking to me, your brother,' Joe said. 'Mammy never comes round about anything.'

'Why ask the road you know then?' Tom said. 'She is bad as she always was. She'll never change and I suppose it's best you are prepared for that.'

When the cart drew up in the cobbled yard just a few minutes later, Gloria was appalled by the place, but Ben was enchanted. He thought the cottage was like a pretend house, for it was like no house he had ever seen before. It was a squat, low building that didn't look big enough to live in, and it was painted white and had yellow straw stuff for a roof and a door that he saw opened in two pieces.

Chickens roamed freely about the cobbled yard, pecking constantly, two dogs ran barking from the barn, and lots of cows looked over the fence of a nearby field and lowed gently.

'Past time for milking and they are letting me know about

it,' Tom said with a smile as he leaped from the cart and lifted the case and bag as if they weighed nothing at all. 'Come away in.'

Gloria was surprised that Joe's mother hadn't appeared to greet them, though Joe had warned her that she was one on her own and didn't operate under the same rules as the rest of society.

'Mammy,' Tom called as he entered the cottage, 'they're here.'

'D'you think that I am deaf and blind, or what?' Biddy growled out from her position by the fire. She didn't get to her feet, not then and not even when Joe followed his brother and stood framed in the doorway side by side with Gloria with Ben in front of them.

Gloria peered through the gloom. She hadn't realised that the room would be so dim, and she saw the light came from one small window at the far end.

However, she could see the old woman sitting in the chair glaring about her as if she hated the whole world and everything and everyone in it. She ignored Gloria and Ben, and spoke only to Joe.

'So, you have decided to come home at long last?'

Even forewarned, Joe was appalled at his mother's rudeness in not even acknowledging Gloria and Ben, let alone welcoming them. He walked to stand in front of his mother and spoke stiffly. 'As you see, Mammy, the prodigal returns. When that happened before, didn't they kill the fatted calf?' He looked pointedly towards the grate where the fire was almost out and there wasn't even a pot of water hung over it to boil up.

Tom followed his gaze. 'Dear, dear,' he said, crossing to the hearth. He poked more life into the dying embers and threw some pieces of peat onto it. 'I'll make you a cup of tea for now,' he said, filling the kettle with some of the water in the bucket by the door, 'and we will have some proper food when I have finished the milking. Is that all right for you?'

'That's fine, Tom,' Joe said.

But his mother snapped, 'Just tea, d'you see? No fatted calf for the likes of you, who only came home because there was no other place he could go to.'

Joe stared at his mother, then said, 'And it is lovely to see you too, Mammy, and, as you see, I have not come alone.'

As he spoke, he crossed to the doorway where Gloria still stood with Ben, uncertain what to do, and put an arm around her. 'This is my wife, Gloria,' he said, and with a hand on Ben's shoulder went on, 'And this is our son, Ben, your grandson. Haven't you at the very least a word of welcome for them?'

'I have no need to give them any sort of a greeting,' Biddy snapped, 'because they are only here under sufferance. They are not welcome and never will be.'

Tom gave a sharp intake of breath and wondered what Joe was going to do about such an insult. However, he had no need to do anything because suddenly Gloria was furiously angry, far too angry to allow herself to be intimidated or cowed by some malicious old woman.

She burst out, 'I think you are a very unpleasant and objectionable old woman and I wouldn't stay under your roof another minute but for the fact that my husband, your son, needs to be here.'

Biddy was astounded at Gloria's temerity. She had thought she would be easily handled, but Gloria hadn't finished.

'Now,' she said, 'I don't expect you and I will ever be the best of friends, and that suits me fine, but for Joe's sake, I am prepared to put up with you. However, I will not tolerate rudeness and if you persist in being so insulting, my stay here will be very uncomfortable – and I mean for you, not me and mine.'

'How dare you? You are under my roof.'

'No, Mammy,' Tom said. 'As I said before, Joe and his family are under my roof and I am very glad to have them here. After the way you behaved and spoke, I think Gloria was justified in every word she said.'

Then seeing that his mother was for once in her life speechless, he continued, 'Now the kettle is boiling, I will make tea for us all before I go to milk the cows.'

'Can I help you, Uncle Tom?' Ben asked.

'Aren't you tired out with all the travelling?' Tom asked.

'Yeah, I am,' Ben admitted, 'but it's a sort of fed up, fidgety kind of tired. I shan't mind helping with the milking one bit. I am not too tired for that, honest.'

'All right then,' Tom said. 'I shall be glad of the help, and we will be off to collect up the cows as soon as we have finished our tea.'

THIRTEEN

Gloria found life on the farm just as dreary as she had anticipated. What she hadn't bargained for was coping with such an embittered woman as Biddy Sullivan. However, she was a feisty young woman who had been to hell and back since the day her father had shot himself. She had coped with things that would have felled a lesser woman, and certainly one that had come from such a privileged background, so she was more than able to deal with a woman filled up with malice, resentment and spite.

She didn't enjoy confrontation, though, but despite this, she stood against Biddy from the first, though she thought the old woman might have an apoplectic fit the day Gloria refused to churn for butter. She said the effort was not worth the amount of butter produced, and they could buy butter in Buncrana every week, like many people did.

Biddy ranted and raved, and Gloria watched her dispassionately, wondering if she were seriously deranged. She had certainly never met anyone quite so nasty, and she found living with her hard going. Not that she ever let her see that, knowing instinctively that that wasn't the way to deal with such a person.

She found the only thing that worked when Biddy got in one of her rages was to stop what she was doing and say calmly, 'I see you are not behaving well at the moment.

I will come back when you are in a better frame of mind,' and then just walk away.

That was the last thing that Biddy wanted. She wanted to bully and browbeat Gloria, and it enraged her that she seemed unable to do that. Joe wasn't the same man either. If she started a tantrum with him he would just look at her in a pitying way and say, 'For goodness' sake, Mammy, if you could only hear yourself. This is no rational way to go on at all. Now if you are prepared to talk to me, then I will listen.'

Their reaction totally took the wind out of her sails and she wasn't sure how to handle it. Tom would marvel that Joe and Gloria could control his mother's excessive behaviour so easily.

Gloria knew though it wasn't so easy for Ben to cope with such an irascible and scary woman, and one day not long after they had arrived, she said, 'Ben, does your grandmother bother you much?'

Ben shrugged. 'I keep out of her way. Anyway, she can't help it, Daddy said, because she's mad. Least,' he added more honestly, 'he said that her mind didn't work the same way as other people's, that she was unbalanced. I mean that's as good as mad, isn't it?'

It was, and Gloria herself thought Biddy was mentally unstable. It just wasn't normal to go on the way she did.

'She doesn't like me, anyway,' Ben went on. 'Dad said I'm not to worry about that because she doesn't like a lot of people, but I wasn't worried anyway.'

Just a few days after this, Ben had proof of how much his grandmother disliked him. His father was resting, his mother had gone to Buncrana, and he was helping his uncle in the fields. Returning to the cottage for a drink of water he dashed through the door, tripped on the mat and, in putting out his hand to save himself, knocked a dish from the table.

Ben gave a gasp of terrified shock as he gazed at the bits of broken crockery on the floor.

'You stupid boy!' Biddy cried. She crossed the room in seconds and gave him such a clout on the side of his head he nearly lost his balance.

Ben's hand flew to his ear, 'I'm s-s-sorry,' he stuttered, scared rigid by the look in Biddy's black and baleful eyes.

She seemed not to hear him, as she knocked his hand away, grabbed him by the ear, still sore from the original thump, and dragged him across the room.

His yelp of fear changed to cries of alarm as Biddy suddenly sat down, pulling Ben with her and in seconds she had him across her knee, pulled down his trousers and was paddling his bottom with the sole of her shoe.

Ben's incensed bellows brought his father from the bedroom and his uncle from the fields. When Joe reached the doorway and saw his mother laying into his son, a malevolent smile playing about her mouth as if she was enjoying it, for a split second he really wanted to kill her. He ran across the room and plucked Ben from his mother's arms, pulling up his trousers as he did so. Biddy had seldom seen Joe in such a towering rage. He was so angry that for a moment he couldn't speak, and then he ground out, 'All right, you old harridan, what was that all about?'

'Don't you call me—'

'Tell me why you were knocking seven bells out of my son or I will shake it out of you,' Joe demanded.

Biddy took one look at his enraged face and said flatly, 'He deliberately broke a dish.'

Joe shook his head. 'I know my son a sight better than you do and I don't think that he would do that.'

'He did, I tell you, and it was one that I was particularly fond of.'

'Ben, Joe said, 'did you deliberately break one of your grandmother's dishes?'

Ben shook his head, and through the tears said brokenly, 'N-no, Dad. It . . . it was an accident.'

'I thought as much,' Joe said. 'And did you apologise?'

Ben was crying so hard he couldn't speak, but he nodded vigorously.

Joe forced himself to speak calmly as he turned to his mother. 'Ben unintentionally broke a dish and apologised immediately. That should have been the end of it. Let's get one thing clear here, Mammy, if there is any chastising to be done, then Gloria or I will attend to it. You lay one hand on my son again and you will be sorry. And, incidentally, we do not punish for accidents.'

Tom recounted all this to Gloria when he spotted her at the head of the lane.

'And where are Joe and Ben now?' Gloria asked.

'Joe took the lad for a walk,' Tom said. 'He said it was to keep him out of Mammy's way till you came home.' He gave a rueful grin. 'I also think he needed to put some distance between himself and Mammy for a wee while.'

'Neither of us has ever struck Ben,' Gloria said. 'There had never been any occasion to.'

'I have never been one to advocate beating children anyway,' Tom said. 'I had too much of it when I was growing up, and Joe the same. In fact I broke the cane Mammy used on us in two halves and threw it on the fire when she used it on Molly.'

'Wasn't she thirteen when she first came here? A bit old for that form of chastisement I would have thought.'

'Of course she was,' Tom said. 'She had her one hell of a life here, though I did what I could, and eventually she learned to stick up to Mammy herself.'

'I am sure that she soon became friends with you, though,' Gloria said. 'Look how Ben loves you. He used to trail after you from dawn till dusk, and I have you to thank for the way he settled so well and happily into his life here.'

'I enjoy his company,' Tom said. 'So what I do with Ben is a pleasure not a hardship, and there is no need to thank me. In fact, he is a fine boy altogether. I envy Joe two things and that is a wife and child.'

'Why did you never marry, Tom?' Gloria said. 'You have so much to give, and you would have made a wonderful husband and father.'

'You have met my mother and can still ask that question?'

'Your mother!' Gloria exclaimed. 'You mean you didn't marry because your mother wouldn't have approved?'

'Not totally, no,' Tom said, and then added with a note of relief in his voice, 'Here's Joe and Ben coming along the road. I'm sure they will want to talk to you, and I'd best get on with the hay.'

Gloria watched him go, wondering what the other reason was that he hadn't married. Then she turned to face her husband and son and saw that Joe had walked the bad humour out of him and was smiling. She said, 'Hello, you two. Tom has been telling me there were high jinks up at the house today.'

'There was, Mom,' Ben said in a high indignant voice. 'Wait till you hear.' And all the way down the lane, he regaled her with the tale she had already heard from Tom.

Gloria found Biddy very subdued when she went into the house and she set about preparing the dinner, knowing that the old woman would have done nothing towards it.

Later, as they ate, Gloria said, 'I met Helen Mortimer in the town today. You know, she used to be McEvoy?'

'Did you?' Tom asked. Helen's mother, Nellie McEvoy, was the postmistress, and she and her husband, Jack, were great friends of his. 'Terrible business with Helen's husband never coming back from Dunkirk.'

'Yes, especially when they only had two days together first,' Gloria said. 'I felt really sorry for her, and then for his family to be completely wiped out just last year. Dreadful time the girl has had.'

'Nellie thought she had died too when there were no letters, and her sister, Margaret, who moved to England with her, couldn't find her at all either,' Tom said.

'Yes, Helen had had a complete nervous breakdown,' Gloria said, 'and little wonder. She said it was ages before she could even remember who she was. Anyway, the psychiatrist suggested that she come here to get away from the bad memories.'

'Wasn't it Birmingham where she was?' Joe asked.

'Yes, and for years,' Gloria said.

'Used to city life, she will probably find Buncrana a little slow and sleepy now, like you do,' Joe said. 'Maybe the pair of you will be company for one another.'

There were plus sides to living in Ireland, Gloria decided, as the days passed. She had never seen Ben as happy as he was that first summer in Donegal, particularly after his father had put his grandmother in her place. Gloria had also seen a steady improvement in her husband week by week, and towards the end of August he had begun to help Tom around the farm again, happy to do it because idleness had never sat easy on his shoulders.

Gloria was very pleased to have the friendship of Helen Mortimer. She had been very lonely before she had met her because she had little in common with most of the women in the town. She hated their insular provincialness, and it showed, and the inconsequential, small-minded gossip both bored and irritated her. There had been suspicion amongst the townsfolk about her from the beginning because she was American and therefore 'foreign', whereas Joe had been accepted back into the fold as though he had never been away.

Helen, despite being born and raised in Buncrana, had been away from it for some years and had seen and done other things, and so now she was almost as different from those living there as Gloria was. The two women gelled from their first meeting. They met at Mass each Sunday morning and would often arrange to go for a walk on a Sunday afternoon if the day was a fine one. Every Saturday, when Gloria went to Buncrana, she would call into the post office for a cup of tea and chat with Helen and her mother, Nellie, and sometimes her younger sister, Cathy.

'They're very alike, the two girls,' Gloria said one Saturday as the Sullivans sat eating dinner. 'They have the same shape to their faces and the same deep brown eyes and hair. Helen, I suppose due to city life, combined with what happened to her, hasn't the rosy cheeks of her sister, but both despair of their freckles.'

Tom chucked. 'Those freckles have always been the bane of Cathy's life. Molly told me many a time that she was always on about them.'

'Oh, yes, Cathy said she used to be such a friend of Nuala's daughter, Molly,' Gloria said.

'They were,' Tom said. 'They were thick as thieves, the pair of them. And now Cathy is engaged to one of the Guardsmen stationed here, and I don't know whether Molly is alive or dead.'

'They speak of her with such fondness, despite the fact that she hasn't written to them either,' Gloria said.

'It would be hard to talk of her in any other way,' Tom said with a sigh. 'She was a lovely girl and as pretty as a picture.'

'Lovely girl my arse!' Biddy spat out. 'She was the Devil's spawn, that one, and gone to the bad like her mother before her.'

'I have had just about enough of this,' Joe thundered, banging his fist on the table so hard Ben nearly jumped out of his skin. He pointed at his mother and said, 'You sit there all day like a venomous snake spitting your poison over everyone.'

'You have no right to speak to me that way.'

'I have every right,' Joe said more quietly. 'And it should have been said years ago.'

'You have no respect.'

'Your attitude negates any respect I might have had for

you, Mammy,' Joe said. 'Let's examine what Nuala actually did that has caused a canker of resentment to grow inside you, because as far as I am concerned she didn't go to the bad at all. That girl hadn't a bad bone in her body. All she did was fall in love.'

'And who with?' Biddy screeched. 'A man of another faith. And that news killed your father.'

'No,' Joe said. 'The two things might be totally unconnected. Daddy was on borrowed time – the doctor had told him that – but he never took it easy like he was told to. He could have died in the fields alongside me and Tom. Would it then have been our fault?'

'Of course not,' Biddy snapped. 'But Nuala—'

'Didn't even know that Daddy had a bad heart,' Joe said, cutting across his mother. 'If you hadn't insisted on protecting her as if she was a child then the outcome might have been completely different. So, maybe you're to blame for Daddy's death.'

'Don't be so ridiculous!'

'Why should anyone be to blame?' Gloria asked. 'People die all the time. When my mother died it was no one's fault. Should I have said, my father's suicide contributed to it, or the precarious way we were living?'

'When I want your opinion, I will ask for it,' Biddy snapped, looking contemptuously at Gloria.

Gloria met her gaze levelly as she countered, 'And I was under the impression that Ireland was a free country and that anyone can express an opinion without approval being sought first.'

Biddy was completely flummoxed and had no reply ready and Joe almost laughed at the expression on her face, but Tom put in, 'You're right for the moment, Gloria, but whether we stay free or not is out of our hands. If England loses this war, the six counties too will be under German control. What chance do you think Ireland will have then?'

'Bugger all!' said Joe. 'That's what.'

Gloria shivered suddenly. Here, in this little backwater of Ireland, it was hard at times to remember that there was still a war being fought on numerous fronts and that the survival of them all depended upon Britain's success.

It was only a couple of weeks after this that Gloria thought that Biddy might be ill, though her voice was as vitriolic as ever, as Joe said when Gloria mentioned her concerns to him.

'Joe,' she said, 'that is no measure. I think when they are nailing her coffin lid down she will be letting rip to someone or other.'

'Aye,' said Joe with a grin. 'Probably Tom.'

'Almost certainly Tom,' Gloria replied grimly. 'And that means that you have drawn the short straw because it is you that must talk to your mother.'

Now that Gloria had brought it to Joe's attention he had to admit that his mother didn't look right, but she refused to acknowledge she was ill and said firmly that she had no need of a doctor.

'You did your best,' Gloria said with a sigh, 'but we'd do well to keep an eye on her.'

This made them all more vigilant and so, a fortnight later, when Biddy suddenly keeled over as she was standing by the hearth, she would have fallen in the fire if Joe hadn't caught hold of her. He declared he was off for the doctor, and Gloria and Tom changed the beds around so that Biddy could have the end room for more privacy.

The doctor lost no time examining Biddy. Then he assembled the family and said all he could do for her was try to keep the pain at bay. Gloria wasn't that surprised, though she could see that both Tom and Joe were stunned.

'Poor you,' Helen said the following Saturday when Gloria mentioned how sick Biddy was. 'How long does the doctor say she has?'

'Not long,' Gloria said, 'but you know the woman is so

contrary that she would hang on just out of spite. And it's me mostly that bears the brunt of her ill humour, of course.'

'I don't know how you'll put up with her,' Helen said. 'I think that you deserve a medal.'

'Shall I let you into a little secret?' Gloria said. 'So do I.'

There was little change in Biddy in late October when Tom came home from Buncrana with a letter that he said was from Molly.

Joe was surprised at his brother's sober demeanour. 'I thought you would be near standing on your head,' he said, 'hearing from the girl after all this time. It means at least she is not dead.'

'Aye,' Tom said slowly. 'That's the only good thing about it. You'd best read it yourself and then you'll understand better,' and he passed the letter over. Joe took it and Gloria, intrigued, read it at the same time, over his shoulder.

'It doesn't say anything,' Joe said when he had finished. 'I mean, it just states the bare facts, like her grandfather is dead and she found Kevin in an orphanage. There is no explanation of where she has been these past years or what she has been doing or anything.'

'What she doesn't say is more important than what she does,' Gloria said. 'I think that girl is hiding some secret that she thinks is too terrible to share. She has written this to assure you she is alive and so is her brother, and she certainly doesn't want anyone to find her because she has put no address on the top of it.'

'What d'you think it means?' Tom asked.

'I have no idea,' Gloria said. 'All we can hope is that she will write again later and explain everything.'

Over a week since the appearance of that strange letter and early one morning, Joe had taken the churns to the head of the lane to await the creamery lorry while Tom was cleaning out the byre. Joe saw the postman first.

'Tom about?' he asked Joe.

'Aye. Why do you want him?'

'I have a package for him,' the postman said, pulling a small parcel from his sack. 'Nellie McEvoy said I was to give it to him direct.'

Joe could never remember any of them getting a parcel before and so he looked at it curiously.

'It's from England,' the postman said.

'You'd best give it to Tom then, hadn't you,' Joe said. 'The byre is where you'll find him.'

Tom was just as perplexed as his brother to receive a package, though he had no intention of opening it until the postman had gone. Joe called into the byre a little later to see if Tom was finished to find the man in floods of tears, the opened package at his feet.

'Tom, what in God's name ails you?'

Tom raised his tear-stained face and silently handed Joe the package. Joe read the letter first. It began with an acerbic attack on Tom for allowing Molly to go alone and unprotected to Birmingham and finished by saying that he was sending him the cuttings from the newspapers of the trial in case Molly hadn't told them everything, and that he was making arrangements to see her immediately. It was signed, Paul Simmons.

Joe didn't know who Paul Simmons was. He withdrew the press cuttings and within a few minutes of reading them he understood his brother's tears. He felt his own eyes fill up and a large lump lodge in his throat as he read of his young, naïve niece, arriving at New Street Station, Birmingham, at the start of the worst raid the city had experienced. She had been understandably terrified and glad to be befriended by two men who promised to look after her.

Instead, they lured her to a flat where they had her pumped so full of drugs she had trouble remembering her own name as they preened her for the whorehouse. A man called Will Baker rescued and hid her, at great risk to himself and his family. However, she knew too much to be allowed to go free and, later, brutal louts tracked her down and made an attempt on her life that very nearly succeeded.

'God, Tom,' Joe said brokenly. 'I don't know what to say.'

'You didn't know Molly, of course, but honest to God, Joe, she hadn't a nasty bone in her body,' Tom said. 'And she was innocent. She would have no idea that the men who pretended they would care for her made a living scouring train stations for young girls on their own. She would never imagine things like that could happen.'

'God, Tom, I am a lot older and more experienced than Molly, and I was unaware of things like that happening,' Joe said. 'And who is Paul Simmons?'

'Paul Simmons is the injured officer Molly's father put his life on the line to rescue in the Great War,' Tom told his brother. 'One of his legs had been shattered and so he ended up with one leg shorter than the other. When the war was over he found driving difficult and he sought out Molly's father and offered him a job as his chauffeur. He owned an engineering works, just like your Brian Brannigan. Anyway, after Nuala and her husband died, Paul took an interest in the children. Molly is set to inherit a great deal of money when she is twenty-one, and Kevin too, of course, in his turn. Mammy knows nothing about this, or about the allowance that Simmons has been paying Molly since she was fourteen. With the help of Nellie McEvoy she had saved most of it and that was how she was able to afford to pay the fare to Birmingham.'

'Well, from the tone of the letter, you are not this Paul Simmons' favourite person at the moment.'

'Oh, Joe, I deserve that and more,' said Tom. 'When I think of what Molly has gone through . . .' Tom shut his eyes for a moment and then went on, 'And then, not only to suffer it, but to stand up and tell perfect strangers what had happened to her. The courage that took beggars belief.'

'I agree with you there,' Joe said. 'But I don't see how you can hold yourself responsible. How d'you think this Simmons chap is going to contact Molly, anyway? D'you think he has her address?'

Tom shrugged. 'If he has, he is not likely to give it to me. But it said in the cuttings that she worked at Castle Bromwich Aerodrome, so maybe he will get in touch that way.'

'Well, couldn't you do the same?'

'I will when Mammy . . . Well, I couldn't leave her the way she is.'

'Tom, you have given her more than half your lifetime,' Joe said. 'You owe her nothing.'

'She is my mother,' Tom said simply. 'Bad as she is, I can't leave her now.'

Three days later, a letter came from Molly to Tom. She wrote that Paul had been to see her and told her of the letter that he had sent to him. She told him there was no way that he or anyone else could have stopped her doing what she felt she had to do. She blamed a lot of what happened at the station on her own stupidity and naivety, and she felt very ashamed of her part in it and that was why she had not been in touch sooner.

She also went on to say that she had Kevin with her now and she had met a wonderful man called Mark, whom she would like her uncle to meet as he had become very special in her life.

'Now,' Joe said, handing the letter back to Tom, 'will you stop beating yourself about the head for something you couldn't prevent?'

Tom smiled and said, 'I'll do my best, but the first thing I will do, now that Molly has sent me her address, is write a long letter to her and say I will be over to see her as soon as my mother is buried.'

FOURTEEN

In the middle of December, in the throes of one of her many tantrums, Biddy suddenly went stiff and her eyes rolled in her head. Gloria and Joe were in with her at the time and Gloria sprang away from the bed. 'Is she dead?'

Joe felt for the pulse in her neck and said, 'No, but something has happened, and so I am away for the doctor.'

The doctor, who was surprised that she had held on to life so long, said Biddy had had a stroke, and a bad one. When it was established that she had no movement below her neck, Joe asked Gloria if she wanted her transferred to the County Hospital as the doctor had recommended. 'I don't,' Gloria said. 'I have bruises and pinch marks on my arms and a graze on my cheek from where she threw the pepper pot at me only yesterday. I will find her easier to deal with in the state she is in now, as long as either you or Tom will be around to help me turn her.'

'You are a marvellous woman,' Joe said. 'Mammy never had a good word for you.'

'She didn't have a good word for many people,' Gloria said. 'Look how she used to harangue Tom.'

'Well, she can't do that anymore,' Joe said. 'Tom won't know what to do with himself.' And then he added with a grin, 'Maybe we should yell at him on a daily basis to make him feel at home.'

'I don't think that will be necessary,' Gloria said. 'And

get from under my feet. I have to prepare a meal for your mother. If you have spare time on your hands, you might go down and tell the priest what has happened. Your mother sent the poor man from here with a flea in his ear about a fortnight ago and he's not been back since.'

Gloria tended Biddy for seven more weeks until her death. She knew it was hard on her to lose the power of speech, and she would feel her malevolent eyes boring into her often. Sometimes, she would refuse the food, or spit it back at Gloria, and for the last fortnight she refused to take the painkillers the doctor prescribed, and ate less than a bird.

'She is in pain, she must be,' Gloria said after the third day. 'I can see it in her eyes. Maybe she should go to the hospital after all.'

'Why, so they can force feed her and compel her to take her medication?' Tom said. 'I think she has had enough, and who could blame her for that?'

'But we can't just leave her suffering,' cried Gloria.

'We can,' Joe said. 'She knows what she is doing. Tom's right, it really has got to be her decision, but I will ask Father Finlay to come up and give her the last rites, I think.'

'Aye,' Tom said. 'That would be a good idea. I tell you, it's a powerfully quiet house without Mammy roaring in it all the time.'

'Well, I did suggest that Gloria and I shout at you on a daily basis in case you missed it, but Gloria wasn't keen.'

Tom laughed. 'Miss it?' he repeated. 'Aye, I miss it all right, like you might miss a headache when it is over. You two couldn't take the place of Mammy because you haven't enough anger and resentment in you and thank God for it.'

Biddy died on a cold blustery day at the very end of January. No one had been to Mass that day, though it was Sunday. When Ben asked why, his dad had said that it was because his grandmother was on her last legs.

213

His mother came into the kitchen then and said to Tom and Joe, 'I think that you had better come through now.' Seeing Ben watching her, she added, 'Do you want to see her, Ben?'

He shook his head vehemently. 'I don't have to, do I?'

'No,' Gloria said. 'I thought you might want to say goodbye, that's all.'

'Is she dying?' Ben asked. 'Dad said she was.'

'Yes, she's dying, Ben.'

'I'm glad.'

'Ben . . .'

'I don't care, Mom,' Ben said. 'I don't even care if that makes me wicked. She was wicked too, and horried. She shouted at people all the time, especially Uncle Tom, so why shouldn't I be glad that she's dying?'

Gloria didn't have an answer, and as they went through to the bedroom Joe told her to leave Ben alone. 'Many people will feel the same as he does, but while an adult will wrap it up nicely, a child says it straight. To be honest, he was often scared rigid of her when she got in one of her rages.'

'She still scared me sometimes,' Tom admitted. 'And she had me a nervous wreck when I was Ben's age, and for long enough after it too. Joe will verify that, and I was always too scared of her to stand up for myself. So don't be that hard on Ben, for if I am honest I am glad too it's nearly the end.'

Biddy's shallow breathing was the only sound in the room. Tom gazed across at her lying prone on the bed, and though her face was contorted in pain, he felt no shreds of regret or compassion for her suffering.

Gloria, though, remembered her mother's passing and she thought however bad a person was, death was a lonely path to travel. And so she sat on the chair beside the bed and took up one of Biddy's withered hands. Joe marvelled that she could do that. He didn't want to go anywhere near

214

the dying woman and he stood at the end of the bed and waited until the breathing finally stopped.

Gloria laid Biddy's arms across her chest as she had done to her mother and said with a sigh, 'I can't help thinking what a wasted life she had. What is the point of living if you take joy in so little?'

'Don't tell me you feel sorry for her?' Joe asked, astounded.

'No,' Gloria said, 'I can't feel sorry for her because she really was almost unbearable at times, but now it is over I can feel it in my heart to pity her.'

'You are a better person than me then,' Tom said. 'For the only thing I feel is relief that my ordeal is over.'

'Anyone in the whole world could understand that,' Joe said. 'I couldn't have done it. God Almighty, I would have strangled her if I'd been in your shoes.'

'No, you wouldn't have,' Tom said with a smile. 'You had a much better way of dealing with her than I had.'

'Well, how you dealt with your mother is neither here nor there now,' Gloria said. 'And here's Father Finlay striding down the lane. Will you let him in, Joe, before Ben tells him that his grandmother is dying and he's as pleased as punch and nearly turned cartwheels around the room because of it?'

'Aye,' Joe said, and left the room with a smile on his face.

Biddy was buried four days later on a bleak Friday morning in February 1943, when snow tumbled relentlessly from the grey overcast sky. There were so few mourners there was no point really in having a proper wake, and though Tom and Joe's hands were pumped many times, Gloria heard not one person express regret at Biddy's passing.

'We're away to Grant's Bar to sink a few jars,' Joe said as the few people started to move away. 'We shouldn't be too late.'

'All right,' Gloria said. 'I'll make for home. Jack McEvoy

will be over to do the milking shortly anyway, and if we are to go into Biddy's old room tonight then it needs a thorough clean, for it smells of disease and death.'

When Joe got home that night, he was very glad Gloria had the end room ready for the pair of them, because he had a tale to tell that was not for Ben's ears. He was now sleeping in the other room with his uncle, as he had when they first arrived, and fast asleep when Joe tiptoed through to their room and got into bed beside Gloria, glad she wasn't asleep.

'Tom told me something coming home tonight and I was so shocked that I thought it was the beer talking,' he said to her.

'And you're sure now that it wasn't?' Gloria asked with a wry smile.

'No,' Joe said. 'And I'm telling you if I had been legless, what he had to tell me would have sobered me up totally, because Tom said when he was a boy, he killed a man.'

'He what? Gloria almost shrieked, as she shot up in the bed.

'Shush,' Joe cautioned. 'This is for your ears only. I certainly don't want Ben to get wind of it.'

'But, Joe, Tom wouldn't hurt a fly,' Gloria said. 'It must have been some sort of accident.'

'In a way,' Joe said. 'You remember when I told you about my sister Aggie being raped by the dancing teacher McAllister, and having to run away when she found herself pregnant?'

'Yes.'

'Well,' Joe said, 'that's who Tom killed – McAllister.'

'Well, I would say he was no loss,' Gloria said. 'But I still can't see Tom killing anyone.'

'Listen,' said Joe. 'The day McAllister died was the first Sunday since Aggie had gone missing. Tom heard him commiserating with our father for Aggie running away from home like that and worrying her parents. Tom said he was raging at the hypocrisy of the man. So when he saw him on his horse on the road below him later, when he was out for a walk, he suddenly wanted to make him pay for what he had done.'

'I'd have wanted to get even, as well,' Gloria said. 'But how did he do it?'

'Well, he knew he was bound for a neighbour's house where he would teach the fiddle, and to get to that house he had to pass through a place where there are trees on either side of the road, where the road narrows and bends slightly. Tom thought if he tied a rope between the trees just after the bend, he might be thrown from the horse and break his leg or something. In the end, he took from the barn some metal twine that we used for mending fences, but McAllister's wife had followed him and when she saw what he was about, she tried to stop him.'

'Why? Didn't she know what manner of man her husband was?'

'Oh, she knew all right,' Joe said. 'She told Tom he had been at it for years and she would love him to get his come-uppance, but not at Tom's hand.'

'Why not?'

'Well, if Tom had just injured McAllister, he would have a good idea who had wished him harm, because Tom was the only one who knew about Aggie. His wife said the man would take great delight in shouting from the roof-tops how Aggie had been begging and pleading for him to have sex with her for months, and then one night he couldn't help himself. Then the sacrifice Aggie made running away to protect her family would be for nothing. And Tom could be in serious trouble, maybe arrested himself and transported.'

Gloria nodded slowly. 'Yes . . . it's monstrously unfair, but that's the way it would have been.'

'But she was too late,' Joe said. 'Tom told me that he was untying the wire from the first tree when the two of them heard the drumming of the horse's hoofs. When the galloping horse hit the wire, it fell to its knees, and McAllister flew through the air and fell awkwardly, breaking his neck.'

'Oh God!' Gloria said, guessing the panic that would be running through the adolescent Tom. 'What did he do?'

'Tom was in too much of a state to think,' Joe said. 'McAllister's wife took charge. She told him to hide the twine, and it is probably down the well to this day, while she would go home and inform the Guards that her husband had ridden out on the horse and that it had come back without him.'

'And they got away with it?'

'Aye,' Joe said. 'But then as I told you before after the letter to McAllister's sister came back, Tom hadn't a clue what Aggie had done or where she had gone and that has been eating away at him for years. Then Molly went to the selfsame city years later and also disappeared for a time, and then we find out absolutely dreadful things happened to her. To Tom it must be like history repeating itself. I know Tom won't be happy until he sees Molly for himself.'

'Nothing to stop him now.'

'No,' Joe said. 'I hope he doesn't go just yet, though, because there are two calves ready to drop and I don't fancy tackling the births on my own. It's years since I was at a birthing.'

'And if you and I don't get some shuteye soon, there will be no point in going to bed at all,' Gloria said to him.

'I know, but I'm still all churned up.'

As they snuggled together, Gloria suddenly said, 'Does Tom mind you telling me all this?'

'No,' Joe answered. 'He said there should be no secrets between husband and wife.'

Gloria said nothing more, but she knew now the real reason that Tom had never married. If he met a woman that he loved enough to want to marry he would have to tell her the tale he had told Joe that night, and he couldn't have risked that. Poor, poor Tom, she thought, and she fell asleep with that thought running around her head.

Joe envied his wife, for though his eyes were gritty with tiredness, a large knot of guilt had lodged in his heart that drove sleep away. He went over Tom's words again and again, bitterly aware of the burden that he had carried for years, which had ruined any life he might have had.

He had also protected Joe from it all. But when he was grown and could have shared the burden, Joe went off to America and it was only then, before he sailed, that Tom told him what had really happened to Aggie. The rest he had kept lodged in his heart until now.

They had both had to cope with the distress of their father's death and the alienation of Nuala, but instead of working alongside Tom as they helped one another get over these things, Joe had decided he couldn't stick at it any longer. Oh, he had convinced himself that he had some justification, that it was pointless working on a farm that would never be his, though he had known that Tom would always have seen that he was all right and compensated him for his years of work. No, he knew that the attitude of that old harridan that they had buried that day had been one of the main reasons he had fled the land of his birth, although he knew that by doing so he was condemning Tom to a life of hell.

What if the positions had been reversed, he asked himself, and Tom had disappeared from the scene and left him to it? Could he have coped as well? God, no! He knew he couldn't, and he would have bitterly resented Tom for leaving him in the lurch. Tom was a nicer person than he by far, and he knew that if there was any way that he could ever go even partway to repaying Tom for the disservice that he had done to him then he would take it and welcome.

Gloria had had her hands so full with Biddy, especially when the stroke had paralysed her, that she had hardly been able to leave the farm except to go to Mass. She had seen the McEvoys, and especially Helen, there of course, but it had only been for a few minutes. So that first Saturday after Biddy's funeral, Joe told Gloria to get herself ready to go to Buncrana and that he was dropping her in, leaving Ben in the care of his uncle.

Gloria was ridiculously excited to be visiting the small market town, and Joe watched her shining face and dancing eyes with amusement. The past weeks had been very demanding and draining for her, and he knew it would do her good to get out and about again.

Helen appeared to be watching for her, and barely had Gloria alighted from the cart than she pounced on her. 'I am so glad you came today,' she cried. 'I was so hoping that you would. You must come up to our house right away. We have two people there who want to meet you.'

'What people? Who are they?' Gloria asked.

Helen laughed. 'You must come and see.'

Gloria looked across to Joe, who raised his eyebrows quizzically and said with a sardonic grin, 'I should go up, Gloria, and satisfy your curiosity.'

'I will then,' Gloria said, but as they started up the hill to the post office she said to Helen. 'Will you give me some clue as to what this is about?'

Helen laughed at Gloria's perplexed face. 'All right,' she said. 'We have two visitors in the house, officers from the American Naval Base in Derry. They are called Petty Officers Morrisey and Meadows, and they want to meet you because Mammy told them you were an American.'

'But what are they doing at your house?

'Mammy asked them up.'

'Why?'

'You know my mother and you can ask that?' Helen said with a laugh. 'They had come to look at the place they said because they'd heard how pretty it was. They had a Saturday off together and decided to come and see for themselves.

They told my mother this when they went into the post office. She left Cathy to carry on, and took them into the living room and fed them tea and cake. In the conversation your name came up, and they said they would like to meet you and so now you are as wise as me.'

Gloria's mind was still teeming with questions, but at the post office she went inside with a little trepidation. The two men, very smartly dressed in their uniforms, stood up as Helen and Gloria came into the room. Gloria was impressed by that because it showed they at least had good manners.

'Here's Gloria now,' Nellie said, turning to greet the girls. 'Come away in, my dear, and meet some of your fellow countrymen. This is Mr Meadows and Mr Morrisey. This is Mrs Gloria Sullivan.'

'How d'you do?' Gloria said, as she shook hands with the men, who were both tall and good-looking. Both were dark-haired too, though Morrisey's mass of brown curls looked as if the US naval barber has tried to tame them and failed. He also had beautiful dark brown eyes, ringed with very long black lashes, and they lit up in appreciation as he shook hands with Gloria. It was a firm handshake too, the sort that Gloria liked, as he said, 'How d'you do? How very British is that?'

At his words, Gloria was transported back to New York. Not to the teeming tenement building they could barely wait to leave, but her life before the Wall Street Crash, and she felt a wave of homesickness flow over her. 'You are from New York?' she said, almost breathlessly.

'I sure am, ma'am,' Morrisey said. 'And I am so pleased to meet you.'

'You must tell me how New York has fared since I left,' Gloria said. 'I have often wondered, for it was in terrible difficulties when we were forced to leave and set sail for England.'

'England?' Morrisey said. 'So what are you doing here in Ireland?'

'Oh, that's a long story,' Gloria said.

'Well, no time like the present for telling it,' Nellie said. 'I'll make a cup of tea to help it all along.'

Gloria smiled as the door closed behind Nellie. 'Bet you are awash with tea when you would rather have coffee, and I could also bet you haven't the slightest interest in my life story.'

'Wrong on both counts,' Morrisey said. 'First of all they haven't the slightest idea how to make coffee in this country, and secondly I would love to know why a girl from New York is buried in a backwater in Ireland like this one, however pretty it is.'

'Well, it was a decision forced on me,' Gloria said, 'for I am a city girl at heart.' So Gloria began her tale. She didn't stress the privilege of her earlier life, but she did say that her father had been the owner of an engineering factory and had dabbled in the stocks and shares for years. 'Eventually, well, I suppose he got greedy. He lost money, tried to recover himself by borrowing more and more, and when the market crashed in October 1929 he lost everything.'

Morrisey saw the sadness behind Gloria's eye as she remembered those days when her whole world had crashed about her ears. The men didn't notice Nellie coming in with the tea tray, for their eyes were fixed on Gloria as Morrisey cried, 'Everything? You lost everything?'

'Everything,' Gloria confirmed, 'And because my father couldn't face what he had done to us, he shot himself.'

'Dear God, that's terrible!'

'It was, Mr Morrisey, very, very terrible,' Gloria said. 'I loved my father so much and could hardly credit what he had done, yet the horror of it was just beginning.'

'Gloria, I had no idea it was so bad,' Nellie said. 'What did you do?'

'There was nothing we could do, Nellie. We were destitute.'

'So many had their fingers burned at that time,' Morrisey said. 'My folks have a garage and I trained as a mechanic,

222

as my father did. After the Crash things were tight for a while but we got by. Luckily my parents had not invested in anything. My father didn't believe in stocks and shares. He maintained that there was only one way to get rich and that was to work damned hard.'

'He would get on well with my husband who fortunately thought playing with stocks and shares was a mug's game,' Gloria continued. 'It was hard for him that though he had done nothing wrong, and I don't think had ever owed a penny piece all his life, he was held responsible for my father's debts because he was made a partner in the business on our marriage. It seemed like every day there were further revelations, more debts uncovered, and Joe shouldered it all. But even Joe couldn't do the impossible and when he couldn't get a regular and permanent job we eventually ended up in a tenement building.'

She didn't need to describe the squalor and degradation that they had descended to, because Morrisey knew all about those tenements. It seemed almost incomprehensible to him that this beautiful young woman should have been forced to live in such penury, although he knew that she wasn't the only one by any means.

'We waited for things to improve,' Gloria went on. 'But they didn't, and we had a child to care for, so after my mother died we set sail for England. I wasn't a bit keen on London at the start, to tell you the truth, but yet I got to love it, and then war was declared.'

The two petty officers listened, horror-stricken, as Gloria described a city bombed to bits, with terrified people bedding down anywhere, even the underground, to try and keep themselves and their families safe. And they learnt of her husband, Joe, helping the regular firemen fight the raging fires in the teeth of those terrifying raids.

Gloria spoke softly of the dear friends she had lost, and then the awful day that Joe had been terribly injured. 'Our home had been destroyed by then,' she said sadly. 'I was so upset about it at the time. We lived on the floor of a mission hall with countless others, but it was definitely was not the place to take a sick man who needed peace and quiet to fully recover from injuries that had almost killed him.'

'And so that is what brought you to Buncrana?' Morrisey said softly.

'My husband came from here.'

'You sure seem to have had a hard time of it.'

Gloria shrugged. 'Believe me, I think every town and city in Britain has people who have suffered just as much as I have, or more,' she added, glancing at Helen. 'But now Joe is fully fit once more, and we must soon look to what to do with the rest of our lives, for I do not want to stay in Buncrana for ever.'

'I guess not,' Morrisey said. 'It's pretty, I grant you, and maybe a grand place to bring up a family, but there isn't much entertainment to be had.'

'Nor employment either,' Helen said. 'Everyone has to leave here to have the chance of a job and life of their own. I have two brothers in Detroit and I was in Birmingham until fairly recently. My elder sister, Margaret, is still there.'

'At least we haven't got to worry about our families when we are away,' Morrisey said. 'Because there are no raids in America.'

'And have you a family, Mr Morrisey?'

'Not a wife or child of my own,' Morrisey said. 'I didn't want to get serious with anyone with this war in the air. I knew it was only a matter of time till we were sucked in. But I have my parents to fret over.'

'And you, Mr Meadows, – have you a family?'

'No,' Meadows said, 'just my parents and two younger sisters.'

'Do you still hanker after New York, Mrs Sullivan?' Morrisey asked.

'I do,' Gloria said. 'I don't say too much about it to Joe because I know he feels guilty about dragging me away from the place I was born and bred, although there was no alternative at the time.'

'Tell us about modern-day America now,' Helen said. 'My brothers are hopeless at explaining things.'

'America is now trying to reinvent itself after the biggest slump it has ever had,' Morrisey said. 'Many, like Gloria's father, lost all they had and the economy was turned on its head, but the years before the Crash, the twenties, I remember as a magical time.'

'How old were you when it happened?' Gloria asked.

'Twenty-three.'

'So was I,' Gloria said. 'And married by then. But, just before I was married, I had what Joe refers to as my year of madness. There were not enough hours in the days for all the things I wanted to experience after years in a convent school. Even the years after our marriage were marvellous, with the cars we drove, many friends and every entertainment imaginable available. Whenever I look back I see it as a time of frivolity and fun.'

'But didn't they have prohibition?' Nellie asked. 'My sons spoke of that.'

'They did,' Morrisey said. 'And isn't that the stupidest thing, to try and stop a whole country from drinking?'

'I wouldn't like to be the fellow who proposed that in Ireland.'

'That's what Joe said,' Gloria said with a smile.

'It didn't work, of course,' Morrisey said. 'It made things worse, not better. And the gangs that once ran riot in New York rose up again because they were in charge of the bootlegging. That's the name for the illegal liquor brought in. The New York cops knew what was going on and would turn a blind eye unless there was any trouble.'

Morrisey and Gloria went on to tell Helen and Nellie about the movies and the dances, the concerts and theatres. They spoke of the jazz music that gripped the nation for a while and the very vibrancy of the place, and they were filled with nostalgia for a time that would never return.

'America will survive though,' Morrisey said. 'But after a war of this magnitude, nothing will ever be the same again, I wouldn't have thought. I mean, I never imagined in a million years that I would be here in Northern Ireland and part of the American Navy. I am just glad that I am not one of the fighting forces. I am a mild-mannered man in the main.'

'I think many are that way in peacetime,' Gloria said, remembering Red McCullough. 'Wartime causes different strengths to come into play.'

'You are right, of course,' Morrisey agreed. 'I am just glad that the American Naval Department decided that it was more beneficial for Meadows and me to impart our skills to the young sailors and so I teach mechanics and Meadows teaches them about electrics.'

'I hear tell that that camp you are staying in is a fine place,' Nellie said. 'I have never seen it myself but a few men from Buncrana were at the construction of it.'

'It's some sight all right,' Meadows said.

Morrisey put in, 'Would you like to see around it? We could arrange it and it would be to sort of thank you for your kindness and hospitality.'

'Oh, I don't know . . .' Nellie said. 'Anyway, would we be let?'

'Yes, it will be fine,' Morrisey said. 'We have a fair few civilians working at the camp already – in the library, the launderette and the barber's. Oh, and the canteen, of course.'

'You have all those things on the camp?' Gloria asked, amazed.

Morrisey laughed. 'Yes. Come and see for yourself. We could go back now and clear it with the bosses, and be back to fetch you in a car this afternoon, if you like.'

'Oh, that would be great,' Helen said. 'I would really like to see it, wouldn't you, Gloria?'

'But what about Joe?' Gloria said. 'I think I will give it a miss. I can't just go swanning off.'

'You hardly had time to do any swanning off at all when you were looking after Joe's mother,' Nellie pointed out. 'And I bet Joe won't mind a bit.'

'Oh, all right,' Gloria agreed cautiously. 'I will ask him, but I'm promising nothing.'

'OK,' Meadows said. 'If you could be here, say . . . about half-past two or so?'

'All right, but if I am not here, don't wait for me. And now I best go buy the things I came into Buncrana for in the first place.'

As they made their way home, Gloria told Joe about meeting the American men from the base, and them offering to show her, Helen and Nellie around the camp.

Joe heard the wistful tone in her voice as she went on, 'I still miss America, though I hadn't realised how much till I talked with these men, Morrisey particularly. He was born and bred in New York, and had that particular inflexion in his voice. And it was just lovely to hear that again.'

'I can understand that,' Joe said. 'New York was your home.'

'And this is yours,' Gloria said. 'And though I know that both you and Ben are happy here, I can never look upon it as permanent.'

'It will be very hard to start afresh in a strange place where I would not only have to find a job, but somewhere to live too,' Joe said.

'I know you can't wave a magic wand,' Gloria replied. 'Just as long as you know that I could never settle here.'

'I understand that,' Joe said. 'But while we are here do you want to see around the naval base?'

Gloria shrugged. 'I'm easy, to tell you the truth,' she said. 'It's Helen that's mad keen, and Nellie is nearly as bad. The two men have been filling their heads with tales of the facilities on offer at the camp and they want to see for themselves.'

'It's probably not half as good as they say it is,' Joe said, and then added with a grin, 'You know what they say about all these Americans and how boastful they are.'

Gloria punched Joe playfully on the arm. 'Watch it, you. And shall I go or stay away?'

'Well, I can't see the harm in going for a look.'

'Right,' said Gloria with an emphatic nod of her head. 'I will then.'

FIFTEEN

Gloria never forgot her first sight of Springtown Camp. Neat rows and rows of metal huts with rounded roofs that Morrisey told her were called Quonset huts were set to one end. In front of them was a vast open space where wide paths dissected lawned areas. They led to the central point where the Stars and Stripes fluttered from a large flagpole. The sight of that actually caused a lump to form in Gloria's throat.

Seeing how moved she was, Morrisey said, 'Doesn't it do your heart good to see that flag flying here?'

Gloria nodded. She couldn't trust herself to speak, but she had never ever thought to see the Stars and Stripes fluttering in Ireland, even in the British-ruled six counties. But there was no time to stand and stare, for Meadows was leading them into the building, where a long, wide and airy corridor stretched out before them, doors opening off it.

The first room, the library, was stacked floor to ceiling with books of every size and description. At the tables many men sat reading or studying.

'I think a library is a very good idea,' Helen said as they all left the room. 'My husband, John, was in the British Army and he never had access to such facilities. I know because he was an avid reader and he used to ask me to choose books to put in the parcels I sent him. I never knew if I got it right, unless he asked for something specific.'

'It's not just good for reading for pleasure, though,' Morrisey said. 'Some of my students are in there. Here they have the books they need to hand, and peace and quiet in which to work. Believe me, peace and quiet is what many crave for in a busy military camp.'

'I can well believe that,' Nellie said.

Meadows opened the next door, saying as he did so, 'And this is the fellow who has the men in the camp half scalped, the barber.'

It was like a barber's shop like you might find in any high street, Gloria thought as she surveyed the barber lathering a man's chin. The barber was obviously well used to the sailors' banter, as he had a large grin on his face as he replied in a broad Irish accent, 'Away out of that. If you want to know what scalped is I will demonstrate it willingly.'

'Now you've cooked your goose,' Morrisey said. 'There'll not be a hair left on your head the next time he gets you in that chair. Isn't that right, Paddy?'

'It is right enough,' replied the barber. 'And indeed I might not wait until I have him in the chair to give him a quick tidy-up.'

'Huh,' Meadows said, laughing. 'I would like to see you try.'

Morrisey, with a good-natured wave to the barber, closed the door as he said to Meadows with a sardonic grin, 'I wouldn't argue with the barber if I were you. He that wields the scissors has the power as far as I am concerned. Now, ladies,' Morrisey said, turning to the three women, 'this next is a place that might interest you. The launderette.'

The launderette fascinated the three women as the assistant explained the function of each machine to them. Gloria sighed as she thought how long the washing took her at the little cottage, especially as every drop of water had to be fetched from the well. She'd had to wash every day after Biddy had been taken ill because she had become incontinent. Nellie spoke for them all when she said, 'Well, I wouldn't mind how much washing I had to do if I had a couple of those in my kitchen. I could have the lot finished in no time at all.'

'Quite a few women who work on the camp get their washing done here,' the assistant said. 'I do it for them. For half a crown they have the washing done, and I add another shilling if they want it dried.'

'What a boon that would be to working mothers,' Gloria said as they crossed to the other side of the corridor.

Morrisey opened double doors to reveal a theatre complex, with plush tiered seats in front of the small, but very serviceable stage.

'This is where they put shows on for the men,' he said. 'They have all sorts of entertainment laid on. And through here,' he went on, leading the way, 'is the most important room in the camp, the canteen.'

It was a massive place and Morrisey pointed out the soda fountain and said to one of the women behind the counter, 'Can you pour us all an ice-cream soda, Joan?'

'No problem, sir,' the woman said.

Gloria watched as she poured a drink for them all and then astonished the three women by putting a scoop of ice cream in each one, saying to Gloria as she passed one to her, 'I don't suppose that you are new recruits?'

'No, we're just here for a look-round,' Gloria said.

She took a sip of her drink and found it quite delicious and she told the woman so.

'Glad you like it,' Joan said. 'Since I've worked here I have tasted things that I've never had before. Tell you what, these Americans look after their men.'

'I know,' Helen said. 'We hardly believed what we have seen so far.'

'You're not from round here then?'

'Not Derry, no,' Gloria said. 'We live in Buncrana.'

She noticed that Helen had wandered over to the windows

231

where her mother stood between the two men and they were pointing something out to her. She was about to go over to join them when the woman said, 'Buncrana isn't that far away. I don't suppose you are looking for a job at all? We're pretty short-staffed here.'

Gloria laughed. 'You surprise me. Isn't every young girl in Derry breaking her neck to get in here?'

The woman smiled back. 'Maybe they are, but they don't particularly want young girls. With all these young men about it's asking for trouble.'

'Yes, I suppose it is.'

'It's more mature women they are after,' Joan said. 'Anyway, while the young girls might want to come here, their fathers are dead set against it. There is plenty of work for young girls as machinists in Derry at the moment, for the shirt factories are now turning out the uniforms as well, and the pay is good. Fathers seem to prefer that type of work for their daughters.'

'Yes,' said Gloria, watching a stream of sailors enter the room. 'I can see why.'

The woman moved away to take her place again behind the counter as Helen came up to Gloria. 'What was all that about?'

'The woman was telling me how short-staffed they were,' Gloria said. 'She thought we might be after a job. She says they prefer older, more mature women to work at the camp.'

'Mature, is it?' said Helen with a laugh. 'That leaves the pair of us out then.'

With the calves born and most of the spring planting done, Tom was ready to be off to England to find Molly in mid-March. It was so early the sun wasn't right up, and it was still a little dusky, but Tom was catching the mail boat that sailed at seven thirty and Joe was driving him as far as Derry. Despite the early hour, Gloria and Ben had got up to bid Tom farewell. Ben was quite tearful as he hugged his uncle.

Gloria said, 'You come back soon, Tom Sullivan. Don't you be tempted by the delights of the big city.'

'There's never a fear of that,' Tom said with a laugh.

'Let's away then,' Joe said. 'Derry is a fair step, especially with this horse, and the train waits for no man.'

Tom pulled himself up beside his brother and with the flick of the reins they were away.

Gloria gave a sigh. Tom was a quiet and mild-mannered man, and yet she knew the place wouldn't be the same without him, and she would be glad to see him back again where he belonged.

She wasn't the only one to feel that way. Tom wished the ordeal was behind him too and he said this to Joe. 'Course,' he went on, 'you would hardly understand how I feel. Travelling from place to place is probably nothing to you, but I am as nervous as a kitten.'

'Well, the only place I chose to go to was America,' Joe pointed out. 'London, and even here, was forced on me because of circumstances.'

'Aye, I know that, but you seem to be able to settle really well in any place.'

'Well, this was my home.'

'But sure, that was many years ago. You are nothing like the young fellow that went away from here. How could you be when you have had so many different experiences and all? Many men here are like me – dull old sticks who have never left the place of their birth and have no real desire to, and a lot of their wives are the same. You seem able to fit in anywhere, but I know Gloria doesn't feel the same way at all.'

'She doesn't,' Joe said. 'She would like to leave here now that I am recovered, but even she doesn't know how that is to be achieved. I mean, the world is still at war and though the bombing raids have eased considerably, they have left devastation in their wake. I would like to bet that more than a few people in many cities in England are living in some form of temporary accommodation, and if we left here I would have to find somewhere to live as well as a job. Added to that, Ben definitely doesn't want to go. He was badly frightened in London, and the peace and tranquillity of this place is what he needs right now. Gloria sees that too.'

'So here you'll have to stay then, for the time being at least?' Tom said.

'Looks like it,' Joe said, trying to hurry the plodding horse. 'Will that bother you at all?'

'Why should it bother me?' Tom asked. 'I am glad you're here. With Mammy the way she was, few people ever came to the house and she gave out to me if ever I left it for any reason. I often felt the lack of company, and I was as pleased as Punch when Gloria wrote and asked if you could all come here until you should be completely recovered. I am sure that eventually you will leave, but until that time comes I will treasure this time that we have together.'

There was a lump in Joe's throat as he thought of Tom toiling ceaselessly as one lonely day folded into another, and became weeks and months and then years, and for what? He must have thought at times of his pointless existence, but it would serve no purpose to speak of that now. Instead he said. 'We owe you a lot, Tom, and both of us are aware of it. If and when we leave here I know that Ben will miss his Uncle Tom that he loves dearly.'

Tom's face lit up. 'Ah, it's a fine boy you have there.'

'I know it,' said Joe. 'He is the very light of my life, and Gloria's too, of course.'

'And mine as well,' Tom said. 'In a way he is lucky that so many people care for him, but then he is an easy boy to love.'

Again came that stab of guilt that Tom would never experience fatherhood, never know the love of a woman, and Joe could think of nothing further to say as the horse plodded along the road towards Derry. They settled into silence as the miles unfolded.

Eventually the station came into view. Tom wrinkled his nose as the smoky, damp air of the station assailed his nostrils and he surveyed the waiting train. It was like a panting beast, he thought, watching the smoke billowing from the front of it and hissing steam seeping along its wheels.

'You'll be fine,' Joe assured him, sensing his nervousness. 'Follow the rest of the people and you'll not go far wrong.'

'Huh, you don't know me.'

'Are you kidding?' Joe replied. 'I know you very well, and I also know you are not as green as you are cabbage-looking, so hurry up and get on that train or it will go without you. You'll be a seasoned traveller when you get back.'

'I doubt that.'

'And take all the time you need,' Joe said, putting his arms around his brother. 'Give my love to them all and look after yourself.'

'I will,' Tom said. 'Oh, I will indeed.'

Six days later, with Tom expected home, Gloria told Helen of the strange telegram that had arrived at the cottage.

'Is that all it said?'

'Yeah, just that he was unavoidably delayed and he would explain it all in a letter later.'

'But what on earth can have delayed him?'

Gloria shrugged. 'Your guess is as good as mine. Joe is worried for, as he said, it is just such an odd thing for Tom to do. He will be on tenterhooks until he hears more. He was all for writing to Molly but I said not to. Maybe whatever has delayed Tom has nothing to do with her, or maybe he doesn't want her to know of it. I'm sure he will write and tell us all as soon as he can.'

However, it was over a week later, with Ben asking every day when his uncle was coming home, that Tom eventually wrote, and Joe was almighty glad that Ben had gone to school by the time Gloria handed him the envelope.

The letter ran to pages and pages, and Gloria watched the colour drain from Joe's face as he read. At one point he felt for the chair and sat down heavily as if he wasn't sure his legs would hold him up any longer.

When he finished, the eyes he turned on Gloria were moist.

'What is it, Joe?' Gloria asked anxiously.

'What isn't it?' Joe said. 'You know the life of drugs and prostitution those perverts had mapped out for Molly?'

'Yes.'

'Well, that has been Aggie's lot for years,' Joe said. 'Tom found her on the streets. Actually, she propositioned him.'

'Ah, dear God!'

'Tom has her away from the place now, thank God,' Joe said. 'Here, you had best read it for yourself.'

As Gloria read the letter she felt the blood in her veins run cold as she imagined the despair of the young girl arriving in Birmingham to find the woman she had been sent to, the only one able to help her, gone. Tom said she would have perished if it hadn't been for the kindness of the prostitutes that took her in and cared for her. When salvation of a sort was offered to her by a man called Levingstone, who wanted to marry Aggie despite the fact that she had 'entertained' punters in his club, he had been killed by a man named Finch.

Tears were trailing down Gloria's face as she cried brokenly, 'Ah, Joe, what this poor girl has suffered all her life and through no fault of her own . . .'

'I know,' Joe said. 'Two men have tried to destroy Aggie's whole life – McAllister and this bloody slimy bastard Finch. If you read on, you will find that when Aggie tried to break out of a life of prostitution it was Finch again that abducted her and forced her back onto the streets by filling her full of drink and drugs and then withholding them. I tell you, Gloria, if I have my way he is not going to get away with it.'

Gloria didn't blame Joe one bit for feeling so angry. Hell, she was angry herself, though she didn't know the poor woman personally, but for such things to happen to an innocent young girl was almost unbelievable. She remembered the cuttings from the newspaper about Molly, who had been rescued just in time from a fate like Aggie's, and she felt sick with disgust that such things should go on in a so-called civilised society. Tom at least knew where his duty lay.

I was powerless to prevent Aggie making the headlong dash to Birmingham in 1901, for I was just a boy. Now I feel it is my place to stay here, doing the job I was unable to do then, and that is care for my sister for as long as it takes.

'Dreadful, isn't it?' Joe said.

Gloria nodded dumbly.

'Obviously he can't think of coming home just yet.'

'No,' said Gloria faintly. She could understand that Tom couldn't leave until she was better, but how long would that be? And what then? Would he just say goodbye and come home? She shook her head and fought down her panic because she felt as if strands were winding around her, holding her down to the farm for ever.

'Gloria, is anything the matter?' Helen asked her friend the following Saturday, as they walked the main street of Buncrana. 'You seem burdened down with sadness.'

Gloria hesitated. Joe had said that the news in Tom's letter was family business and that was how it must stay, but surely that didn't extend to the McEvoys. Jack and Nellie were good friends of Tom, and they knew all about Molly. Tom had even taken them the cuttings from the papers and they had been as horrified as he was. So she said, 'We got a letter from Tom the day before yesterday.'

'Did it say why he was delayed?'

'Oh, yes,' Gloria said miserably. 'He explained it all very well and I will tell you because if I don't tell someone I will go mad. First, though, I must have your solemn promise that you will not breathe a word of it to another soul, apart from your parents and possibly Cathy.'

'You have that, of course,' Helen said. 'The McEvoys are very good at keeping secrets, but it does sound terribly mysterious.'

'Believe me, the things Tom told us of were not mysterious, they were disgusting and depraved,' Gloria said. 'The very night that Tom was booked to come home he found Aggie.'

'Aggie?' Helen said. 'Was she was the sister that Mammy said was supposed to have run off with the gypsies, though she never believed it?'

'She ran off with no gypsies,' Gloria said. 'Though, God knows, she might have fared better if she had. It wasn't Tom that found Aggie, to be absolutely accurate, it was Aggie found Tom.'

She went on to tell Helen what had really happened to the girl. 'Can you imagine her despair, Helen, when she found the woman who was to help her gone?'

'Oh God! That poor girl . . .'

'And without the prostitutes befriending her she would have died.'

'I know,' Helen said. 'You don't think about that side of prostitutes, do you? They must have the same feelings as everyone else.'

'Well, to be honest, I have never spent much time thinking of them at all,' Gloria said. 'Yet I suppose in a way she had fallen in with possibly the only ones in that city who wouldn't judge her, and who cared for her when she lost the baby.'

'And in doing so they sealed her fate,' Helen pointed out.

'Yes, they did that all right,' Gloria conceded. 'I imagine few girls sucked into such a life would have a brother like

Tom who, once he found out what his sister was doing, was willing and able to help her.'

'But how did Tom recognise her?' Helen asked. 'There is a blackout in England.'

'Someone was waving a torch about,' Gloria told Helen. 'It lit up Tom's face for an instant and Aggie knew who he was.'

'I have never heard anything so tragically sad,' Helen said. 'I have tasted unhappiness and loss and so have you, but my heart bleeds for that poor woman and what she has gone through all her life.'

'Yes, and it all traces back to that bloody dancing teacher McAllister,' Gloria said.

'Quite,' Helen said with feeling. 'Mammy said he died shortly after. Good riddance, I say. God Almighty! The damage he did to poor Aggie.'

'McAllister's wife told Tom that Aggie wasn't the first and probably wouldn't have been the last either. Think of how many young lives he might have ruined.'

'Aye,' Helen said with a sigh, then added in a quiet voice, 'The wife didn't . . . well, you know, do him in, like?'

It was on the tip of Gloria's tongue to tell Helen the truth, but she stopped herself. That secret really had to be kept within the family. Even years on, there could be dire consequences for McAllister's wife and Tom. So she said, 'I have no idea how McAllister died, and after all this time it hardly matters.'

'No, it doesn't, of course, and at least Aggie is out of it now, though she has lost so many years.'

'Yet Tom says she bears no resentment to anyone,' Gloria went on, as they walked a little faster. 'She's just as he remembered her from a boy and Tom is staying with Aggie for as long as it takes. I hope they're back soon. I am not completely heartless but, God, I am bored out of my brain.'

'And me,' Helen admitted, looking up and down the narrow main street. 'People seem to stagnate here. Some people like that, of course.'

'I am not one of them,' Gloria said. 'I used to have a job when we were in London. I miss the company, and the money too would be useful. The trouble with children is that they grow and nothing Ben wore last spring and summer will look at him now. And he says his shoes are pinching his toes.'

'Well,' Helen said, 'you and I must put on our thinking caps and find something the two of us can do.'

The weeks passed, Easter was over, and they were nearly at the end of April. Joe was still fretting about Finch and how he couldn't be allowed to get away with what he had done to his sister.

'Don't keep on about it,' Gloria snapped one day. 'It doesn't do Ben any good to hear it, for one thing, and as you don't even know where the man lives, you can't do anything even if you wanted to.'

'I do now,' Joe said triumphantly, shaking out the letter he had got from his brother just that morning. 'Paul Simmons, that man that Molly's father worked for, found out. He even knows where he hangs out in the evening.'

'So is he to be involved in this too?'

'No,' Joe said firmly. 'I told you before, this is family business.' Then he smiled and went on, 'Anyway, according to Tom, the only one of the family that Paul Simmons wants to get involved with is Aggie.'

'What do you mean, get involved with Aggie? How?'

'You know,' Joe said. 'The normal way. They're fond of one another.'

Gloria hadn't met Aggie, but she had read the letter Tom sent them describing the condition of Aggie when he had first seen her. He said she was just skin and bone, her fine hair steel grey and hung round her face in greasy trails, and she was dressed like some old trampish woman. The image he depicted had stayed in Gloria's mind and she was stunned that a woman like that, and one who had been on the streets, could be found attractive by any man.

'Does he know everything?' she asked.

'Of course he does,' Joe answered. 'It wasn't her fault, Gloria.'

'I know that,' Gloria said. 'It's just that some men aren't that concerned with whose fault such things are.'

'He has offered Tom a job in his factory as well,' Joe said. 'Tom was getting very strapped for cash, and he wants to stay in Birmingham until Molly's wedding, at least.'

'And then what?'

'Then he said we will look at the whole thing again.'

Gloria sighed for she had guessed as much. 'And what d'you intend to do about this man Finch, Joe?'

'What do you think?' Joe growled out. 'He has to pay for what he did to Aggie, and this time it's down to me!'

'How d'you work that out?'

'Tom dealt with McAllister, the first man who abused Aggie,' Joe said. 'And, poor fellow, it coloured his life ever after. Finch is mine. Thank God I have got my strength back.'

'Joe, surely this isn't the way,' Gloria reasoned. 'It's monstrous that you should undertake some sort of vendetta like this. You are not in the Wild West of America now. Let the authorities deal with it.'

'They wouldn't believe Aggie,' Joe said. 'Why would they? They would see her as a street woman, while Finch is probably a pillar of the community. He's certainly rich, and we know how many doors money opens, and he's influential. He's what many would see as a fine upstanding man and they would take his word every time against a depraved street woman.'

'But, Joe,' Gloria insisted, 'you can't do this kind of thing. Meting out justice yourself is against the law. You could get into big trouble or get hurt, or both, and in the end it might make things worse not better.'

'I'll have to take that chance,' Joe said. 'Tom will be with me, but I want him to take no hand in it. I want to beat that man to pulp myself.'

'Ooh, don't,' Gloria said. 'Violence isn't the way, surely.'

'It is the only way with scum like that,' Joe ground out. 'The only language a man like him understands. I can't believe you, Gloria. You read what he did to my sister. What did you think I was going to do to him, shake him by the hand?'

Gloria shook her head. She had hoped that he never found out where the man was, and felt annoyed at Paul Simmons for passing the Sullivan brothers information, for he must know they would act on it. But then if Joe was right, and he was keen on Aggie, maybe he too thought the man should get his just deserts.

'Joe,' she said, holding on to his arms and staring into his eyes, 'listen to me. I don't want you to do this. It's wrong and it's dangerous, and if you have any feeling for me at all, then give it up.'

Joe shook his head. 'Sorry, my mind is made up. This is for Aggie.'

'You are putting the wishes of a sister you haven't seen for over forty years above the welfare of your wife and child. Do we count for nothing?'

'I am surprised that you even have to ask that question,' Joe said. 'You mean the world to me. You should know that.'

'Then give up this mad notion,' Gloria cried.

'No,' Joe said gravely. 'I am afraid I can't do that. This isn't something Aggie has asked me to do or expects me to do. She will know nothing about it until the deed is done.'

Gloria remembered back to the time that Joe decided to volunteer as an auxiliary fireman, when she acknowledged that once he had made up his mind, wild horses would never make him change it. She had tried and failed to prevent him doing something then that had nearly taken his life. Then he had seemed to have no thought in his head for her or Ben, and this was the same. Joe could see nothing except that he had to avenge the violation of his sister. He didn't seem to care that it was against the law.

'Joe, listen to me, please!' she begged. 'You could end up in prison for this.'

Joe shrugged. 'So be it.'

'I see. So where does that leave me and Ben?'

'I have to do this, Gloria.'

'I say again, Joe, where does that leave Ben and me?' Gloria almost hissed. 'Don't you have a duty to us first?'

Joe stared at his wife. She had no siblings so how could she possibly understand the bond that held them together and the guilt he felt that Tom had borne the brunt of all of Aggie's problems so far? He had been no help to either of them, and that thought was eating away at him. It seemed to supersede everything else. 'I would feel less of a man if I was to let this go now, or let Tom deal with it like he did last time,' he said at last.

'I'll tell Ben that then, shall I?' Gloria said. 'Like I will tell him the same if you end up in a hospital bed, or even on a mortuary slab, as you could do. It can't have escaped your notice that this man Finch is dangerous. He has already killed the man that Aggie was to marry. What will he do to you?'

'I think that I am well able for Finch.'

'Are there no words I can say that can turn you away from this mad notion?' Gloria asked.

'None,' said Joe. 'The decision is made. The die is now cast.'

Gloria knew it was, which made her feel helpless and frustrated. That night she cried herself to sleep, the first time she had done that since she had landed in Ireland.

A few days after this, with Joe and Gloria barely speaking, Joe told Gloria that he had arranged for Jack McEvoy to take over the milking that weekend, as he intended to go to England.

'Didn't he find that strange?'

'No, I told him that as I was not going to be able to get

243

to Molly's wedding, because we had already decided that you and Ben will go in my stead, I wanted to meet Molly, who Tom keeps on about, and check out the chap she is marrying. He didn't think that strange at all.'

'Yeah,' Gloria snapped. 'Well, I think that he would take a different viewpoint altogether if he knew what you would really be at.'

'Well, he'll never know that, will he?' Joe said warningly.

'Don't look at me like that, Joe,' Gloria snapped. 'Though I abhor what you intend to do I will tell no tales. Quite apart from anything else, I would be almost ashamed to.'

'When I told you about Tom, you said you could understand that he wanted to make McAllister pay for what he had done,' Joe said.

'I know, but Tom didn't intend to kill the man,' Gloria said. 'Though I know that it's a good job that he did.'

'Tom was just a boy of thirteen,' Joe told her. 'That was why he couldn't meet McAllister on equal terms. Between me and Finch it will be different.'

SIXTEEN

The day before Joe was due to leave, Gloria called at the post office and asked Helen to go for a walk, giving the excuse that it was too nice an afternoon to miss. It had been a lovely day, but the truth was she was too churned up about Joe, and relations between the two of them were so strained she couldn't have stayed in the cottage a moment longer.

Helen knew that there was something ailing her friend, and though she had no idea of Joe's intention, she did think Gloria's strange mood might have something to do with the fact that Joe was going to Birmingham. She thought Gloria might unburden herself once they were away from other people and so she suggested they walk by the River Crana, which flowed on the edge of the town.

'Good idea,' Nellie said, overhearing this plan. 'Do you both good to get a bit of fresh air, especially you, Gloria, for you are as white as a sheet.'

The two set off down the hill, the sun warm on their backs, the promise of hotter days to come. Even to Gloria's jaundiced eyes the countryside had never looked lovelier. The trees were heavy with fragrant blossom, and the hedgerows alive with colour. When they reached the shore they wandered down to the harbour, empty of fishermen today, and the water was sparkling in the sunshine.

It all seemed peaceful and tranquil, and it seemed almost

inconceivable to Gloria that in the morning Joe would be going off to Birmingham for the express purpose of beating someone to pulp. She felt sick with fear for him, and also slight disgust at what he intended.

'What is it?' Helen said. 'I know something is bothering you.'

Gloria turned to face Helen, seeing the concern on her face. She wanted to tell Helen everything – not just what Joe was about, but also how it had changed something in the way she felt about him. She fought with her conscience, but before she was able to say anything, she saw Helen's face light up and she said, 'Hello. What brings you this way?'

Gloria spun round and saw Morrisey and Meadows coming towards them and knew the moment to tell Helen was gone.

'We were looking for you,' Meadows said. 'Your mother said we would find you here. We have a proposition to put to you.'

'Oh, yes?' Helen said, smiling at Meadows archly, her eyebrows raised in enquiry. 'And what sort of proposition would that be?'

'Well, we were wondering if either or both of you want a job?'

'I do,' Helen said, turning for home. 'I would be a lot happier, because I feel bad living off my parents. But what sort of work are we talking of, and where?'

'Springtown Camp has vacancies in the canteen at the moment,' Meadows said.

'Are you mad?' Helen said. 'We would get ourselves talked about.'

'And I am married,' Gloria stared flatly.

'That doesn't preclude you,' Morrisey said. 'You wouldn't be the only one there. In fact, they like married women.'

'Yes, but Joe would never stand for it, would he, Gloria?' Helen asked.

Suddenly Gloria remembered Joe's set face when he told her what he was going to Birmingham for, and that none of her pleading had moved him one jot. He hadn't asked her opinion – far from it – so why should she value his or his permission either?

'I had a job in London, she said defensively.

'Not in a camp full of sailors you didn't,' Helen said. 'Anyway, just because there are vacancies there is no guarantee that we will be offered a job. They'll likely have hundreds after them.'

'Not that many,' Morrisey said. Then he turned to Gloria and said, 'That time you went for a look around you were talking to a woman in the canteen, remember?'

'Yes, Joan I think her name was.'

'That's right,' Morrisey said. 'Joan Reilly. She is the manageress and she remembered you.'

'After all this time?' Gloria said incredulously. 'I only saw her for a few minutes and that was months ago.'

'They've been run off their feet at times in the canteen, because in January a construction battalion arrived at the base but they weren't given any extra staff to cope with the inflated numbers. Then last week two girls announced they were leaving and Joan remembered you two,' Morrisey explained. 'She said you were just the right sort of age and she thought you both very suitable, especially you, Gloria, because she said you could speak the lingo.'

'I would like to have a go,' Helen said. 'I think I might enjoy it, but I wouldn't go without you, Gloria.'

'Well, I'd like to try for a job too,' Gloria said. 'The money would be very useful and as a few people travel to Derry to work just now they have the trains organised to cope with it.'

'Anyway, if you are interested she would like to see you Saturday afternoon.'

Gloria remembered that Joe would be in England then,

and she pushed down the thought that he might be dead, dying or arrested and said, 'I think I could make that.'

'Well, we can certainly go up and see the woman on Saturday,' Helen said. 'No harm done if we decide to go no further with it. D'you really think Joe will let you do this?'

Gloria shrugged. 'To be honest,' she said, 'I really don't know what Joe thinks of anything any more. But I shall put it to him at the first opportunity, and stress how important it is for me to have this chance.'

'You might have an easier job with Joe than I will have talking Mammy round,' Helen said. 'She is bound to disapprove.'

However, Nellie had seen the restlessness in Helen and knew that she was too active a girl to be idle. If she didn't find employment soon, she might return to Birmingham, and Nellie didn't want her going back to a city full of dark memories. Maybe to take a job only six miles from her home would be a solution of sorts, and if Gloria was to go too then they could look after each other.

That night, as soon as the chores were done and Ben in bed, Gloria told Joe about meeting the petty officers and the proposal they had put to them both. However, she didn't mention going up to see the place on Saturday afternoon, though the words were hardly out of her mouth anyway when Joe nearly bit her head off.

He was incensed. 'What d'you mean they offered the pair of you a job at the Springtown Camp in Derry?' he cried.

'Ssh,' Gloria cautioned. 'You'll disturb Ben. He'll probably not be asleep just yet.'

'Never mind that,' Joe said irritably 'What's this all about?'

'You know what it's about,' Gloria said. 'I told you plainly. That's just how it happened.'

'Well, I hope you told them straight that it is out of the question.'

'No,' Gloria said quietly, 'I didn't, and don't shout at me.'

'Good God, woman, you damned well need shouting at,' Joe exploded. 'You can put that hare-brained notion right out of your head.'

'I think not,' Gloria said. 'I don't need your permission.'

'This is monstrous, Gloria,' Joe thundered. 'Jesus, I am a mild-mannered man, God knows, but you are enough to try the patience of a saint. You will take no job in any camp, American or otherwise. You will not shame me like this.'

'Oh, yes?' Gloria retorted. 'What about you shaming me? How d'you think I will feel if, because of this stupid scheme you and your brother have cooked up, you end up dead or in gaol?'

'Is that what this is all about?' Joe cried. 'Tit for tat?'

'No, it isn't,' Gloria almost hissed. 'But how many times have you made up your mind about something without discussing it with me and not given a cent for how I might feel about it?'

'This isn't about me,' Joe snapped, feeling they had gone off the subject. 'It's about you and this totally unsuitable job.'

'I don't happen to think it is all that unsuitable.'

'I can't believe that I am hearing this,' Joe said. 'You are not taking it and that's that. You must obey me in this.'

'Oh, yes?' Gloria said sarcastically. 'Why is that, exactly?'

'Gloria, I am your husband.'

'Yeah, that's right,' Gloria snapped back. 'That doesn't make you my bloody keeper.'

Joe regarded his wife and saw just how furious she was. Her eyes were flashing fire and so although he was angry and outraged himself, he knew their yelling at each other would achieve nothing. So he said in a conciliatory manner, 'You must see, Gloria, that this will not do at all. Anyway, aren't there girls the length and breadth of Derry to work in the place?'

'There are no girls queuing up to work at the camp,' Gloria said. 'The woman I spoke to in the canteen the time we were taken to look around it said a lot of parents wouldn't let their daughters work there, and prefer them to go into the shirt factories. And the commander at the camp prefers older, more settled women rather than flighty girls with all those young men. I wouldn't be the only married woman there, and Helen is mad keen but wants me to go with her.'

'Helen is single.'

'Yes, she is,' Gloria agreed. 'She's a respectable widow and not seeking a husband amongst young Yankee sailor boys.'

'Why the hell did they think of you and Helen anyway?'

'The time we went to see around the camp we were taken into the canteen. The manageress asked us if we were looking for a job. She said we were just the type of woman they would go for at the camp, especially me because I am American. Now they have two girls leaving and the manageress remembered us. The two petty officers came to tell us that because they know where Helen lives. They just told us about the vacancies and asked us if we are interested. I imagine it will be up to the manageress, or the camp commander, or both, whether we would be offered a job or not.'

'But you would like to work there, wouldn't you?' Joe said. 'I can see it in your eyes.'

Gloria nodded. 'Yes, Joe. And I will tell you one of the reasons why. If we ever move from here, we will have to start again and we can't do that without money. I can just about manage on what you give me each week. There is nothing to save at all.'

Joe knew that.

'I mean, Ben is always needing new clothes and shoes,' Gloria went on. 'The boy is growing and I will not send him to school like some sort of ragamuffin.'

'I'm not suggesting that you do,' Joe said stiffly.

'Well, where is the money to come from, Joe? Answer me that?' Gloria demanded. 'Shall I pluck it out of thin air or what?'

'All right then,' Joe said. 'But why the camp? Why don't you do what the other girls are doing and go into one of the shirt factories?'

'I don't know if they have any vacancies,' Gloria said. 'And anyway, I want to be surrounded by American people again and hear the sounds of home, because I still miss it, even after all these years.'

Joe listened to the wistfulness in Gloria's voice, yet he shook his head as he said, 'You know, if I agree to this, many of the townspeople will be scandalised. For Helen it will be bad enough, but for you, a wife and mother, to take up work in a camp full of young, unattached men, would be completely untenable to them, whatever argument we put up to justify it.'

'I know,' Gloria said, 'but they have never taken to me anyway, so it's no odds. Helen really is my only friend, and if she goes to work at the camp and I don't, where will that leave me?'

Joe was silent as Gloria's words sank in. None of those in Buncrana had seen the courageous side to Gloria that he had, and all that she had put up with. This was the first time that she had ever asked for anything for herself, and something too that would help the family.

'Joe, what are you thinking?'

'Of our lives together,' Joe said. 'It has been a bit of a roller coaster of a ride so far, I think. I never really expected you to conform to Buncrana's standards. It would have been like trying to fit a square peg into a round hole. But then, I had never envisaged that we would ever come back here to live.'

Gloria shrugged impatiently, 'So, what are you saying, Joe?'

'Well, I understand all you say about the job, but with me going off in the morning it isn't something we need to decide here and now, surely. I need to give some thought to it. When this business is over this weekend, we will talk again.'

'There's no time for that,' Gloria cried. 'The vacancies will likely be gone unless I act fast.'

'I can't help that.'

Anger pulsed through Gloria's veins again. 'No, and you don't care either,' she yelled. 'That's what you hope: that they are gone and so is my chance.'

Joe didn't speak. He felt that he had conceded a great deal by even agreeing to think about a potential job for Gloria in a military camp, never mind prepared to talk it over with her on his return. He knew it was far more than many of his friends in Buncrana would do and Gloria still wasn't satisfied.

He was suddenly furiously angry with her and he strode across the room and snatched his jacket from the hook behind the door.

'And where are you going now?' Gloria demanded.

'Out,' Joe said. 'To walk the bad humour off myself before I say something I will probably regret later.'

Joe left the next day, straight after he had done the milking, and Ben got up early to see his father off.

'Can I come with you as far as the station?'

'You'll be late for school.'

'No, I won't,' said Ben. 'It's hours yet.'

'See what your mother says.'

'Why don't you?' Ben said.

Joe looked at Gloria framed in the doorway of the cottage. He had the urge to take her in his arms and forget the quarrel, but he knew Gloria might reject his embrace and he couldn't have borne that.

'The lad wants to come as far as the station,' he said. 'That all right?'

Gloria didn't answer him. She had expected Ben to ask that, and she looked directly at him and said, 'You come straight back, mind.'

'I will.'

'Here, put your coat on,' Gloria said, taking it from the back of the door and handing it to him. 'It's early enough to be chilly.'

As Ben shrugged himself into it, Joe glanced over his head to Gloria and said, 'Goodbye, then.'

Gloria met his gaze levelly. 'Goodbye, Joe.'

Joe sighed and as he picked up his case, he saw Ben's eyes full of reproach, staring at him, and knew that he should have risked Gloria's reaction and bid farewell to her properly. Oh, well, too late now, he thought as he turned on his heel and strode up the lane with his son beside him.

'You will come back, won't you, Dad?' Ben asked his father earnestly.

'Course I'll come back, Ben,' Joe assured him. 'Why wouldn't I come back?'

Ben gave a shrug. 'I don't know why. But maybe it's what grown-ups say, like Uncle Tom did. He never came back, did he?'

'Well, he had some unfinished business to attend to,' Joe said. 'I told you at the time.'

'So what if you have some unfinished business as well?'

'I won't.'

'How d'know?' Ben persisted. 'I mean, Uncle Tom didn't know before he went, 'cos you said he was due back when he sent that telegram.'

'With Tom something came up at the last minute,' Joe said, and added with a smile, 'And, no, before you ask, the same thing won't happen to me.'

'And you'll want to come back?'

'Why wouldn't I want to come back?'

'Because you're not friendly with Mom,' Ben said flatly. 'I heard you shouting at each other last night.'

Joe was about to brush him off when he saw Ben's big eyes staring at him and knew that if their arguing had entered into his life, then he deserved at least a semblance of the truth. 'Your mother and I have disagreed over something, that's all,' he said. 'You and your friends must have disagreements sometimes.'

'Yeah, we do,' Ben said. 'But we make it up again, and you and Mom haven't yet.'

'We will, Ben. Honestly we will.'

'Mom says that you should never let the sun go down and still be angry with someone,' Ben said.

'That's sound advice, Ben,' Joe said. 'Pity your mother and I didn't follow it.'

Gloria watched till Joe and Ben were out of sight and then she turned and went into the cottage, her heart full of regret. She didn't approve of what Joe intended doing, but at the very least he risked being injured. What if something happened to him and she had let him go without so much as a kind word? That stupid quarrel, she thought, could have been handled differently.

She had the urge now to take to her heels and run after Joe and say she was sorry, bid him a proper farewell and urge him to take care.

But she remembered his speculative eyes on her as she had stood in the doorway. Surely if he had any feeling for her he would have made some move towards her. Obviously something was wrong in the very fabric of their marriage. She sank into a chair before the fire, put her head in her hands and wept.

As the train drew nearer to Birmingham, Joe told himself to put all thoughts of Gloria and the job in the camp to one side, because he was on a mission. The whole purpose of this weekend was not just to see Molly, but to help Tom track Finch down and deal with him, and as soon as possible. He had no room in his mind for anything but hatred for the man.

Tom was waiting for him at New Street Station, as Joe knew he would be, and he was delighted to see his brother was a more contented and happier man than he had ever seen. They had the carriage to themselves on the train that was taking them on the last leg of their journey, to Boldmere Road in Sutton Coldfield, and Joe was glad of it because he wanted to impress upon Tom that Finch was his problem and that he would deal with him.

First, though, Tom pointed out some of the bomb damage as the train travelled out of the city centre. 'I was shocked to the core when I first came. I wasn't surprised at the numbers of dead and injured, though of course it was a terrible tragedy, but I was surprised, looking at the destruction, that so many were left alive,' he said.

'It is a terrible way to live,' Joe told him. 'Cowering night after night in a shelter as Gloria and Ben did, hearing the droning planes above you and the whine and whistle of the bombs and the crashes of the explosions. It was small wonder that Ben was a nervous wreck when he first went to Ireland, but the very worst thing of all was the loss of so many good friends. Even Ben lost friends he was at school with.'

'That must have been dreadful.'

'It was,' Joe said. 'And often I had to deal with the aftermath of the raids, trying to rescue as many as I could. Gloria doesn't know the half of it. I couldn't ever bring myself to tell her. It would upset her so much. It's an horrendous way to wage war on innocent men, women and children. But another innocent victim is Aggie, and Finch is going to pay for what he did. So don't forget, this is my fight.'

'Joe, I don't think you know what you are taking on.'

'I do,' Joe insisted. 'You keep watch. I don't want the two of us to end up in gaol.'

'I told you what happened to that man Aggie was engaged to marry.'

'Yes, but as you also said, Finch knows nothing about us,' Joe reminded him. 'We have the element of surprise.'

'Are you absolutely sure about this?'

'As sure as I have ever been about anything.'

'Come on then,' Tom said, as the train slowed. 'This is Wylde Green. Boldmere Road is only a step from here.'

'No sign of much bomb damage here, at any rate,' Joe said as they walked through tree-lined roads.

'No, Sutton Coldfield got away light in comparison to some places,' Tom said. 'No industry, you see, though they have camps of soldiers Jerry mustn't have known about. And here we are,' he went on, opening the little gate that led to a very small garden, the large house set back only slightly from the road.

He opened the door and led the way up the first flight of stairs then the second, saying as he did so, 'I was lucky to get this. I was desperate to get Aggie away and I had searched all morning. I was in the estate agent's when a young man came in to drop keys off. We got talking, as you do, and he said he had just finished renovating this house, which had been turned into three flats, and he understood the top one was empty if I was interested.'

'You were lucky.'

'I know I was,' Tom said. 'Property is at a premium, and any with money are doing what my landlord has done: buying up big houses and converting them.'

'Makes sense.'

'I'll say,' Tom said. 'I'd do it myself if I had the wherewithal.'

Aggie had heard them on the stairs and now she opened the door. Joe looked at the woman he hadn't seen for over forty years. It was a very emotional moment, for he never thought he would see Aggie again in the whole of his life.

She was still slender, and though her hair was streaked with grey strands and her face showed the march of the years, her eyes were dancing in her head, and her voice just as soft as he remembered.

'Welcome, Joe. A thousand times welcome,' she said.

Then she threw her arms around him and hugged him tight and his eyes grew moist as he realised that, despite all that had happened to her, the essence of Aggie was still there.

He could not understand the mind of the man who would wish to hurt and abuse such a lovely person, and fury against Finch coursed through him. He hid it well, though, for Aggie must have no idea of what he intended to do that night.

After a meal, Tom asked Aggie if she minded him and Joe going out for a few jars. Aggie had no objection at all, but didn't say that she had a date with Paul Simmons that evening, for their relationship was tentative and very new.

'You won't be lonely on your own?' Tom asked anxiously.

'I am not a child to be minded,' she said with a smile. 'Go and enjoy yourselves.'

'Aggie is another like you,' Joe said as they reached the street. 'She hasn't a nasty bone in her body.'

'And with Finch dealt with, the last shreds of fear will fall from her,' Tom said. 'Let's hope that will be tonight.'

Tom had the name of the club that Finch used and he and Joe located it easily, as it was on one of the roads off Broad Street that led down to the canal. It wasn't open and they didn't expect it to be, for people went to these places when others were thinking of going to bed. Not wanting to be spotted hanging about, and also to waste time, they went off to a nearby pub, not to drink too much, but just enough to fuel the rage building up in Joe.

It was as they finished their second pint and the clock read ten o'clock that Joe said, 'Let's go. I'm ready.'

He knew what Finch looked like, for Tom had shown him a picture from the *Evening Mail* where he had been photographed opening something or other, but in the blackout the darkness was almost complete. Joe wondered if they might not recognise him until it was too late, but a bonus was they could go right up by the door and the few now beginning to filter into the club wouldn't know they were there.

Finch came by taxi. They heard his nasal tones as he talked to the taxi driver. Then he got out and turned on the torch he held to see the money in his wallet, and they knew they had their man and that he was alone.

Joe stealthily moved forward. He waited until the taxi had driven off and Finch was almost at the door of the club, and then he pounced. Finch, taken totally unawares, gave a yelp of surprise and alarm, before a hand was slapped across his mouth so hard that he felt his teeth bruising his lips. The other arm held him so tightly that he was having trouble drawing breath and was unable to struggle much, as Joe virtually carried him to the towpath where he threw him to the ground with force.

He then pulled him to his feet and began pummelling into him. Tom melted into the darkness to watch the shadowy figures who were illuminated duskily now and then by the moon peeping out from behind the clouds. He saw Joe punching Finch from side to side, parrying his efforts to defend himself with ease.

Joe suddenly powered a hefty punch to Finch's abdomen. 'That's for Aggie,' he ground out, and Finch groaned and staggered, but recovered his balance as the name reverberated in his head.

After extensive searches had failed to locate Aggie, he had assumed – everyone had assumed – that she had thrown herself into the canal, and he had been annoyed that she had escaped his clutches. Now it seemed the bitch was still alive and this man trying to use him as a punchbag had something to do with her escape. With an angered cry he fell upon his assailant with renewed vigour.

Joe was ready for him, however. He punched Finch hard in the face, and then dealt another to his abdomen, doubling him up. The next blow caused Finch to fall to his knees.

Then his hands, which he put out to save himself, came in contact with a hefty lump of wood on the ground and he got to his feet clutching it.

'Look out!' Tom called when, just for a moment in the moonlight, he had seen Finch circling Joe with the wood held menacingly in his hands.

'Come on, big boy,' Finch taunted. 'Let's see what you are made of now.'

Joe lunged and Finch caught him a mighty blow to the side of the head which might have rendered a lesser man unconscious, but Joe was so angry he was only momentarily stunned, which gave Finch time to deliver a stinging blow to his shoulder. Joe staggered and struggled to regain his balance, and Tom gasped. But Finch too was tiring and when Joe saw him raise the club again, he ducked beneath it and drove first his right fist and then his left into Finch's unprotected stomach.

He fell to the ground and Joe was on top of him immediately, wrenching the wood from his hands. For a moment he raised it and had the desire to bring it crashing down on Finch's head. He saw that Finch anticipated this. He had shut his eyes and was whimpering in fear, and his whole body was shaking. Joe looked at him in disgust, threw away the wood, and heard it plop as it hit the water in the canal. Finch, seeing that he was off guard for a moment, caught him with a left hook that snapped his neck back.

Joe said later that was when a sort of red mist filled his mind and through it he saw his lovely, kind and gentle sister being subjected to incredible abuse at the hands of the man beneath him. By God, he thought, he would make him pay for that.

He dragged him to his feet. 'Now fight fair, you slimy bastard,' he growled out, and launched into him immediately.

After that, Joe didn't hear Finch's groans or moans. Nor did he feel any punches that made their mark as he pummelled his prey without mercy until he fell to the ground in an unconscious heap. Then he lifted his boot and kicked him and would have done so again, but Tom came forward and put a hand on his arm.

'Hasn't he had enough?'

'Not while he breathes, no.'

'Joe . . .' Tom knew what it was to take another's life and he didn't want Joe to have that on his conscience.

'Don't pretend that this is some decent human being that I am kicking the shit out of,' Joe said angrily. 'He is a brutal, filthy rat, and rats deserve no mercy.'

'And you have given him none,' Tom said gently. 'But it's over now. Let's go home.'

Tom's words, soft though they were, permeated Joe's brain and he shook his head to rid himself of the red mist.

'You all right?' Tom asked.

Joe nodded. 'I am now.' He looked at the unconscious man in a heap on the ground in front of him and he said, 'Is he dead?'

Tom bent over Finch to check that a pulse was still beating in his neck. 'No, he is alive,' he said, getting to his feet. 'Come on. Let's get out of here quick.'

That's when they heard the scraping scratching noise and they were immediately alert. They didn't turn on their torches, but they had no need to because the moon was full and now uncovered by cloud. They could plainly see the derelict warehouses and the remains of a factory, and in the middle of that, sitting on a crate, cleaning his whiskers, was a rat.

Joe sighed with relief and gave a rueful smile as he said to Tom, 'Aren't we the big men? Frightened of a bloody rat.'

'Aye,' Tom agreed. 'But let's away now. To hang about here is madness.' They started up the road and hadn't gone that far when they heard the unmistakable sound of a tremendous splash.

They looked at one another in alarm and then dashed back

down to the towpath. It was deserted, but they both heard the sound of running footsteps disappearing into the night. Tom ran to the canal and playing his torch on the water, saw the body of Finch being sucked under, and he watched dispassionately until it had quite disappeared.

'Someone disliked the bastard as much as we did,' Joe said as he joined his brother. 'See anything?'

'Aye,' said Tom. 'I saw the slimy toad being sucked under the water, and good riddance, I say.'

'And me,' Joe agreed. 'Finch is no loss to the human race. Let's go and tell Aggie that she can sleep easy in her bed now.'

'Yeah,' Tom replied. 'And I think that gentle sister of ours will proper give out to you when she sees your face. I only caught a glimpse of it in the light from the torch, but it looks a right mess. You be glad of the blackout and let's hope that we have the carriage to ourselves on the train. We wouldn't want any fellow passenger to become curious as to how you got so battered-looking.'

SEVENTEEN

Aggie was so angry and disappointed when she saw the state of Joe's face when he and Tom arrived home that night. She felt that he had tainted the evening that, up until then, she had thought almost magical, because she had had a wonderful time with Paul, in fact she could never remember enjoying herself so much and then Joe, who hadn't been in the country five minutes, arrived home in such a state.

She knew Joe had been in a fight. She had seen enough street brawls in her time to recognise his injuries, and she gave out to him good and proper.

It was only when the men impressed upon her what they had done and were able to promise her that, though Joe hadn't killed Finch, someone else had finished the job, was Aggie able to believe that at last the man was dead and gone.

'All the women who worked for him hated him,' she said.

'Well, for them, and especially you, it is over,' Joe told her. 'You are free of Finch and can go forward with your life now.'

Both Joe and Tom were amazed when Aggie began to cry.

'Aggie, I thought you would be pleased,' Joe said in consternation, and Tom was similarly dismayed and confused.

However, Aggie's face was lit up in a way the men had never seen before, though the tears continued to trickle down her cheeks as she said, 'I am pleased, you pair of eejits. God, don't men know anything?'

Tom thought he would never understand women if he lived to be a hundred. But, ever the peacemaker, he said, 'Shall I make us all a cup of tea and we'll tell you all about it?'

Aggie wiped her eyes and nodded. 'I'd like that. And there is no rush either, because it will take me some time to get this man's face to rights.'

The next day Joe was stiff and sore, and his face still a mess despite Aggie's ministrations. They were due to go to Molly's that day and they took a tram for most of the way because the house beside the aerodrome was a tidy distance. Aggie caught the conductor's eyes on Joe more than once, and she thought it little wonder, for he looked as though he had gone ten rounds in a boxing ring and come off the worst.

She didn't underestimate either the pain or discomfort that he must be in, nor the courage it must have taken to tackle Finch in that way and so enable her to live the rest of her life in peace and free from fear. She knew that she would always owe him a debt for that. And Tom too, not only for taking revenge on McAllister, which she was unable to do, but also for lifting her from the gutter and caring for her so well that she was now able to face the world again. Together her brothers had given her a future and she knew she would never forget that.

Joe wasn't at all sure that if he had been in Tom's shoes that night when Aggie accosted him he'd have acted the way that Tom did. Would he have wanted to be seen with the depraved and gin-sodden woman Tom described, let alone claim a kinship with her and take her in and look after her? He knew he just might have walked away, and he was filled with shame for even thinking that way.

'What are you thinking about, Joe, that is putting such a frown on your face?' Aggie asked.

Joe had no intention of telling her, but he did say, 'I was just thinking that I need to send a telegram to Gloria.'

'Did she know the plan the two of you had hatched up?' Aggie asked quietly.

Joe smiled and said just as quietly, 'She did, and she wasn't best pleased. Gave out to me good and proper, but whatever she said, I know concern about me was at the root of most of it and I don't want her worrying unnecessarily.'

'We can get off the tram before we get to Molly's,' Tom said. 'There's a parade of shops nearby and I know there's a post office because I posted some of the letters to you from there.'

And that is what they did. The telegram was short and to the point, Joe would tell Gloria all when he got back and so he just wrote, 'JOB DONE. ALL IS WELL.'

Tom went into the post office with his brother and when they came out he had a big grin plastered on his face. 'You should have seen the way the woman behind the counter looked at Joe,' he said to Aggie. 'I think she thought that any minute he would start demanding money with menaces.'

'I'm not really that surprised,' Aggie said. 'Maybe you'd better go ahead and warn Molly, Tom. I would hate her to think that Joe always looks like this.'

Joe agreed, and so when he met Molly for the first time she made no comment about his appearance. And neither did the man in air-force blue by her side. Joe brushed away the hand Molly had extended for him to shake and gave her a hug instead, saying, 'I am so pleased to meet you at last, my dear, and I agree with Tom. You are so like your mother it is almost uncanny.'

'Thank you,' Molly said. 'I take that as a compliment.'

'Good,' Joe said. 'For that was how it was meant.' And he turned to the young man and held out his hand. 'And you must be Mark?'

'I am, sir,' Mark said. 'And very pleased to meet you.'

Joe saw that the man had good manners and heard he was well spoken, and his handshake was firm, and while he admired all those things what really reassured him was the love that seemed to spark between the two young people. Tom said Molly had met her soul mate and Joe thought she probably had. He recalled the way he and Gloria had parted, and regretted it bitterly. He hoped that they could mend their marriage when he returned home.

Molly led the way indoors. Joe was looking forward to meeting the boy, but Kevin had not been warned about Joe's face and so he took one look at him and said, 'Crikey! What happened to you?'

'Kevin! Don't be so rude.'

'I'm not,' Kevin said, affronted. 'I'm just asking a question. How can that be rude?'

'It's personal and—'

'Molly,' Joe said with a smile, 'it's natural to be curious. For all Aggie's care, I am not yet ready for respectable company.'

'So what happened then?'

'Kevin!'

Joe didn't answer straight away. Instead, he asked, 'How old are you, Kevin?'

'Thirteen.'

Joe glanced across at Molly with his eyebrows raised and she knew what he was saying, that he wasn't sure the tale he was going to tell was suitable for a lad of thirteen. However, Molly had told Kevin everything that had happened to her while he was in the orphanage, and she had answered his many questions as honestly as she could, and so she said, 'Whatever it is you have to tell us, Kevin should hear too. He has been through so much already. And he knows that what he hears he mustn't repeat.'

Kevin flashed his sister a look of gratitude as Joe said, 'All right then. I look this way, Kevin, because yesterday night I was in a fight.'

Kevin's eyes grew as big as saucers. 'Golly, were you really?' he exclaimed. 'Who did you fight?'

'A very bad man,' Joe said. 'And one who hurt your Aunt Aggie very much.' And then Molly, Mark and Kevin listened open-mouthed to what Joe had done the previous night and why, and none of them blamed him one bit.

'I don't think that you can really understand the relief I felt at the news that that man was dead at last,' Aggie said. 'My feelings for that man went beyond fear and beyond hate. The thought that he is gone and that he can never hurt me or mine in any way ever again is almost unbelievable. I am still coming to terms with it, like I am coming to terms with the fact that if I hadn't accosted Tom that time in the street, I might not be here now, surrounded by my lovely family.'

They all heard the catch in Aggie's voice and though there was a lump in Molly's throat as well, to give Aggie time to compose herself she said, 'I'm glad we are all here together today too because I want to talk about the guests at our wedding.'

'What about them?' Tom asked.

'I want to invite the McEvoys,' Molly said. 'I've explained why to Mark.'

'I am looking forward to meeting them,' Mark said. 'Molly says that Nellie and Jack McEvoy were substitute parents when she lost her own.'

'Aye, they were,' Tom agreed. 'And Cathy was her best friend.'

Aggie knew the McEvoys were from Buncrana, though, and as she felt her budding self-confidence seeping away she asked fearfully, 'Would they judge me? I shouldn't want my tale spread all around Buncrana, and it would be hard for the rest of you too to rise above the shame of it.'

'The only shame in this is that it has been allowed to continue for so many years,' Joe said fiercely. 'None of what happened to you is your fault.'

'That isn't how people will see it, Joe. You know that,' Aggie said.

'Many people are like that,' Tom said. 'If they heard one hint of this they would say that there was no smoke without fire. But the McEvoys are different. Over the years they have kept many secrets for us and I would trust them with my life.'

'Right,' said Aggie with an emphatic nod of her head. 'If I have your word, Tom, that is all I need.'

'They are a lovely family altogether,' Joe said. 'Their elder daughter, Helen, is a good friend of my wife, Gloria. Her husband didn't some back from Dunkirk and then his entire family were wiped out in the Birmingham blitz. Small wonder Helen was ill. When she came back home to recover, as I did, she met up with Gloria and they soon became the best of friends. Gloria missed the pace of life in London because she is a real city girl, and so is Helen now. The two of them stick out like sore thumbs in Buncrana.'

'Well,' Aggie said, 'the country life is not for everyone.'

'I think deep down she really is homesick at times,' Joe said. 'She was delighted to meet with two American petty officers a couple of months ago in Buncrana. They had come over from the naval base in Derry and Nellie took them under her wing.'

'Oh, she would,' Molly said with a smile.

'Yes,' Joe agreed. 'Anyway, one of them was from New York. Gloria said she didn't realise how much she missed the accent until she heard it again, and the upshot of all this was the three women, Nellie, Helen and Gloria, were shown around the camp. Then just before I came away, these petty officers told Helen and Gloria there are jobs going in the canteen at the camp if they wanted to try for them.'

'Gosh,' Molly said. 'Is she going to?'

'Oh, I don't know,' Joe said. 'I wasn't best pleased at first, to tell you the truth, but after this weekend I promised her we'll talk about it. Anyway, you will meet her soon, and Ben too, for they are coming over for the wedding. Will you look after Ben for me, Kevin?'

'Course I will.' Kevin said, delighted that he would get to see his cousin. 'How old is Ben now?'

'Nine,' Joe said. 'Just one thing, Kevin. Ben will not be told the truth about Aggie. He is far too young to know about things like that.'

'I'll say he is,' Kevin said. 'I mean, he's just a kid really.'

Tom bent his head to hide his smile as Kevin went on, 'What you going to tell him?'

'There won't be any explanation needed,' Aggie said. 'Just say I'm Aunt Aggie and let that be the end of it.'

The next day, Tom took Joe around the city centre for he was booked on the night boat and hadn't to catch the train until half-past nine that evening. Although some of the bomb damage was extensive, Joe noticed an air of defiance, such as people still trading in the market hall in a place Tom called the Bull Ring, although the roof had been blown clean off.

'That's the Brummie spirit,' Tom told Joe later as they each nursed a pint of Guinness in a city centre pub. 'You are looking at a battered city, but when this war is all over it will be rebuilt and I think I would like to be here when that happens.'

Joe stared at his brother for a moment, then said, 'What exactly are you telling me, Tom?'

'I am saying that I am just beginning to realise what life is all about, and that is family, surely,' Tom said. 'I have no children of my own, nor never will have, and that is a burden that I must carry, but here I have a sister I had given up for lost, a niece I met and learned to love in 1935, and a nephew that I am just getting to know. Added to that I have a first-class job with a fair and generous boss and I am happier than I have been in years.'

And he looked better, there was no denying it.

'But what of the farm?' Joe asked.

'Well, that's another thing,' Tom said. 'I have worked on that farm since I was a child, and for what? After my day it will fall into disrepair because I have no one to pass it on to, while you have a son.'

Joe shook his head. 'I am no farmer, Tom,' he said. 'We are just scraping by, and Gloria is no farmer's wife. She hates everything about it, particularly the primitive conditions we live under.'

'Ben likes it well enough.'

'Ben is just a child. Of course he likes it. He hasn't the concerns and worries of his parents, and why should he have, but he may not love the land so much when he is fully grown.'

'And then again he may.'

Joe shook his head. 'Gloria will never stand it.'

'All right,' Tom conceded. 'Maybe that is asking a lot of you all.' Then he looked at Joe steadily and said, 'Many years ago, you wanted to try your hand in America and I gave you the wherewithal to do that. Now I am not reminding you because I am calling in favours, but because you might understand the urge to have a chance of trying something new.'

'Aye, of course,' Joe said. 'Despite all that happened, I was always grateful to you for giving me that opportunity.'

'That is what I am asking of you,' Tom said. 'Give me one year to see if this really is the life I want, while you keep the farm ticking over. If then we both feel neither of us wants the farm any more, it can be sold and the money split between us two.'

'It's your farm, Tom.'

'I will split it,' Tom insisted, 'and that will give you, Gloria and Ben the money to set up somewhere else.'

What could Joe do but agree? He owed his brother a debt. Anyway, Tom had endured hell on earth for years one way and another. Surely he deserved some happiness in his life, and a year wasn't really that much to ask?

'All right,' Joe told his brother. 'I will run the farm for one year.'

'And after that we can talk again,' Tom said, and he grasped Joe's hand and shook it warmly.

All Friday evening, Gloria worried about Joe and what might have happened to him. She knew that he would seek Finch out at the earliest opportunity, because that was the type of man he was.

She had the idea, though, that this Finch character would not play by any sort of rules. These sort of people thrived on brutality and she feared he would soon make mincemeat of both Joe and Tom.

Then again, someone could have overheard the men talking, or maybe caught sight of the fight developing and informed the police. She looked at the clock. Maybe even now they were in police custody. She expected any minute to hear the heavy tread of the Garda boots in the cobbled yard, and the thump of a fist on the cottage door.

Exhaustion drove her to bed in the end, where she tossed and turned, listening out for any unexpected sound in the night. But nothing untoward had happened by the time the sun nudged its way over the horizon, and Gloria heaved herself out of bed, for Jack McEvoy would be making his way to them shortly to start on the milking, with Ben helping him as it was the weekend. She felt like a piece of chewed string and reminded herself that she had an interview in Derry that day, though she didn't feel a bit like it.

She had to feign enthusiasm in front of Jack, though, but she was glad when he had the job finished and was on his way home.

'When will Dad be home?' Ben asked later as he ate his breakfast.

'I have answered that question twice already,' Gloria said.

'And the answer will be the same no matter how many times you ask it. Your father is travelling on the night sailing on Sunday, and you will be in school by the time he arrives home on Monday morning.'

'I could have the day off?'

'No, you could not. Anyway, all your father will be fit for is sleeping, because it is unlikely that he will have had much rest on the boat or train. You'll see him in a better frame of mind when you come home from school.'

Gloria hoped what she told her son was true, because she didn't know what she would do if Joe didn't arrive. She kept herself busy to stop her mind thinking of all the things that could have befallen her husband and it was past midmorning when she sat down with a cup of tea and glanced out of the window with a sigh. If only it was Monday morning already.

And then, she felt as if all the blood in her body had frozen, because riding down the lane was the telegraph boy. Ben hadn't noticed him, and Gloria had to force herself to cross the room and open the door.

Then Ben was aware of something unusual happening and he slid off his chair and joined his mother as she took the telegram from the boy with hands that shook, and tore it open. 'JOB DONE. ALL IS WELL.'

Gloria felt relief flow all through her. 'Any answer?' asked the boy and Gloria shook her head dumbly and shut the door with a sigh.

'What's it mean?' Ben said, scrutinising the telegram, which Gloria had left on the table.

'Daddy had a job to do for Uncle Tom and he was just telling us that it was finished,' Gloria said.

'Oh, is that the "unfinished business" then?' Ben asked, remembering the conversation he had had with his father before he left.

'Unfinished business?' Gloria repeated.

'Yeah. Dad said that Uncle Tom couldn't come home

271

when he said he was going to because he had some un-finished business. So if the job is done now, maybe Uncle Tom will come back as well?'

'I don't know about that, Ben, but your father will be here.'

'You already said that he would,' Ben pointed out, 'before you got that message.'

'Yes, well now I am certain of it.'

'You mean you—'

'Ben, I want to go to Buncrana, and today not tomorrow, so go and get ready and stop plaguing me with questions,' Gloria said.

Ben sighed, but did as he was told because when his mother spoke like that she meant business. There were still lots of things he didn't understand. In his experience, though, grown-ups were good at changing the subject just as he was trying to get to the bottom of things.

'Helen's in the kitchen,' Nellie said, opening the flap so that Gloria could go through to the back where the living accom-modation was. 'Leave Ben in here with me. He can count the money for me and stamp anything that needs stamping.' Gloria could see that Ben was more than agreeable to that and so she left him and went through to see her friend.

'Those two petty officers are coming to take us down in a car,' Helen told her. 'They phoned Mammy this morning to tell her.'

'So we will at least arrive in style?'

'I'll say,' Helen said. 'I'm a bit nervous, are you?'

'Yes,' Gloria said. 'But by going to see this woman, we are not committing ourselves, are we? We might not like the thought of it in the end.'

'Yes, or she might not like the look of us, at viewing us a second time,' Helen said.

'Mmm,' Gloria said. 'Then I'd say the woman was hard to please.' And the two laughed together.

Afterwards, though, Gloria thought that Joan Reilly's approach to the interview to work on a military base was casual in the extreme, for it was more like an informal chat than the gruelling interview she had expected. Joan took a particular interest in Gloria and then asked about their experience with canteen work. They had none, and Gloria was sure that that would count against them, but Joan just said, 'Well, it's fairly basic stuff that I'm sure you will pick up quick enough. In fact, I think that you will fit in very well. Could you begin work Monday week?'

Neither woman could believe it was so easy, and as the men drove them back to Buncrana, Gloria's stomach gave a lurch at the thought that she had yet to tell Joe what she had done.

It was almost ten o'clock on Monday morning before Gloria saw Joe trudging slowly down the hillside towards the road, and she felt her heart almost burst with relief.

Joe was on the road by the time she reached the head of the lane to meet him, and as they drew close she saw that his eyes were swollen, his lips puffy and his face bruised and battered. 'Oh, Joe,' she cried, 'I have been so worried about you.'

Joe put his arms around his wife and tried not to wince as she squeezed his shoulder. But she saw the look of pain flash over his face and pulled back.

'What is it?'

'Nothing much,' said Joe, putting his other arm around Gloria as they began to walk towards the lane. 'My face is the worst, but that bugger Finch picked up a piece of wood and took a couple of swings at me and so I have a gash on my shoulder and a lump the size of a duck egg on my head. But they don't worry me,' he said, seeing the look of concern on Gloria's face. 'The man is now dead and gone.'

Gloria looked at him appalled. 'You killed him?' she said.

'No,' Joe said. 'But someone else did.' And he told her what had happened.

'And you saw nothing?'

'No, though we heard someone running away, but you know what the blackout's like. I shan't lose any sleep over it either. On the plus side, our Aggie is lovely, and that Paul Simmons is a fine bloke and fair besotted by her, and you only have to see Molly with Mark to how much in love they are.'

'I can't wait to meet them all.'

'Not long now.'

They had reached the cottage before Joe told Gloria about Tom's proposal.

'And you have agreed to this already?' she said.

'Well, yes,' Joe said. 'I know I should have discussed it with you—'

'Yes, Joe, you should have done.'

'It was sort of forced on me,' Joe said defensively.

Gloria shook her head. 'Tom would never force anyone to do anything, and he would quite understand that you had to come home and discuss such a proposal with me before saying yes.'

'Oh, come on, Gloria,' Joe said. 'It isn't as if we have made any plans to leave or anything.'

'Not likely to, without money behind us,' Gloria retorted. 'But that is not the issue here, Joe. You just don't seem to get it, do you? It's about showing respect for me, for my feelings.'

Joe, though, was only too aware of what he owed Tom and he said to Gloria, 'D'you know, when Tom gave me the money to go to America, he did it without any conditions. I know in many ways it put him in a fix to do without my help on the farm, but he never said a word about that. He wished me Godspeed. His heart must have been heavy, for the work-load would have increased and the only companionship he got was from an evil-tempered, malicious old woman.'

'I know all this.'

'You know nothing,' Joe said firmly. 'You put up with my mother for months, whereas Tom put up with her all his bloody life until, thank God, she died and released him. Yet never in all the letters Tom sent me was there any hint of resentment and all he felt was happiness for me as my fortunes increased. He worried himself sick when we were going through it in New York, and there was no hint of smugness about his concern. Then he was happy to welcome us when we needed to come here.'

'I know that Tom is a lovely person and I don't know any man that is kinder.'

'Well, then, don't you think that this lovely, kind man deserves a stab at happiness?' Joe asked. 'He is free for the first time in his life and he has asked me to do one thing for him, and that is biding here for one year so that he can decide whether he wants to farm again or not. It might not be an easy decision for him to make, for the farm has been in our family for years and Tom was brought up knowing that he would eventually inherit it. You can't just throw all that in the air. He needs to take his time, think it through.'

'All right,' Gloria said. 'I hear what you say and I have news for you too,' she added as nonchalantly as she could. 'I have taken that job in the canteen at the Springtown Camp. I'll need something if I am stuck here for at the very least another year and it will be a chance to save.'

'You have taken the job there already?'

'Yes. I start next Monday at half-past nine.'

'I thought we were to discuss this when I got home?'

'You weren't here,' Gloria said. 'Helen and I had to see the canteen manageress on Saturday. She offered us jobs and we accepted. We had to make the decision there and then. You could say it was sprung on the two of us, the same as happened with you and Tom.'

'There is no comparison.'

'I think there is, Joe,' Gloria said. 'And anyway, that is

neither here nor there. What's done is done, and just as I have to live with the decision you made, you have to live with the decision I made. And as far as I am concerned, that is the way it is.'

EIGHTEEN

Gloria had been working three weeks at the camp when Joe decided enough was enough. He felt he had almost been tricked into allowing her to go in the first place, Gloria had used his agreement against him to get her own way.

The men of the town thought him crazy when he told them where Gloria was proposing to work and said quite categorically that none of their wives would have been allowed to take such a job. Nor could he imagine any woman that had been born and bred in Buncrana, and lived there ever since, wanting to do such a thing. Joe had always thought he wouldn't care about the opinion of the towns-folk, but he found he did, because he hated being made to look like a fool.

It wasn't to be borne, he decided. However, Joe knew that Gloria wasn't like the wives of the men in Buncrana who would just stop doing a thing because their husbands said they must, and he was unsure how to tackle her. He had gone over what he intended to say as he milked the cows that evening and it had sounded all right. But later, when he sat facing Gloria, after they had eaten and Ben was in bed he knew that he had begun badly with a belligerent, almost hectoring tone, yet he couldn't seem to stop himself.

'Since you began at that job I have to scratch around at dinner-time to make a bite to eat for myself. I have never had to do a thing like that before,' he said to her.

'I leave it as ready as I can,' Gloria protested. 'I usually leave broth or something like that. All you have to do is put it on the fire and get a few slices of bread. I also pack Ben's lunch box.'

'Well, soup and bread are hardly enough nourishment for a working man, are they?' Joe said. 'I am used to having my main meal in the middle of the day and now it's in the evening, and late too by the time you get in and then have to cook it.'

Gloria shrugged. 'Well, there is nothing I can do about that and as you are in a complaining mood I will tell you something else to get your teeth into. The canteen works a rota system and next week it's my turn to work the weekend.'

'Work the weekend?' Joe repeated almost in disbelief. 'Good God, Gloria. Whoever heard of a wife and mother doing that?'

'It's part of the job,' Gloria said. 'Would you have us tell the men they are to have nothing to eat all weekend?'

'But if you work on Sundays, when will you go to Mass?'

'The early one,' Gloria said, 'while you're doing the milking.'

'So who is going to make breakfast for me and Ben when we come in from the later Mass?' Joe demanded.

'God Almighty!' Gloria cried in exasperation. 'I knew there was something up with you because you have been going round with a face that would sour cream for days. You're not some bloody helpless imbecile, Joe, though you are acting like one at the moment. It will only be every seventh week that this happens. Can't you and Ben look after yourselves for once?'

'We shouldn't have to,' Joe complained. 'That's the point. Nothing is the same since you started this job.'

'No, I'll say it isn't,' Gloria agreed happily. 'Now I am saving money in the post office each week.'

'You don't even bake any more,' Joe complained. 'Everything is shop bought.'

'Nellie McEvoy has been buying shop bread and cakes for years, she told me herself,' Gloria said. 'So why is it all right for her and not for me?'

Joe couldn't really answer that and instead he said, 'You don't even do your own washing these days. It's taken out for some stranger to do.'

Gloria shook her head almost incredulously. 'I can't believe I am hearing this. At the camp there is a launderette, a place where there are banks of machines and dryers for the clothes, and women engaged to do the laundry for you. I take my bags of dirty washing there in the morning and pick them up at the end of the day, washed, dried and folded so that sometimes it doesn't need ironing at all, and all I have to do is put it away. All the women there do the same thing. Now tell me, Joe, why should I stop doing that and do it here instead? Every drop of water would have to be hauled from the well – buckets and buckets of it to fill the huge boiler – and then I would need to spend hours pounding the clothes in the poss tub before putting the whole lot through the mangle and hanging it out on the line in the orchard. And then I would have to empty the boiler and clean up. It will take nearly the whole of one day just to wash the clothes, and a large portion of the next to iron them all. Surely to God as long as the clothes are clean does it matter what method is used to achieve that? Anyway,' she said, with a shrug, 'there are only so many hours in a day, Joe, and I have no time for that sort of palaver.'

'Yes, but that's just it,' Joe said. 'If you stayed at home you would have plenty of time.'

'Huh, I might have great swathes of time,' Gloria conceded, 'but I would lack the enthusiasm to engage in that back-breaking and mind-numbing experience if there was any sort of alternative.'

'Well, there wouldn't be if you didn't work at the camp.'

'But I do work there and will continue to do so.'

'Gloria, I have already said I don't want you working there any more.'

Gloria gave a nonchalant shrug and tidied the teacups onto the tray, not looking at Joe. 'If you don't like it, then you must get over it. Isn't that the attitude you displayed to me when I objected to you intending to beat a man to pulp? Objecting to the type of job a person does is not in the same league as that really.'

'Gloria, I can't believe that you will defy me like this.'

'Oh, can you not?' Gloria said, banging down the tray, now blisteringly angry. 'Well, I have never heard you behave like this before either. And these aren't even your words; they are words fed to you by the people, particularly the men, of Buncrana that have seeped into your brain. Tell you what, Joe, one of the prime reasons for doing this job is for the extra money. You find me another job in Derry that pays the same and with the same benefits, and I will give up the camp tomorrow without a qualm.'

Joe was silent, but Gloria saw the resentment and fury smouldering beneath his eyes. She said, 'Joe, what is happening to us? After all we have been through, we are throwing angry words at one another about a job of work. If the people of the town are bothring you, then you must deal with it because we really do need the money I earn. Added to that, you said often to me, when I was struggling to cope with things, that we could make it if only we stick together. Does that still hold water, Joe?'

'Of course.'

'There isn't an "of course" or there wouldn't have been such an argument,' Gloria pointed out. 'I need to work and that involves both of us doing our bit and not moaning if you have to make your own meal or see to Ben when I'm not here. It's not such an onerous task. When the year is up, and Tom decides one way or the other, we will have money to enable us to go wherever we want and start again.'

'Tom said if he decides not to come back, then he will sell the farm and split the proceeds between us.'

'Even if Tom does decide that, I should say that farms

might take some time to sell,' Gloria said. 'This way we are assured of money in the bank. What do you say?'

What could Joe do but agree? That night he lay in bed beside his slumbering wife and knew that he would be the butt of the jokes in Buncrana. He had claimed to the fellows in the market and the pub that he would tell Gloria she had to give the job up, and now he would have to confess that she hadn't, and wouldn't, and he could almost hear their laughter.

'Are you looking forward to Molly and Mark's wedding?' Helen asked Gloria the first week of June.

'You bet,' Gloria answered. 'And at least now I am working, Ben and I can have new clothes, and we won't be turning up at Molly's wedding looking like two country bumpkins.'

'You'll probably be the best dressed people there,' Helen said. 'Remember there is the points system on clothes in England.'

'I know,' Gloria said. 'When that came in a couple of years ago, I found I was using up my allotment and sometimes Joe had to get things for Ben because he was growing so much. Then I had to use heaps to buy things for Joe so that he could leave the hospital, because everything he possessed was crushed in the remains of the flat. I can't remember the last time I had anything new.'

'Well then,' said Helen. 'Make the most of this occasion.'

'Oh, don't worry,' Gloria said. 'I intend to.'

However, Gloria could find nothing to suit her in any of the dress shops in Buncrana, and so she did as Nellie advised and bought material for the dressmaker to make up into something she really wanted. The material had a satiny feel to it, and was mainly lemon, but with a swirling mix of colours as well, and she also bought plain lemon for the jacket.

The dressmaker turned out a beautiful outfit. The dress

finished at the knee and it had a scooped neckline trimmed with lace, and it clung to her body until just below the waist, where it fanned out in gorgeous little folds. The softly tailored jacket draped over the shoulders made the whole thing complete. She had navy shoes to match the handbag and hat she was borrowing from Nellie McEvoy, and when Petty Officer Morrisey heard that she was going to a snazzy wedding in England he gave her a pair of nylon stockings as a gift. She was almost speechless with pleasure, but didn't tell Joe where she had got them from.

Gloria tried on her outfit for Joe, spinning around so that the dress flared out and then settled against her nylon-clad legs, but when she caught sight of his glum face she suppressed a sigh. The outfit looked far more expensive than it was, and Joe was annoyed that Gloria had used some of the money that she said they desperately needed on such an outfit for herself, and new clothes for Ben too.

'Say something, Joe,' Gloria pleaded. 'How do I look? Will I do?'

Joe thought that Gloria was absolutely stunning, like some sort of film star. Few would believe that she was a wife and mother who lived in a small and primitive cottage in the North of Ireland. And suddenly that annoyed him.

So what he said was, 'And how much did that little lot cost you?'

Gloria was upset because she knew she looked good and she had wanted Joe to be proud of her, and so she snapped back, 'Not as much as if I had bought a ready-made rag in the town.'

'Ah, yes, but none of the dresses that suit every other woman was good enough for you, were they?' said Joe mockingly.

Gloria noted Joe's glowering face as she said rather sadly, 'No, no, they weren't, and I make no excuse for that. It's the type of person I am. The person you married.'

She turned away and made for the bedroom to change back into her everyday clothes.

Joe was sorry now that he said the harsh and scornful words; sorry he had dimmed the light in her eyes. He almost called her back and said so, but he hesitated too long, and Gloria shut the door behind her and the moment was lost.

For all that, Gloria enjoyed the wedding. She had met all the family the evening before at Molly's house, and the next morning she took her place in the church beside Ben. She saw Mark, the nervous young groom that she had met the previous night, get to his feet with his best man as the strains of the Wedding March were heard. She turned her head to see her beautiful niece begin the walk down the aisle arm in arm with Tom, and it was the absolute pride in Tom's eyes that brought tears springing to her own.

The couple stood before the altar, facing one another, and the love they had for each other seemed to radiate out of them. This gave Gloria a cold feeling in her heart because she realised that she didn't feel that way for Joe any more. But, she told herself sternly, this wasn't about her but about the young couple at the altar, and she pushed her own problems aside and prayed earnestly for their happiness.

At the reception later, she had many comments and compliments about her clothes. Ben too was as smart as paint, for Gloria had bought him a proper little grey suit and, worn with a pure white shirt and a striped tie, it looked the business. Gloria realised that Helen had been right about the difficulties of getting anything halfway decent to wear in war-torn Britain at that time. She thought Molly had been very sensible to take Mark's mother up on the offer of borrowing her wedding dress.

Molly looked a picture in it too, for she was a very beautiful girl, Gloria thought, and couldn't have been more welcoming. She also liked her brother, Kevin, who took Ben under his wing immediately, as he said he'd promised his Uncle Joe he would.

But it was Aggie Gloria was totally intrigued by. She was like an older version of Molly, and Gloria thought must have been a real stunner when she had been younger. She was still extremely attractive and, with the life she had led for years, Gloria considered that was truly amazing. She also found Aggie to be just as kind and gentle as Joe had said, with no bitterness in her at all.

Her eyes seemed to dance in her head, especially when she gazed across the room at Paul. That night, in bed in Molly's house, Gloria examined her feelings about Joe. She still cared for him. She had been worried about him over the whole Finch business, for example, but she certainly didn't feel the same way about him as she had once upon a time. It was as if the love between them had melted away. And she suddenly felt sad and lonely.

Gloria had been home four weeks when there was a letter from Aggie. Joe read it as he ate the breakfast that Gloria made for him and Ben before she left for work. 'Aggie and Paul are getting married,' Joe said.

'Well, that's no surprise,' Gloria said. 'When is it?'

'The twenty-third of October.'

'Great!' Ben burst out. 'Can I go? Will Kevin be there as well, like last time?'

'Kevin will undoubtedly be there,' Joe said. 'But I don't know if we're going yet.'

'Why not?' Ben and Gloria said together.

'These things have to be considered.'

'What is there to consider?' Gloria said. 'Your sister is getting married and she wants you there, and really that is all there is to it.'

'Well, there's the farm to see to.'

'Ask Jack McEvoy again,' Gloria suggested. 'I'm sure he wouldn't mind. He said he enjoyed himself last time. And it's not as if the McEvoy family will be asked to Aggie's wedding. I mean, they barely know her. In fact, I hardly know her either so I shan't mind staying here if you and Ben want to go on your own.'

'Don't you want to come?'

'It's not a question of wanting or not wanting,' Gloria said. 'It's the practicalities of it. Look, I have to go soon or I'll miss the train. I haven't time to discuss this, but it would make sense for me to stay here. It's a lot to expect Jack to come here and do the milking and go home without a bite to eat. And then I would have to book the time off work and take the loss in pay.'

'So,' Joe said truculently, 'your job comes before your family?'

'I didn't say that,' Gloria protested. 'Nor meant it either, but if you want to take that attitude then I can do nothing about it. Nor can I discuss it any more because I will be late for work.'

Helen laughed when she saw her friend's disgruntled face as they met at the station to catch the train to work. 'What's up with you?' she said. 'Got out of bed the wrong side?'

'Definitely, I think,' Gloria said, and told Helen of the letter that had arrived that morning and of the words she had had with Joe over it. Helen couldn't see the problem. 'Why can't you both go together?' she said. 'We can cope for a few days without you.'

'I suppose,' Gloria said, struggling to be honest. 'The truth is, I don't want to go anywhere with Joe at the moment, and particularly nowhere near his family.'

Helen was perplexed. 'But why not? You said you enjoyed Molly's wedding and they couldn't have been more welcoming.'

'I did, and they were. But just at the minute, I don't want to go into the midst of Joe's family and pretend everything is fine and dandy between us when it isn't. They'll soon work that out.'

'You have just had a few words, that's all.'

'No,' Gloria said. 'I don't mean just now. I realised at Molly's wedding that my feelings for Joe had changed.'

'In what way?'

'The most basic way there is, Helen,' Gloria said. 'I don't think I love Joe any more, and it is nothing to do with the odd spat. It's far deeper and more important than that. I feel concern for him, the same as I would feel for a friend, but the love just isn't there any more. It's like a dead marriage.'

'I feel so sorry for you, Gloria,' Helen said. 'You have been through such a lot to get to this point.'

'I know that,' Gloria cried. 'In a way that makes the whole thing worse. I mean, I probably wouldn't be here today if he hadn't rescued me at the docks over twenty years ago. And after Daddy killed himself, Joe was marvellous. I don't honestly know what Mother and I would have done without him. So I know what I owe Joe, and I'm grateful to him and respect him as the father of my child, but I don't think I love him, and the realisation of that hurts me.'

'I really don't know what to say,' Helen replied. 'Have you talked to Joe about this? Asked how he feels?'

'Helen, Joe is a man,' Gloria said. 'And you know what that means. He probably isn't aware that there is a problem.'

Joe did know, however, and he was saddened to see the marriage that he once thought so wonderful falling apart around his ears. But he had no idea what to do about it, and so as one week slid into the other he hoped that it would right itself eventually.

However, the situation got worse instead of better. They tried not to argue in front of Ben – in fact, they seldom argued – but Ben could often feel the antagonism in the air.

And so when his mother steadfastly refused to travel to Birmingham for Aggie's wedding, although Ben expressed regret, secretly he was pleased. There would just be him and his dad, and his dad was always in a better mood when his mother was not around.

*   *   *

In fact, while Ben and his father were enjoying the delights of the wedding reception, Gloria was at a dance put on for local people by the servicemen at the camp. Gloria and Helen had heard about it about three weeks after the letter had come inviting them to Aggie's wedding, when Joan asked them if they would come to serve up the food. 'You will get paid, and generously,' she encouraged. 'I've done it a few times.'

Gloria looked across at Helen, read the excited anticipation in her face and knew she wanted to do it. She also knew that it was same day as the wedding and so there was nothing stopping her either, so she said, 'I don't think we'd mind, but the trains don't run much after dusk.'

'Oh, they'll fetch you,' Joan said. 'I'm sure they will because they bring in women from the outlying areas anyway.'

'Oh, well, I'll do it then,' Gloria said.

'And me,' said Helen. 'I shall look forward to it.'

Returning to the counter for the midday rush, Helen said, 'Are you going to mention this to Joe?'

'Are you kidding?' Gloria said. 'And give the old moaner something else to gripe about? I'm telling him nothing and what he doesn't know can do him no harm.'

'I wonder why they are having it here anyway,' Helen said, as they began serving vegetables to the men in the queue.

'What do you mean?'

'Well, a couple of the girls told me the Guild Hall in Derry was the place to go,' Helen said.

A young sailor, hearing this, said, 'Have you been to the Guild Hall?'

'That's hardly likely when we live six miles in the opposite direction,' Gloria said drily. 'What's wrong with it?'

'It's all this waltz and foxtrot rubbish.'

'What sort of dancing do you do then?' Helen asked with a smile. 'The cancan?'

'No, don't be silly,' the sailor said. 'We jitterbug.'

'What's jitterbugging, when it's at home?' said Gloria.

'Just about the greatest fun in the world, that's what,' said the first man's neighbour in the queue. 'We are going to show these Derry girls a good time.'

'I can't wait to see what this jitterbugging is all about,' Gloria said when the sailors had moved away.

Morrisey, arriving at the counter at that moment, overheard what Gloria said and asked, 'Are you two ladies going to be at the dance?'

'Yes,' Gloria said. 'But only to serve the food.'

'Oh, I'm sure there will be ample time for a dance or two.'

'We wouldn't have the least idea how to do those sorts of dances anyway,' Gloria said.

'I would like to wager that most of the women who come here the night of the dance won't have the least idea either, but it's easy to learn.'

'I'll take your word for it,' Gloria said. 'But I think I will stay behind the counter.'

'Ah, we'll see,' said Morrisey, with a large wink to them both.

The day of the dance the canteen was unrecognisable. Bands of men had been decorating it all day with streamers and balloons and such, but when Helen and Gloria went in that night, the room was transformed.

A wide stage had been set up at one end, and bandsmen with their brass instruments were taking their places on it. In front of this a large area of the floor had been left clear, obviously for dancing, and around the edges on both sides were some of the canteen tables, now with white cloths on them and lit candles at their centres.

When the music began it was new and vibrant, some of the tunes reminiscent of the jazz that Gloria had enjoyed in New York. She watched the sailors teaching the Derry women to jitterbug and longed to be amongst them, for it was music a person would love to dance to.

But the evening wore on and the canteen workers were kept very busy. Eventually the crowds thinned out a little, though the bar set up to the side of the room was still doing a roaring trade and the dancing seemed to get wilder and wilder.

'I should say some of these women will have sore heads in the morning,' Gloria said to Helen.

'You could be right,' Helen replied. 'Some of them seem crazy about the Americans. I was talking to a girl the other day and she said that when they came here first, it was like Hollywood had come to Derry.'

Gloria laughed. 'When in actual fact they are just men and, like any other men, after one thing. If the girls allow their heads to be turned, they are silly. D'you think we can start clearing away now? This lot will be finished in half an hour or so.'

'I think so,' said Helen. 'The food is more or less gone, and tea and coffee don't seem to be the preferred drinks just now.'

'No indeed,' Gloria smiled. 'Come on then. We'll get this done in no time.'

It was as they were putting away the last of the dishes that Morrisey came to find Gloria. Meadows was with him, but it was he who spoke to Gloria. 'I've come to claim the dance I promised you earlier.'

'I gave you your answer then,' Gloria said. 'I don't know how to do dancing like this.'

'Your friend doesn't seem to have such inhibitions,' Morrisey said. He was right, for Gloria saw with astonishment that Helen had allowed herself to be swept up and out onto the makeshift dance floor with Meadows.

Gloria shrugged. 'She is a free agent.'

'Mrs Sullivan,' Morrisey said, 'I am suggesting dancing with you, not making love to you. Being married surely doesn't preclude having fun?'

Oh, yes it does, Gloria might have said. Certainly in my case.

She didn't say this, but it did set light to a little spark of defiance. She would be doing no harm dancing with a man, and wasn't it what she'd longed to do all evening? 'You'll have to show me how,' she said.

'It will be my pleasure,' said Morrisey. 'Trust me in this. You will pick it up in no time.'

And Gloria did pick it up and found that she thoroughly enjoyed herself. She hesitated when the last waltz was announced, but when Morrisey drew her into his arms she went without protest. Strangely, she felt comfortable there, as if it was the right place to be, as if she had come home at last, and she fought the longing she had to lay her head on Morrisey's shoulder.

Morrisey felt the tension in her ease. He held her closer and she allowed him to, but he didn't go further than that. He was greatly attracted to her, so much so that had she not been married he would have asked if he could see her again. However, she was already spoken for, and that, as far as he was concerned, was that.

NINETEEN

Joe and Ben came back on Tuesday morning and Gloria had arranged to go in to work late so that she would be there to cook their breakfast when the pair came home. She saw them as they came into the yard, and opened the door.

Ben's face was white with tiredness, she noticed, but when he saw his mother he ran towards her and, despite being a big boy of nine, he hugged her tight. She looked up at Joe, wanting to put her arms around him too and try to chase away the coldness that had grown up between them. The look he gave her, however, didn't encourage that. She knew he had not forgiven her for refusing to go to the wedding. She saw it in the set of his face and the stiff way he held his body as if he had drawn a barrier up between them.

Ben was too excited and tired to notice. 'Mum, you should have been there,' he cried. 'It was great. And yesterday Molly let Kevin have the day off school so he could take me round and show me the place.' He gave a short laugh and added, 'Kevin said I should come every week 'cos usually Molly won't let him have even an hour off school.'

'You like Kevin, don't you?'

'Yeah, he's real good fun. I like them all – Molly and Mark, Aunt Aggie and Uncle Paul, and Uncle Tom, of course. They are all smashing.'

'Take off your coat and leave everything else until later,' Gloria said. 'I will have a bowl of porridge for you in no time, and then I think it would be a good idea if you have a little sleep.'

'I don't need to sleep, Mom,' Ben said. 'I'm not a bit tired.'

'No, of course you're not,' Joe said to his son sarcastically, 'but I am tired and while I'm sleeping you will lie on your bed and rest yourself. There will be no one to listen to your chatter anyway, because your mother will be running off to that job of hers just as soon as she can.'

Gloria turned from stirring the pan of oatmeal she had added water to and said, 'We agreed that that was what I should do.'

'There was no agreement to it,' Joe complained. 'You tell me what you want me to do and I go along with it for the sake of a quiet life.'

'A quiet life!' Gloria burst out. 'Fat chance anyone has of a quiet life here with you carping and complaining at every turn.'

The words were out before Gloria could bite them back, and she saw Ben look from one to the other, his eyes full of confusion and his shoulders hunched, as if he was protecting himself from a fresh onslaught. Gloria hated herself for dragging him into the centre of their discontent and Joe made it worse.

'Any man would complain,' he snapped. 'Haven't I reason enough? I am the laughing stock of Buncrana, do you know that?'

Gloria laughed, but it was a hard, bitter laugh. 'So the people in Buncrana don't like the way we run our lives,' she said, 'as if it's any of their damned business anyway. So what odds? I don't give a tuppenny damn for their opinion.'

'You would care if you had made any effort to get on with them.'

'But I don't want to get on with them,' Gloria said. 'The McEvoys apart, I have no time for any of them. They are narrow-minded and have far too much time on their hands

– time enough, anyway, to mind everyone else's business as well as their own.'

Joe had opened his mouth to make a rejoinder to this when Ben suddenly said, 'Please don't fight any more.'

Both Gloria and Joe were ashamed. Gloria knew she shouldn't have retaliated to Joe's jibes. Whatever her differences with Joe, was she not mature enough to say nothing until Ben was out of the way at least? What a homecoming.

'I'm sorry, Ben,' she said as she laid the table for the breakfast. 'We won't argue any more. Tell me what Birmingham is like.'

Ben looked across at his father first to see if he was going to continue to quarrel, and Joe smiled, although it was an effort, and more like a grimace. But Ben was satisfied.

'It's good, Mom,' he said. 'Kevin took me on a tram right into the city centre yesterday. We went to this place called the Bull Ring and there were loads of barrows selling all sorts of things. There's a Market Hall as well, like the one in Buncrana, only this one hasn't got a roof because the Germans blew it off. Kevin said it was better before the war when Saturday night was entertainment night.'

'Helen said something about that to me too,' Gloria said.

'Well, Kevin only went a few times 'cos he was only small, but he said he would never forget it,' Ben said. 'He said all the stalls were lit with gas flares and it looked like fairyland, and there were men walking about on stilts and that. He said there was an Indian fellow with no clothes but a sort of nappy thing, and he used to lie on a bed of nails and invite women to stand on him.'

Ben caught sight of his mother's incredulous face and cried, 'It's true! That's what he said, and when I asked Molly she said it was right. And she told me there was a sort of boxing booth and people were invited to see if they could beat the champ. Her parents never let her watch that, but she never heard of anyone that had done it, and there was a man tied up with chains too, and he used to get free when the people watching had put a pound in the hat.'

'I bet the war and blackout and everything put paid to that,' Gloria said. 'And after this war the world will never be the same again.'

Later, as Gloria ate dinner in the canteen, she told Helen what Ben had said about the Bull Ring.

'Did you not get time to take a peek yourself when you were over for Molly's wedding?' Helen asked.

Gloria shook her head. 'There wasn't time. I'm glad Joe and Ben took an extra day.'

'It's worth a look,' Helen said. 'Even now it has an atmosphere that is all its own. But before the war, it was the place to be on a Saturday night.'

'Kevin told Ben all about it,' Gloria said.

'Yes, you could go with little money in your pocket and still have a good time,' Helen said. 'There were stalls to buy whelks and mussels and things, if you got peckish, and the hot potato man, of course, and then as the night wore on the musicians would come – accordions mainly – playing the tunes for the dances we used to do at home, and then they went on to music-hall songs. Then the Sally Army would arrive, banging their drums and shaking their tambourines and belting out the hymns, and collecting up the down-and-outs – you know, the sort of people most would cross the street to avoid.'

Gloria nodded. 'But what did they do with them?'

'Oh, they took them back to the citadel, which is what they call their church, and gave them a meal. But tell me, how did Joe enjoy himself?'

'Hard to tell,' Gloria said, putting down her knife and fork and looking straight at her friend. 'All I can say is that he has come back in the same black mood he left. I don't know quite why he is behaving the way he is. He must know there is something wrong because we never used to go on like this.'

'You might have just hit the nail on the head,' Helen said. 'Maybe he knows only too well that things are nowhere right between you, and being a man he's burying it and pretending that everything in the garden is rosy and that's what's making him short-tempered.'

'You could be right,' Gloria conceded. 'I mean, I feel like my marriage is dead, but when did it die? When did the love we had for one another seep away, and why weren't we aware of it and took steps to stop it happening?'

'I don't know,' Helen said. 'But I am sorry for both of you.'

'Nothing has happened,' Gloria said. 'Nothing major, I mean. Me working at the camp gives Joe something to focus his anger on, but really I think you were absolutely right: he is as confused and unhappy as I am. Ben, though, loves us both and so we must muddle on together as best we can.'

Joe was acutely aware how unhappy Gloria was, and three days after he returned from Aggie's wedding he faced the fact that his unreasonable behaviour and the anger he had directed against Gloria was little to do with her at all. It had, however, a lot to do with how guilty he felt about sailing off for America and leaving Tom to it.

His guilt had increased since he had met Molly, Kevin and Aggie, and he realised that he had done them all a severe disservice by his selfish attitude. If he had stayed on at the farm he could have gone to England, seen Nuala and told her what had happened to their father. He could have then kept in contact and have got to know the children a little. He could certainly have helped and supported Molly when she had come to live on the farm. In fact, if Tom had told him about Aggie earlier he might have even gone searching for her.

And yet how could he regret marrying Gloria, which he wouldn't have done if he hadn't gone to America? He had been crazy about her, and together they had a son. Yet now he faced the fact that that all-consuming love and passion seemed missing from their lives.

Some couples never experienced such love, Joe told himself, and yet they go on year after year, living together as he and Gloria would have to do if the flame that had been extinguished between them could not be ignited again. But he couldn't keep snapping at her and expect her not to react.

So that night, as they sat having a drink before bed, Joe said in a normal voice, 'Paul and Aggie are after another house, you know.'

Joe hadn't spoken to Gloria normally since before he went to the wedding, and she was pleased. She wondered if he was over his moroseness and knew that if he was going to act in a reasonable manner then life wouldn't be so bad after all.

'Why?' she said. 'Hasn't Paul already got a fine house in Edgbaston? Aggie was telling me all about it.'

'He has, but he wants them to choose a house together. Added to that, Edgbaston is on the other side of the city and I think that now Aggie has found her family, and in particular Nuala's children, she doesn't want to live that far away from them.'

'I can understand that,' Gloria said. 'She does seem remarkably close to them both, but Molly told me she and Mark were moving too; that she was only caretaking that house for the best man's family.'

'Yes,' Joe said. 'Terry's Sallinger's mother and sisters went to stay with relatives, with the war so bad, but now, with the bombing over, they want to come back. And anyway, Molly and Mark want their own place, and as Paul said, it is best to buy before the war is over. Everyone else will be house-hunting then.'

'Wise advice.'

'Yes, and it isn't as if they have any money worries,' Joe said. 'Paul settled a sizeable sum on Molly when she reached twenty-one. Anyway, they have found a house: a three-bedroomed semi on Chester Road. Molly showed me over it the day that Kevin took young Ben into Birmingham. It's not that far from the airfield and on a direct tram stop, and it's empty so they are moving in just a week or two.'

'So that has all worked out for them,' Gloria said. 'Have Aggie and Paul anywhere in mind?'

'Yes. They have their eye on a big property on Eachelhurst Road.'

'And that is close by?'

'Very,' Joe said. 'The house Molly and Mark have backs onto a park called Pype Hayes, and if you walk diagonally across the park you come to Eachelhurst Road.'

'And where is Tom's flat in relation to these places?'

'Not far away,' Joe said. 'Though of course it won't be his place much longer.'

'Why not?' Gloria asked, and a *frisson* of hope stirred in her. 'Don't say he's coming home?'

'No,' Joe said with a small sigh. 'No sign of that yet. Anyway, Aggie is adamant he stays with them while he decides his future, and for good if he wants to make Birmingham his home.'

'Oh right . . . ,' Gloria's innards were fluttering with excitement as she said, 'When's this move taking place?'

'Well, it's hard to be specific when you're buying houses,' Joe said. 'But Aggie and Paul definitely want to be in for Christmas, and Tom will probably move in sometime in the New Year.'

'So there will be a two-bedroomed flat going begging that no one knows about but us?'

'What are you getting at?'

'This is our chance,' Gloria said. 'We could leave here and move to Birmingham with everyone else. Finding a place to live was a real stumbling block to that plan, wasn't it? You'd get a job easy enough, I'd say. I mean, if all else fails you could always ask Paul. He got a job for Tom.'

'I can't do that,' Joe said. 'Though I will never be the

farmer that Tom is, I gave him my word that I would stay for a year and I cannot just walk away from that.'

'Even if that means we lose the flat that would be perfect for us?'

'Yes. A promise is a promise.'

'Joe, you can't just view it like that,' Gloria cried. 'Places like that will be like gold dust to get hold of. If you can't renege on the promise you made to your brother, then let me and Ben go and take up the tenancy of the flat, and you can join us when you—'

'Are you mad?' Joe exploded. 'Let you and Ben go alone? First it was working in a camp full of servicemen and now it's living apart altogether. 'Are you really so tired of me, Gloria?'

What shocked Gloria was that she couldn't have answered 'no' and meant it. She saw Joe suddenly as a dull old man, and unbidden into her mind came the image of Morrisey with his full head of thick dark curls, his laughing brown eyes and his sardonic grin.

'Does your silence answer that question?' Joe asked.

'You know how I hate living here.'

'I would say Tom hated living with our mother,' Joe said, 'but he put up with that for years because there was no alternative. Can't you view this the same way?'

'No,' said Gloria. 'Because my name is not Tom Sullivan.'

Things did not improve between Joe and Gloria as winter took hold of the land. Each thought the other selfish and unfeeling, and as Christmas approached they were barely speaking. Again Gloria found that the job saved her sanity, for she knew she was well liked and valued for the work she did. She began to dread going home to her morose husband and her confused and unhappy child.

In fact, she looked forward to seeing Morrisey each day. Things had changed between them since the dance, and each time Gloria saw him she went weak at the knees and her stomach lurched. Although nothing had happened between them, she knew that Helen would have tumbled to her pre-occupation if she hadn't found herself besotted with his friend Colin Meadows.

She talked about him all the time and her eyes shone whenever she spoke his name. Gloria became worried that Helen might be heading for further heartache. She certainly had it bad.

'Oh, Gloria, when he is near me I can scarcely breathe, and I can feel my heart thudding against my ribs,' Helen said one day in mid-December. She turned to Gloria, her eyes were sparkling. 'I haven't felt this way since . . . You don't think me awful, after John?'

'Of course you're not awful,' Gloria said. 'Why should you be? John is dead and gone and you have a perfect right to a life of your own. All I worry about is that you might get hurt again. I mean, how does he feel about you, Helen?'

'I don't know,' Helen admitted. 'Sometimes I feel that it isn't possible to love someone as much as I do without them feeling something for me too.'

Gloria smiled grimly. 'It is very possible, believe me,' she said.

'What about you?' Helen asked.

'What about me?'

'I think Morrisey has a fancy for you.'

'Nonsense,' Gloria said dismissively, 'but whether he has or not is neither here nor there. God, Helen, don't you think I have troubles enough at my own door without looking for more?'

Later that night, after Ben has gone to bed, Gloria asked Joe if they could talk.

'Well, of course we can talk,' Joe snapped, and added before he could stop himself, 'We can talk any day in the week, but you usually never have two words to say to me.'

He was sorry as soon as the words were out and they

hung in the air as Gloria gave a sigh and a shake of her head. Then she said, 'Please, Joe, I don't want it to be like this.'

Joe thought that Gloria was going to talk about the state of their marriage, which his mind recoiled from discussing and so he was surprised and relieved when she said, 'The men on the base are putting on a Christmas party for the children of Derry this coming Saturday, the eighteenth.'

'So? How does that affect you or me?'

'They have asked me to help and said that I can take Ben,' Gloria said. 'He hasn't had anything like a party since the year we first went to London, before the war, and toys and even basic food became unavailable. He barely knows anything about Father Christmas. Have you any objection?'

'You mean you are asking my opinion?' said Joe sarcastically. 'You totally floor me. I would have said that my opinion in anything was of no account.'

'Stop feeling so bloody sorry for yourself,' Gloria snapped, angered at last by Joe's attitude. 'All right, if that is the sort of mood you are in, I will make the decision. I am taking Ben with me and that's an end to it.'

'Of course you are,' Joe said. 'You always do as you please, and I am the mug for putting up with it the way I do.' He strode across the room as he spoke, took his coat from the back of the door and slammed out into the night.

As he walked he wondered why he was so cross. Not because of the child going to a party. He would be a poor father if he could begrudge the boy a bit of fun and lightness in his life. It was really the high-handed approach to everything that Gloria adopted. She would decide a thing and that was that. He thought that somehow things were coming to a head. Before war had been declared he'd told Gloria that he felt the country was balanced on a knife edge, and now he felt that his marriage was in the same state. And he also felt he had just as little control to change the course of events. He returned home a worried man.

* * *

Ben was almost speechless with surprise when Gloria told him he was going to a Christmas party.

'They told me that first they are putting on a variety show for all of you, then you have the special party tea, and then you'll see Father Christmas, only they call him Santa Claus.'

'Some of the kids at school say that Father Christmas isn't real,' Ben said.

'And what do you say?'

Ben shrugged. 'I'm not sure.'

'I'll tell you what I am sure of,' Gloria said.

'What's that?'

'That every child who does believe will get a present.' She added with a smile, 'Are you sure now?'

'You bet I am,' Ben replied, and his grin nearly split his face in two. 'Presents! Oh, boy!'

Gloria was to learn that the Christmas parties for the children had begun in 1941. Five months before the attack on Pearl Harbor, civilian technicians and construction engineers arrived in Derry to build the naval base, and their kindness to the children had endeared them to many of the Derry people. And that first year they took over the Rialto Cinema and entertained 7,200 children, and Santa Claus arrived in a beech wagon throwing sweets.

'Gosh!' Gloria exclaimed when she heard this in the canteen one day at work. 'I wonder how they catered for so many.'

'It doesn't bear thinking about, does it?' Helen said with a shudder.

'Like my worst nightmare, that,' one of the other women said.

'Aye, you got to hand it to them,' said another. 'Must have nerves of steel. Harder job, I'd say, than facing the enemy.'

There was laughter at this, and then Gloria said, 'Where does it all come from – all the fancy food, the sweets and the toys and everything?'

'Your neck of the woods,' the first woman said. 'America, where else? It was a shock for many coming here and seeing how the people were living, and when they told them back home apparently they couldn't do enough to help.'

'I'm so glad they did,' Gloria said. 'I have never seen my son so excited about anything.'

Gloria had seldom worked as hard as she did at that party, for she had never seen so many children gathered in one place before. After the party tea, there was a conjuror to entertain the children while the ladies cleared away before the arrival of Santa Claus. When everything was done, Gloria slipped outside for a breath of air.

She wasn't feeling too good. She had a pounding headache, probably brought on by the row she had had with Joe that morning before she and Ben had left. It hadn't been helped, of course, by the screams and shouts of hundreds of excited children, and she leaned against the wall and closed her eyes, welcoming the blasts of cold air hitting her face. 'Penny for them.'

She knew the voice, she wasn't even surprised, and she opened her eyes to see Morrisey smiling at her. 'You don't want to share my thoughts, Officer Morrisey,' she said.

'Well, they sure as hell aren't making you happy,' Morrisey said. 'And isn't it about time that you started calling me Philip?'

'I couldn't.'

'Sure you could. It's an easy enough name to say.'

'It's not that.'

'Well, what is it?' Morrisey asked. 'Your name is Gloria and mine is Philip. What's the harm in using our given names?'

'None, I suppose.'

'So?'

'All right,' Gloria said with a smile. 'Your name is Philip.'

'Yes, and now that we have that established, Gloria,

haven't you heard about a problem shared being a problem halved?'

'Yes, but that won't help in this case.'

'How can you be the judge of that?'

Gloria wasn't going to admit the real cause of her unhappiness and so she said instead, 'I hate living in Buncrana. The place stifles me.'

'I understand it,' Phillip said. 'I would die a death buried in a place like Buncrana for years, however pretty it is.'

'The point is that we have the possibility of leaving here soon and Joe won't even consider it,' Gloria said.

'Oh, yeah? How come, when living here is making you so unhappy?'

'Oh, it's all tied up with a sort of pact he made with his brother,' Gloria said, and she went on to tell Philip about the money that Tom had raised for Joe's fare to America and the promise Joe made that they would stay in Buncrana for a year until Tom made up his mind what he would do.

'He should never have made that promise without asking you first,' Phillip said.

'Maybe not,' Gloria replied, 'but he did, and that is that, and he would rather chop off his right arm than break a promise he made to his brother. But if we don't take this flat I just can't see us ever leaving here. Anyway, I must go in now, and I'm sorry for burdening you with personal issues. It was wrong of me.'

'Why was it?'

'Those are not things that should be spoken of outside the family, and should never be brought to work.'

'Why not?' Philip asked. 'I don't know your husband and probably will never meet him, but what you have said maybe explains how sad you look at times.'

Philip held her trembling hands as she tried to leave, and said, 'Don't be afraid of me. I would never hurt you and I know that you are married and therefore spoken for, but

303

I have to say that you are the most beautiful woman I have ever seen, and your husband should tell you that often.'

'Please, Philip, you're embarrassing me.'

'I'm sorry,' he said, dropping his hands.

Gloria knew that she had to leave this man, to get away while she still could. 'Please let me go,' she said.

'Not until I tell you how much I love you,' Phillip said. 'I have only just acknowledged the depth of feeling that I have for you. It's been eating me up inside for weeks, ever since we met, really, but more particularly since the dance.'

'You mustn't say these things, Philip,' Gloria told him, stepping away from him.

'Even if they are true?'

'No, they mustn't be true,' Gloria cried. 'Philip, I can offer you nothing.'

'I know that,' Philip said. 'It doesn't help.'

'You must see that this is wrong?' Gloria said. She was aware of her heart thudding against her ribs and a weakness affecting all her limbs. She sighed and ran her clammy hands down the overall she still wore, and said in a voice that shook slightly, 'I will leave you now.'

Philip reached out and drew Gloria into his arms. Then he bent his head and kissed the tears from her cheeks that she hadn't been aware she had shed. She gasped and for a second their eyes met and they stared at one another. She saw the love light shining in Philip's deep dark eyes and knew it was mirrored in her own. 'Oh, Philip,' she cried, and she could no more have prevented the kiss than she could have prevented the sun from shining.

As their lips met, it was as if an explosion happened inside Gloria. She knew her innards were on fire for Philip Morrisey and her heart felt heavy, for she knew this man was forbidden to her. So she kissed him with everything in her for she knew that that kiss would have to last her a lifetime. When they eventually broke away they were both breathless and yearning for more. Gloria realised that she had reached a turning point and she had to put the brakes on because the sin was all hers. She was the one already committed.

Neither was aware of the passage of time, that the conjuror was long finished and that Santa Claus had given Ben a football. It was the very thing that Ben had wanted for years, and he was so full of exhilaration at getting such a magnificent present he had wanted to show his mother.

But she had been nowhere to be seen in the building and so he had gone in search of her. And he had found her, in the arms of another man and kissing him.

Ben thought all kissing between men and women disgusting and sloppy, and he didn't even like his own parents engaging in it. Not that he had seen them doing much of it lately, but that didn't give his mother the right to go around kissing other men. But he didn't know what to do about it, and in the end he slunk back inside.

Helen looked at Ben's unhappy face and said, 'Did you find her?'

Ben shook his head. He certainly didn't want anyone else to know what he had seen. However, just after Ben had gone into the main hall with the other children, Helen saw Gloria and Philip come in together.

One look at their flushed faces and Gloria's tousled hair told its own tale and caused prickles of apprehension to run down Helen's spine. She knew her friend was playing a dangerous game and she wondered how much Ben had seen, for something had badly disturbed him.

TWENTY

'What's the matter with Ben?' Joe asked Gloria, the evening before Christmas Eve. 'He hasn't been himself for days.'

Gloria had been aware that there was something up and she had an idea that it was something that had happened at the party, for he had been tetchy on the way home, though she had no idea what it was.

'How would I know?' she said to Joe. 'He's said nothing to me, but it's you he usually talks to if something is bothering him.'

'Yeah, it is,' Joe agreed. 'But this time I can barely get a word out of him.'

'I bet what Father Christmas leaves on Christmas morning will put a smile on his face,' Gloria said.

It ought to, because into his stocking that year the silver sixpence, bar of chocolate and apple would be joined by a yo-yo, a bag of marbles, and a tin whistle, which Joe said he would teach him to play. But pride of place, on the bedroom floor would be the fort and lead soldiers that had belonged to Helen's brothers, which Nellie thought Ben would like.

'Well, it might,' said Joe. 'But then again it might not. I thought he would be over the moon to have a ball of his own, but he has barely looked at it since he brought it home.'

'I know,' Gloria said. 'He can't seem to care less about it.'

Ben could have told his mother that every time he took

the ball in his hands, he would see her wrapped in that man's arms, and so he had no desire even to pick it up. But he didn't say this because he kept that secret tight inside him, and that was where it was going to stay.

Initially, he had intended to tell his father about it, and almost did the following evening as they'd milked the cows in the byre, but he stopped himself. He had the feeling that to put what he saw into words would make things worse, not better, so he decided to say nothing and try to forget it had ever happened.

When Gloria had told Helen of Ben's strange behaviour over the ball, she remembered seeing the boy's amazed, joyful face when Father Christmas gave it to him, when he had been so overwhelmed that he almost forgot to thank him. But when she met him later, he looked confused and upset. He claimed he hadn't been able to find his mother and yet she had come in with Philip only a short time afterwards.

What would it achieve, though, if she told Gloria this now? So, what she had said to Gloria was, 'Christmas will give him a boost, you'll see, and he would probably like you at home as well. We are lucky to get Christmas Day and Boxing Day off.'

Gloria said nothing because she wasn't looking forward to it one bit. All she could think was that she wouldn't see Phillip for two whole days. Since the kiss on the day of the party, she had avoided any situation where she might be alone with the man who disturbed her senses so much. She knew she had to do that because she was so greatly attracted to him that she couldn't trust herself.

She knew he was aware of how she felt, for she had seen it in his speculative eyes, but he never made any sort of approach to her or made things awkward for her in any way. He knew as well as she did that neither of them could risk any sort of relationship developing between them, for that would lead to heartache for both of them, and she didn't dare think of the damage to Ben if it should leak out.

Just to see Philip in the canteen or around the camp was enough to set her pulses racing, and she felt quite bereft at the thought of not catching sight of him at all for two days. She found herself wishing the holiday was over and she was back at work. Immediately she felt guilty. What sort of mother was she who didn't want to be with her child on Christmas Day? She really had to get a grip on herself.

First, though, they had Christmas Eve to get through.

It started badly with a row with Joe before she left that morning. 'The sailors have to eat on Christmas Eve as well, you know,' she snapped. 'You just think yourself lucky that I have the next two days off, because the canteen is still open and I am not the only married one there.'

'It's not right,' Joe said stiffly. 'In the New Year we will have to rethink this whole business of your job at that camp.'

Gloria gave a hard brittle laugh. 'Think all you like,' she said, 'but I will not give up my job and, anyway, I couldn't really afford to and you know it. My wages are what buys much of the food to put on the table and so you stick to the high moral ground and we will all go hungry.'

Joe was silent because he knew that Gloria spoke the absolute truth. The harvest had been a poor one that year because the weather had been wet. Added to that, the milk yield was well down, and the death of the farrowing sow and all her piglets had been a blow. There was still the vet's bill to pay. Without a sizeable proportion of Gloria's wages the winter would be a very lean one.

Joe felt the helplessness he'd felt in New York when he couldn't afford to provide adequately for his family and this frustration caused him to rap out, 'Go on then to your precious job. It's all you seem to care about anyway.'

'And can you wonder at that?' Gloria had said quietly as she lifted her coat from behind the door. 'Remember, as the trains are running only a skeleton service today, Helen and I are getting a lift home, so I might be a little later than usual.'

'Does Joe mind you working Christmas Eve?' Helen said as they settled themselves in the train.

Gloria sighed. 'Joe minds about everything almost as a matter of course. But I have already decided that I will not let Joe's attitude spoil things for me.'

'Good for you,' Helen said. 'We only have the one life so we might as well try and enjoy it while we can.'

When they finished for the day, there was a little buffet arranged for the workers with food that many hadn't seen in years, particularly those from Derry, who had their food-stuffs rationed. They tucked into proper sausage rolls, huge pork pies and slices of ham and pork. Even proper bread and butter was a treat when the usual bread was the grey National Loaf, and butter just a distant memory. And all this was followed by mince pies, chocolate log and Christmas cake.

There was punch to drink, and though the other women claimed it was delicious, Gloria and Helen viewed it rather dubiously. Colin and Philip waved their caution aside.

'There is alcohol in it,' Colin said, 'but not that much. A couple of glasses will do no harm at all.'

'Don't worry,' Philip said. 'We have no desire to drive the pair of you home singing.'

'Are you taking us back then?' Helen asked.

'Yes,' Colin said. 'Does that worry you?'

'No. Should it?'

'Let's wait and see, shall we?'

Philip's eyes met Gloria's suddenly, and his smile caused her knees to quake.

The previous time they had travelled in the car with the two men, the petty officers had sat at the front and the woman at the back, but that day Colin, who was driving, called Helen to sit up beside him, and Gloria and Philip got in the back together. Gloria's whole body was trembling and she wasn't surprised when Philip's arm slid around her. She didn't repulse it, though in her heart of hearts she knew she should have done.

She had allowed him to hold her once before, and ended up kissing him, and though it was too wonderful to truly regret, she knew she shouldn't have done it. Whatever she felt for him, she must go no further because soon she would be past the point of no return.

So, if she felt like that, why didn't she slip out of his arms now? She didn't understand herself at all, because she did the exact opposite and let her body sag against Philip's with a sigh. Philip heard the sigh and smiled to himself, and he cuddled Gloria closer, a thing he had fantasised about doing for so long.

They talked of generalities until they reached the streets of Buncrana, and then to Gloria's surprise Colin stopped the car at the bottom of the hill and got out.

'Got to be the driver now, sweetheart,' Philip said as he disentangled himself. 'Come up and sit beside me.'

'But why are you driving?'

Philip smiled. 'Colin has other things to do,' he said, adding to Colin, 'Pick you up later, buddy. Same place.'

Colin, with his arm tight around Helen, gave a wave, and Philip drove up the hill and along the road towards the farm. As they neared it, Gloria felt misery envelop her and she knew that she didn't want to go home.

When she sighed this time, Philip knew that it wasn't a sigh of contentment and he said, 'What's the matter?'

'Nothing,' Gloria said. 'Well, at least nothing special. I am just fed up with everything.'

'I think,' said Philip, 'that it is more than that. I believe you are deeply unhappy.'

'What makes you say that?'

'It's in every line of your body,' Philip said. 'And sometimes in your face and manner. You were made for joy and laughter, Gloria. Your smile would light up the room and your eyes are the most beautiful that I have ever seen. I would like to see them dancing with delight. You deserve to be happy.'

'Does anyone really deserve that?' Gloria said. 'I married Joe of my own free will when I was nineteen and I promised to love, honour and obey him for richer, for poorer, in sickness and in health, till death parts us. Nowhere does it mention that I should be happy in that marriage, though I was for many years, and now Joe is an unhappy as me.'

'Gloria, you can't go on like this.'

'I can, Philip, and I must,' Gloria said. 'Eventually the war will end and you will return to the States, and I will try and breathe life into a dead marriage.'

'Less than a week ago I told you that I loved you,' Philip said.

'Yes,' said Gloria. 'But that will change nothing, nor will the fact that I love you too.'

'But—'

'Philip, I am married to Joe for life, and mother to Ben,' Gloria said. 'And however much I love someone else, those facts don't change. When I think of you leaving, to be honest, I feel sick, and yet it will happen and then this madness, this fantasy, will end too.'

'It doesn't have to be like this.'

'For me it does,' Gloria said almost angrily. 'What d'you think I should do? Walk away into the sunset with another man and leave behind the one I have chosen and my poor unhappy child?'

'Does Joe love you?'

'Now, I don't know,' Gloria said. 'Oh, he did. Once there was no doubt of it, and I also loved him, couldn't ever imagine life without him.'

'It's a funny do altogether – love,' Philip said. 'People have been writing poetry and songs about it for years and yet no one really understands it. Maybe it's like a flower, and if you don't tend it and care for it, then it dies.'

'That's what it feels like,' Gloria said, nodding. 'Like it's all withered up inside me.'

'And you will wither up too in the end,' Philip said. 'You said that you will try and breathe life into a dead marriage when I eventually leave for the States. How will you bring back to life something that is dead and gone? Living that way will destroy you. It would destroy anyone. Gloria, you only have the one life.'

'I know. And I have chosen the path it must take. In the Catholic Church there is no room for a second chance.'

'So you will sublimate your life for a man who no longer loves you and a boy who will one day grow up and leave you anyway?'

'Yes,' Gloria said. 'That is the way it must be. Leave me here now at the head of the lane, Philip. Don't come any further.'

Philip stopped the car and turned to Gloria. 'I think you are making a grave mistake, but I will respect your decision, though it's breaking my heart.'

And mine, Gloria might have said. She couldn't trust herself to speak, however, and neither could she trust herself to stay alone with Philip any longer. As she slipped from the car and began walking down the lane towards the farmhouse, the tears began to seep from her eyes and she had to stop before she went inside to wipe the evidence away.

The next morning Ben was truly delighted with all that he had been given, especially the fort, which he had never expected, and Gloria was glad to see the shadows fade from behind his eyes. She did all that was expected of her. She walked to Mass with the family and bid everyone a Merry Christmas, and when she took Communion at the rails she felt justified in doing so because she had made it clear to Philip that there was to be no dalliance between them.

Outside the church, with the Mass over, Gloria could see that Helen was buzzing with excitement over something. When Gloria raised her eyebrows in enquiry, however, Helen gave a shake of her head and Gloria knew whatever news she had she didn't want it shared with others. Gloria would probably have to wait until the day after Boxing Day to find out what it was all about.

Back home it was as if Gloria and Joe had decided to bury their differences for Christmas. After a wonderful dinner, Joe showed Ben how to work the yo-yo, and before it was time for the milking, he gave him his first lesson on the tin whistle.

When Gloria went to bed that night, she felt more peaceful than she had in a long time and wondered if Joe would reach out for her that night. Sex between them had become a memory of pleasure shared, but she would have welcomed some closeness between them that night. However, Joe was ages coming to bed and she was only drowsily half awake when he did slip in beside her. Then he turned on his side and went fast asleep.

Joe wasn't actually asleep, he was lying listening to Gloria's even breathing. He had desired her that night more than he had done in ages, but there were unresolved matters between them that couldn't be swept aside by sex. In fact, he thought it might muddy the waters further.

The day after Boxing Day, Gloria met Helen on the road. 'OK,' she said. 'Spill the beans. I am dying with curiosity.'

Helen was only too happy to tell someone. 'Colin has asked me to marry him.'

'Marry you?' Gloria cried. 'That is just terrific news.'

'Ssh,' Helen cautioned, because they were nearing the station. 'No one must know yet.'

Gloria was puzzled. 'Why not? Has he already got a wife in America?'

'No,' Helen smiled. 'I'll tell you when we get in the carriage.'

'If we get one to ourselves,' Gloria answered. 'I will burst if I don't hear all before we get to Derry.'

'How d'you think I feel?' Helen hissed. 'I have had to keep it to myself all over Christmas.'

There were, however, few passengers travelling at that time of day and as soon as they were settled, Gloria said, 'Go on then. Why all this cloak and dagger stuff?'

'It's because of Mammy. Daddy too, of course, but mainly Mammy.'

'Nellie would be pleased for you. Any mother would be,' Gloria said.

'Aye, she would. Well, one part of her would be, anyway.'

'Well, then . . .'

'Think, Gloria,' Helen said. 'My mother gave birth to five children. I have two brothers already in America and a sister in Birmingham. Added to that, when the war is over and Cathy marries her guardsman, she could end up living anywhere. In fact, the only thing she is sure of is that her husband will not be stationed down the road in Buncrana. So how is my mother to feel when I tell her that I am to marry a man that will take me to America when the war is over?'

'I do see what you mean,' Gloria said. 'And it is hard on them when you put it like that. So what are you going to do?'

'Keep it quiet for now, at least,' Helen said. 'What is the good of making them miserable before they have to be? Anyway, I am marrying an American Protestant in a registry office, a marriage that will not be recognised in the eyes of the Church. I can't see either of my parents being over the moon about that either, can you?'

'No, but why should you be denied this second crack at happiness?'

'I know,' said Helen. 'I love Colin so much, and I long to marry him. I want children too, Gloria, before it is too late.'

'God, Helen, you have years yet.'

'Yes, well, I want them while I am still young enough to enjoy them,' Helen said. 'Colin feels the same. We both want children straight away. Of course, the priest won't see that at all. To him I will be unmarried, my children bastards and my feelings of no account. If Mammy knew of my intentions she might even send him to talk some sense into me to try and prevent me leaving these shores.' She looked at Gloria, then went on, 'Really, Gloria, I can do without pressure like that. Like you say, I want a second crack at happiness. I don't honestly think that is asking too much.'

'It isn't,' Gloria assured her. 'And I hope the pair of you will be very happy. You deserve to be.'

In January, Helen said to Gloria, 'Colin is really fed up with this hole-in-the-corner relationship. He wants to take me out properly – you know, go to the pictures or "movies" as he calls them, take me dancing and things like that. He's tired, he says, of just seeing me in stolen moments when our lunch hours coincide.'

'You can see his point, Helen.'

'Yes, I can, but what excuse can I give Mammy for coming back into Derry in the evening?'

'I know that you don't want to upset your parents or anything,' Gloria said, 'but aren't you being just a bit melodramatic about all this? I mean, your parents know Colin; nearly know his life history.'

'I know, but I can't tell them yet.'

'Well, I think it is plain daft,' Gloria said. 'You are a grown woman and entitled to a life, and you should tell your parents that.'

'Oh God, Gloria, I am not as brave as you,' Helen said.

'Then tell your mother that you have got friendly with one of the other single girls at the canteen and you have decided to sample the night life of Derry a time or two,' Gloria suggested.

'Oh, Gloria, that's a great idea,' Helen said. 'Why ever didn't I think of that?'

Nellie and Jack expressed great surprise when Helen proposed going back to Derry to go to the pictures. 'Haven't we got a good enough cinema here?' Nellie said.

'Yes, of course, but the better and newer films are in Derry first. Anyway, this girl Chris that I am going with lives in Derry.'

'And her father will bring you home, you say?'

'Yes, he promised.'

'He must be a good man and a caring father to be doing that,' Nellie said. 'You must bring him in so that we can thank him.'

'It would be too late,' Helen said desperately, and then, remembering what Gloria had said about being a grown woman, she added, 'Anyway, do you not think I can and should deal with this myself? You don't need to thank the man on my behalf. I am no longer a child.'

'No, no, of course not,' Nellie said placatingly.

'We were not implying any such thing,' Jack said, 'and we have no objection to your going out into Derry a time or two. Not that we have any right to object, for, as you say, the decisions you make are your own now. I am pleased that you are taking up the threads of life again.'

'And so am I,' Nellie said stoutly. 'You work hard enough, and all work and no play is no good for anyone.'

Helen recounted all this to Gloria as they made their way to work. 'So it's all plain sailing for you now, and you will make Colin's day,' Gloria said.

Helen agreed, then added, 'What happened between you and Philip on Christmas Eve? I know you are fond of each other . . .'

'Nothing,' Gloria said. 'I laid it on the line for him and he has kept well away since.'

'Yes, he has,' Helen agreed, 'and most people on the camp are suffering for it.'

316

'What do you mean?'

'I mean he is like a bear with a sore head,' Helen said. 'Colin said the young sailors that he teaches mechanics to don't know what has got into him. He has heard them talking and apparently they were saying that they have never known him like this. Being lads they presume some woman is at the back of it, but they have no idea who it is.'

'Phillip will have to deal with it as I have to do,' Gloria said. 'Does he think he is the only one suffering?'

'Ah, Gloria, I am so sorry for you,' Helen said sympathetically.

'You know what?' Gloria said, with a rueful grin. 'I am sorry for myself as well, but as my mother used to say, what can't be cured must be endured and that is how I have to look at the life I have mapped out for myself.'

'Why don't you and this girl Chris ask Gloria along to the pictures a time or two?' Nellie asked Helen one Saturday in mid-February as she made herself ready for her date with Colin. 'The girl looks right peaky to me. Likely a night out would do her good.'

Helen was nonplussed for a second or two, and in the end mumbled that she didn't think Joe would like her to do that.

'Don't see why not,' Jack said to his daughter. 'Do Joe good too if he came up to Buncrana a time or two and had a few pints and a chat with his neighbours, the same as Tom used to do. He might loosen up a bit then perhaps.'

'Are things all right between Joe and Gloria, d'you know?' Nellie said to her daughter.

'Why do you ask?'

'Well, Gloria often looks as if she has the weight of the world on her shoulders,' Nellie said. 'And Ben is a bag of nerves.'

'I think they are going through a sticky patch just now,' Helen replied.

'This isn't a recent thing – not with Joe, at any rate,' Jack said. 'God, I have never seen such a change in a man. Tom, for all he had to go through with that mother of his, was always pleasant and used to come up to Grant's Bar on a Sunday night with the rest of us and thoroughly enjoy himself. Joe, on the other hand, goes no place now, and barely bids people the time of day when he strides about the town. Before he left for America, he was the life and soul of every gathering and could sink a fair few pints if ever he got his hands on any money, and Tom was seen as the quiet one. Joe was off to the socials and flirting with all the girls and there were more than a few broken-hearted when he left.'

'You are recalling a man who was as free as a bird,' Nellie said. 'Now he has a wife and child – responsibilities. He is bound to be different.'

'Not this different,' Jack said. 'I would have said that the time he was injured in London hurt more than just his body, and yet when he first came home, despite the pain he was often in, he was like the old Joe and always had a cheery word for everyone.'

'Gloria said that too,' Helen said. 'You know, about slotting into place here as if he had never been away, and it was her that was the distrusted outsider. But now I really must go,' she said, picking up her bag. 'I will miss my train if I'm not careful.'

On the way to the station, Helen reflected on her parents' words. She knew what was the matter with Gloria. She was pining for Philip and yet she was adamant that she mustn't see him.

And Gloria didn't see him. He never even came into the canteen any more. She didn't know where he was eating, but she was glad that he kept away and told herself that it was a good thing.

Then the dreams began, strange, lurid and disturbing dreams that in the cold light of day she was ashamed of, and yet each morning, from the minute she opened her eyes, the longing for Phillip almost overwhelmed her.

Sometimes she was so full of misery it was difficult to rise from her bed. She felt she had nothing to look forward to. Joe watched her and worried about her, for she seemed steeped in such gloom even the light had gone from her eyes.

He knew that he was semi-responsible for Gloria's unhappiness and yet he could see no way that he could now retrieve the situation, because though she was still there in person, he knew that she had left him a long time before and gone to a place where he was unable to reach her.

This knowledge made him almost as disconsolate as Gloria. Eventually Joe's unhappiness spilled over into the weekly letters he sent to his brother. Tom kept asking him what was wrong. Joe never replied to these questions, because he hardly knew himself.

On Monday 24 April 1944, as Gloria and Helen travelled to work, Helen suddenly said, 'I'm getting married on Thursday.'

Gloria just stared at her. 'This Thursday?' she said at last. 'Why so soon?'

'Colin says there is something big happening on the South Coast of England,' Helen said. 'That's why.'

'What sort of something?'

'Well, they are told nothing official, you understand,' Helen said. 'But there are plenty of rumours, and the prevalent one is that Allied troops are massing at the coast. That can mean only one thing.'

'Invasion?'

'Right,' Helen said. 'Anyway, Colin said before the balloon really does go up and all leave is suspended, or they are shipped out to some other place, he wants it made legal between us. He has a forty-eight-hour pass coming up, and has arranged a special licence so we're all set. We are telling Mammy and Daddy tonight and I don't relish that one bit. What I want to know is, will you be my witness?'

'I don't know how Joe will view that,' Gloria said. 'With doom and gloom certainly, but that is how he looks at most things.'

'Go on,' Helen pleaded. 'You are the only real friend I have here. If you don't do this for me I will have to have a complete stranger by my side.'

'What about Cathy?'

Helen shook her head. 'If Mammy and Daddy feel they can bear it, I want them to come and that means someone must look after the post office. Anyway, with Cathy being so much younger than the rest of us, and me being in England so long, I don't really know her nearly as well as I know you. What I do know is that she will take her stance from Mammy, and Mammy will disapprove, so she will too. I don't want someone feeling that way to stand at my side.'

'Of course you don't,' Gloria said, feeling for her friend. 'Your wedding should be joyful, wherever it is, and you want people there who will wish you well.'

'So you will do it?'

'Yes,' Gloria said. 'Joe doesn't even have to know anything about it. It'll be just as if I was going to work except that under my coat I will have my wedding clothes.'

'Oh, Gloria, I can't tell you how much it means to me,' Helen said in obvious relief. 'I can tackle Mammy and Daddy with a better heart now.'

The next day, though, Helen had swollen eyes and said it had been worse than her worst nightmare telling her parents because her mother, as Helen had predicted, had been so upset.

'I was breaking my heart,' she told Gloria. 'And Colin didn't know how to handle the situation at all. He had never seen Mammy like that. She had always been so kind to him and Phillip, and she was looking at him as if he was the devil himself.'

'What were they like this morning?'

'Stiff,' Helen said. 'Very proper, you know. The point is,

nothing will change after Thursday, except that I will be married to Colin. He will have to live on the camp and I will still have to stay at Mammy's until something is decided about the wives of the servicemen. It is going to be very awkward for me if they refuse to accept the situation.'

'They'll come round,' Gloria told her reassuringly. 'What you told them was bound to come as a shock. When they have time to think about it they will be different again, you'll see.'

The following morning, Helen told Gloria the priest was waiting for her when she got home from work the previous evening, but even against him she stayed firm. 'I said that I had a perfect right to a life of my own and also a perfect right to choose who would share it with me,' she said to Gloria. 'And there was nothing he could say or do to turn me away from the man I loved, or convince me that I was making a huge mistake. Cathy had a go at me later for being so rude to the priest. I tell you, Gloria, Thursday can't come soon enough for me.'

The morning of the wedding, just before Ben was due to leave for school, Gloria said to him, 'I have to tell you something, a secret.'

'What? I'm really good at keeping secrets.'

'Helen is getting married today.'

'Gosh! Is she?' Ben said. 'Why is that a secret?'

'Because Helen is marrying a Protestant and so she's not getting married in a church. Now do you see?'

Ben nodded. He understood that well enough.

'I'm going along to support her because we are friends,' Gloria said.

'And you didn't tell Daddy because of it being a secret?'

'That's right,' said Gloria. 'But you can tell him when you come home from school because I might not be back by then.'

'All right then,' Ben said. 'See you later.'

Gloria watched her son run up the lane and set off just a few minutes later, knowing that when she alighted at the station she would have to make a mad dash across the city to get to the registry office in time. She was in fact five minutes late, and an official told her that the groom and the best man for the Mortimer/Meadows wedding, along with guests, were already in the room and awaiting the bride.

Helen arrived a few minutes later in a beautiful cream suit and a matching hat with a little veil. Gloria stepped forward in the foyer and kissed her on the cheek, saying as she did so, 'You look gorgeous.'

'Do I?' Helen said. 'Thank you. That makes me feel better. I'm so nervous my mouth has gone all dry.'

'You'll be fine once you are in the room,' Gloria told her. 'And Colin is in there waiting for you.'

'Oh, well, here goes then,' Helen said, and she walked into the room, Gloria following. The only other people there beside Phillip and Colin, she noticed, were Helen's parents. Jack was in a suit that was a little tight for him, and Nellie in a blue costume that had seen better days. Nellie's eyes were full of sadness and Jack's reproach. Gloria turned her eyes from them and stood beside her trembling friend as the groom and best man joined them.

It was as the couple went forward to take their vows that Gloria realised who Colin's best man was and found that she was looking into the velvet-brown eyes of Phillip Morrisey. Her face coloured, but Phillip's tentative smile started the familiar tug in her stomach and she could hear the beat of her heart.

Suddenly Philip reached out a trembling hand and she looked into his eyes, so full of trepidation. She felt a shiver run all down her spine and this set her whole body quivering with desire for the man standing bedside her. She knew too that if she took hold of Philip's hand, she would be lost to all reason, even all decency for love of this man. And yet as their eyes locked together she grasped it tight.

Nellie's startled eyes met those of her husband.

TWENTY-ONE

When the wedding service was over they all had dinner in a hotel, and afterwards Gloria couldn't remember a thing she had eaten. When she had touched Philip's hand in the registry office, a tingle shot all through her arm and she had almost gasped at the power of it. She sat opposite Philip at the meal later and drank in the sight of him. It was as if she was coming alive again, a coldness being replaced by warmth that seemed to be filling every part of her.

People spoke to her and she hardly heard what they said, for she had eyes and ears only for Philip. She knew then that her life would have no meaning if she did not have this man in it.

After the meal, Helen and Colin were making for a hotel in Southern Donegal where they would spend their wedding night, and then Colin would have to return to camp. He had the loan of a staff car and offered Jack and Nellie a lift home in it, but Jack said stiffly that he already had a lift organised.

Colin watched them stride up the street, disapproval evident in every line of their bodies, and he said ruefully, 'Somehow I don't think that I am on the favourites list with Helen's parents. Now, then, Gloria, do you want a lift home or are you going to go all starchy on me as well?'

'Not home, no,' Philip said. 'But if you drop us the other side of the border then I would be grateful.'

Colin said nothing but his eyebrows raised quizzically and it was Helen who said to Gloria, 'That all right?'

Gloria nodded, because yearning for Philip was so coursing through her body she was incapable of speech.

They were dropped on a country road just past the little town of Muff. They didn't need to speak. Shafts of desire were stabbing at Gloria and she went into Philip's arms as if it was the most natural thing in the world. Together they watched the car drive away.

'Oh, my darling,' Philip said. 'How I have longed for this moment. But I need to be sure you really do want this.'

Gloria felt as if her nerve endings were jangling. Still holding hands and as if by tacit agreement, they began walking up through the hills as Gloria said, 'I have never been so sure of anything in my whole life. How much do you love me, Philip?'

'With every fibre of my being. I love you so much that even now, if you say, as you did before, that it is wrong, I will walk back to Derry with you and set you on a train to Buncrana with no harm done except to my heart, which will be shattered into a million pieces. It would destroy me, but I would rather that than see you disgraced. That way, your reputation would be intact and your conscience clear.'

'And my heart would be bleeding for you,' Gloria said. 'Why did you put your hand out to me in the registry office?'

'Oh God, I don't know,' Philip said. 'It was as if my feelings overwhelmed me. When I saw you there, I just had to try to touch you. After what you said last time I wasn't sure that you would take it.'

'I couldn't not,' Gloria said. 'I love you so much.'

'You said you loved me before,' Philip said tentatively, 'and yet . . .'

'I am still a wife and mother, Philip,' Gloria said. 'None of that has changed, but now I know that I am only half a person without you, that I truly cannot live without you. My life is of no account without you in it.'

'You don't know how long I have waited to hear you say those words,' Philip said, swinging her round to face him and kissing her tenderly.

'I want you to make love to me, Philip,' Gloria said. 'Listen to me, I am shameless. I am craven with lust for you, because I feel as if I'm on fire, and I will die if you do not satisfy this ache inside me.'

'Oh, my darling!' Philip cried, and his mouth met hers. Clasped together, they sank down into the grass and Philip felt yearning in every line of Gloria's pliant body. As their kisses intensified he could feel her heart thumping in her chest and felt his own excitement mount.

Phillip, however, had to be sure. 'You know that this will change things for always?' he said, as they lay together.

'Yes, yes, I know,' Gloria said impatiently. 'I don't care any more, I love you so.'

'Oh, my darling girl . . .'

Gloria felt as if her innards were on fire. ' Philip,' she cried, 'please hurry.'

She began tearing at her clothes and Philip put his hands around her agitated ones and said, 'Take it steady. Let me undress you.'

Gloria, her nerve ends tingling, let her arms fall down by her sides and Philip slowly and sensuously removed her clothes. She had to bite her lip to prevent herself from urging him to hurry and eventually she lay naked before him.

But Philip hadn't finished, and he undressed totally too before covering Gloria's body with his own. They lay skin to skin and Gloria sighed in contentment.

Though Philip knew that Gloria was ready, he wanted to take her to the peak of arousal, and so when their lips met, he let his tongue dart in and out of her mouth, while his hands caressed her between her legs and she gasped aloud. His lips went on to kiss her neck and her throat, and his hands continued to caress her body, fondling her breasts, sucking at her nipples, until Gloria moaned and groaned in ecstasy. 'Please, Philip,' she cried. 'Oh, please, I can't bear it.'

Philip smiled as he entered his beloved. Gloria had given herself to him totally and they moved together as one. Gloria's passion rose higher and higher, until she felt as if she was drowning in exquisite rapture, such as she had never felt before and never wanted to end, and she cried out over and over. She acknowledged that while sex with Joe had been good, sex with Philip was beyond her imagining, and when it was over, she was completely and utterly sated.

Philip watched her with a smile playing around his mouth that lit up his eyes. 'You are truly and utterly beautiful, and I love you so much,' he said.

'Oh, Philip . . .'

'Get dressed, my darling,' Philip said. 'There is much to talk about.'

'Yes,' Gloria said, beginning to get into her clothes. 'I am joined to you now. Whatever the obstacles, they can be overcome, because without you I don't exist.'

'Think carefully about what you are saying,' Philip said. 'I don't want to force you into anything.'

'Did you force me just now?'

'No, but . . .' Gloria's heart went out to Philip, gazing at her with anxious eyes, and she realised that despite the rapturous sex they had just enjoyed, that joined one to another, Philip was still afraid that she might walk away from him. She had done this before but it was far too late to do that now, even if she had the desire to. She took his face between her hands, looked deep into his dark eyes and said, 'I belong totally to you now, and I love you so much I ache.'

'What of your husband? Your son?'

'I don't know if Joe won't be as pleased as I am that our sham of a marriage will soon be coming to an end,' Gloria said. 'Neither of us is happy with things as they are. But Ben, of course, will have to come with me, wherever that is.'

'That is the point, darling,' Philip said. 'You won't be able to go anywhere until we are married.'

'But I am already married,' Gloria said. 'And there is no divorce in Ireland.'

'We have no time to wait for divorce anyway,' Philip said. 'No one knows what is going to happen with all this hullabaloo on the South Coast. The point is, if invasion is on the cards, I would say most of the young sailors will be part of it. If that happens my job here, like Colin's, will probably be at an end.'

'And mine too, I suppose,' Gloria said 'But where will you be sent?'

Philip shrugged. 'I don't know. I might be recalled to the US, or drafted someplace else, and if they do that, unless we are married, you will have to stay here.'

'Oh God,' said Gloria in dismay, 'what are we to do?'

'There is only one thing to do, as I see it,' Philip said. 'And that is to get married as soon as possible in Belfast or some place like that where you won't be known.'

'Could we do that?'

'Well, we shouldn't do it,' Philip said. 'I mean, it's against the law and not at all the sort of wedding I want for you, and if there were any other way I would take it, but I think in the circumstances this is the only thing to do. How do you feel about it?'

Gloria thought about what Philip had suggested with a sort of shocked disbelief. She was a law-abiding person, and even in her wilder youth had never broken the law or come anywhere near it, apart from sneaking the odd, illicit drink at a speakeasy. She didn't want to break the law now, either. Every fibre in her being cried out against doing something that would break all the rules of propriety.

Philip watched Gloria's troubled eyes and her furrowed brow, and felt his heart sink. Was it one step too far for Gloria? He was afraid to ask, afraid to break her mood of concentration.

Gloria in fact was telling herself that she was some sort of hypocrite. After all, didn't it offend the rules of propriety not only to leave Joe in the lurch, but to take his son away too? She didn't underestimate the blow that would be for him. Yet she was balking at the thought of marrying her beloved bigamously, although she knew in her heart of hearts that it was the only way forward if they were to have any sort of a future together.

And so she smiled at Philip as she said, 'I don't mind anything as long as we can be together.'

Philip let out a sigh of relief. 'My darling girl, don't worry,' he assured her. 'We can legalise the whole thing once we reach the States. And once we are married, I will try and get you somewhere to stay in Belfast and come and see you as often as possible.'

'But what of my son?' Gloria said. 'I can't drag Ben to Belfast and if I did, Joe would try to find him. What if he were to succeed and see what we were about? He could spill the beans about my not being free to marry and that would put paid to me travelling to America and maybe an end to our freedom because, as you said, bigamy is a crime.'

'I do see what you mean,' Philip said. 'And it just could happen like that. So what do you recommend we do?'

'Go on as we have been,' Gloria said. 'I will stay at the farm until all the arrangements to travel to America are in place.'

'I hate to think of you sharing another's bed.'

'Well, that is all I do,' Gloria said. 'Sex between Joe and me stopped a long time ago.'

'Even so . . .'

'It is the only way, Philip, and the safest for us too,' Gloria said.

Philip nodded his head resignedly because he knew that Gloria spoke sense. 'Anyway, the first thing I'll need is a special licence,' he said. 'And I don't know how long that takes. Then it is just a question of waiting for a suitable ship to take you across the Atlantic. Now we best get back. Do you want to walk back to Derry and catch a train?'

'No,' Gloria said recklessly. 'I want to walk across the hills, holding hands with you.'

'Then we will,' Philip said, hauling her to her feet. 'And we will have to step on it because time is getting on and I will be on a charge if I am late back at the camp.'

Gloria was even more distant when she returned from Helen's wedding and yet in a strange way she seemed happier in herself. Joe wasn't at all comforted by this change in her. In fact, he was alarmed because he knew he hadn't done anything to warrant it.

Then she began spending a couple of evenings a week with Helen in Derry. She hadn't asked Joe if he minded her doing this, she had told him that she worked hard and she deserved some time off and she was going into Derry where there was more entertainment to be had.

For the first time Joe wondered if she was seeing someone else. He knew that he should at least have challenged her about it, if not forbidden her to go, further shaming him. It was what every other man in Buncrana would do, but strangely he couldn't seem to summon up the energy, though he realised that it was one more thing the men of Buncrana would laugh at him for.

The fact that he said nothing about Gloria's outings to Derry to see Philip just convinced her that Joe didn't care two hoots for her, and he wouldn't care that much when she eventually left him altogether. Strangely, she was saddened by this. She had known Joe since she was fourteen, and now she was thirty-seven and had been married to him for almost twenty years. She often lay sleepless in bed beside a slumbering Joe and went over their lives together.

They had coped with years of plenty, followed by many years of penury and deprivation; they had crossed continents and been able to deal with the rigours of war and the tragic loss of many dear friends. Not when their home was destroyed, nor even when Joe's life had hung in the balance had she felt their love for one another had been threatened, especially as during these turbulent years they had reared a much-loved son. She had thought their marriage would last for ever and yet after less than two years in Buncrana their love had drifted away like so much mist. She still didn't know why or how she could love another man so passionately that she couldn't imagine life without him.

She knew that when she sailed for the States, Joe would probably not see her again, nor Ben either, or at least not for many years. She pushed down the guilt that threatened to engulf her at that point because she knew if the positions had been reversed, it would have torn the heart out of her.

The room where she and Philip were to be married a month later was bare and cold, and apart from the two of them and the registrar, the only other ones in the room were Helen and Colin. As the marriage had drawn nearer, Gloria had been very nervous of going through with it, certain that someone would find out; she knew bigamy carried a prison sentence. In the end, even Joe had remarked on how jumpy she was. On the day itself, she was certain that someone would turn up and denounce her in some way. Helen told her not to worry, but she couldn't understand how fearful Gloria was.

Even as they stood before the registrar, Gloria's senses were on high alert. Any moment she expected the doors open, the marriage stopped, and she and Philip hauled off by the police.

There was no sort of specialness to the occasion at all. The registrar seemed in a rush as if he couldn't wait to get the ceremony over with as quickly as possible, and he rattled through the vows. They responded just as quickly and in a matter of minutes it was over.

'You may kiss the bride,' the registrar said, and Philip took her in his arms.

Gloria didn't feel like a bride – she didn't feel married at all – but she told herself not to be so stupid. She had known how it would be for she had seen Helen marry in a similar way in Derry, but she couldn't help feeling flat and deflated.

Unbidden came into her mind the day she married Joe and what a wonderful day it had been from start to finish. She tried to smile at Philip but he had seen her face, and guessed some of her thoughts. He put his arm around her and said, 'Think of that, my love, as just a process to enable us to spend the rest of our lives together. Once we get to New York, I will get lawyers to sort all this out and start divorce proceedings. When you are free I will marry you again, and properly, in any place you choose.'

'I know,' Gloria said, giving herself a mental shake. 'I know I am just being silly. The point is, it's done now and all I have to do is wait.'

'That's all,' Philip said. 'But that is the hardest job in the world.'

'These rumours about troops massing on the South Coast of England are worrying, aren't they?' Helen said to Gloria as they made their way to work in early June. 'Margaret has got to hear about it now. Not that she can say much in her letters without the censor cutting it all out.'

'I know,' Gloria said. 'Tom wrote that he had heard the whole of the South Coast was out of bounds to civilians.'

'And the whole of the camp is on high alert.'

'Yes, Philip said that too,' Gloria said. 'Something is afoot, all right. I just hope it won't delay plans for us to leave here. Philip has had a letter from his parents. They say they are looking forward to meeting me, and I can hardly wait.'

A few days later, on a Wednesday evening, the droning of planes was so loud Gloria and Joe went out of the cottage to see what was going on. They saw hundreds of planes in the air.

'They're emptying the airfields,' Joe said excitedly. 'If we go up to the top of the hills we might see what is happening to the ships on the Foyle.'

The two of them stood and watched the fleets of ships leaving the Foyle and sailing out against the sky. Gloria shivered and it was not from the chill of the night, but Joe's words. 'This is it, then. Make or break. We will know soon whether they have made a grave mistake or not.'

The next morning, the canteen was very quiet and Gloria thought of the young sailors that had sailed out the previous night to who knew what danger. There had been ships sunk and sailors lost on convoy duty before, but this time so many sailors were putting their lives at risk. Mid-morning they were told of the newsflash from Reuter's News Agency that announced, 'Allied Armies began landing on the coast of France this morning.'

The paper that Gloria bought on her way home from work spoke of Operation Overlord, or D-day. The paper claimed it had been a success, though later they were to hear of the many who gave their lives to achieve victory.

The year that Tom asked for to make up his mind about the farm was past, and he came back in July and told them after great deliberation he had decided to relinquish the farm, and that it and all in it was to be sold as soon as possible. However, he hadn't been there long when he saw that Joe and Gloria were trying to cope in a marriage that was in tatters, a marriage that once had been rock solid.

'What's up with you?' he asked his brother. 'I knew there was something amiss and asked you in every letter.'

'How could I explain this?'

Tom immediately felt guilty. He wondered if his inability to make up his mind, therefore forcing Joe and Gloria to remain on the farm, had anything to do with their unhappiness with one another.

He was more certain this was the case when Gloria said,

'I understood you were going to move in with Aggie and Paul, but you haven't done so yet.'

'No,' Tom said. 'Aggie is lovely, and you couldn't get a nicer man than Paul, but I thought they needed more than a few months together before I landed on them. I thought I would give them a year at least of living together and then as it became apparent that I was going to sell the farm, I thought the flat would do as a start for you and Joe and young Ben, if you wanted to move to Birmingham, as Joe had said you might. Accommodation of any sort is virtually impossible to find in Birmingham at the moment.'

Gloria smiled ruefully. Tom's offer had come too late. It would take more than an apartment in Birmingham to save their marriage, especially when her heart now belonged to another.

It was harder for Gloria to get away to Derry in the evenings with Tom in the house – without raising suspicion, anyway – and each day she longed for news of the ship to take her to America.

Everything was winding down at the camp, and Gloria and Helen were given notice as only a skeleton staff was being kept on.

'Colin and I are leaving too,' Philip said, when he went into the canteen one dinner-time and Gloria told him she had been given her cards. 'We're being recalled. We more or less expected it because, with most of the young sailors gone, our jobs are really at an end.'

'Any idea where you are going?'

'America, at first,' Philip said. 'Then who knows? It would be nice if I was in America for the duration but I doubt it. I am more than ready to leave here now. The canteen won't have the same attraction without you in it.'

'I'm sorry to be leaving, to tell you the truth,' Gloria said. 'I will miss the other women. And to be absolutely honest, I really don't relish being at home with Joe day after day. Thank God that Tom is there too. He tries valiantly to keep an even keel in a house that is turned on its head.'

'Can't be for much longer,' Philip said. 'And, in the meantime, decide how you are going to break the news to Ben. I'd like to bet that he will not be overjoyed, and if we're not careful, once Ben knows, this whole thing could blow up in our faces.'

'I know,' Gloria said. 'And that's why I'm not telling Ben that he is going to America till the last minute. I'm going to let him think he is going to Birmingham.'

'Do you think that's wise?' Philip asked. 'I imagine he will be very angry with you if you do that.'

'Wise doesn't come into any of this,' Gloria said. 'And I don't care how angry Ben is. This is the only way that I can see of doing it, and the safest way for us because, by hook or by crook, I will have Ben on that ship.'

Philip said nothing. Gloria must know her son, but he reckoned that if someone had tried to take him away from his home without telling him when he was Ben's age, he would have been as mad as hell. He suddenly felt sorry for the boy, who had had no choice in any of this, and vowed to try to make it up to him just as soon as he could.

In early August, Helen came to meet Gloria with a smile on her face.

'You have heard about the ship?' Gloria burst out.

Helen nodded. 'Colin told me last night. There will be a liner in Belfast Harbour in just under a fortnight's time. Couldn't be better because we will have worked our notices by this Friday.'

'Ooh,' said Gloria. 'I can hardly wait.'

'I'm the same,' Helen said. 'I just can't wait to see America, anyway. You'll have show me round.'

'God, Helen, I'd hardly know the place now,' Gloria said. 'It will be like a voyage of rediscovery for me as well, but we will certainly meet up as often as possible.'

That night over dinner, Gloria began her plan of action.

She mentioned taking Ben for a little holiday in Birmingham. Ben's excitement was such that Joe couldn't find it in his heart to refuse him, though he did wonder what game Gloria was playing now. Tom was unaware of any undercurrent, however, and he was almost as enthusiastic as Ben was.

'I will write to them tomorrow and make the arrangements, shall I?' Gloria said to Joe.

He nodded. 'Aye, I suppose you may as well.'

Everything seemed to go Gloria's way. The morning she was to leave was the day Joe and Tom had arranged to sell the calves to a neighbouring farmer and they had them ready loaded on the cart. She knew it would be difficult for them to drop her and Ben off at the station in Derry.

'Why worry?' Gloria said. 'Aren't I well used to going into Derry by train anyway?'

'Are you sure?' Tom said. 'It seems an awful way to go on, with us not even leaving you at the station.'

'We'll be fine,' Gloria assured him. 'I have Ben to look after me, for as he is fond of telling me, he is a big boy now, in double figures.'

Ben grinned, though he blushed in embarrassment and said a little gruffly, 'Can we go or we'll never get there?'

Ben's excitement lasted until they reached Derry and there a car was waiting for them. Helen was there too, and a naval officer she introduced as her husband, Colin, was in the driver's seat. The man beside him was introduced as Phillip. Ben didn't recognise him as the man he had seen kissing his mother and assumed he was a friend.

'In you get, Ben,' Gloria said. 'These kind men are giving us a lift to Belfast.'

'Belfast?' Ben cried. 'Not Dun Laoghaire? I thought you said that Belfast was a military port?'

'We have to use Belfast because the boat is bigger.'

'Satisfied, Ben got into the car, squashed between the two

women. As it drove off he wondered what Helen was doing there, but then he remembered his mother saying that Helen used to live in Birmingham too, and so he said, 'Are you going to Birmingham as well, Helen?'

'No, Ben,' Helen said. 'I am going to New York. That's in America.'

'I know,' Ben said. 'That's where I was born.'

'Of course.'

'Would you like to go back and see it?' Gloria asked.

Ben considered that, then said, 'I wouldn't mind going on a visit.'

'Wouldn't you like to live there?'

Ben shook his head. 'I wouldn't mind living in Birmingham,' he said. 'Uncle Tom says Molly is having a baby. Isn't that good? Kevin will be an uncle.'

Gloria let Ben's voice flow over her because his words about a baby brought to mind the secret she was nursing. She hadn't had a period since the first time she had made love with Philip on 27 April, and now it was 15 August. She had never even contemplated pregnancy and refused to believe it at first. They had waited years for Ben, and he was now ten. There had been no sign of a baby since, and she'd thought she was barren. But she couldn't be, for now she was almost sure that she was carrying Philip's child. She hadn't had any opportunity to tell him since she had begun to believe that it might be true, but she intended to do that before the boat sailed that day.

As arranged with Colin, she stopped on the way to send two telegrams from the post office: one to Molly in Birmingham, to say that they had been unavoidably delayed and she would write later; and another to Joe, 'DO NOT WORRY. BEN IS WITH ME AND HE IS SAFE.' Then she sat in the car as the docks loomed closer and told Ben where they were really going.

'But you said we were going to Birmingham,' he complained. 'I don't want to go to New York.'

'You'll love it, Ben. It's where you belong.'

'No it isn't,' Ben said angrily. 'And you shouldn't have lied to me.'

'I had to do that, Ben, because, you see, we are not going for a holiday,' Gloria said. 'We are going there to live.'

'I'm not,' Ben said determinedly. 'I won't. And what about Dad?'

'You must come with me,' Gloria said, 'because I am your mother.'

'Don't I have a say in any of this?' Ben cried, and Gloria was not the only one to hear the tears behind Ben's words. 'Don't you care what I want?'

'I'm afraid I can't, Ben,' Gloria said. 'Sometimes adults have to decide what is best for you.'

'That isn't fair,' Ben said, and tears rolled down his face. 'Are we going by ourselves, just you and me?'

Gloria swallowed deeply before saying, 'At first there will be just you and me. Later, Philip will join us, but he has to stay in the American Navy until the war is over. He will be your new father.'

Philip wished that Gloria hadn't said that. He couldn't hope to be a father to a boy of Ben's age, especially as Gloria had said often how much Ben loved his own father. He wasn't a bit surprised when Ben ground out, 'I don't want a new father. I already have one.'

Philip turned to face Ben and said, 'Sure you have, and I would never try and take his place, but I sure hope that we can become buddies.'

Ben glared at the man and then suddenly there was a flash of familiarity. 'I know you,' he said. 'I saw you kissing my mother the day of the Christmas party.'

Both Gloria and Helen gasped, but Philip met Ben's outraged gaze and then said simply and without the slightest hint of shame, 'I sure did. I love your mother very much.'

What could Ben say to that? He knew against grown-ups he didn't have a chance. He would be taken wherever they wanted him to go, just as if he were a parcel or something, as if he had no feelings of his own. Tears prickled the backs of his eyes but he was too angry to cry, and resentment burned against his mother for taking him to some strange place just because she wanted to go. He felt sunk in misery and was already missing his father that he knew he wouldn't see again for years and years. He felt a yawning emptiness inside him at that thought, and he sank back on the seat with a sigh.

Gloria heard the sigh and she felt for his hand, but he pulled it away. Though she was hurt she accepted that the child was very upset and vowed she would do all in her power to make it up to him. By the time the boat docked in New York Harbour she would have won Ben round, she was sure.

Joe and Tom had just returned from the neighbour's farm when the telegram was delivered and Joe was confused by it.

'I know Ben is with Gloria,' he said to Tom. 'Where else would he be?'

Tom shrugged. 'Maybe she wanted to reassure you.'

'No, Tom, there is something fishy about the whole thing,' Joe said.

An hour later Jack came almost running down the lane. 'Molly has been in touch with Aggie and she phoned the post office,' he said. 'Apparently, she received a telegram to say Gloria and Ben had been delayed and she wondered if anything was wrong.'

Joe felt his blood run cold. He looked at Tom and said, 'So she hasn't taken Ben to Birmingham then. So where the hell has she taken him?'

'Where could she take him?' Tom said. 'She would never harm the boy.'

'I know that,' Joe said. 'But where is he?' He turned to Jack. 'Maybe she confided in Helen. The two of them are as thick as thieves. Could I go and ask her if she can shed some light on this?'

'Helen left this morning with that American husband of hers,' Jack said. 'Apparently there is a ship moored in Belfast to take all the wives of American servicemen over to the States.'

Joe felt as if a large lead lump had landed in the pit of his stomach. He remembered the times that Gloria had gone into Derry and he had wondered if she had been seeing someone else. He suddenly felt sick and he knew just where his son was.

'That's where Gloria has gone,' he said. 'She will be on that bloody ship with my son.'

'You could be right,' Jack said, 'because sitting beside Helen's husband in the car was his mate. His name is Philip Morrisey. At Helen's wedding he was one witness and Gloria another, and Nellie and I saw them holding hands. Then later, at the meal . . . well, I wondered if there was any funny business going on.'

'Funny business or not, she is not taking my son to America,' Joe said.

'She can't,' Jack said. 'Helen said they have to be married to be aboard those ships. That's why they had to marry in a hurry.'

'Then she has false papers,' Joe said. 'But I will stake my life that that is where she has gone.'

'Then you have got her,' Jack said. 'She is in big trouble.'

'Do you think I care a bloody fig about that?' Joe snapped. 'All I'm interested in is getting Ben back. How can we get there fast, Jack?'

'Hughie, the taxi driver in Buncrana, will take us, I'm sure,' Jack said. 'I will tell him that it is a matter of life or death.'

'It might well be,' Joe answered grimly. 'For if I find that one of those men at that camp has anything to do with the disappearance of my son, then I will break every bone in his bloody body.'

TWENTY-TWO

All the way to the docks, Gloria talked to Ben about the delights in store for them both when they reached the shores of America.

Philip butted in at times too. 'You will be staying with my parents for a little while,' he told Ben. 'They sure are looking forward to meeting you, buddy. And I am sure before too long you'll be my right-hand man. I used to love helping my father when I was a kid.'

'Yeah, well, I like helping mine too on the farm in Buncrana, because that is where my father is,' Ben said. 'I don't want to be your right-hand man or anything else either, because you are not my father.'

'Ben . . .'

'Don't you tell me off,' Ben exploded. 'He isn't my father and never will be, and you can't make me think any other way.'

'I understand how angry you are,' Philip said reasonably. 'This has been forced on you and it's a bit of a shock I'm sure. I really will try to make things as easy as I can for you. And then, when you are sixteen, we'll get a licence and I will teach you to drive. What do you say to that?'

Ben was going to say that for him sixteen was a lifetime away, but before he could say anything, Gloria burst out, 'Oh, Ben! Won't that be just wonderful?'

Ben glowered at them both and then turned to his mother

coldly. 'I suppose it would be all right if I had wanted to go to America in the first place,' he said. 'But I didn't, and I still don't. What's Dad to do if I just go off and leave him?'

There was an uncomfortable silence. In her heart of hearts, Gloria was concerned how Joe would cope with the loss of his beloved son. However, it was no good admitting that to Ben and so she said instead, 'He'll be all right, Ben.'

'No he won't,' Ben said. 'And you know he won't. You can't leave him like this. It isn't right.'

He had upset his mother, he knew, because her face had a crumpled look, as if she was going to cry, but Ben didn't care. He was glad that she was upset. She deserved to be. He wanted to scream and shout at her that she had to stop all this and go back home where she belonged, but there was no time because they had reached the dockside.

It was extremely noisy, heaving with people laughing and shouting and weeping and hugging one another, and porters with laden luggage trying to get through the crowd. Children ran about shrieking and screaming, either in excitement or fear, and babies wailed at the strangeness of it all.

Philip helped them unload everything from the car, and Colin went off to park it while Philip organised a porter. Ben thought of darting away and losing himself in the crowds, but he knew they would soon root him out. He had to be cleverer than that. Anyway, his mother had a hand on his arm as they followed the porters, who had their luggage piled high.

Ben remembered Kevin saying that you had to play adults at their own game. 'When you are a kid,' he'd said, 'they can make you do things you don't want to do because they are bigger and stronger, and everyone believes them over you, so kids have got to learn to box clever.' So Ben knew that if he didn't want to find himself in America, he had to get off the boat, and to be given the freedom to do that meant convincing his mother that he had accepted the fact that he was going to the States to live with her.

341

When they eventually got through the crowds and he saw the troopship bound for America moored at the dockside, he was impressed enough to say, 'Wow!'

Gloria smiled at him. 'Some ship, isn't it?'

'You bet. Look at all those decks!' Ben cried, pointing at them towering one above the other, with three black funnels on top of that.

There were two officers at the top of the gangplank checking the marriage lines of all the women going on board, and Gloria was mightily glad that Ben was so fascinated with the ship that he didn't notice this or he would certainly have something to say on the subject.

They were sharing a neat little cabin and Ben thought that if he really did want to go on this trip to America, he would have enjoyed living and sleeping in it for the time that they would be afloat. The cabin had four bunk beds in it, and beside each one was a set of drawers and a tall cupboard. They put their things away quickly and went out on deck, where Colin joined them.

Gloria looked at her son and said, 'We're going home, Ben. Aren't you the tiniest bit excited too?'

Ben nodded. 'A bit, yeah,' he said. 'It will be nice, I suppose, to see the place where I was born. Anyway, I haven't got a lot of option, have I? I still feel sorry for Dad, though.'

'You can write to your father as soon as we get to New York,' Gloria promised.

Yeah, Ben thought sarcastically, that will really help him. But what he said was, 'Can I explore the ship a bit?'

Gloria looked at all the people. She didn't really want Ben leaving her side. On the other hand, she wanted to spend the last few precious moments with Philip and was desperate to tell him before he had to leave the ship, that he was going to be a daddy, and so she said to Ben, 'All right, but don't go too far and for heaven's sake don't get lost.'

'I won't,' Ben assured her, moving away, but with the number of people aboard he was soon hidden from her.

She opened her mouth to call him back, but Philip said, 'He will be all right, you know. He's a big lad now and it is natural to want to explore.'

'I know,' Gloria said. She glanced across at Helen and Colin and, seeing them absorbed in each other, she said, 'I'm glad Ben is out of earshot for a few minutes, actually, for I have something to tell you that is for your ears alone, at least for now.'

'What?'

'Can't you guess?' Gloria said, and then, seeing Philip's consternation, she gave a little laugh and said, 'I have good reason to believe that I am carrying your child.'

She watched the incredulous joy flood over Philip's face and then he said anxiously, 'Is it mine?'

'Of course it's yours,' Gloria said. 'I told you, sex between me and Joe stopped a long time ago. But even if he had tried, how could I have let Joe make love to me when my heart belonged to another? You must have no doubts, my darling. This is your child that I am carrying.'

She looked into his beautiful deep brown eyes as she spoke and saw them moisten with tears at her words, and her heart turned over with love for him. He reached out for her as he said, 'Oh, my darling girl, that is probably the best news that I have ever received in my life. I never dreamed . . . Oh God, darling. It really is the icing on the cake as far as I am concerned.'

Gloria was glad that Ben was away as she allowed herself to be hugged tight, and laughed when Philip planted little kisses all over her face, and then was transported to Paradise as Philip kissed her properly. She knew she would have felt constrained with Ben watching.

Ben had seen enough, however. He watched them laughing and hugging and kissing, and knew it was so terribly wrong. He began traversing the ship while thoughts tumbled around in his head.

He wondered how long his mother had been seeing this

man Philip. From what he had witnessed the night of the Christmas party, it had been going on from then, at least.

He imagined his father alone in the little whitewashed cottage and tears burned in the back of his throat. Somehow he had to get off that ship and go back to him. He didn't want to leave his mother either, because he loved her too, but she wasn't acting like a mother because mothers stay with their husbands and she was prepared to walk away. She wanted a new life with a new man and he wanted no part in that, he decided.

In the end he had found what he wanted, and that was a gangplank as far away from his mother as it was possible to be. It was on the lower deck too, and used only by the sailors to load the ship with cargo. He smiled to himself, then went back to his mother.

'Where have you been?' Gloria asked.

'Right on the highest deck,' Ben said, the lie tripping easily off his tongue. He didn't mind lying to her. She had been lying to him long enough, and he frowned at the casual way that man had an arm draped around his mother's shoulders. 'You can see for miles,' he went on. 'That's where I want to be when the ship pulls out, when I say goodbye to Ireland.'

Gloria heard the sadness in her son's voice and she said, 'You do that, Ben, though it isn't goodbye for ever. I'm sure you will come back one day on a visit.'

Ben didn't answer; there wasn't time, for the hooter had sounded the signal for those not travelling to leave the ship. Gloria suddenly realised that she wouldn't see Philip for maybe months and her attention was all for him.

'Can I go now then?' Ben asked, and Gloria gave him a perfunctory wave.

'Yes, but come back here afterwards. I'll wait for you.'

Ben gave a nod and watched his mother in the American's arms again, clinging to him as they kissed.

He melted into the crowd and then, once out of his mother's sight, hurried as fast as he could, jostled by the disembarking passengers. From his hiding place he watched the quayside fill with those leaving the ship and saw the sailors beginning to unwind the hawsers.

Soon he knew they would raise the gangplanks and then it would be too late. He leaped up and ran down the short plank. One of the sailors shouted at him, but he paid no heed, and when another on the dockside tried to grab him, Ben twisted out of his grasp and was soon lost to view.

Joe was finding it hard to come to terms with the fact that his wife, his Gloria, had run away from him with another man. As the car sped on its way to Belfast, he examined his behaviour over the last months and knew that he was partly to blame for Gloria's dissatisfaction, which had eventually driven her into the arms of another.

'I refused to see how hard she was finding things,' he said. 'When she started working at the camp she made me a laughing stock, and yet we needed her money to survive. That I couldn't provide properly for her and Ben cut me to the quick.'

'I knew there was something the matter,' Jack said. 'I said to Nellie that you were nothing like the Joe I remembered, or the Joe that first returned, even taking into account the injuries you were suffering from. But even so, you can't take the total blame for this, you know.'

'I agree,' Tom said. 'It isn't your entire fault, Joe.'

'You know her, Tom,' Joe said. 'Would you say that Gloria would ever have done this without provocation?'

'I have to admit this is the very last thing that I expected Gloria to do,' Tom said. 'I knew she disliked the country and everything, but I would have said she loved you totally.'

'That is what I am saying,' Joe said morosely. 'I killed that love. You saw how it was between us and I spoke of this before to you. I wanted her to be more like the women in Buncrana. Just how crazy is that? She was a free and independent spirit and I choked the life out of her. I see it all now. Tom, you know that we have been unhappy for months. Maybe this man, whoever it is, made her feel more valued than I did.'

'Many of us are only truly valued at our funeral,' Hughie the taxi driver commented. 'That's life. Don't give you the right to run away when the going gets tough.'

'But that's it. She didn't,' Joe said. 'You wouldn't believe how bad it was in the tenement of New York and then the blitz in London.'

'What about bringing you here and managing Mammy the way she did?' Tom said. 'Giving credit where it's due, she was truly amazing then. Huh, I'd say if anything was going to send her into the arms of another man, then that would have been it.'

'If I had my time again I would do it all differently,' said Joe, 'and realise, as she did, that us two were the important ones, and how we handled our family was our business, and the townsfolk's opinion shouldn't matter a jot.'

'That was easier for Gloria to do,' Tom said. 'She came in as an outsider and didn't know the people. You were hailed as the returning hero to the place where you had been born and reared, where you had friends.'

'Is it too late?' Jack said. 'Could you not put it to her, as you have to us here in the car, and say you're sorry? I wouldn't have said that Gloria bears grudges.'

'And I have the flat in Birmingham going begging,' Tom put in.

Joe shook his head. 'This is what I should have done months ago. I should have explained how I felt and why, told her how sorry I was, and supported her and valued the contributions she was making to the family's finances. Now I fear it is much too late for Gloria and me.'

'Well, regardless of whose fault it is, I think the important one at the moment is Ben,' Tom said.

'Yes,' Joe agreed. 'She can't take the boy. If she wants to leave me that is one thing, and one I will deal with. But there would be no point in going on without my son.'

Tom heard the despair in his brother's voice and he sighed. 'Let's hope we are in time then to get him off that damned ship before it sails.'

However, they hadn't even found a place to park the car when they heard the hooter, and Joe knew he had failed and he would not see his son again for many years. He felt as if he had been stabbed in the heart.

He got out of the car, stumbling like an old man, and Tom turned away from the agony etched on his face.

'Sorry,' Hughie said, though Tom and Jack knew he couldn't have done any more; as it was, he had driven like a madman.

Joe didn't even hear him, nor feel the hand that Jack put on his shoulder as a gesture of support. He wandered away from them all onto the dockside as if he were in the throes of drink.

'Go after him, Tom, for God's sake, lest he do something stupid,' Jack said. 'The man's not in his right mind at all.'

Tom knew that as well as anyone. Joe's eyes were trained on the ship moving, as yet quite slowly, away from the harbour.

On board that ship Gloria and Helen were waiting for Ben to join them. 'I don't expect him to come back until the shores of Ireland are just a blur in the distance,' Gloria said.

'Did you tell him to come back here?' Helen asked.

'Yes,' Gloria said. 'It seemed the wisest plan.'

'Yes, it was,' agreed Helen, and when they had waited another few minutes, she wandered over to the rail. The ship was gathering pace now and the dockside emptying fast. 'Can you still see Colin or Philip?' Gloria asked, joining her.

'No,' Helen said. 'But they hadn't time to hang about. They were due back at camp.'

Then Gloria, scanning the dockside, caught sight of the lone figure staring, staring out at the disappearing ship. She knew immediately who it was. 'Look,' she said to Helen, 'that's Joe!'

'Are you sure?'

'Oh, yes,' Gloria said emphatically. 'I have been married

347

to him for long enough to recognise that stance, and there's Tom beside him.'

'How did they know where we were?'

'No idea,' Gloria shrugged, turning away, because the sight of Joe had filled her with guilt. 'I wish Ben would hurry up. I want to see if I can get us a meal somewhere. I'm famished.'

'Oh my God! Look!' Helen cried suddenly.

Gloria turned, and to her horror saw that another, smaller figure was approaching her husband. 'Dear God!' she cried and turned anguished eyes to Helen. 'What am I to do?'

Helen shook her head helplessly. There was nothing they could do.

'What has he done?' Gloria cried. 'How did he get off the ship, and why?'

'I don't know, Gloria.'

'But I can't go to the States and leave my son behind.'

'You can do little else just now,' Helen pointed out. 'I would think the captain would take a very dim view of turning this big ship round to pick up one young boy who doesn't want to travel to America anyway. He told you that plainly, and had he wanted to go he wouldn't have left the ship in the first place.'

Although what Helen said made sense, Gloria barely heard her. She felt an actual pain in her heart that was so powerful she fell to her knees with a heartbreaking cry, and Helen kneeled beside her and held her friend as she wept.

Ben hadn't been able to believe his eyes when he saw his father just standing there. He had thought that he would have to hitch all the way home and so he stepped from his hiding place and said, 'Hello, Dad. What're you doing here?'

Joe spun round in total shock at seeing the son he thought he had lost standing in front of him. 'Ben?' he cried. 'I thought you were on the ship.'

'I was, but I don't want to go to America and have a new father. I want to stay with you and so I got off.'

Joe put his arms around his son and held him tight. Tears ran down his face and his heart felt lighter than it had done in ages. Suddenly, he felt Ben stiffen and he followed his gaze. A little way from them was a naval officer staring fixedly at Ben as if he couldn't believe the evidence of his own eyes.

Joe stepped away from his son and faced the man. 'Are you Philip Morrisey?' he asked, and the man nodded. 'I am Joe Sullivan,' Joe said. 'And you are my wife's fancy man. I should knock you to the floor for what you have done, but I won't do that because I want to know how you secured a passage for Gloria to travel to America. I understood only wives could travel on that ship, and she is still married to me.'

There was no point in lying, and Philip said, 'We went through a civil ceremony in Belfast.'

That shook Joe. Even though he knew that she would have had to do something like that to get on the ship in the first place, the fact that she had actually gone through a marriage ceremony when she was still married to him shocked and hurt him. It showed him just what lengths she was prepared to go to for this American sailor. It wasn't the behaviour of the Gloria he knew, the one he had been married to for years. That Gloria had been as straight as a die and would never do anything underhand.

Philip saw the look in Joe's eyes and, despite his strong and ardent love for Gloria, he felt such sympathy for the man whose eyes were pain-filled.

'I could make things very difficult for you both if I had a mind,' Joe said. 'No one would blame me, for bigamy is a crime that carries a prison sentence. Many would say that you have stolen my wife away, but that isn't true, for I know the decision to leave had to be her own and I know she hasn't been happy for some time. However, Ben doesn't want to go with her and he has made that patently clear, and so he will stop with me. If you make trouble for me, or try to take Ben through the courts, then I will whisper into someone's ear. If you agree to leave Ben in my custody, then I will say nothing and if Gloria wants a divorce then she can have one. Perhaps when you are writing to her you will tell her this.'

Philip knew that Joe was right. He had the potential to make a great deal of trouble for both of them. But Philip knew Ben's place was with his father and he had to make Gloria see that. 'I'm sure that Gloria will see leaving Ben with you as the best solution,' he said.

Ben tugged on his father's arm. 'Let's go home, Dad.'

Joe turned away from Philip and his moist eyes softened as they lighted on the son he loved so much. Despite Ben's age, Joe lifted him into his arms and said, 'We will go to the cottage, Ben, and pack up all our things and move them to Tom's flat in Birmingham, and that will be our home now. What do you say to that?'

'Oh, you bet, Dad,' Ben said. 'That is just terrific.'

'And as soon as I get rid of the farm I am coming to join you,' Tom said, stepping forward as Philip walked away.

Ben put one arm around his father's neck and one around his uncle's, and said, 'That will be better still.'

The three of them stayed like that for a few minutes and watched the ship sail out against the sky.

Ben was squeezed into the back of Hughie's car between his father and Jack McEvoy, with his Uncle Tom in the front, and he listened to the banter and ribaldry between them. He took no part in it, though, because he felt saturated in misery with the realisation that he might never see his mother again.

Joe was so light-headed with relief that he had his son back with him again that at first he didn't notice Ben's silence.

Then, as they turned into the lane, Tom said, 'You and

Ben would do well to leave here as soon as possible, because your lives won't be your own when this news breaks in the town.'

'Your brother is right,' Hughie said. 'And though no one will hear it from me, these things get about.'

'And you know I can keep my own counsel when I have to,' Jack said. 'But this is a bad business altogether, and Hughie is right: someone will get hold of it before long.'

Joe knew the two men were right, and that, because Gloria had sailed for America and, as they saw it, abandoned both husband and child, then she would be hanged, drawn and quartered by the women of Buncrana. There was no way he could even begin to justify what she had done to their satisfaction, and that would be no help to Ben, whom he was sure still loved his mother.

In fact, now he came to think about it, Ben had been remarkably quiet altogether on the way home, and as the car drew up in the yard before the cottage and they climbed out, Joe said to his son, 'After we have eaten I will go down to the station to make arrangements, and then we will start to pack. All right?'

Ben nodded dumbly, Joe's eyes met those of Tom over the child's bent head and they both knew that he was too distressed to speak. The meal that Tom had on the table only minutes later was one of Ben's favourites: thick rashers of home-cured bacon and golden-yolked eggs with soda bread and thick creamery butter, but Ben moved it around the plate and actually ate very little of it.

Tom and Joe kept the conversation going, mainly about the arrangements, because the ensuing silence if they didn't was uncomfortable.

'Only book the passage for you and the boy from Derry,' Tom said. 'I'll take you that far and when you have that organised I'll send them all a telegram in Birmingham for they will be wondering what's afoot.'

'What will you say?'

'Don't worry,' Tom said. 'I'll leave all the explanations up to you. All I'll say is that the arrangements have changed and that you will be coming over with Ben, and give them the time of your arrival at New Street. I'm sure one of them will be there to meet you.'

'Probably,' Joe said, 'and the whole lot of them will be stunned by what has happened today. It won't take me long to pack, when all is said and done, because I have just realised that Gloria must have a whole case of Ben's clothes that are on their way to New York at the moment.'

'That won't be a problem,' Tom said. 'Molly said before I left that she is keeping anything still wearable that Kevin grows out of for Ben. With the rationing on clothes, it's the very devil to keep them decently clad when the child is still growing. Kevin has slowed down now, which is just as well, because he stands nearly five foot ten in his stocking feet.'

'Does he really?'

'Aye,' Tom said. 'You have never seen such a change in a boy. His voice has broken as well. The child is growing into a man.'

'I'm looking forward to seeing him again,' Joe said. 'Has he done with school now?'

'He could have left in July, for he was fourteen in March,' Tom said, 'but Paul convinced him to stay another year.'

'And then what?'

'Then he starts an apprenticeship to be a tool-maker,' Tom said. 'Paul is arranging it for him. Molly would have liked him to go on and matriculate – even university, if he wanted – but Kevin is no academic. He is not a stupid boy, but book-learning is not for him and Paul knows that as well as I do. Tool-making is a good job, anyway. They are the craftsmen of the factory.'

'How about that then, Ben?' Joe said to his son. 'Your cousin, Kevin, is almost a working man.'

Ben wrinkled his nose. Kevin, the working man, didn't sound half as much fun as Kevin the boy, but he was too dispirited to make much of it and he shrugged and muttered, "S all right, I s'pose.'

'What is it, Ben?' Joe said, thinking it was better to face what was eating him openly.

Ben raised his eyes, looked at his father, and said, 'Why did you let Mom go away like that?'

'I didn't let her go, Ben,' Joe said. 'I didn't know what she intended.'

'You must have done, else you wouldn't have been there at the dockside.'

'That was because of the telegrams your mother sent,' Tom said, and explained them to Ben.

'So what do we do now?' Ben asked.

'I told you,' Joe said. 'We are making for Birmingham just as soon as it can be arranged.'

'I mean about Mom,' Ben said agitatedly.

'Ben, your mother is on her way to America,' Joe said. 'What do you want me to do?'

'Make her come back.'

'I can't do that.'

'Yes you can,' Ben insisted. 'Or go to America and fetch her back. You can 'cos you said to that man Mom is still married to you, and married people live together.'

'Ben, I—'

'If you don't do it, if you don't make her come home,' Ben said desperately, 'then I might never see her again.'

Tom plainly heard the distress in Ben's voice, saw it mirrored in Joe's face, and decided that neither of them needed his presence in the cottage.

Barely had the door closed behind Tom when Ben said brokenly, 'I want Mom to come home, Dad.'

'I know,' Joe said, and tears rained down his own face as he admitted, 'So do I, but she's not going to.'

'Oh, Dad . . .' cried Ben. Joe gathered the weeping child onto his knee and let him cry out his fear and his pain, and they took comfort from one another.

TWENTY-THREE

Ben hadn't realised just how much he would miss his mother. A fortnight after he had come to Birmingham to live it had got no easier. The loss of his mother was like a constant ache inside. Everyone was very kind to him, tiptoeing around him as gently as if they were circling an unexploded bomb. Even his father was like that with him and sometimes it made Ben want to scream.

He knew he had made the right decision, that was the annoying thing. He knew he couldn't have borne it if he had gone off with his mother and left his father all alone in Ireland, but he resented the fact that he had been forced to make that decision. Or any decision at all. He blamed his mother for that. She was the one who had left, but she wasn't there and so it was usually his father who bore the brunt of his ill humour. And he bore it all without complaint. He didn't get angry and tell him off as he would once have done, and that unnerved Ben too. He viewed starting a new school with no enthusiasm at all.

Joe knew how Ben felt and understood his anger. He too grieved for Gloria, but alone in his bed at night. He had no one to discuss his feelings with because from the first he had said to the family that though Gloria had gone, there had been faults on both sides, that Ben still loved his mother and it wouldn't help him for them to start pulling Gloria to bits.

'Easy to say,' Molly said to Aggie one day. 'But just to walk out on him like that . . . I mean, everyone goes through sticky patches in their marriage, but you don't just give up and walk out.'

'Ah, but it wasn't just a sticky patch, was it?' Aggie said. 'Not to put too fine a point on it, she was carrying on with an American. I got on well with Gloria when she came over for your wedding. I could see, though, that she was intrigued by the attraction Paul felt for me. I saw her speculative eyes on me more than once.'

'Why?'

Aggie shrugged. 'I imagine she was wondering how Paul could feel that way about me when I had spent years on the streets.'

'That was hardly your fault,' Molly said.

'I know that, but it doesn't alter the fact that I was a prostitute,' Aggie said. 'As I recall, it took me some time to understand and accept that Paul was taking me warts and all, so I can hardly blame others for being surprised. I think in the end Gloria accepted how it was between us. I liked her, though, and I thought she liked me, and I was a little disappointed that she didn't come to my wedding.'

'Maybe by then she had bigger fish to fry,' Molly said. 'And I notice that you say "liked", not "like". How do you feel about her now?'

Aggie thought for a moment, then said, 'Till Joe turned up at my door with Tom that time to deal with Finch, I hadn't seen him for over forty years. I had shared no part of his life. To see him go through all this upset now hurts me. Whatever he says, he is suffering. It is often etched on his face, and he looks quite grey at times. And there is Ben, a confused, angry and unhappy Ben, who he is also trying to cope with. I know that Joe said there were faults on both sides, and I dare say there were, but she has gone and Joe is left to pick up the pieces.' Aggie shook her head. 'It is hard to feel the same about her and not blame her totally.'

'Do you think she should have taken Ben with her?'

'Good God no,' Aggie said. 'Joe couldn't have borne that. What the woman should have done was stay put and get on with mending her marriage and rearing her child. You know,' she went on, 'one thing I will always regret is not having a child of my own, and I suppose that's why I was so dumbfounded that Gloria should just walk away from her son.'

'Ah, Aunt Aggie . . .'

'And then I met Paul's sister, Isobel,' Aggie said. 'You know what a lovely gentle and softly spoken lady she is, and though they would have liked more, she had just one son, Gregory. They both adored him.'

'Yes,' Molly said. 'And he died at Dunkirk.'

'Yes,' Aggie said. 'And I got to wondering whether it was better to have no children at all than to give birth to them, nurture them and watch them grow up, learn to love them with all your being and see them killed like that, so young, their lives full of promise.'

'I don't know that I could bear it,' Molly admitted. 'Paul told me Isobel's husband never got over it.'

'No,' Aggie said. 'He died three years ago. He had influenza and people recover from that all the time. He should really have been able to fight it off. Isobel said it was as if he had given up.'

'And then Isobel became Uncle Tom's fancy piece,' Molly said with a large grin.

'You know he did no such thing,' Aggie said, giving her niece a tap on the hand. 'You are a tease and when you say that in front of Tom he goes bright red.'

'I know,' Molly said with a laugh. 'It's such a temptation to tease him because he blushes so easily. And he does go out with Isobel.'

'Only when Paul and I go too,' Aggie said. 'And you know that was because after her husband died Isobel was very sad and lonely. Before Paul met me he would take his sister out and about to the pictures and theatre, or out for a meal, and he didn't want her to feel pushed out so he asked Tom as company for her. That's all it was.'

'Of course,' said Molly with a knowing smile. 'Maybe that's how it began, but you never know. After all, they're both two lonely people.'

Aggie shook her head. 'Tom is not the marrying kind,' she said. 'We all know why now, but he'll hardly change, and Isobel is certainly not looking for any entanglements, though she does like Tom.'

'Everyone likes Tom,' Molly said. 'And he is so pleased about this baby he is like a dog with two tails.'

'And me,' Aggie said. 'I can hardly wait.'

'I can see I shall have to watch the pair of you or you will have the child ruined,' Molly said to Aggie with mock severity. 'And you're not the only ones either. Kevin is cock-a-hoop about being an uncle.'

'Let's hope that Ben takes some interest in the baby too,' Aggie said, 'for that child needs something to cheer him.'

'Yes,' said Molly almost fiercely. 'And I hope his mother is proud of herself, wherever she is.'

The liner took almost a week to reach New York and the agonising pain of losing her son never left Gloria, so she was glad of Helen's support.

'What breaks my heart most,' she said to her one day, 'is that he ran away from me. He chose Joe.'

'You must see it from his point of view,' Helen said gently. 'In his opinion you have Philip now, and Joe has no one. He actually said that to you.'

'I know,' Gloria said miserably. 'I didn't think that it would hurt this much. And then there are Philip's parents, who have arranged to meet me. They are expecting Ben, and I thought he might break the ice a bit.'

'Oh, he might have done more than break the ice,' Helen said ruefully. 'Especially as he didn't want to go to America in the first place. He could just blurt out that you are still married to his dad or something like that. I mean, you didn't intend to tell them that straight away, did you?'

'No,' Gloria said. 'And you're right: Ben could and probably would blurt that out, especially if he was angry enough. That would have been just dreadful. Phillip has told me to say nothing for now. He will explain it to them when they have got to know me a little. And when he hears what Ben has done he will know what we have to do to get him back.'

'What d'you mean?' Helen said. 'Ben has shown you plainly where he wants to be, so why not leave him be now?'

'No,' Gloria said determinedly. 'You don't understand. You're not a mother yet, and Ben is just a child, so what does he know? His place is with me. I couldn't go through life without Ben.'

Helen suddenly felt immeasurably sad for Joe and she said gently, 'Not even for Phillip?'

Gloria met Helen's gaze levelly. 'I didn't think that I would be called on to make a choice.'

'Can't you feel the tiniest bit sorry for Joe if you try and take Ben away from him?' Helen said. 'And won't Ben be miserable if you force him to come to a place he never wanted to come to?'

'Ben will get over it,' Gloria said dismissively. 'Children are very adaptable. As for Joe, how the hell did he know I was on that ship? I didn't even tell them at the canteen when we left – you know, when we had that bit of a leaving do. Everyone was making plans for what to do with their free time and arranging to meet up and everything, remember, and I just went along with it.'

'I know you did,' Helen said. She added, 'I told no one either, so it's a mystery how Joe found out, but I bet he thought at first that Ben was on the ship.'

'Yes,' said Gloria grimly. 'And that is where he should be. Ben's place is here with me.'

Helen said nothing further. She had no wish to alienate her friend, but she privately thought that she was piling up a heap of trouble for herself and a whole lot of misery for Joe, who had done nothing wrong.

As the ship pulled into the New York harbour, Gloria and Helen weren't the only ones scanning the photographs of their new families and trying to identify them among the many people on the docksides waiting to welcome the Irish wives their sons had chosen.

The gangplank was lowered to a cheer from the women and children aboard, and they began to shuffle forward.

'Can you see your people?' said Helen suddenly.

'No,' Gloria said, 'not yet anyway. Philip's father said he would wear a pink carnation.'

'Did he really?' said Helen with a laugh. 'I think I've spotted mine, anyway. Over to the side a little. Can you see?'

'I think so,' Gloria said. 'Oh, I am going to miss you.'

'How d'you think I feel?' Helen said. 'It will all be strange to me.'

'And me too after all this time,' Gloria insisted.

'Oh, look, I think that I have spotted your new in-laws, because there's a man over there sporting the biggest carnation I have ever seen,' Helen cried.

Gloria looked in the direction of Helen's pointing finger. The way the man stood so tall and straight reminded her of Philip. She had searched the photograph that he had sent her at the time for any resemblance but much of his face was covered with a trim beard and moustache. 'He used to have hair as dark as mine when I was a child,' Philip had told her. 'Now he is as grey as a badger.'

So was the dumpy woman beside him, Gloria thought, but her eyes in the round, open face looked kindly and the taut muscles in Gloria's stomach relaxed a little. She knew whatever these people were like she would have to live with them until the war was over and Philip demobbed.

She shivered suddenly, and Helen said, 'I'm scared stiff too.'

'This must be one of the hardest things I have ever done in my life,' Gloria said, and the two girls embraced, and tears squeezed from Gloria's eyes and trickled down her cheeks. Her stiff backbone came to her rescue and she pulled herself from Helen's arms, wiping the tears away from her cheeks impatiently. 'This won't do. Here we are on the edge of maybe the greatest adventure of our lives, when we will become involved with the relatives and friends of the men we love, and all we can do is weep. What madness is this?'

'It is mad,' Helen agreed. 'It isn't as if we will never meet again. Anyway, Colin's parents look friendly enough to me, and he always speaks about them with such fondness.'

'So does Philip,' Gloria said.

There was a sudden surge forward and Gloria was at the top of the gangplank. Unbidden there flashed into her head the memory of Joe's first day in that brave new world more than twenty years before. Then he had risked his own life to save the life of a young girl. If he'd failed neither Gloria nor Joe would be alive today.

She owed Joe her life and she suddenly felt sorry for the blow she had dealt him. He hadn't deserved her to run out on him the way she had, and she faced the fact that had she succeeded in taking Ben to New York with her, it would have destroyed him. Ben wanted to stay with his father, he had indicated that as strongly as he could, and she knew, though her heart felt as heavy as lead despite her spirited words to Helen, that it might be better to leave him there after all.

She approached Philip's parents and shook them both by the hand, saying sincerely as she did so, 'I am so delighted to meet you at last. Philip told me so much about you.'

Philip's father, Richard, introduced himself and his wife, Mary, and Gloria noted his gruff voice, realised he was as nervous as she was, and she warmed to him.

She saw the woman relax a little – with relief, Gloria guessed as she kissed her on the cheek – and say, 'We are delighted to meet you too, dear, and may I say, I think my son has chosen well. You are very welcome and you may call us Mom and Dad, or Poppa if you would like to, though if you find that awkward, Mary and Richard will do just as well.'

'I thought there was to be a child?' Richard said. 'Your son?'

There was no way Gloria was going to tell them that Ben had run back to his father, but what she did say, careful to keep any trace of sadness from her voice, was, 'I decided to leave Ben with his father just for now, until I get myself settled.'

'Oh,' said Richard with a slight frown, 'I was looking forward to having a child about the place once more.'

Gloria almost told them then of the child she was now sure she was carrying, but she stopped herself. It was too early. There might be a moment when she would need such news. It might sweeten the pill when Philip explained that they weren't legally married.

'Did your son not mind?' Mary asked. 'Especially with you going so far away and everything.'

Gloria shook her head. 'No. Ben loves his father and Joe is a fine man. Just because it didn't work out between us doesn't mean that he hasn't always been a very good father. His brother is at the farm now because he is selling up and he is another favourite of Ben's. My son is quite happy, I assure you.'

Mary pursed her lips and Gloria saw it and knew she thought it odd of her to leave her child behind when she had gone to live in another continent entirely. But she said nothing further.

Richard stepped forward and, picking up the cases, said, 'Come. We will get a cab. Is this all you have?'

Gloria knew that most women, even Helen, had far more

possessions than she had for starting their new life, but to take more than she had done would have aroused suspicion. There again Gloria had an explanation. 'There was very little to buy in the way of clothes and things in Buncrana – it's such a small place – and in Derry the clothes are rationed, but because I don't live there I had no ration card. Philip said to leave any major clothes buying until I got to New York.'

Mary nodded her head and said, 'I see that, and if you can't find anything to suit in New York, then you are hard to please indeed.'

Gloria laughed. 'I don't think it will be a problem here. Maybe you could help me,' she added.

Mary's homely face coloured with surprise and pleasure. 'I would be delighted, my dear,' she said. 'There is nothing would give me greater pleasure that that.'

Gloria relaxed still further. She had made the first move to friendship with Philip's mother and she wanted it firmly established with both of them before Philip broke the news that they had committed bigamy.

The taxi ride home was uneventful. Richard and Mary pointed places out to her, and though Gloria remembered some, others were very new. She looked about her with interest. She really did feel as if she was coming home, back where she belonged.

Richard and Mary Morrisey lived on the outskirts of New York in a pretty little bungalow with a little garden all around it.

'Oh how lovely!' Gloria exclaimed as she stepped from the taxi. 'What a charming place you have. But,' she added as she looked all around, 'I understood there was a garage?'

'There is,' Mary said. She jerked her thumb and said, 'Over yonder wall. We didn't want it too close to the house. I know it is how we earn our living and all, but I don't want to smell grease or gasoline all the day long. Come in and I will make us a drink.'

The bedroom assigned to Gloria, which she would eventually share with Philip, was huge, and it was as she went to the window to look at the view that she found the letter.

'That came the other day,' Mary said from the door.

'But who's it from?'

'Why, Philip, of course.'

'Is it?' Gloria said. 'I've never seen his handwriting, just his signature.'

'It's to welcome you, I suppose,' Mary said. 'I will leave you to read it in peace and then if you would like to freshen up, the bathroom is right next door. Supper will be on the table in about half an hour. Is that time enough?'

'Plenty of time,' Gloria said, anxious for Mary to be gone so that she could open the letter and read the words written by the man she was already missing.

It wasn't a love letter as such, although at the beginning, Philip reiterated the deep love he had for her and said how much he was missing her. However, he went on to tell her of what had transpired at the dockside and the threat that Joe had made that he would carry out if they should try to gain custody of Ben in any way.

He knew that only women married to the sailors were allowed on the ships. I don't know how he knew, though I suppose he could have found out easily enough. I don't know what he was doing on the dockside either, or how he knew that you were travelling that day. He would hardly have told me if I had asked. I mean, I wasn't his favourite person and I wouldn't have been at all surprised if he had really gone for me. He did mention knocking me to the ground and in a way he would have been justified if he had done, but he didn't lay a finger on me in the end.

I was so shocked to see Ben there when I had thought him safe aboard ship with you and Helen, and he was hugging his father as if his life depended on it. And, honey, he sure loves that man. It was written all over his face. We must give up all thought of Ben joining us in our new life in the States.

Gloria let the letter flutter to the ground. This was the price she had to pay for Philip, as Helen had hinted at on the ship. Soon Gloria would start a new life, with a new man whom she loved dearly, and in time she would hold a new baby in her arms, a baby made through the love expressed between her and Philip. However, her beloved son Ben would have no place in that life, and that fact hurt so much she felt a sharp pain in her heart and guessed that she would carry it for always. She felt guilt drag at her, for she had been unfair to the child forcing him to choose between her and Joe.

So even without the threat of exposure she already accepted the fact that Ben should stay with his father, for both their sakes. She would not relinquish all claim to him, however, and she knew that Joe would not expect her to because he wasn't a cruel man. Maybe Ben could come on a visit when the world was a more stable place. For now she would write to him every week so that he would know that he also had a mother who loved him dearly.

TWENTY-FOUR

When Joe got the letter from Gloria saying that she agreed to Ben staying with him, he was so relieved. He had a dread of dragging her through the courts and washing his dirty linen in public, as it were, though he would have done so if he had been forced into it, for Ben's sake.

He hadn't a bother about her writing to Ben or the boy writing back. He knew how much she loved Ben too, and thought the correspondence would be beneficial to both of them. Ben, however, didn't feel the same way at all.

'Why should I want to write to her just because she has sent you the address?' he asked his father truculently.

'I just thought you might, that's all.'

'Well I don't.'

'Look, Ben . . .'

Ben leaped to his feet and faced his father angrily. His face was crimson and his eyes were flashing fire just the way his mother's used to, Joe thought with a sinking feeling in his heart. 'Don't you dare to tell me off, or tell me I should understand. She should be here with us where she belongs. You didn't even care. You just let her go.'

'I couldn't stop her,' Joe said helplessly.

'You didn't try,' Ben said accusingly.

'She had made up her mind, Ben,' Joe said. 'Believe me, nothing I said would have made any difference.'

'So, why bother getting married when you can just walk away if you get fed up?'

Joe didn't really know how to answer Ben, but he tried. 'Life isn't as cut and dried as that, son. You know that your mother was never happy in Buncrana.'

'Yeah,' Ben said. 'I knew that, but she didn't just leave Buncrana. She left us.'

'She just fell in love with someone else and, to be honest, Ben, that upsets me too.'

Ben's eyes were full of confusion. 'If you were upset, why didn't you tell her?'

'Well, by the time I realised that things were that serious she cared about him, that Philip Morrisey, more than she cared for me.'

'And me,' Ben said.

'No, not you, Ben,' Joe contradicted. 'Your mother loves you and she always will. Never doubt that. She wanted to take you with her.'

'Yeah,' said Ben. 'But I didn't want to go and she wouldn't listen, and that man was going to be my new father. No one asked if I wanted one or seemed to bother with the fact I had a dad already that I was quite happy with. No one does that to someone they care about.'

'It's difficult to understand, I know.'

'Don't say that I will understand it all when I am older,' Ben said. 'I hate it when people say that.'

'All right then,' said Joe. 'I won't.'

'It's what you meant though isn't it?'

'Probably,' Joe said and added almost impatiently,' But look, son, if we talk from now till doomsday it won't change anything. Your mother has gone. She now lives in America and will not come back. She has moved out of our lives and you must accept it, as I must, because there is nothing else to do. She wants to keep in touch with you, though, and wants to write to you and for you to write back. So how about it?'

'No,' Ben said determinedly. 'You said she has moved

out of our lives and that I must accept it. Well then, she can stay right out of my life. I don't want to write to her. I don't want anything more to do with her and she must accept that because it is the way I feel.'

The following Saturday, with Kevin and Ben dispatched to the Palace Cinema in Erdington, Joe popped in to see Molly and was delighted that Aggie was there as well.

'Both boys get off all right?' Molly asked.

Joe nodded. 'Tell you the truth, it was a change to see a smile on Ben's face. He is so angry. I have never seen him like this before.'

'His mother has never left him before,' Molly pointed out. 'You must see it from his point of view. His life has changed beyond all recognition. He has been taken from a rural idyll in sleepy Buncrana to live in a flat in a bustling city – not to visit, but to live in for always. He will have to make new friends, start a new school, and learn to live without his mother. It's tall order.'

'I know it is,' Joe said. 'And I do feel for the lad. The point is, he is adamant about not writing to his mother and I don't know what to do. I mean, I don't think that it is appropriate for me to write to her. Anyway, what would I tell her – that Ben wants nothing to do with her? I don't think that would be helpful.'

'No,' said Aggie, putting the kettle to boil. 'But if you do nothing won't Gloria think that you have forbidden the boy to write, or told him nothing at all?'

'Better that than have her think the lad has turned against her,' Joe said. 'That might break her altogether.'

'Do you still care for her, Uncle Joe?' Molly asked.

'In a way,' Joe said. 'I got into the habit of caring for her. I couldn't take her back, though. The girl that I fell in love with is not the same person as the one who sailed away to America. It would never work for us now and so all I hope is that she is happy in her new life.'

'You are a very special man, Uncle Joe,' Molly said admiringly. 'Many left the way you were would hope that she would roast in hell.'

Joe gave a rueful smile. 'Don't you get polishing up my halo now. The title of saint in this family belongs to Tom, and, God, will I be glad to see him back.'

'You can say that again,' Aggie said with feeling, looking to see if she had any biscuits. 'D'you know when it is likely to be?'

'Not long,' Joe said. 'The farm is up for sale now, and there has been a fair bit of interest. He can leave it all in the hands of the solicitor soon and come back. I bet Paul will be glad to see him.'

'He will,' Aggie confirmed. 'But he knows these things can't be completed in five minutes and so he told him to take all the time he needed. Actually, most of his concern has been for you and Ben. He said to tell you that there is a job for you in the factory when you are ready.'

'I know, and I will be glad of it,' Joe said. 'I thought it better not to start right away, but to get Ben settled first. As you say, it has been one hell of a change for him. Once the schools start up again, and I get him into that, I will feel happier about leaving him. It's only another week.'

'Where are you sending him, Boldmere Road?'

'No, St Nicholas's, the Catholic school,' Joe said. 'It is only on Jockey Road no distance away.'

'Kevin was changed from the Catholic school when I left,' Molly said. 'Kevin said the priest and Granddad had an up-and-downer about it and the priest went away with a flea in his ear. Kevin stopped believing in God, you see, after Mom and Dad died.'

'Ah, can you wonder at that?' Aggie said. 'The poor child.'

'Yes, I know,' Molly said. 'It would have been better for him if I had been left here with the both of them. Granddad could have had the tenancy of Mom and Dad's house changed over, just as he wanted to, and I could have seen to all of us. The next-door neighbour would have helped. She was terrific when Mom was so ill in hospital for weeks before she was killed, and she showed me how to do lots of things.'

'So, it would have been better for you too,' Joe pointed out.

'Yes, I suppose,' Molly said. I often thought that when I was in Buncrana, but then I would never have met you and Uncle Tom. There would be a whole branch of the family neither Kevin nor I would know.'

'And if Tom hadn't come over to see you then he wouldn't have found me and rescued me from the gutter,' Aggie said. 'I would likely be dead by now, and instead I am married to a lovely man and surrounded by my family, which is soon to have a new addition to it.'

'Not that soon,' Molly said. 'There's another five and a half months yet. I think nine months is an awful long time to wait.'

'Gloria used to think that when she was having Ben,' Joe said. 'But just think, Molly, the war might be over by the time the child is born.'

'A peacetime baby,' Molly smiled. 'But do you think that the war will be over that soon? I don't know. It seems to have gone on for ever.'

'I know,' Joe agreed. 'But we really have got to be near the end now.'

'I don't know so much,' Molly said. 'What about those pilotless bombs falling all over London?'

'The ones they call doodlebugs, because of the noise they make?'

'Those are the ones. People say that when the noise stops they just drop.'

'Must play havoc with the nerves,' Joe said. 'Pity those poor people who have already suffered the blitz.'

'I gather that folk are leaving the city in droves.'

'I don't blame them,' Joe said. 'And yet now I know the

London spirit, I know that for everyone who leaves there will be twenty or thirty stay and battle it out.'

'At least we can be thankful that they don't reach this far,' Aggie said.

'That's what they said at the beginning of the war about the ordinary bombs,' Molly reminded her aunt. 'They soon realised they were wrong.'

'Well, you may be sure that if they could reach here they would have done so by now,' Aggie said. 'But wherever they land I pity the poor people.'

'Think Jerry cares a jot for that?' Molly cried with a shiver. 'Look at those death camps that the Allies are liberating now. What the Nazis did to the Jews – it's, well, it's inhuman. How can one human being inflict so much pain and suffering on another?'

'Not to mention gassing thousands of them,' Joe said, indicating the story in the newspaper on the table before them.

'But we shouldn't be surprised,' Aggie said. 'Certainly not Molly and me, anyway. We have both been subjected to men's brutality.'

'You're right there,' Molly said. 'Look at the way Finch treated you.'

'Well, he'll hurt no one ever again, thanks to you,' Aggie said, turning to Joe, teapot in hand.

'If I hadn't done it Tom would have,' Joe said. 'I just think he had done enough already – that Finch really was down to me. Gloria couldn't see that. I knew that she was worried for me, worried that I might get into trouble or hurt – killed, even. I accepted her concern and yet I couldn't do what she wanted and just walk away, pretend that what had happened to my sister was no concern of mine. I've thought since, though, that the first cracks in our marriage began then. If I had handled things differently when I came home, we might have been able to ride out the storm.'

'But we'll never know that,' Molly pointed out.

'No, and it's very easy to be wise after the event,' Aggie put in.

'I suppose,' Joe conceded. 'Anyway, as Tom said, it is all water under the bridge now.'

'And talking of Tom,' Molly said, handing round cups of tea, 'I bet when he comes back, you will meet his lady love.'

'She's talking about Isobel, Paul's sister,' Aggie said, with a sigh.

'Oh, he mentioned her,' Joe said. 'He said she was a lovely lady and a good friend.'

'And that's all they are – friends,' Aggie said. 'Though Molly would just love it to be different. There was not and is not any romantic entanglement at all.'

'Maybe there wasn't at the start,' Molly said, with a wink at her uncle, 'but how do you know that it hasn't developed between them since?'

'Yes,' Joe smiled, playing up to his niece's banter, 'These strong silent types are the ones you have to look out for. Haven't you ever heard the expression "still waters run deep"?'

'I don't know which is worse, you or Molly,' Aggie said in mock exasperation, taking a seat at the table and handing Joe the milk jug.

'Well, I am intrigued by the woman, anyway,' Joe said. 'She must be an irresistible type, this Isobel, because Tom would usually run a mile if a woman even spoke to him.'

'She is fairly ordinary-looking,' Molly said, 'but very nice, and she likes Tom.'

'Everyone likes Tom,' Joe said. 'That's no measure of anything.'

St Nicholas's Catholic School was as far removed from the cosy national school in Buncrana as it was possible to be. Ben watched the swarms of children playing in the playground before the first bell and decided that he didn't like it one bit. He strode across the playground with his father, aware that many of the children paused in their games to watch him curiously, and the hairs on the back of his neck prickled with apprehension.

Inside, the headmaster, a Mr Beaufort, was a large, jovial man, who welcomed Joe and Ben as if they were long-lost cousins he had been waiting to see for ages. Ben's eyes slid across to his father and he wondered if he was taken in by his attitude. He himself certainly wasn't. He had met teachers like Mr Beaufort before, and guessed he would be the very devil if he was to get on the wrong side of him.

Ben heard the clang of a large bell outside, and watched the children stand as still as statues and then, when the bell rang for a second time, form lines at each of the doors. He sat and watched his father fill in the relevant forms with the headmaster and listened to the muted sound of children entering through the nearest door and the receding tramp of their feet as they marched down the corridor. He felt a lump of dread settle into his stomach.

With the formalities completed, the headmaster said to Joe, 'I haven't had the records from the other school yet, but your boy looks a bright one. Were you thinking of putting him in for the eleven plus?'

Joe shook his head with a smile. 'You'll have to explain what that is.'

'It's an exam that the children take at the end of this year and it determines whether they go to grammar school and go on to matriculate,' Mr Beaufort said. 'Ben can then go on into the sixth form and take further exams called the Higher School Certificate when he is eighteen. They are the passport to university, should he wish to go.'

Joe had never thought that far ahead for Ben. He said, 'I don't know whether Ben is capable of that or not.'

'If he isn't, then he will go a secondary modern school for a different type of education,' the headmaster went on.

'Kevin goes to one of them,' Ben said suddenly. 'He said it's all right as far as any school is all right.'

'Kevin?' the headmaster enquired.

'His cousin,' Joe said.

'Ah,' said Mr Beaufort, speaking directly to Ben, 'your cousin is right. An education in a secondary modern school is excellent for some children. All I am saying to your father is, if you have the ability, then a grammar school gives you more opportunity.'

It was the word 'opportunity' that seeped into Joe's brain. He remembered Brian Brannigan holding out the hand of opportunity to him and that he had grasped it. It was up to him to help his son in the same way and so he said, 'I hear what you say, sir. I would like him to have the chance of taking this eleven plus, if he is bright enough. That all right with you, Ben?'

Ben shrugged. None of it was all right, but when did that ever matter? Ben was taken down to join his new class, accompanied by the school secretary, a position the school in Buncrana hadn't needed. Joe had stayed talking to the headmaster and Ben knew why he was being shuttled out of the way: his father was going to tell the headmaster about his mother and what she had done. He burned with shame that anyone had to know, but his father had been firm that the school had to be told. 'It is your mother who has done wrong,' he told Ben when he complained. 'You have nothing to be ashamed about.'

'Course I have,' Ben had cried. 'The others will take the mickey.'

'But why?' Joe was genuinely nonplussed.

'They just will, that's why,' Ben said. 'Well, you tell the headmaster the truth if you want to, but I am going to tell anyone who asks that my mum is dead. It isn't really a lie either, because she might as well be.'

All this went through Ben's head as he stood by the teacher's desk that first morning. Her name was Miss Tranter and she was young and quite pretty and, Ben guessed, not all that strict. However, as he looked around at the sea of faces he knew straight away who he would have trouble with and that was a group of boys at the back of the class. He saw them nudge one another in delight and knew they viewed him as a new boy to bait, and knew too he was in for a tough time in the playground.

Ben had been at school just over a fortnight when Tom came home. Joe was immensely glad to see him. Tom had always been a firm favourite with Ben, and Joe was greatly worried about him because he seemed to be worse, not better, since he had begun at the school. Joe had hoped that he might have made friends and begun to settle to life in Birmingham, but that hadn't happened yet, and if ever Joe tried to talk to him about it he always claimed he had homework to do.

Ben did tell his father that as the records hadn't come through from the school at Buncrana he had been given an aptitude test, which had showed him to be grammar school material and so he had homework every night and he would disappear into his room and stay there. From then too, he would never let his father into the bathroom when he was washing or in the bath. It had never bothered him before but he knew he would have a hard job explaining away the bruises and abrasions on his body to his father's satisfaction should he catch sight of them.

Joe had made enough fuss about his constantly grazed knees. 'Goodness, Ben!' he exclaimed a few days previously when once more his scraped knees had been covered with a plaster. 'What's the matter with you? You never used to be this clumsy. Can't you keep on your feet at all?'

It's hard, Ben might have said, when the legs are kicked from under you. What he did instead was growl at his father, 'I fell over, that's all. I didn't do it on purpose or anything, so what you're giving out to me for?'

'It's just . . . Ben, is anything the matter?'

'I told you there isn't,' Ben cried. 'So why don't you leave me alone?'

Joe had great hopes that Tom might break through the hard shell that Ben had wrapped all around himself, but as one week slipped into another, Ben seemed to distance himself further and further away from them all.

Even Kevin had tried to find out what was wrong, to no avail. 'You have to get over this, mate,' he said.

'Why?'

'Look, I know what it's like to lose your mother,' he said more gently. 'It is just about the worst thing that can happen in the whole of your life and it hurts like hell. But in the end you have got to face it, because nothing you do will change it.'

'Your mother died,' Ben hissed, 'and I know that was sad and everything, but she had no choice. My mother chose to go away and leave me and leave my dad. She preferred some stupid American that she had only just met to us. You have no idea how that feels.'

It wasn't just the lack of his mother that was bothering Ben, but also what was happening in the school. The very things that had made him popular in London worked in the opposite way in Birmingham.

His accent now was a mixture of American with an Irish lilt, not at all like the Brummie accent, and something else to tease him about. His good looks appealed to many of the girls so the bullies called him a sissy. He was also bright and keen to learn and, like his father, quick to pick things up. While this endeared him to the teachers it enraged the bully boys on the back row.

Each morning, as he turned in the gate as late as he dared to be, he would feel as if he was entering a hostile battleground, and the knot lodged in the pit of his stomach would tighten as he saw those boys elbowing one another as they saw him arrive.

There was no hope of avoiding them at playtime, for if one wouldn't spot him, another would, and they would congregate round him and start jeering. Anything could start them off. They even mocked him because he had no mother. It was useless to try to defend himself, though he attempted this when the jeering and name-calling escalated into blows. In the beginning the girls in the playground had tried to intervene and stop the fighting, but it made matters worse and their intervention was just another stick to beat him with. Now they watched helplessly.

Going home too was a trial. He always left the building like a bat out of hell, but the bullies often caught up with him and would continue what they had begun in the playground. He would arrive home with his clothes in complete disarray, often with a rip in his shirt or jersey. His father was always annoyed with him about the state of his clothes, reminding him he only had so many coupons a year to buy him everything he needed and urging him to take more care.

Then he would often ask him if there was anything the matter. Ben would shake his head because there was a great deal the matter but nothing that his dad could help with. There was one person, though, that he was strangely drawn to and that was his Uncle Tom's friend Isobel, whom he called Aunt Izzy. He couldn't understand why this was and yet while she seldom said much, he felt that she was sympathetic towards him.

Isobel was a kindly lady, like Uncle Tom. Her brown hair, which she often wore in a soft roll at the nape of her neck, was streaked with grey, but her deep brown eyes in her honest and open face missed little, and he wasn't a bit surprised that she was so friendly with his uncle, for, as his dad said, they were made in the same mould.

Isobel wasn't a great talker. She had been the younger sister and had let the elder one talk for her. Then she'd married a voluble man who had taken over where her sister left off, so Isobel had learned to listen and found a person learned a lot about another by observation. She found out too at an early age that sometimes what a person did was a better indicator of what was going on in their head than what they said.

And so she knew that it wasn't only the loss of his mother that was making Ben so unhappy, it was something else as well. She guessed it was to do with school because it was the only place Ben went, and yet Joe said he had no trouble with the work and was in line to sit the eleven plus. Isobel didn't badger him with questions, though she knew he was suffering, because she also knew that he wasn't ready to say anything yet.

As the bullying continued, Ben worked even harder. He knew that none of his tormenters would be sitting the exam and the only way to get rid of them, as he saw it, was to make sure he passed, so he took extra work home. He even took work home to do over Christmas because the exam was in two parts, the first part to be held in the town hall in January.

By Christmas the end of the war seemed as far away as ever. Since September, the beleaguered Londoners had been attacked by a new hazard: V-2s, pilotless like the doodle-bugs, but which were even more dangerous as they made no noise at all.

'I feel so sorry for the Londoners,' Joe said. 'The blitz was shocking, wasn't it, Ben?'

'I'll say.'

'Do you remember it well?' Isobel asked, and Ben nodded vigorously.

'I'll never forget it,' he said. 'Dad was a volunteer fireman and it was usually just me and Mom down the shelters.' He stopped. He never spoke about his mother, but now that he had, the memories came flooding back. He remembered the feel of her arms around him and how comforting they were when he was so scared, and how brave she was in the teeth of the most terrifying raids. He could even remember the smell of her as she held him close. The loss of her stabbed his heart as keenly and as painfully as it had in the early days.

Isobel looked into Ben's anguished eyes, guessed at the thoughts tumbling about his head and felt her heart turn over for the young boy. She knew this had been a particularly poignant time for him, the first Christmas without his mother.

Isobel wasn't surprised when Ben suddenly leaped to his feet and made for his room.

When Isobel got up to follow Joe said, 'I should leave him be. He gets over these moods on his own.'

'I don't think he is in a mood,' Isobel said. 'I think he is finding the memories almost more than he can cope with. Maybe he needs the comfort of another human being in the room.'

'He might be rude to you,' Joe warned.

Isobel shrugged. 'It doesn't matter if he is,' she said. 'I have very broad shoulders.'

Ben lay spread-eagled on the bed and he continued to lie there though he knew that Isobel had entered the room. She made no comment, just sat down on the chair beside the bed. The room was virtually silent and yet it wasn't uncomfortable. Instead it seemed to radiate peace, and as Ben lay there he felt all the tension seeping out of his body.

Eventually he turned over on his side and regarded Isobel as she sat on the chair as if she had all the time in the world. 'Why aren't you interrogating me with questions?' he asked in the end.

Isobel smiled. 'Is that what you would like me to do?'

'No,' Ben said. 'I'd hate it, but that's what most adults do all the time.'

'Maybe I'm not like most adults.'

'No, you're not,' Kevin said. 'So why did you come in here then?'

'I had the feeling that the memories you had were suddenly too much to bear,' Isobel said. 'I have been there too and sometimes it helps to have someone with you, especially if they know what you are going through.'

'What were your memories then?'

'Of my son . . . my husband,' Isobel said. 'There are so many memories that comfort me now, but it wasn't always like that.'

'Did they die?'

'Yes, Ben,' Isobel said.

'But that isn't the same,' Ben argued. 'That's like Kevin's mother and father, and I know it's sad but it isn't the same. They had no choice in it, but my mother chose to go off.'

'My son, Gregory, chose to go in the army,' Isobel said. 'He didn't have to. He was only seventeen and he lied about his age. He could have deferred it too, for he had a brilliant future ahead of him, a place in medical school virtually guaranteed, which he was due to start the following year. But he didn't listen. I could have gone to the recruitment board with his birth certificate and they would have released him.'

'Why didn't you?'

'Because it wasn't what he wanted,' Isobel said. 'He wouldn't have been happy.'

'So what happened to him?'

'He died at Dunkirk,' Isobel said. 'My husband, Gerald, never got over it. He collapsed when the telegram came and was never fit for work again, and I nursed him till he died in 1941.'

'So do you think your son was selfish?'

'Perhaps a little.'

'Well, he only thought about himself, didn't he?' Ben said.

'Yes, he did,' Isobel said. 'But lots of people do that.'

'Like my mother.'

'Yes, but that didn't mean that she didn't love you, Ben. Gregory loved us very much, but he still went. Your mother wanted to take you with her, remember.'

'Dad would say that is like having your cake and eating it.'

'I suppose it is.'

'And, anyway, I didn't want to go,' Ben said. 'How could I go and leave Dad on his own?'

'Your mother will know that now,' Isobel said. 'She must love the American very much, but there won't be a day goes by when she won't miss you, and even perhaps wishes things had worked out differently.'

'How do you know all this?'

'Because I miss Gerald and the son we had for just such a short time every day, and it is as if there is a hole in my heart where they used to lie.'

'Yeah,' Ben said. 'That's what I feel like too.' He looked up at Isobel. 'You know, no one has ever spoken to me like this before.'

'The thing to remember, Ben, is that whatever bad situation you are in, there will be someone in the world even worse,' Isobel said.

'So I just have to put up with things.'

'Yes, Ben,' Isobel said. 'If you can do nothing to change the situation. That's exactly what you must do.'

Ben thought about Isobel's words and knew she spoke the truth. He had to accept that his mother had chosen to go away and live a different life in America and there was nothing he could do about it. He had missed her so much at Christmas; though they had spent the day at Molly's, with Uncle Tom as well, he felt like there was a gaping hole inside him.

He accepted now that that was something he had to deal with on his own. His dad couldn't bring his mother back, which was really what he would like him to do, and so it was no good getting cross with him because it didn't help anyone. As for the bullies at school, as long as he passed the eleven plus, he would leave them far behind, so in a few months his life was bound to be better than it was now.

He slid off the bed and Isobel said, 'Now where are you going?'

'Back into the living room,' Ben answered. 'I'm getting on with it, like you said.'

TWENTY-FIVE

Early in January, with the schools not long back after the Christmas holidays, Isobel took Ben into Birmingham to the town hall so that he could sit the first part of the eleven plus. She had offered to do this, knowing that Joe hated missing time from work. Molly was too near her time to go far from home at all, and Aggie was reluctant to leave her.

Isobel was quite glad it had fallen to her because the more she had to do with Ben, the better she liked him. He was waiting for her and they set off into the raw, bleak day. The skies were gunmetal grey with thick oppressive clouds and they both shivered as they hurried to the tram stop.

'Tell you one thing,' Isobel said a little later as they boarded the tram, 'after the exams are over, we will go out for a slap-up lunch, or at least what passes as a slap-up lunch in war-torn Birmingham.'

'Haven't I got to go back to school then?' Ben asked, knowing that if his father had brought him, he would have delivered him back to school as soon as he could so that he could get back to work.

'Not at all,' Isobel said. 'Goodness me, no. After an exam like that you need feeding up. And in weather like this that means something that sticks to your ribs.'

Ben grinned at her. The day was already sounding better.

'How are you feeling?' Isobel asked.

'All right, I suppose.'

'You do want to go to grammar school, don't you?' Isobel asked. 'It's not something that you have been forced into?'

It had been a concern of Isobel's and yet she knew that she hadn't any right to express an opinion about it. Ben, however, allayed her fears straight away. 'No, I really want to go. In fact, I can't wait.'

'You have to pass the exam first.'

'I know, but the teacher said I had a good chance,' Ben said. 'And I have done extra work, more than the others mostly.'

'How many are taking it then?'

'Just one other boy and two girls from our school,' Ben said. 'They're all right. It's not them that I have problems with.' Ben gave a gasp as he realised that he had said the words aloud. He could have bitten his tongue out. What an idiot he was.

Isobel glanced at Ben's red, agitated face and said, 'So who do you have problems with?'

Immediately it was like there was a shutter across Ben's face. 'No one really,' he muttered.

Isobel knew Ben was lying but didn't pursue it. He had enough on his plate for now, but she stored the subject away for later.

Ben had never seen so many desks as were in that hall that morning. He was told they were arranged alphabetically, which meant that his desk was probably in the last row. He hadn't noticed that his shoes had a squeak until he walked almost the length of the room and then up and down the rows, searching for his name. The desks were all singles, he noted, and each one far enough apart from its neighbour to ensure there could be no copying. As he took his seat the teacher began laying out the papers face down on the desks. He knew what they would be because his teacher had explained about the verbal reasoning tests, and before

Christmas they had practised these over and over, as they had the English and arithmetic tests, which he knew would follow.

When Ben first turned over the paper, for a moment the words swam before him and he was gripped by panic. He couldn't do this. He would make an utter fool of himself. He told himself not to be so stupid. This was the day he knew would come, that he had been working towards for months, and he picked up his pen and began.

After the exam, the candidates were sent into the reception area to meet up with the people who had come with them.

'That your mum?' a boy asked Ben, pointing his finger at Isobel, who had spotted him across the room and was waving.

Ben didn't know how to explain Isobel. It sounded strange to say that he was a friend of his Uncle Tom's. 'I haven't got a mom. She's dead. That's my Aunt Izzy,' he said as she approached.

Isobel heard what Ben said and wasn't surprised, because it was far better for him to say his mother was dead than to say that she had run off with someone else. So she made no comment, but instead just said, 'You survived it then?'

'Just about,' Ben said. 'And I'm starving.'

'Me too,' Isobel said. 'Let's go.'

A little later they were studying the sparse menu in the city-centre restaurant.

'Spam fritters, mashed potato, swede and carrots,' Isobel said. 'It's not quite the banquet I had in mind, but never mind. It will probably be better than poor man's goose, which I happen to know is liver, or Lord Woolton pie.'

'Ugh, I'll say,' Ben said with feeling. 'And at least we know what Spam is.'

'Oh, I dispute that,' Isobel said with a laugh. 'No one knows what Spam is. All we can say is that it is edible and we know of no one who has died from eating it.'

'It'd better be Spam then,' Ben said with a resigned sigh.

A short time later, as they attacked the meal, Isobel said, 'Do you want to talk about the exam or not? I don't mind either way.'

Ben laid down his fork and said, 'You know, Aunt Izzy, you are the oddest grown-up I know.'

Isobel smiled and said, 'Am I supposed to take that as a compliment?'

Ben nodded. 'You're not full of questions like lots of grown-ups.'

'Well, I think that sometimes people have to get things fixed in their own head before they want to share it with others,' Isobel said. 'And some things they might not want to share at all, and then I don't think they should be forced to.'

'That's it exactly,' said Ben. 'And really there isn't much to say about the exam. It was hard as I expected it to be, but I did my best and I hope that I did enough to pass, but we will have to wait and see and that's all there is to it.'

'Right,' Isobel said. 'That's the exam dealt with. Anything else you want to talk about?'

'Y . . . yes,' Ben said hesitantly. 'You probably won't answer, though.'

'Try me.'

'Are you going to marry Uncle Tom?'

'No, I'm not, Ben, but what made you ask?' Aggie said.

'Well, you are friends with him, aren't you?'

'Yes, I am,' Isobel said. 'And proud to be because he is a lovely man. But he is just that, a friend.'

'Will you ever marry again?'

'I'm not looking for anyone else in my life,' Isobel said. 'I had a lovely marriage to a wonderful man, and I really think that there is no way that that could be repeated. But I'm not against marriage for other people.'

'Uncle Tom used to say that he wasn't the marrying kind.'

'No,' Isobel said. 'He is happy single. He told me he has

never been happier nor more content than he is at the moment, and Paul said he took to factory work like he had been born to it.'

'He likes working for your brother,' Ben confided. 'He told me that.'

'Paul's a kind man,' Isobel said. 'He owes your family a debt because if Molly's father hadn't crawled in to save him that time in the First World War he wouldn't be here today.'

'Molly told me about that,' Ben said. 'And Kevin said a bit. Must have been brave, their dad, mustn't he?'

'I'll say he must have been,' Isobel said. 'Two of my brothers, both older than Paul, had already been killed, and with each one I saw my parents age a little more. Mind you, we didn't know our brothers much because my sister and I were so much younger, and then when they were eight they were sent away to school.'

'I wouldn't like that much.'

'It's how it was,' Isobel said. 'No one ever questioned it. There are seven years between Sarah and Paul and so she was only about a year old when he went to join his brothers. I am two years younger again and they always seemed quite grown up to me. Anyway, that was all a long time ago and there has been a lot of water under the bridge since then. I know something far more interesting from your point of view.'

'What?'

'I happen to know that they have apple pie and custard on the menu for once. Have you room for it now you have cleaned your plate?'

'Are you kidding?' Ben said with a grin. 'For apple pie and custard I would always have room.'

'Well, you're better than me then,' Isobel said. 'Because I haven't the smallest space left, but I will buy it for you with pleasure. I love to see a boy with a good appetite.'

Ben tucked into the pudding, which he described as delicious, with gusto, and Isobel let him enjoy it.

He had almost finished when she suddenly said, 'Is someone bullying you at school, Ben?'

There was no lead up to the question and so Ben was taken completely unawares. He was about to make an emphatic denial when his eyes caught the concerned ones of Isobel and he lowered his head and mumbled, 'Yeah, a bit. How d'you know, anyway?'

'Something you said before the exam. What's it all over?'

Ben shrugged. 'Anything and everything.'

'Why don't you tell someone?'

'That's a daft thing to say,' Ben said. 'You know I can't do that. And I wouldn't mind it so much if it was one to one, but there are three of them. The others join in sometimes, but I think they only do it because they are scared that, if they don't, they might start on them next. But none of them are sitting the eleven plus and so if I pass, they won't be able to bully me any more.'

'They should be taught a lesson before that,' Isobel said. 'Bullies are nasty people and usually cowards. We have fought a war for five years now because of a bully.'

'Maybe someone will bully them in the secondary school,' Ben said. 'It would serve them right. And you know what? I'd laugh if I got to hear about it.'

'And so would I,' said Isobel.

Just over a week after this, Molly gave birth to a baby girl that she called Nuala in memory of her mother. Ben was very impressed with the baby. He had never had much to do with babies and had no idea that they were so small, or helpless, or so perfect. He could quite understand Kevin's pride in her, which was almost as great as Mark's.

Ben was ticked pink when she was laid in his arms, and he held the little child as gingerly as if she was made of delicate bone china. He noted the fine down on her head, the slightly pink cheeks and the baby-blue eyes trying so hard to focus that a pucker had developed between them, and he envied Kevin being her uncle.

'Well, you're her cousin,' Kevin said, when Ben said this.

'Am I?' Ben asked. 'I thought I was your cousin.'

'You are,' Kevin said. 'That's how it works. You're my cousin and Molly's, and because of that you are the baby's second cousin, but still a cousin.'

'I'm glad,' Ben said, 'because she is lovely, isn't she?'

'She isn't half,' Kevin said. 'Molly said she can see that Nuala will be able to twist me around her little finger before she is much older, and you know what? I wouldn't mind that a bit.'

'I won't mind either,' Ben said.

'I am glad, though, that I will be out at work soon,' Kevin said. 'Molly and Mark shouldn't have to provide for me now that they have a baby to see to.'

'I won't be working for ages,' Ben said.

'If you get to grammar school you won't,' Kevin told him. 'When do you hear if you passed that exam or not?'

'The teacher said we will be sent the results by early March,' Ben said. 'If I have passed the first part of the exam, the second part is taken at my first choice of school.'

'St Philip's?'

'That's right.'

'It's over the other side of the city.'

'Only just,' Ben pointed out. 'Anyway, I had to put a Catholic grammar school as my first choice and that is St Philip's. Aunt Izzy can't understand it either.'

'Well, she wouldn't,' Kevin said. 'She's not a Catholic.'

'Neither are you.'

'No,' Kevin said. 'Not now I'm not, but I still sort of know how it works.'

'Aunt Izzy says Bishop Vesey's in Sutton Coldfield is a good school,' Ben said.

'She's nice, isn't she, Aunt Izzy?' Kevin said. 'I wonder if she will ever get together with Uncle Tom.'

'She says not.'

'Don't say you've asked her?'

'Yeah, I did,' Ben admitted. 'The day of the first exam. I didn't think she'd answer but she did. She said that she is very fond of Tom and proud to be his friend, but she isn't looking for anyone else and neither is he.'

'Ah, but you know what grown-ups are,' Kevin said. 'They don't always tell the truth, do they? I mean, they often tell us what they think we'd like them to say instead of being totally honest, which we would prefer.'

Ben nodded his head. He knew exactly what Kevin meant.

Just over a fortnight after little Nuala was born, Ben was in his bedroom settling to do his homework when his father came into the room. 'Can I talk to you, Ben?'

Ben was wary. 'What about?'

'Your mother.'

'No.'

'Ben . . .'

'No. I don't want to hear anything that she has got to say.'

'Look, Ben,' Joe said sternly, 'I know your mother ran out on you and I understand it was hard, but it was really me that she was leaving, not you. She has not suddenly developed two heads, or even stopped loving you.'

'Huh!'

'Ben, she's written to you every week,' Joe said, and saw his son's eyes widen in astonishment. 'I have kept all her letter – unopened, of course – just in case you want to have a read of them some day.'

'Small chance.'

'Listen, Ben,' Joe said, 'this morning she wrote to me saying she had a feeling that you weren't getting the letters because she had never got a reply. She accused me of keeping the letters from you, which I had been doing in a way, and asked that you at least be told the latest news.'

'And what's that, as if it matters?'

'Your mother has given birth to a baby girl,' Joe said. 'She was born a week ago and they are calling her Rebecca Norah. She is your half-sister, Ben.'

Ben felt as if he had been kicked in the stomach. Somewhere in that vast continent of America his mother had had a baby, his sister that he would never see, or hold, or learn to love. He knew he would get to know Molly's baby much better than the one his mother had had. It wasn't right, and it was just one more thing to blame his mother for.

'Good job I didn't go with her when she said she wanted me to,' he told his father. 'There will be no place for me in her new life now.'

'Love isn't like that, Ben,' Joe said. 'You don't have just so much of it so if you love someone you have no love left for another.'

'How d'you know anything about love anyway?' Ben demanded. 'You told me that you still loved Mom when she went away. And why are you being so reasonable? Anyone else would be hopping mad.'

Joe wondered about that himself. Whatever she had done, though, for her sake and Ben's he didn't want her totally to lose the son he knew she still loved.

Children, however, view the world as black and white. In Ben's world his mother had been bad running away from them in the first place, and then made it worse by having another baby. 'It's all disgusting anyway,' he said. 'And I want no part in it.'

'Can you not write just a short note to your mother?' Joe asked.

Ben shook his head. 'No. Why should I? I don't care about some baby that she has had in America. She might be my half-sister but I'll never know her. She will be like a stranger to me and so will Mom in the end, and I don't care.'

Joe knew that Ben cared very much – his anguished eyes

spoke for him – but he knew that it would do no good to try to reason with him because he was too hurt to listen.

Isobel, whom Joe confided in, agreed with this. 'Did you have any idea that Gloria might be pregnant when she left?' she asked.

'I didn't think she could,' he said. 'I mean, there had been years before we had Ben, and nothing since.'

'There is no possibility that the child could be yours?'

'No. None whatsoever,' Joe said. 'Sex between us was just a distant memory for months before she left. And even though I guessed that she was having some sort of affair – though, I didn't know how far it had gone – with Gloria's problems I would never have imagined that it might end up with her being pregnant.'

'So it was a shock for you?'

'Well, yes.'

'So how much more of a shock must it have been to Ben?'

'Immense. I see now.'

'And you expected Ben to be delighted with the news?' Isobel asked with a wry smile. 'To clap his hands with delight and write a letter to his mother congratulating her on the birth of his baby sister that he probably won't even see for years.'

'Put like that it is ridiculous,' Joe said. 'So what should I do, do you think?'

'With Ben, nothing, I would say,' Isobel advised. 'Time, as they say, is a great healer. Let Ben come to the realisation that though his mother has a new life and family in America, she still wants contact with him.'

'And you think he will do that in time?'

'I have no idea,' Isobel said. 'But it is the only thing to do. At the moment he is one angry and hurt boy. If you want to do something then you write to Gloria.'

'I have always avoided that.'

'Yes, I know. And I accept what Gloria did upset you a great deal, but it cut Ben to the quick. You should put aside any resentment you still have clinging to you for the sake of the son you share. If Ben won't write to her then you write. Tell her how he is, his likes and dislikes; tell her about the exams he is taking for the eleven plus. Paint a picture of the child she left behind so that when she does write she has some idea of the person she is writing to. Oh, and remember Ben is only a boy. I know he has your strength of character and will not be won over by showering him with goodies but he does need to know that his mother is thinking about him. Maybe she could buy him something really nice for his birthday, for he had virtually nothing at Christmas, like many more in this country at this time.'

'Do you know,' Joe said admiringly, 'if we had people like you in government then we wouldn't need to have wars ever again.'

Isobel smiled and Joe saw suddenly, and with a little surprise, how pretty she was when she did so.

'Maybe I should have been the one chosen to talk to Herr Hitler that time in Munich,' she said.

'You couldn't have done worse.'

'Ah, Joe, just think what life would have been like without this devastating war. I would have probably still have Gregory and Gerald, and you, Gloria and Ben would in all likelihood be in London enjoying life together.'

'Yes. Isn't it a pity we can't roll back the years and have another crack at it?' Joe said.

'It is indeed,' Isobel said wistfully.

Isobel was worried about Ben, because the pressure and worry of the exams was enough stress without the bullying going on at school, and coping with losing his mother, and in the end she sought the help of Kevin.

Kevin was angered that Ben was being bullied, though surprised because he was a tough little nut and as strong as an ox from the work on the farm and the good food they'd had in plenty.

'I would have thought he could give a good enough account of himself,' he said to Isobel.

'Maybe he could if it was just one to one. In fact he said that to me,' Isobel said. 'But there are three of them, he said.'

'Cowardly bullies then.'

'Isn't that usually the way?'

'Yes, I suppose it is,' Kevin agreed. 'What do you want me to do?'

'I don't really know,' Isobel said. 'I think I am the only one that he has told about the bullying and though he didn't actually tell me to keep it a secret, I know he would hate me to blab about it.'

'Does Uncle Joe know, or Uncle Tom?'

'I doubt it,' Isobel said. 'I feel sure they would have said something if they did. Joe, I think, would probably go storming down to the school and that is the last thing that Ben needs right now. I thought that maybe you could sound him out. He is so immensely fond of you.'

'I'll take him up town next Saturday morning,' Kevin said. 'How's that? Away from the house he might talk more.'

'Thank you, Kevin,' Isobel said. 'I knew that I could rely on you.'

Kevin didn't wait till Saturday to speak to Ben. On reflection he thought it was a long time to delay if he was in trouble of any sort. So Monday afternoon he left his school via the back wall after afternoon registration and made his way to Chester Road, where he caught a tram to Boldmere and was waiting nearby Kevin's school when the bell went.

He semi hid behind a tree, not wanting Ben to catch sight of him until he was able to see what was happening. Ben didn't see his cousin as he sped past, because behind him he could hear the pounding feet of his pursuers.

Ben shot up Boldmere Road, fear lending wings to his feet, and Kevin, loping easily behind them, turned the corner to see that Ben had been grabbed by two of the bullies. Ben's progress had been hampered by a clutch of mothers with prams, babies and small children, who had stopped to chat. The two boys who had grabbed Ben began dragging him towards an alleyway that led to the back of the shops, and Kevin noticed another boy, bigger and beefier than the two who had grabbed Ben, chugging behind them and breathing heavily because he was more than a little on the plump side.

The alleyway opened on to storage yards and the two boys still held Ben fast as the stouter one eventually caught up with the others. The smaller of the two turned to him and said, 'What we going to do with him then?'

'Teach him a lesson,' said the stouter boy. He pushed his face right up to Ben's and hissed, 'You brought this on yourself. I told you what you had to do.'

Then Kevin saw him power his fist into Ben's unprotected stomach so hard that Ben's knees crumpled, and had it not been for the boys holding his arms he would have fallen. Kevin decided enough was enough, and with a howl of rage he flew down the entry. The two smaller boys scattered, but the other one, whom Kevin thought was probably the ringleader, wasn't quick enough, and Kevin grabbed him and yanked his arm up his back until he yelped in pain and fear.

'You lay one hand on my cousin again and I will give you the same back doubled,' he said to the trembling boy. 'You got that?'

Then as the boy gave no reply to this he gave his arm another twist. 'I said, have you got that?'

'Yeah, I got it,' said the boy breathlessly. 'Let me go. You're breaking my arm.'

Kevin released the pressure slightly as he warned, 'It'll be your bloody neck I break next time if I catch you at this type of caper. I will be keeping an eye on you from now on, so watch out.' He released the boy then with a push, and the boy staggered and then began to run down the alleyway, rubbing his arm as he went.

Ben was looking at his cousin with a kind of awe. 'You were just terrific, Kevin.'

Kevin shrugged. 'I hate bullying,' he said. 'Was it the same thugs split your lip?'

Ben nodded as the two began to walk down the alleyway and up Boldmere Road to the flat.

'Why?' Kevin said. 'What was that big kid talking about? What did they want you to do?'

'Shoplift.'

'What?'

'Pinch sweets from the shop,' Kevin said. 'They said if I did they would lay off me. I actually considered it as well, 'cos I thought that no one really cares about me any more.'

'How do you work that out?' Kevin said. 'For your information, mate, I am risking the cane coming to sort you out today. I bunked off school. How else would I be there when school finished?'

'I dunno,' Ben said. 'I thought you might have had the day off or something.'

'The only ones who have days off are Catholics, who have Holy Days,' Kevin said. 'State schools don't give days off, and if I have been missed I am for the high jump. But now I am here tell me who else couldn't give a monkey's about you?'

'Well, you know . . .'

'This is all to do with your mother, isn't it?'

'I suppose.'

'Look, Ben,' said Kevin, 'it don't matter whether your mother dies or runs off. The fact is, she ain't here now.'

'I know that,' Ben said scornfully.

'All right then, I will tell you something that you don't know,' Kevin said. 'When my mom died I hadn't seen her for nine weeks because she got pneumonia. The day she died, well, that was the day she was discharged from the hospital and Dad went to fetch her in Paul's car. The neighbours were all there, a party tea done and everything, and I never saw either of them again.'

Ben heard the catch in his voice and for the first time realised the level of Kevin's suffering when he had been only five years old.

They reached the flat. Ben opened the door and they went inside before Ben turned to Kevin and said, 'I'm sorry for what I said before, Kev, about it not being so bad for you and everything because your mom died and mine ran away. That was a horrible thing to say.'

''S all right,' Kevin said magnanimously. 'It hadn't long happened then, and I think you just wanted to hurt someone else like you'd been hurt. But I'll tell you what I envy you for.'

'What?'

'That you can remember your mother,' Kevin said. 'Sometimes I can hardly remember what mine looked like. Uncle Tom said to look at Molly because she is the spit of our mum, but it's not the same. And there's my dad as well. They are like shadowy figures to me and I wish they weren't, and I would love it if my mom and dad were in America rather than dead and gone.'

'You think I should write to her, don't you?' Ben said, and when Kevin nodded, Ben went on, 'She's had a baby, you know? And they got married when Mum was already married to Dad.'

'I know,' Kevin said. 'Uncle Joe told Molly he's getting divorced as soon as possible. He said it will be best for the baby.'

'But I don't think you can get divorced as a Catholic.'

'Maybe not,' Kevin said. 'But you can in law and that's what matters. And it would be better for your sister.'

'Half-sister.'

'Don't split hairs,' Kevin said.

'Anyway, it won't mean anything to me, will it?' Ben said.

'Not if that's the way you think, it won't.'

'She's in America and has a little baby. I can hardly send her a letter.'

'You should ask Aunt Gloria all about her, and they don't stay babies for ever,' Kevin said. 'When Molly went to Buncrana, I missed her lot and I couldn't really write properly so Granddad said to send her pictures. So I used to draw things for her that she said often made her cry because if I drew our house I put Mom and Dad in the picture too. Point is, Ben, that little baby might really want to have a big brother who cares about her when she is older, but you are the only one who can decide this. She can't. She is helpless and innocent.'

After Kevin had gone, Ben went over and over his words. That night, after they had eaten, Joe said he was going into the bedroom to write a letter. He had put it off all weekend and hated to do it now. He had never written to Gloria before and didn't know the kindest way to tell a mother that their child did not want to have any communication with her, and he rose from the table with a heavy heart.

Ben swallowed deeply before saying, 'Are you writing to Mom?'

'You know I am, Ben. One of us has to.'

'Maybe both of us should and if you leave the letter open I will put a note as well.'

Joe's eyes met his son's over the table and he smiled his slow and easy smile as he said, 'D'you know, son, that is the best idea I have heard in ages.'

Before Joe left to write his own letter, he put a pile of letters beside Ben's plate. 'They are from your mother,' Joe told him. 'As I told you, she wrote every week.'

'I only agreed to send a letter for the baby's sake, not Mom's,' Ben stated flatly. 'If she cared about me she wouldn't have gone, so I'm not interested in anything else she has to say.'

'Well, that's up to you,' Joe said. 'They're there if you want them. That's all I'm saying.'

TWENTY-SIX

Ben had intended leaving the letters on the table when he went into his room to do his homework, but for some reason he picked them up too. He wasn't going to read them, though, he thought as he laid them on the chest of drawers in his room. He hadn't time. He had masses to do.

He turned his back on the letters, sat down at his desk and opened up his arithmetic homework book. The figures danced before his eyes and he couldn't seem to make either head or tail of the problems. The urge to read what his mother had to say to him niggled at him so much that in the end he decided to read just one, the first one she had written, and then settle to his homework.

Over an hour later, he was sitting on his bed, the letters scattered around him, some of the words smudged from the tears that had fallen from Ben's eyes. Gloria wrote as she spoke, so that Ben could almost imagine her in the room as she reminded him of the time the two of them explored London together, stirring up his memories of that time together.

He would never forget the blitz, but some of his mother's letters brought that terrifying period to life again and he recalled struggling from his bed, alerted by the siren's wail. He was often still half asleep and trying to struggle into a siren suit that seemed to have more arms and legs than he needed. And then hurrying through the streets alive with ack-ack guns barking into the night sky, lit up by the incendiary bombs already dropped and the beams of the roving search lights, hearing the drone of planes and often the crump of bombs exploding not that far away.

The fear had been like a living thing inside him, lodged in his stomach or crawling down his spine, and sometimes he would shake so much his teeth would chatter together. And his mother was always there beside him suffering too, and probably just as scared as he was, but she never showed it, and when she held him tight he always felt better.

They would stumble home hours later when the all clear went, the skies usually alight with fires burning, and sometimes they would see tongues of flames licking the smoky air that also smelled of cordite and gas and brick dust. Gloria also spoke of the night his father was injured so badly he almost died, and that terrible night when Tottenham was hit and the flat destroyed.

Do you remember the burning, glowing mounds of rubble were all around us that night, Ben? And we had to clamber over seeping sandbags and dribbling hosepipes, and then seeing the utter desolation of the whole area where our flat had once stood?

That was the reason they had had to go to Ireland in the first place, but apart from his horrible grandmother he had loved Ireland. He knew that his mother didn't, though, and he had felt sorry about that. Gloria freely admitted that in her letters, and why she started work at the naval camp: 'I was very lonely and a little homesick for America, and the money was needed, anyway.'

Maybe the money was needed, but Ben knew that from his mother starting work there, his father became unhappy and then the rows began. Gloria touched on this a little and then went on to say how she had met and fallen in love with Philip Morrisey.

It wasn't anything either of us were looking for, and you were the last person in the world that I wanted to hurt, and yet I know I did and that pains me very much. I am also so very sorry that I made you choose between your father and me. That was absolutely wrong and a cowardly thing to do and I bitterly regret it. I fully support the decision you made to leave the ship, but there is not one day goes by when I don't think of you and wonder how you are doing, and I would love it if you would write to me, even just now and again, and let me know what your life is like.

That was the last letter Gloria had written before the one to Joe telling him about the birth of the child. Ben could feel his mother's sadness rising up from the page. She had missed him as much as he had missed her, and despite what she had done he realised he still loved her dearly.

Letters were a poor substitute for having his mother come back to live with them again, but it was better than nothing. Ben remembered what Kevin had said that day. Ben could only imagine the big hole losing both his parents had left in Kevin's life, and he hadn't even the comfort of letters to fill the gap even partially, and yet Kevin had risen above the tragedy and he must do the same.

He had to accept that even if he had the power to force his mother to return to them, she would be desperately unhappy. Her life now was in America with Philip. Reading through the letters again he realised that she was happy in her new life. He wrote that he loved her and missed her and was surprised by the news of the baby.

Maybe, when the baby is older, you will tell her about her big brother who lives in England and one day we might even get to meet.

When Joe popped his head around the door a little later, he saw the tear trails on Ben's face and the letters strewn on the bed.

'All right?' he said.

'Yeah,' Ben said. 'It was just remembering it all again, but I'm all right now.'

'If you ever want to talk about your mother or discuss anything, don't feel that it would upset me,' Joe said gently. 'I know you must miss her sorely at times.'

Ben looked at his father with gratitude. 'I'll remember that,' he said. 'And thanks, Dad.'

Ben worked harder than ever at school. He had told his mother about the exam and wanted to pass because he knew that she would be so proud of him if he did. It was much easier for him at school now, because the bullies gave him a wide berth. Ben knew that Kevin really couldn't keep much of an eye on him, but they didn't know that. They all thought that if he had a cousin like that, then it was much healthier to leave Ben Sullivan alone.

In early in March he learned that he had passed the first part of the eleven plus. The second part was to be held at St Philip's School the following Saturday, the tenth.

'As it's a Saturday,' Joe said, 'I can go with you this time.'

'Can Aunt Izzy come too?'

'If she wants,' said Joe. 'Though she might already have plans.'

'It's just that it's a long time to wait,' Joe said. 'Aunt Izzy went on a tour around the shops last time because it was in town. She found that restaurant that she took me to later for lunch, but I don't know anything about St Philip's and you might get really fed up on your own, and anyway, she is really nice.'

'She is,' Joe agreed. 'I will ask her, and if she is doing nothing she will probably be keen to come as she took you to the first one.'

Isobel was delighted to be asked and she readily agreed to accompany them both. The three of them set off early on Saturday morning because they had to take the tram to the terminus in the city centre and then take one out along the Hagley Road, Edgbaston, on the other side of it. 'Thank God it's dry,' Joe said as they waited for the Edgbaston tram. 'Though this wind is enough to cut a body in two.'

'I couldn't agree more,' Isobel said, tucking her scarf in tighter. 'But don't you think it too long a trek for a young boy to make every day?'

Joe was inclined to agree. He said nothing to Ben, and though he hoped he had passed the exams, he didn't really want him to pass with enough marks to get his first choice. Bishop Vesey's in Sutton Coldfield, which was his second choice, would be much better for him, he thought. However, it wouldn't help to say this now and so instead he said, 'He's young and fit and, remember, he won't be the only one.'

'I suppose,' Isobel said. 'But what time will he have to set off in the morning to get here on time?'

'No earlier than me, that's certain,' Joe said, and added with a wide smile, 'because I work for that slave driver of a brother of yours.'

Isobel's smile was just as broad as she replied in like manner, 'You do indeed.' She lifted her head as she spoke and as her amused eyes met those of Joe, the laughter was suddenly stripped from the pair of them and Ben felt as though they had suddenly formed a magic circle around themselves and he was on the outside of it.

It was gone in an instant, and the tram arrived, and by the time they were seated Ben thought he had imagined the whole thing. But he hadn't. Both Isobel and Joe had been aware of the attraction that had flowed between them and Joe was the more shocked of the two. When he had watched the ship sail out against the skyline, taking away the only woman he had ever loved in his life, he had felt his heart like a cold, dead weight inside him and had honestly thought that it would stay like that until the day he died.

But some electric current had passed between him and Isobel, causing that same heart to thump against his ribs. He knew he had no right to feel like that about anyone, least of all Isobel, who he counted as a good friend. Was he some sort of beast that he couldn't view a woman in any light other than a sexual one? He was very glad that Isobel hadn't been privy to his thoughts.

But Isobel had felt the pull too and knew that the look in Joe's eyes was probably mirrored in her own. When she had told Ben that she was looking for no man to share her life she had spoken the truth, so she had been taken unawares by the attraction she had felt towards Joe. Suddenly, they felt awkward with one another and a silence grew up between them.

In an effort to break it, Joe said, 'It's a nice enough journey out to this school anyway, for this is a fine wide road.'

Isobel was grateful for Joe remarking on something so innocuous and innocent. 'Yes, I always liked it too,' she replied. 'Gerald and I used to drive down this road to visit Paul when he lived in the house in Edgbaston. I always thought it a lovely road, so near to the city centre and yet lined with trees like a country lane.'

Joe laughed at her but gently. 'It's like no country lane that I've ever seen,' he said. 'If you want country lanes, Ireland is the place for you.'

'D'you know I have always wanted to go there and never made it,' Isobel said. 'Gerald was always too busy building his business to take time off to have any sort of holiday.'

'One day I will take you to Ireland,' Joe promised.

Isobel looked at Joe and opened her mouth, but before she could say anything, Ben said, 'Not without me you won't. If you are going to Ireland, then I am coming too.'

'Did I suggest going without you?' Joe said.

'No,' said Ben. 'But you never made it clear I was going either.'

Whatever remark Joe was going to make to this was never given, because the conductor came up to tell them that they had reached their stop.

At the school, as it was a Saturday, the staffroom was made available to those who accompanied the boys while the exams were in progress, and as the day had turned out blustery as well as cold, Isobel and Joe decided to take advantage of it.

'Did Ben like Ireland so very much?' Izzy said, as they settled themselves down for the long wait.

'Yes, he did,' Joe replied. 'Though he was glad enough to get away when we did, before the news broke about Gloria and Philip Morrisey. In a small place like that . . . well, let's just say that our lives wouldn't have been worth living. They'd mean well and their sympathies would have been with us and everything, but both of us were too raw to have dealt with it just then.'

'I can totally understand that.'

'What Ben really would like to return to, I think, is the life before all the upset happened, maybe before Gloria's job at the Springtown Camp, but that life will never come again and even the farm will be in new hands soon.'

'Has Tom a buyer then?'

'More or less,' Joe said. 'And he will insist on sharing the money. I don't know what I will do with my share.'

'Did you make no plans?'

'Not plans as such, no,' Joe said, 'because I didn't know that Tom only stayed on here so that I could come over here with Gloria and Ben and take over the tenancy once he decided what to do with the farm.'

'Yes, he told me that too,' Isobel said.

'By the time he told us this, relations between Gloria and me were stretched to breaking point,' Joe said. 'And though I didn't know it, she must have been pregnant with Philip

Morrisey's child and making plans to leave. I had it in mind to buy a house, mainly so that Ben will have something when I am gone, but now I am having a rethink.'

'Oh?'

'Well, I will not have enough to buy a house outright,' Joe said. 'I would have to have a mortgage and I am hesitant to tie up all my cash in paying it back. It would mean hefty repayments, because I am fifty-five years old. I have only ten years more in employment. In the meantime, if Ben passes this exam and proves to be bright enough to go to university, a lump sum might be useful then.'

'I think there are grants and things,' Isobel said.

'Maybe there are, but if Ben makes the grade, I want him to have the same as the other students.'

'What will Tom do with his share?'

'Put it in the bank, if I know Tom,' Joe said. 'He'll be moving in with Aggie and Paul, that I am sure of. It's been on the cards for ages. He only stayed on with me this long because Ben was in such a state.'

'You must have been devastated too when it happened?'

'I felt so saddened that our lives together were over,' Joe said. 'My immediate concern was to get Ben away here as soon as possible. It was when we arrived that the whole thing hit me, but then Ben needed me and I couldn't really give way at all.'

'You did a good job,' Isobel said. 'Ben is a fine boy. One you can feel proud of.'

'I am proud of him,' Joe said. 'I always have been. And I suppose the sensible thing for me to do would be to invest most of my share of the money and stay on at the flat.'

Isobel thought of the bungalow that she had lived in alone since her husband's death. It was far too big for her, and both Sarah and Paul had urged her to sell up and find somewhere smaller, but all her memories, good and bad, were tied up in her home and she loved it dearly. It had three bedrooms, enough room for Joe and his son, and she would love to have a man about the place again and to see a boy grow to manhood in a world of peace. She also knew that it would be totally inappropriate for her to mention this to either of them and she found herself saying instead, 'Yes, I think that that will be the best solution all round.'

A fortnight or so after this, Molly said to Tom, who had popped round one day as he was wont to, 'Don't think I'm mad or anything, but is there anything going on between Isobel and Joe?'

'Funny you should mention that,' Tom said. 'There is nothing going on, as such. Well, not that I've seen, and Ben has said nothing either and I'm sure he would have done, but I've not seen Joe the way he is now in years. There is a light dancing in his eyes and a spring in his step, and he reminds me of when he was a young lad in Buncrana and going out to the socials.'

'Well, Isobel too is like a young girl,' Molly said. 'And then last Sunday after dinner, with the boys upstairs and you putting Nuala to bed, I made a pot of tea and took it into the living room. Uncle Joe and Aunt Isobel were in there. They were doing nothing wrong, weren't even sitting together. Joe was in one of the armchairs and Isobel on a corner of the settee, but I saw the look that passed between them before they realised that I was in the room. It was so . . . sort of bittersweet in a way. It brought a lump to my throat, to tell you the truth.'

'Do you think they are aware of it?' Tom asked.

'They must be,' Molly said. 'They might not have admitted it even to themselves, but there is a certain something between them.'

'Maybe it is time for Joe to take my place and accompany Isobel, like I used to, so they get to know each other a little better?' Tom suggested.

Molly nodded. 'It would do him good, anyway. He hardly goes across the door. I mean, if Joe doesn't want to leave

Ben in the flat on his own, he can come here. He's hardly away from the doorstep, anyway. Mind you, I don't think that it's me that's the draw. It's more likely Nuala.'

Tom smiled. 'He really loves the child.'

'I know,' Molly said. 'He is very sweet with her and when she does something like when she smiled at him for the first time, he was bowled over and he told me he wrote to his mother and asked if Rebecca did that yet. Gloria wrote back that she did and sent him some photos to prove it. Of course, all this worshipping at the cradle of Nuala is doing her no good at all. I said to Mark, the sooner this war is over and we can be a proper family again and give Nuala a brother or sister, the better I will like it.'

'It can't be long now,' Tom said. 'Anyone but Hitler would have admitted defeat by now.'

'Hitler is a madman,' Molly said. 'Everyone knows it. I tell you, the ones who find him and hang him from the nearest tree, or lamppost will be doing the world a favour, in my opinion.'

'And in mine,' Tom said. 'And it can't come soon enough.'

'Are you sure that you feel all right about me doing this?' Joe asked Ben anxiously as he got ready in the bedroom. 'You're not in any way upset that I am going to the cinema with Isobel?'

'You asked me this twice already,' Ben pointed out. 'And I said I didn't then. Why should I, anyway?'

'I don't know. I just thought . . .'

'Look, Dad, stop worrying about me all the time,' Ben said. 'You're taking me round to Molly, and then me and Kevin are going to play football in the park, and after he is going to show me the crystal set that Uncle Paul got him. We're going to see if we can set it up and I am stopping overnight with them so why would I care what you do?'

'So you have the evening all planned out then?'

'We sure do,' said Ben in a broad American accent.

'And I should stop being such a worry guts?'

'Yeah, you should,' Ben said. 'I'm eleven, not a baby any more.'

'All right, all right,' Joe said with a mock sigh, 'I know when I'm not wanted.'

'Good,' Ben said with a grin. 'Glad we've got that established.'

Joe was delighted to see his son in such good form, but what he said was, 'You cheeky young whippersnapper! You're not too old for a good hiding, you know.'

Ben looked not a bit abashed. All he said was, 'Are you ready yet? Shall I get my coat or what?'

Joe thought that he was the luckiest man in the world, sitting beside Isobel in the dark of the cinema, as if he had a perfect right to be there, and he hoped that she couldn't hear the thump of his heart that suddenly seemed too big for his body. His mouth was so dry, it was uncomfortable to swallow, and though he longed to take one of Isobel's hands in his, he resisted the temptation and tried to calm down and concentrate on the screen.

The main film was *Lassie Come Home*, and it was less than a quarter of the way through when Isobel said quietly to Joe, 'Wouldn't Ben just love this?'

He would, Joe knew, and so just as quietly he whispered back, 'Let's take him then on Saturday.'

'Thank you, I'd like that,' Isobel said. 'But maybe Ben would like you to himself.'

'No, he always likes your company,' Joe said. He wanted to add, 'So do I,' but he didn't think it was the correct thing to do. So the words hung unsaid in the air.

But that did pave the way for more outings, at least, and after that they took Ben out every weekend as March gave way to April, and still the war rumbled on. Isobel and Joe were unaware that the whole family was watching this love developing between them with great interest. Joe tried to deny the feelings rising inside him every time he even thought about Isobel. He knew that if he had declared his love for her, nothing could happen because he was still a married man, his divorce not yet achieved.

Ben didn't know this, but after Tom left to live with Aggie and Paul, Isobel became an even greater part of their lives.

One day Ben said to her, 'Are you still Uncle Tom's friend?'

'Yes, of course.'

'You're more Dad's friend now, though, aren't you?'

'I am very fond of your father too,' Isobel conceded.

'But you wouldn't marry Dad either, would you?' Ben said. 'Is that because he is just a friend like Tom is?'

'No, it's because I am not looking for a husband and I'm sure your father doesn't think of me like that.'

'Have you asked him?' Ben persisted. 'Because I think he does.'

Isobel felt her cheeks flame with embarrassment as Ben exclaimed, 'You've gone ever such a funny colour!'

'All right, that's a halt to the personal questions,' Isobel said. 'And I must say, Ben, that for someone who doesn't like answering that many questions, you certainly can dish them out.'

'The teacher said we need to ask questions,' Ben said with a large grin. 'That's how we learn, she said.'

'Oh, did she?' Isobel answered grimly. 'Well, in my book you have learned enough. Let's go and find your father.'

TWENTY-SEVEN

Hitler killed himself on 30 April in a bunker in Berlin together with his lover, Eva Braun, whom he had married the day before. This was reported in the papers after Berlin fell to the Red Army on 2 May. Hitler's successor, Admiral Doenitz, then surrendered to the Soviet Army on 7 May and the war that had claimed so many lives was finally over.

Tuesday 8 May, was declared a national holiday, VE or Victory in Europe Day. Euphoria gripped the nation as the realisation sank in of what the end of the war really meant. Church bells, the ringing of which was reserved for warning of invasion, rang out for the first time in years.

Many shopkeepers opened their store of goods that they had kept back for just such a moment. Things not seen for years appeared on the counters, and pubs were open all day. People seemed to have a need to be with other people: some took to the streets and others gathered together with their families. Paul and Aggie opened their house to everyone, as it was the largest. Joe and Ben got off the tram at Molly's and together they walked across the park, pushing Nuala in the pram. They saw people stacking up piles of rubbish, including many of the hated gas masks. For a second or two Kevin wondered what they were doing and then he exclaimed to Ben, 'Oh boy! Look at that. They are building a bonfire.'

That had been another thing banned through the war. 'Can we go?' Kevin asked. 'When it gets darker, I mean?'

'I should think so,' Joe said. 'Though they might not wait for dark to light it because it stays light for ages now.'

'I wonder if there will be fireworks,' Molly said. 'You know, if anyone has a few that they have kept all these years.'

'The shopkeepers might,' Tom said. 'If they had stock in from before the war.'

'Would they be any good after all this time, though?' Joe asked.

'Well, there is not much to spoil, is there?' Tom said. 'The most important thing is whether they were kept dry or not.'

'Ooh, I hope you're right, Uncle Tom,' Molly said. 'I love fireworks. I remember fireworks on Bonfire Night. Do you, Kevin?'

Kevin nodded. 'Just about.'

'We will come out and see afterwards,' Molly promised the two excited boys. 'And any that wants can come with us.'

Aggie, Paul and Isobel were waiting for them all with tables laid out for an impromptu party.

Isobel said to Joe, 'Don't ask where Paul got all the stuff. I tried that and I was told those that ask no questions will be told no lies.'

'Then the only thing is to do justice to the food,' Joe said.

Isobel laughed. 'You're right there. But there is no need to worry. There will be not a scrap left when we let Kevin and Ben loose on it. I think both those boys have hollow legs.'

Joe laughed. The boys certainly did have healthy appetites and he had often blessed the fact that Ben had a good meal at school and he and Tom ate in the works canteen Paul had set up, because it meant the rations went that bit further. But when he said this, Paul said, 'Yes, and I think rationing will go on for many years. We must remember the war isn't totally over yet, because there is no sign of Japan giving in.'

'Yes, and I'd rather fight a German any day than a Nip,' Joe said, and there was a murmur of agreement.

'They mustn't be right in the head,' Tom declared. 'I mean, when you are in the forces, you take on board the fact that you risk your life, but to actually want to die for your country as long as you take as many Americans with you as you can like those kamikaze pilots is almost unbelievable. How do you fight people with that sort of warped mentality?'

'And it isn't only Americans,' Paul said. 'Look at all those captured in Singapore, among other places.'

It was a sobering thought to be celebrating with fighting still going on and atrocities being committed, but then Aggie said, 'I know that it's disappointing and worrying that Japan is still holding off surrender, but if we fret about it from now till the end of time we cannot change that. Let's have this one day of celebration when we realise what everyone in this country has gone through for six long years. For us now it is time to look forward and we ought to mark that, surely. It is not a sin to be happy.'

'Aggie is right,' Paul declared. 'I have a couple of bottles of bubbly put by for just such an occasion and we will drink a toast to the future.'

'Even us?' Kevin asked hopefully.

'Even you, on this very special day, will have a small glass,' Paul said with a smile.

A few hours later a sizeable hole had been made in the food and drink. *Rhapsody in Blue* was playing on the gramophone, Nuala was fast asleep in her pram, and Ben and Kevin were anxious to go back to the park and see what was happening with the bonfire.

'I'll go over with them, if one of you will mind the baby,' Molly said.

'My dear, you don't have to ask,' Aggie said. 'Between us all, we will be fighting over her.'

'You don't have to come with us, Moll,' Kevin said. 'No one does. We ain't babies and I'll look after Ben.'

'I want to see it as much as you do,' Molly retorted, with

411

a smile. 'I'm reliving my childhood. And much too excited to stay in, so let's go if we're going, while Nuala is still sleeping.'

When they had gone, the adults started reminiscing about the war years and Joe told them of his years in London in the blitz, and though he said not a word of the horrors he had seen as a volunteer firemen, he did mention the good friends he and Gloria had that never made it. Isobel, sitting close to Tom, gave a small gasp and he saw the sadness sweep over her face and knew that she was remembering too.

No one else appeared to have noticed and when Tom saw her slip out of the back door he sidled up to Joe and said quietly, 'Isobel has gone outside. Go out to her. She'll be upset, I'm thinking.'

'Then maybe she is best left alone,' Joe said. 'She'd hardly want to see me.'

'Of course she'll want to see you, man,' Tom said impatiently. 'You can comfort her as no one else can.'

'What are you saying, Tom?'

'I am saying that she is eating her heart out for you and I am surprised that you have not seen it yourself when it is so apparent to everyone else.'

'Is it?'

'Yes!'

'But, Tom, I have nothing to offer her.'

'You have yourself and you have your heart,' Tom said. 'I know Isobel too, remember, and I am pretty certain that that will more than satisfy her.'

'I can't even offer her marriage yet.'

'I know that and so does she,' Tom said. 'And I think after this war the world will be changed for good. But I cannot speak for Isobel, so go out and talk to her, for God's sake, and give her some comfort for it is what she needs.'

Isobel was no longer crying, but she had been. Her eyes were still brimful and the sight of her distress tore at Joe's heart. He gathered her into his arms for the very first time, wondering, even as he did so, if she might object to such familiarity. However, far from objecting, Isobel sighed and snuggled into Joe as if it was her rightful place to be, and Joe held her tenderly. When he felt the beat of her heart against his chest he felt as if he was exploding with love.

The power of it took him by surprise and when her saddened eyes met his, he bent his head and touched her lips gently. And then Isobel was kissing him back with all she had in her. There was such beauty and tenderness in that first kiss, and when they broke away reluctantly in the end, Joe wanted more.

However, he recognised that they needed to talk about the shadows in their lives.

'Let's walk a little,' he said, as he put his arm around her shoulders. 'I suppose it was my reminiscences that caused you so much pain, and I am sorry for that.'

Isobel shook his head. 'It wasn't just you. It was the day and everything. I knew I would find it difficult. I mean I had come to the realisation that I will always miss Gregory and Gerald, and that they will always occupy a corner of my heart.'

'That's perfectly understandable,' Joe said.

'I was coping with that,' Isobel said. 'And then suddenly, as you were speaking, the events of that terrible day when I received the telegram came flooding back. I was holding the telegram in my hands and trying to cope with the anguish and desolation that I would never see my son again. Gerald had followed me into the hall, and even if I had been able – for I was beyond speech then – there was no way I could have prepared him for the stark words telling us that our beloved son was dead and gone. I watched the blood drain from Gerald's face and then he sort of folded up at my feet.'

'Heart attack?'

Isobel nodded.

Joe said, 'My father died of a heart attack after a telegram.'

'Tom said something about that,' Isobel said. 'But Gerald didn't die, not then, though he was no good after it. He somehow just faded away. The doctor said he had lost the will to live.'

'Did you love him very much?'

'If I am truthful, when I married him, I didn't love him at all,' Isobel said. 'Our parents had been friends for years and we had known each other from childhood, and it was sort of expected that we would marry. In those days young people, especially young women, usually did what was expected of them, and anyway, I liked Gerald well enough. I leaned to love him, though, because he was a kind and considerate man, and when Gregory was born he was the most marvellous father and I loved him even more because of that. When I see the relationship you have with Ben and the love you have for one another, it brings it all back. It's beautiful to see. Did you love your wife?'

'I did,' Joe said. 'I loved her very much. She was only fourteen when I met her first and she grew up before my eyes and propositioned me. I would never have had the nerve to do it, because I was so much older, and employed by her father, of course. But the love between us died a long time before she left me.'

'Why?'

'Oh, there was a variety of reasons,' Joe said. 'We became two different people wanting different things from life and I know that really she was homesick for America. She left it because she had to, you see, not because she wanted to, and though she did her best she had this hankering for the land she was born and reared in.'

'I can understand that,' Isobel said. 'If you have made the decision to go, it has got to make a difference to your attitude.'

'I suppose . . . And then it got even worse in Ireland because she was so lonely and so isolated, and I did not support her enough. Then there was the pledge I made to Tom. I suppose you heard about that.'

414

'Yes. Tom said that he asked you to give him a year to decide whether he wanted to go back to farming or sell up altogether and move here.'

'And I agreed to that without even talking it over with Gloria,' Joe said. 'I was a much better brother than I was a husband at that time, I see it now. And when she took the job at the American camp I used to moan at her a lot of the time. I didn't want her working there, or anywhere else either, but money was tight and it made me feel a failure that I couldn't provide properly for my family. Instead of talking these things over with Gloria, I would moan as if it was her fault. Gloria ran out on me and it did knock me for six at the time, but there were faults on both sides and I have to take some of the blame for the way she behaved.'

'And me, Joe?' Isobel said. 'What do you think of me?'

'I think,' began Joe and then he said, 'No, I don't think at all. I *know* now that I love you truly.'

'And I love you too, Joe,' Isobel said. 'I told you that in time I came to love Gerald, but not the way I love you. I have never felt this way before.'

'Oh, darling,' Joe said, pulling her to a stop. 'I love you so much.'

Their second kiss was as magical as the first had been, and after it Joe had to bite back a groan of desire.

'What are we to do?' Isobel asked.

'What can we do?' Joe said. 'I have little to offer you. Gloria and I have to be apart at least three years before the divorce is even considered, Gloria told me in the last letter she sent.'

'Well, we more or less knew that anyway,' Isobel said. 'Let us take one day at a time and see what comes of it.'

'Yes,' Joe said. 'That is the best solution and now I suppose we must tell them all inside. Tom said they have been aware of how we feel about one another for some time.'

'Really?' Isobel pulled away from Joe and looked into

415

his face. 'How? We had not even admitted it to one another until now.'

Joe shrugged. 'Maybe they are more astute than we give them credit for. That's what Tom said, anyway. They are all for it anyway, I think.'

'Well, I'm glad,' Isobel said. 'Really, though, it's Ben's reaction I am bothered about most.'

'Ben? Why worry about him?' Joe said. 'He loves you almost as I do.'

'Yes, while he thought I was just a friend.'

'Believe me, my darling girl, Ben will be the least of our worries.'

'I am no girl, Joe,' Isobel chided.

'You are to me,' Joe insisted. 'My own darling girl who I love dearly, and I must kiss you one more time before I share you with the others.'

The family were all pleased with Joe and Isobel's news, and Ben took it all in his stride, even the fact that they wouldn't be able to be married straight away until the divorce came through. Even then, he knew that they couldn't be married in a Catholic church, because divorce wasn't recognised, but then neither could his mother so he supposed that that was sort of fair in a way.

For Ben, life changed for the better. Isobel was around more, they went out together more, and sometimes he and his father went to Isobel's bungalow on Walmley Road on a Sunday, when she always cooked them a lovely dinner. Ben loved that bungalow. It was set back from the road behind tall privet hedges and so the gardens all around it were really private and you felt that you could be miles from anywhere.

When they went to Isobel's Ben often met Kevin and some of his mates to play football in Pype Hayes Park in the afternoon. They were always glad to see Ben because he had a genuine leather football, which his mother had sent to him from America for his eleventh birthday. He had had a bit of a funny feeling when he opened up the parcel and saw the ball.

For a moment he remembered the Christmas party where he had been given a ball, and the gift had been spoiled for him because he had seen his mother kissing one of the sailors from the camp. Now, looking back on it, a kiss didn't seem half as bad as what she had done later, and he'd had to learn to accept that in time. Anyway, a ball was still a ball, and the finest one he had ever seen. It made him a very popular boy indeed and secured him a place in any game going.

His mother had also bought him a shiny brown satchel for grammar school and it hung on the back of his door. Every day when Ben saw it he felt a thrill of pride. Sometimes, though, he would have a shiver of fear that he might have failed the second part of the exam, which had been harder than the first. He really wanted to pass, not only for himself but to make his parents proud of him, and he knew that he would know soon because the results would be out the week after the school closed for the summer.

Kevin left school for good that July and was anxious to start working life straight away, but Molly insisted he had some time off first. 'Once you start you will be working until you're sixty-five and, believe me, the novelty will soon wear off. Spend some time with Ben. Try and take his mind off those results that will be out any day now.'

Kevin didn't mind that at all because he was really fond of his young cousin and they went into the city centre one day to look at the bomb damage, which was considerable. The Bull Ring was still there, but not quite the same, and the shops still had little in them.

'I suppose it will take time to get back to normal, like Paul said on VE Day,' Kevin told Ben.

'Bound to. I reckon it will take years to get it back the way it was.'

'Molly said that it will never be the same again,' Kevin said. 'She said the world will have changed and moved on, and there is really no point in looking back to the way things were.'

'I suppose not.'

'She can't wait for the war to be over properly and for Mark to be home again,' Kevin said. 'Because until the Japanese cave in, as far as the RAF are concerned, the war is not over.'

'Well, there is no sign of that,' Ben said. 'Dad said it could go on for years yet.'

'God, I hope not.'

'Me too.'

'Come on,' Kevin said. 'Let's go home and go up the park. There is nothing to see here.'

'All right,' Ben said. 'And I haven't got to be home till about half five. Aunt Izzy is coming round to cook the dinner, but that's about the time Dad's home.'

'Come on then,' Kevin said. 'That's ages yet and Molly's given me some money for chips for both of us.'

'Oh boy, that's even better news.'

Ben got home that evening before his father, and Isobel came out from the kitchen when she heard the door. 'There's a letter for your father from the Education Department,' she said. 'I've put it behind the clock.'

'Is it the results, d'you think?'

'Can't think of any other reason they'd be writing to him, can you?'

Ben shook his head. He felt as if a large stone had lodged itself in his stomach and he looked at Isobel with eyes full of foreboding. 'What if I haven't passed?'

'You probably have,' Isobel said. 'You have certainly worked hard enough. But if you haven't it won't be the end of the world, will it? I mean, the world won't stop spinning on its axis or anything.'

'I want Mom and Dad to be proud of me.'

Isobel held Ben's shoulders gently as she said, 'They are proud of you, Ben. A child does not have to do something to make their parents proud, and that won't change if you have failed your eleven plus.'

For all her encouraging words, though, Isobel hoped that Ben had passed, not for her own sake, but because it mattered so much to him. She was as anxious to hear Joe's key in the door as Ben was, but she hid it better.

Eventually, though, he was there, and strode across the room, took the letter from behind the clock and split it open straight away. Ben's eyes were full of trepidation as he watched his father scanning the sheet of paper he had withdrawn from the envelope. Then Joe threw down the paper and lifted Ben high in the air. 'You've done it, you clever, clever boy,' he cried. 'You have passed.'

All through the meal, Ben felt as if he was floating on air. He knew he had pleased his father because he couldn't stop going on about it, and even Isobel had hugged him tight and told him how proud she was too, and he felt warmed by their so obvious happiness at his achievement. It didn't matter a jot that he hadn't got his first choice of St Philip's and that he would be going to Bishop Vesey, and Joe was relieved that he wouldn't be facing such a long journey morning and evening.

After the meal, Ben said, 'I will write to Mom now, if you don't mind. I want to do it when I am really excited so she might be able to feel it a bit.'

'I don't mind in the least,' Joe said. 'I have to go home with Isobel anyway.'

'You don't, Joe,' Isobel said.

'Oh yes I do,' Joe contradicted. 'So no argument.'

It was as they were going to the bus stop, arm in arm, that Joe suddenly said, 'I can't believe it. My boy going to grammar school.'

'He deserved it,' Isobel said. 'He worked hard.'

'Yeah, he did,' Joe agreed. 'I've saved all my clothing coupons and most of his to get him fitted out with the uniform.'

'They'll likely have sales at the school,' Isobel said. 'They'll know the situation as well as the rest of us.'

'I'd not want him to start in second-hand clothes,' Joe said rather stiffly.

'Will you listen to yourself?' Isobel said. 'Surely it's the quality of education that is important, not the clothes. Anyway, Kevin wore a uniform of sorts, though not as stringent as that of a grammar school, and every night he had to take it off and hang it up. His uniform was always the better-looking of his clothes. He always grew out of them before they were worn out though sometimes the trousers took a bit of a pasting. Anyway, Ben will need other clothes as well as his uniform, so how are you going to get those if you have used up his supply of coupons?'

'I don't know anything about all this,' Joe admitted. 'Will you give me a hand when the time comes?'

'Of course I will,' Isobel said. 'And here is the bus at last.'

Unless the weather was very cold or wet, they got off the tram at the edge of Pype Hayes Park and walked across, then skirted the golf course. It was their chance to be together, because they had already decided that there would be no canoodling in front of Ben.

They walked hand in hand through the park that warm and balmy evening and suddenly Isobel sighed and said, 'I am so happy, Joe, but I wish the war would end totally very soon. Molly is concerned about Mark and I don't blame her. After all, it is the first of August on Wednesday.'

'Well, I don't know what they would have to do to Japan to force surrender,' Joe said.

Only a few days later, on 6 August, the Americans dropped an atomic bomb on the city of Hiroshima, killing an estimated seventy-eight thousand people. It sent shock waves all around the world. It was hard even to visualise so many killed by one bomb.

Everyone expected Japan to surrender, but when there was no response, another bomb was released over Nagasaki on 9 August and it was estimated that that one killed thirty-five thousand.

Now surely Japan would bend to the inevitable. No country could just stand by and see so many of its people killed. As Isobel said, 'We have made and released a devouring monster and it could be justified only if it brought a speedy end to the war that had already claimed so many young lives.'

But it didn't. The world looked on in disbelief as there was still no response from Japan, and so on 13 August, Allied aircraft launched a huge attack on Tokyo, and Japan surrendered the next day.

'The war is finally over, but at what cost to the Japanese people?' Isobel said a few days later scrutinising the newspaper.

'We can do nothing about the decisions governments make,' Joe said.

'I know.'

'And the Japanese were the aggressors.'

'I know that too,' Isobel said. 'Don't mind me. I am totally out of sorts today.'

'Anything I can do to help?'

She smiled. 'You help by just being there. But I would love to go for a walk, if Ben doesn't mind?'

'Why should I mind?' Ben said. 'I got a couple of good books from the library today, as it happens.'

'I'll likely not be too late,' Joe said, 'though I might as well take Isobel home while I am about it.'

'That's OK,' Ben said.

Isobel had come to a decision. They had barely reached the street when she said, 'You don't have to take me home every night, you know.'

'We've been through this, Isobel.'

'I'm not talking of me going home on my own,' Isobel said. 'I am talking of the fact that I have a three-bedroomed bungalow that I rattle round in, which is plenty big enough for all of us.'

'I couldn't take that offer, much as I would like to,' Joe said. 'If I moved in with you I would ruin your reputation.'

'I don't care about that.'

'You must care.'

'I don't, honestly,' Isobel said. 'Once I craved respectability above all else, but it is a very cold bedfellow. One thing this war has taught me is that life is very short and you have just the one crack at it. We really shouldn't waste any of what we have and live life to the full. Both of us should have this second chance of happiness but I would put no pressure on you. If you didn't want to share a room with me until you are free, I would understand that.'

'And what would you do if I did that?'

'I would wait for you until you were ready.'

'You would do that for me?'

'Yes.'

'But what are you getting out of this?' Joe said. 'What do you want, Isobel?'

'I want to make you happy,' Isobel said simply. 'And I would do whatever that takes. I would welcome you into my bed, if that is what you wanted.'

'You're not worried about making a name for yourself?'

'Not in the slightest,' she said emphatically.

Joe looked at her incredulously, hardly able to believe that, after Gloria, he could love another person so much, or so deeply, and he held her tight as he said, 'Oh Isobel, you are very special, and my own darling, darling girl, and you have achieved your objective, because you have made me happy. In fact, you have made me the happiest man in the world.'

Acknowledgements

Hi to all my readers. Many of you have written following the publication of *A Daughter's Secret* in March 2008, saying how much you enjoyed hearing stories about the Sullivan family whom you had met in *A Sister's Promise*. I hope *A Mother's Spirit* is no exception.

This is Joe's story. As the second son he knows the farm will never be his and after his father's death he strikes out for New York to find his fortune in this brave new world, that promises so much.

Research for this book has been quite phenomenal. Having not had the funds or time to visit New York, I had to rely heavily on the internet. I also used books such as *The Search for Prosperity* by Richard Garrett which deals with emigration from Britain between the years 1815–1930; *Modern America* by Chris McDonald and Jon Nichol goes back to the First World War and traces America's progress through the years.

Joe arrived in 1921; I had to research Ellis Island where all the steerage passengers were first sent. They had to pass a medical and have a good understanding of English and be able to pass some basic tests before they were allowed on American soil. Prohibition was in operation then too, so that had to be researched and as Joe arrived in November, I had to look into Thanksgiving, the reason for it and the special food prepared. Once Gloria was finished with school, I had to delve into the world of the flappers of the 1920s. There was a terrific amount of entertainment to be had in New York at the time and apart from the movies the most popular amongst the young were the dance halls. There girls danced the daring charleston and the shimmy and wore dresses just below, or shockingly just above, the knee and many wore heavy cosmetics, smoked and had their hair bobbed.

It was a fascinating insight into America. I cannot claim this as an original thought of mine, but a fellow writer once said that 'research for a book is like the iceberg effect'. Although the writer has to know as much as possible about a subject to write about it convincingly, the reader is fed only a little of that information, which is blended into the story.

Research about pre-war London and London during the blitz also proved more difficult than I had anticipated and my lovely editor helped there. I also used maps and street plans and the books *London Life in the Post War Years* by Douglas Whitworth and *30s and 40s Britain* by John Guy.

I had already done a lot of research on Ireland and the farm that Joe and Gloria returned to, as this is the third book in the series, but I did dip into *Rekindling a Dying Heritage* by Evelyn Ruddy, which I have used many times before. I also skimmed *The Donegal Corridor* by Joe O'Loughlin and relied heavily on *An Atlantic Memorial – The Foyle and Western Approaches 1939–1945*, now threadbare I have used it so often. It documents Derry through the war years and the American service men that lived in Springtown Camp. Last but my no means least I used *Sutton Coldfield in the Forties* by John Bassett, although I still remember much of how Sutton Coldfield was as I grew up just beside it in the late 1950s, and later lived there for 14 years before moving to North Wales.

So that was it and another book is born, but the series wouldn't have begun at all if it hadn't been for my very astute agent suggesting it in the first place. Thanks, Judith. Immense thanks must also go to the great team at HarperCollins, like my editor Susan Opie and Yvonne Holland for the terrific job they did on the copy-edits and my publicist Kiera Godfrey. The book would be a much poorer one without them, believe me. So thank you all so much.

And I must not forget Judith Evans, who is in charge of all the bookshops in Birmingham International Airport, and Peter Hawtin, regional sales manager at HarperCollins, who together were instrumental in my writing for the publishing house in the first place. Thank you both. I would also like to say hi to my dear friend Judith Kendall, who reads everything I write and says that a packet of tissues should be given away with each book. I suppose that could be arranged.

My family is very special to me, my son and three daughters, their relevant partners and their families. I love them all so much, although I am quite horrified that my beautiful grand-daughter was old enough to take her GCSEs this year, and that her *little* brother is off to secondary school after the holidays. Even the baby of the family, seven-year-old Theo, the one that this book is dedicated to, will join his brother in the juniors in September. I must be getting old, for the days just seem to gallop past at an alarming rate.

My husband Denis needs a particular mention and special thanks because he is my rock. He helps and supports me in so many ways and probably knows me better than anyone, and yet he's still around – amazing! I am so glad that I married him all those years ago.

Heartfelt thanks though go to you, the readers, because without you there would be no point in my carrying on writing anything. So many of you now write and say how much you have enjoyed the books. That is very much appreciated and I hope that you continue to enjoy them. Immense gratitude to you all.

A Sister's Promise

Anne Bennett

Molly's life changes forever when her parents are killed in a horrific accident. Although her beloved grandfather wants to keep her and her little brother Kevin with him in Birmingham, the authorities decide it's best for the girl to live with her maternal grandmother on a farm in Donegal. So Molly is packed off to Biddy Sullivan, a hard, cruel woman who loves to bear a grudge.

Years of hardship follow and just as Molly begins to grow independent, war breaks out. She fears the worst for her grandfather – and what will become of Kevin? He's only ten. So the naïve country girl sets off for her home city, little guessing what perils are to befall her before she can discover her brother's fate…

'Anne Bennett draws on her own background to give emotional depth to an affecting story populated with rich, beautifully drawn characters'   *Choice*

ISBN: 978 0 00 722602 3